Treason in Tokyo

A Reiko Watanabe/Inspector Aizawa Thriller

by

Matthew Legare

Copyright

www.matthewlegare.com

Black Mist Books
Paperback ISBN - 978-1-7323090-4-3
Ebook ISBN - 978-1-7323090-8-1

Cover design by Caroline T. Johnson

Mailing List

Join my mailing list! You'll receive updates, deals, and the free prequel novella, *Conspiracy in Tokyo*! Just visit www.matthewlegare.com.

Thanks!

Author's Note

In addition to using the Western calendar, the Japanese also divide their history among eras named after the reigning emperors. For example, modern Japanese history is comprised of the Meiji Era (1868 – 1912), the Taisho Era (1912 – 1926), the Showa Era (1926 – 1989), the Heisei Era (1989 – 2019), and the Reiwa Era (2019 – present). The events of this novel take place in 1933 or Showa 8. Additionally, there are references to the Tokugawa Era, which covered the years of 1603 – 1868 when the Tokugawa Shogunate ruled Japan through a military dictatorship, reducing the emperors to mere figureheads.

Many Japanese terms that have not entered the English lexicon have been italicized, followed by a brief translation. Those words that have gained familiarity in the West (e.g. geisha, yakuza, shogun) are not italicized.

There are also common suffixes used throughout the novel such as *san* (formal for both males and females), *chan* (informal for females), *kun* (informal for males), and *sama* (extremely formal for both).

In Japan, surnames come before given names (e.g. Watanabe Reiko), but in order to make the story more palatable to Western readers, characters' given names will come before their family names (e.g. Reiko Watanabe).

In Japanese, 'e' is pronounced like 'eh' so Watanabe would be pronounced 'Wat-ah-nah-beh,' Natsume would be pronounced 'Naht-soo-meh,' Miyake would be 'Mee-yah-keh,' Hashizume would be 'Hah-shi-zoo-meh,' and so forth.

Acknowledgments

As with all my novels, I am grateful to my friends and family, my Japanese friends who helped with cultural nuances, my readers, and my other half, Jenny.

January 1933

Eighth Year of the Showa Era

CHAPTER ONE

Ringing bells echoed throughout Tokyo and inside Utako Natsume's ears, numbed from the cold. The Japanese always ushered in the new year by clanging temple bells a hundred and seven times, then once more just after midnight – one hundred and eight chimes for the same number of sins in Buddhism. A silly belief, but her countrymen cherished such superstitions. Regardless, 1933 – Showa 8 – was here, the year the Japanese Revolution would begin.

Beneath a glowing streetlamp, Utako shuffled for warmth, scraping her high heels against a light dusting of snow on the pavement. She pulled her cloche hat down over her ears, shielding them from the frigid air. Utako checked her wristwatch again – five after midnight. The streets were deserted, but this was Kasumigaseki, the government district of central Tokyo. The six story Metropolitan Police Headquarters towered in the near distance and a *koban* Police box stood within eyesight. A risky place for a political assassination.

She looked over again at the Sakurada, the south gate that connected Kasumigaseki to the Imperial Palace. A despicable structure, especially when so many wallowed in poverty. But the people's rage wouldn't be stifled any longer. Just last year, a Korean nationalist had thrown a bomb at the Emperor to protest Japan's occupation of his native country. Unfortunately, that puffed-up Imperial peacock escaped unscathed. Utako and her comrades wouldn't make the same mistake. Explosives were unreliable. Her gloved hands gripped her handbag, feeling the frame of the Nagant revolver nestled inside.

The streetlamp's electric light provided enough illumination to make out Major Taro Kuno several yards away, closer to the Sakurada Gate. Although he wore a gray flat cap and overcoat, Kuno's muscular build and rigid poise marked him as an Army officer. A military man who had been converted to Communism – it was almost too good to be true.

Utako's other comrades – Saburo Genda and Pak Sang-hoon – lurked in the gloomy shadows underneath a pair of snow-powdered trees. No doubt their trigger fingers itched but they'd have their chance soon enough. Wataru Izumi waited nearby in the getaway car, ready to spirit them off afterward. All they needed now was the victim – Marquis Tatsuo Maeda. According to Major Kuno, the withered aristocrat was meeting with the Minister of the Army, General Araki. Being attached to the Army Ministry exposed him to such useful information.

Headlights sliced through the darkness. An automobile cruised out from the Sakurada Gate and onto the bridge, passing over the moat that encircled the Imperial Palace. Utako glanced over to Major Kuno, who inspected the oncoming vehicle with narrowed eyes. He turned back and gave a quick nod, confirming that it was Maeda's private car.

Showtime.

She dashed out from beneath the streetlamp, allowing the car's headlights to engulf her. Summoning her past skills as an actress, Utako became the epitome of a damsel in distress.

"Stop! Please help me!" she cried, waving her arms.

The performance was enough for the vehicle to grind to a halt, just inches away. Through a haze of swirling snowflakes, Utako could make out the stunned chauffeur in the driver's seat, along with Marquis Maeda, glaring at her in the back.

In his black frockcoat, pince-nez spectacles, and top hat, the Marquis looked like a caricature of a Japanese aristocrat rather than an actual person. Fitting, since this wasn't about a man, but a symbol. In her peripheral vision, Utako saw Pak's spindly figure and Genda's hulking frame emerge from the darkness. Major Kuno joined them from the north, covering the vehicle's rear. Marquis Maeda was blocked from all sides now.

"Are you mad?" the chauffeur snapped, rolling down his window. "Get out of the way, you foolish girl!"

Utako stayed silent as she pulled the Nagant revolver from her handbag. All too late, the chauffeur realized what was happening. Pak raised his gun – also a Nagant – and placed a bullet straight through the chauffeur's temple, knocking his cap off. Marquis Maeda gaped in mute horror, as his head darted north, south, east, west, only to face a pistol in each direction.

Utako took aim and fired, the bullet crashing through the front windshield and ripping through Maeda's face. Genda and Pak fired from the sides, cutting through the Marquis' torso. If Maeda wasn't dead already, Major Kuno finished him off with a bullet to the back of his skull. The Marquis twitched and convulsed, bleeding out all over the upholstered seats.

The *koban* became animated, inflamed by the commotion. Two *junsas* in black uniforms and peaked caps emerged, swords drawn. The rank-and-file officers of the Metropolitan Police were rarely equipped with firearms, and those pathetic short swords almost made Utako laugh. She aimed and opened fire, catching one of the *junsas* in the chest. Major Kuno and Pak finished off the other in a hail of bullets.

Utako sucked in a mouthful of frigid air to temper her passion. Killing Maeda was necessary for the Revolution, but it felt mechanical. Killing police officers filled her with a deep, visceral pleasure, especially after what they'd done to her poor Ichiro. Hopefully, there would be many more. But such fantasies would have to wait. Their gunfire would attract the Imperial Guard, a more formidable enemy.

Luckily, another pair of headlights cut through the darkness, accompanied by a ferocious roar. A blue sedan rocketed toward them, sliding to a stop next to Maeda's pockmarked vehicle. Wataru Izumi sat behind the wheel with a cocky smirk on his plump face. Although an arrogant rich kid, Izumi had dedicated himself – and his supercharged Ford Model 18 – to the Revolution.

"Let's go!" Izumi barked, slapping the side door. Kuno, Genda, and Pak obeyed and piled into the idling Ford, but Utako still had one last thing to do.

"Not just yet," she snapped.

Utako dropped the Nagant into her handbag, then pulled out a folded pamphlet, the final ingredient for this assassination.

"Natsume-san," Izumi growled over the rumbling engine, "there's no time to waste!"

Ignoring him, Utako walked back to the automobile, her high heels stabbing little holes in the thin carpet of snow. She reached over the hood and tucked the pamphlet underneath a windshield wiper, conspicuous enough that the Police were bound to find it. After all, she couldn't have those feeble old men in the Japanese Communist Party taking credit for this assassination. If there was one thing she'd learned as an actress, it was that life was grand theater with an unlimited budget.

Utako turned and fled into the waiting Ford, which peeled away from the Sakurada Gate, kicking up plumes of snow behind it. Crammed in between her comrades, Utako peered out the back window, watching the Imperial Palace shrink behind them.

Happy New Year, Tokyo…

CHAPTER TWO

Inspector Kenji Aizawa trudged toward the Sakurada Gate, snow crunching beneath his shoes. An icy breeze slapped against his face, sobering him up after a few Asahi beers. New Year's was the one time when Japanese were expected to lose all inhibitions, and drunkenness was almost a duty. He'd been drinking at a nearby *izakaya* when a *junsa* requested his immediate presence. After all, other detectives were busy celebrating with their families.

As he approached the Sakurada Gate, Aizawa took in the scene. A squad of *junsas* had cordoned off the area, their black uniforms spotted with white snowflakes, drifting down from the darkness above. Two police officers lay contorted on the ground, cushioned by bloody snow. At the center was an automobile, lying inert like some beached whale.

Two figures inspected the car, their breath misting the night air. In his black uniform coat, peaked cap and epaulettes, Superintendent Shinsaku Miyake was the Tokyo Metropolitan Police Department personified. However, his sharp face – stained red from alcohol and the cold – couldn't disguise an irritability, no doubt from having his New Year's celebration interrupted. If Aizawa's immediate superior was at a crime scene at this hour, then the corpse inside that vehicle must have held some clout.

The other figure was a young Army officer – evidenced by his dark brown overcoat, shoulder rank tabs, and peaked cap with black visor and bright red band. Set against the cap band was the usual five-pointed brass star insignia of the Army, but it was also cupped with a bronze wreath design. A simple but effective way to denote that this Army officer was a member of the Imperial Guard, charged with the personal protection of the Emperor.

Aizawa's footsteps crunched as he drew closer, gaining their attention. He snapped a firm salute to both men. The officer stood at attention and saluted in return. Superintendent Miyake didn't reciprocate, but a small nod was enough of a greeting.

"Happy New Year, Superintendent," Aizawa said with a puff of frosted breath.

"Hell of a way to start it," Miyake said. "Sorry to drag you away from your celebrations, Inspector, but I figured you'd be at your usual watering hole."

"It's fine, sir. At first, I thought this was another one of those love suicides."

Months earlier, a Keio University student and the daughter of a wealthy merchant killed themselves at the base of the scenic Mount Sakata. Investigation revealed that the daughter's parents disapproved of their desire to marry, forcing the couple into *shinju* – love suicide. Their tragic romance inspired numerous imitators, usually other young people, unable to marry for social reasons, who killed themselves in a variety of dramatic methods – drowning, poison, and leaping into a volcano. The Japanese people were horrified, but also captivated, by these beautiful gestures of death.

"Two foolish kids jumped in front of the subway earlier tonight," Miyake grunted. "But this is far more important. Take a look inside and see for yourself."

Aizawa peered through the car's shattered windows and found two bodies. A uniformed chauffer slumped over the steering wheel, blood crusted around his temple along with a glaze of frost. A more elegant corpse occupied the backseat, although his frockcoat and top hat had been sliced to shreds in a melee of bullets. The sheer volume of his wounds was enough evidence that he was the intended target and that the others – the chauffeur and the two *junsas* – were poor unfortunates in the way. Snowflakes drifted through the broken glass, whirling about inside the car in an ethereal strangeness.

"Who is he?" Aizawa said, gesturing to the well-dressed corpse.

"The Marquis Tatsuo Maeda," the officer answered.

"Thank you, Lieutenant…?"

"Oh yes, this is Second Lieutenant Endo," Miyake said, "and this is Inspector Aizawa."

Lieutenant Endo and Aizawa exchanged respectful nods.

"Please tell the Inspector what you saw," Miyake said.

"At exactly 0010 hours, Marquis Maeda exited the premises of the Imperial Palace and drove across the south bridge. At 0012, we noticed activity on the other side of the moat, near the Sakurada Gate. Several gunshots rang out. Although the Imperial Guard's duty is limited to the Palace grounds, my men and I crossed the bridge to offer assistance. Unfortunately, we were too late, and the perpetrators had already fled the scene."

"I understand, Lieutenant," Aizawa said, glancing back over at Tatsuo Maeda's bloody husk. "Why was the Marquis leaving the Palace so late? On New Year's, no less?"

Lieutenant Endo remained rigid as a smattering of snowflakes collected on his black visor. "I'm not at liberty to say, Inspector."

Aizawa only grunted but flashed Superintendent Miyake an imploring look. A police inspector might not have enough status to challenge an officer of the Imperial Guard, but a police superintendent outranked this callow lieutenant.

"Come now, Lieutenant Endo," Miyake said. "The Metropolitan Police and the Imperial Army can't keep secrets from each other, especially not in a case like this."

The prodding seemed to convince Endo.

"Marquis Maeda was attending a meeting with General Araki."

"General Araki? The Army Minister?" Aizawa asked. Endo nodded. "Why were they meeting on New Year's Eve?"

"I have no idea. But Marquis Maeda was a member of the Privy Council and met with cabinet members often."

Aizawa forced a calm demeanor while his thoughts raced. The Privy Council was the Emperor's highest group of advisers, offering guidance on matters of state – from whom to appoint prime minister to the interpretation of laws and international treaties. All were decided by this clique of old aristocrats, unelected and unaccountable to the people. Maeda's membership in this group meant an unsettling political dimension had been added.

"Had the Marquis received any death threats?" Aizawa asked. When Endo gave a confused look, he added, "From any right-wing patriotic societies?"

Superintendent Miyake croaked out a laugh. "Marquis Maeda wasn't some weak-kneed liberal. The man was so conservative that he made the old Tokugawa shoguns look like dandies. Besides, we already know who did it."

This time, Aizawa couldn't hide his shock. "You do, sir?"

Sliding a hand into his overcoat pocket, Miyake retrieved a folded pamphlet and handed it to Aizawa. Opening it up, columns of *kanji*, *hiragana*, and *katakana* characters screamed out an angry diatribe.

"To the wolves of the Metropolitan Police,

Japan is a slave society, ruled by *zaibatsu* capitalists, aristocrats, and militarists. These plutocratic cliques use the Emperor as their puppet to keep themselves in power and Japan in chains. The *zaibatsu* enriches itself from the Japanese people toiling in factories and fields for starvation wages.

The aristocracy clings to its unearned privileges, just like the *daimyo* lords of old. And the militarists have begun their march of conquest, using your sons as cannon fodder. All the while, the Japanese people act like docile slaves, hypnotized by the so-called 'Emperor System' into worshipping a false god.

The monster of Japanese Imperialism has devoured Taiwan, Korea, and now Manchuria. Thanks to its ravenous appetite, a new world war looms on the horizon. Only by destroying the slave masters in the home islands can we slay this beast.

With the assassination of Marquis Tatsuo Maeda, we have broken one of these fetters in our quest to bring about the Japanese Proletarian Revolution. Just as the Red Terror destroyed the White forces of Reaction in Russia, so too shall it cleanse Japan! Tremble in fear, enemies of the people! The Red Terror Society shall be utterly merciless!"

Aizawa felt the cold air against his face, now flushed with emotion. The word *okami* could mean "gods" but also "wolves," a slur for the Metropolitan Police favored by left-wing groups.

Handing the pamphlet back, Aizawa asked, "The Red Terror Society? Is that a splinter group from the Communist Party?"

Superintendent Miyake shrugged. "Your guess is as good as mine. I've never heard of them before tonight."

Aizawa circled the car, pausing in front of its hood. Snowflakes fluttered down, but their pace was slowing. Although January was the coldest month in Tokyo, when snow did stick, it often melted within days. But for now, it remained powdery and thick, a natural record of who had come and gone. Heavy footprints had sunk into the snow, showing the outlines of men's shoes and *geta* clogs. But a more delicate pair with pointed toes and thin heels remained in front of Maeda's car.

A woman had been here.

Crunching snow jerked Aizawa's attention behind him. A hulking figure, wrapped in a dark overcoat and fedora, traipsed toward the crime scene. Despite his inconspicuous clothes, a sinister aura accompanied his presence. Recognition set in. It was Inspector Hiroshi Tezuka of the Tokko – the secret police of the Japanese Empire.

CHAPTER THREE

The Tokko Inspector zeroed in on Maeda's car, aloof to Aizawa and the others. Hiroshi Tezuka was more myth than man, the subject of past glories and dark rumors. There were even whispers that he even kept files on fellow police officers.

Although part of the Metropolitan Police Department, the Tokko functioned more or less as an autonomous organization. Its official title – the Special Higher Police – was usually shortened to Tokko, but they'd also earned a more ominous nickname – the Thought Police. The Peace Preservation Law had given the Tokko sweeping powers to maintain order, one of which was the authority to arrest anyone with "dangerous thoughts." That meant anarchists, Communists, or anyone determined to change the *kokutai*, the national order of Japan.

Although they were technically the same rank, Aizawa presented Tezuka with a rigid salute and low bow. Seniority and age always demanded proper respect. Only then did the Tokko Inspector acknowledge him with a brief salute of his own. Tezuka's wide, grizzled face, decorated with a thick mustache, betrayed no emotion. But his narrow, hooded eyes focused on Aizawa. Was this Thought Policeman scrutinizing his mind? Aizawa wondered what Tezuka would find if he pried too deeply.

"Inspector Tezuka," Superintendent Miyake said. "How did you know about Marquis Maeda's death? Don't tell me the Tokko can now read people's thoughts!"

Tezuka gave a gracious smile before saluting both Miyake and Lieutenant Endo. "Happy New Year, Superintendent," he said, his voice gruff like a backfiring engine. "I wish it were off to a better start."

"You and me both," Miyake said with a grin. "Why are you here, Inspector? Out for a stroll?"

Lieutenant Endo stepped forward with a loud crunch of snow. "I took it upon myself to telephone Inspector Tezuka about tonight's incident."

Miyake snorted out a laugh. "Ah, so the Tokko *does* have eyes and ears everywhere! Even within the Imperial Guard!"

Shaking his head, Tezuka said, "It's nothing like that, sir. I've been attached to the Palace in the past few weeks. I've been working a case with Marquis Maeda."

Miyake's hawk-like face glowed with curiosity. "What's the case?"

"My apologies, sir, but I am not at liberty to discuss such details," Tezuka answered, sounding almost rehearsed.

"No, I'd imagine you aren't." Miyake sighed. "Ah well, the less we know about Tokko cases, the better."

Aizawa agreed. When it came to the Thought Police, not knowing was Buddha.

"What evidence have you collected?" Tezuka asked.

Miyake handed the pamphlet over. Tezuka scanned it, then slid it into his pocket. "The Red Terror Society," he said with a contemptuous snort.

"It sounds like they're a splinter group from the Japanese Communist Party," Aizawa said.

Tezuka pocked the pamphlet and returned his attention to Aizawa, reviewing him again with a quick once-over. "A good guess, Inspector, but not exactly. Our recent efforts have seriously hampered the Communist Party's membership, but it still survives as a pitiful underground organization, consisting of a central committee that sends out marching orders to dozens of small, semi-autonomous cells. A few months ago, one of these cells started calling itself the Red Terror Society. My informants tell me that although they're still officially tied to the Party, they operate independently of the central committee. I suspect they were involved with that bank robbery in Yokohama last month."

Aizawa nodded, reflecting on the strange crime wave that had swept Japan. Bank robberies were almost unheard of in Japan until recently. In October 1932, a gang of Communists held up a bank in the Omori suburb of Tokyo, desperately trying to fill the Party's empty coffers. Although the perpetrators were quickly arrested, the audacious crime had spawned numerous imitators, like something out of American gangster pictures. In November, a desperate salesman, shackled with debt, had robbed a bank in Kobe but was soon caught. However, the group who'd plundered a Yokohama bank in December were still at large.

The Omori Bank Incident also gave the Tokko an incentive to crack down on the already-weakened Communist Party. While its leaders vacationed at the Atami Hot Springs, the Special Higher Police launched a daring surprise raid, arresting most of Japan's remaining Communists in a single night. Although the central committee had since been rebuilt, it was a pale imitation of what it had been before. With their organization beheaded, the rank-and-file Reds scattered like rats into the sewers.

"They're getting more daring," Tezuka said. "Now they've graduated to shooting Privy Council members in the shadow of Police Headquarters."

"Regardless, a woman must be among their ranks," Aizawa said, pointing to the snow in front of Maeda's car. Inspector Tezuka circled the vehicle and examined the high heel prints, slowly being buried by a fresh coating of flakes.

"Yes, I know all about her but a good observation nonetheless, Inspector…?"

"Aizawa," Superintendent Miyake interjected. "Inspector Kenji Aizawa. He's the detective from the—"

"The Kusanagi Society Incident," Tezuka finished for him. His mustached face alighted with recognition. "Ah, yes. I remember reading about you in the newspapers. Fine work you did there, Inspector."

"Thank you," Aizawa said, rubbing the back of his head in embarrassment. "I had…assistance with that case."

Reiko Watanabe was the unsung hero of that sordid affair, but the specifics were too strange and too complicated to share. The fewer people who knew, the better.

"You're far too modest, Inspector. Have you ever considered transferring to the Tokko?"

No more than he'd ever considered becoming an *oni* devil or a *tengu* bird demon. Nevertheless, the Tokko were brother police officers and deserved respect. Besides, he couldn't help but admire Tezuka's efficiency and dedication to duty, even if he was a Thought Policeman.

"I don't have what it takes to solve thought crimes. Regular crimes are difficult enough."

"Very true," Tezuka said. "Most police officers don't qualify to join our ranks. They lack certain skills. The Tokko doesn't just punish, we rehabilitate thought criminals."

Aizawa nodded along, remembering the rehabilitation he'd seen. Torture and shame were the twin instruments of the Metropolitan Police, but the Tokko took such practices to new heights.

"I actually served under you once, Inspector," Aizawa said. "During the 3-15 Incident."

Tezuka's face brightened further at the mention of that incident from years past. In 1928, several left-wing proletarian parties won a surprising number of seats in the Diet elections, threatening the *kokutai*. Although the Communist Party had long been outlawed, the government suspected a resurgence of their movement. The Tokko struck on March 15th, 1928, arresting hundreds of Reds in a clean sweep. For years afterward, the underground Communist Party struggled to regain its membership, and now it teetered on the brink of total extinction.

"A proud day for the Metropolitan Police," Tezuka beamed. "You were one of the *junsas* under my command?"

"Yes, sir. The Reds never knew what hit them, eh?"

"We caught quite a few in their bathrobes!" Tezuka said, snickering. "Tell me, Aizawa-san, when did you shed your uniform?"

"I became an inspector the year after, in Showa 4."

"He served under Joji Shimura," Miyake said, inserting himself into the conversation again. Not that Aizawa could blame him. Two inspectors excluding a superintendent was rather disrespectful. Aizawa glanced over at Lieutenant Endo, still as a statue as snow gathered on his brown uniform. He half-pitied the officer, but soldiers were accustomed to standing at attention.

"Ah, yes. I remember Shimura-san." Tezuka shook his head. "Tragedy what happened to him."

"Well, at least our Inspector Aizawa caught the bastard who did it," Miyake said, clapping his shoulder.

Aizawa nodded but said nothing. His former mentor had turned into a bitter enemy before becoming another casualty of the Kusanagi Society. He didn't like where this was headed. Time to steer the conversation back on course and away from his past.

"If there is any assistance I can offer, Inspector Tezuka, I am at your service."

The Tokko inspector held up a hand. "That won't be necessary. As mentioned, I was working with Marquis Maeda on another matter. This is a Tokko investigation from now on." He turned to Miyake. "I'll report my findings to Superintendent Genki Abe."

Mention of the Tokko chief soured Miyake's face, but he forced a stoic composure. "Of course, Tezuka-san. Inspector Aizawa and I will defer to the Special Higher Police."

With the matter concluded, Inspector Tezuka bid them both respectful bows, dismissing them. As they trudged away from the crime scene, Aizawa cast a quick look back. Tezuka had reconvened with Lieutenant Endo. Amid a hushed, conspiratorial conversation, they passed under the Sakurada Gate, back toward the Imperial Palace. What secrets lurked inside that ancient structure? Part of him didn't want to know.

CHAPTER FOUR

Once darkness had swallowed Inspector Tezuka and Lieutenant Endo, Superintendent Miyake paused and heaved a relieved sigh.

"What luck!" Miyake exclaimed, clapping his gloved hands together. "The gods can be merciful sometimes!"

"Sir, I never thought you were one to cede jurisdiction to the Tokko," Aizawa said.

"Don't be a damn fool. Marquis Maeda was a member of the Privy Council. One of the Emperor's personal advisers. If Inspector Tezuka and Superintendent Abe want the responsibility of catching the assassins, they're welcome to it. The pressure they'll face from—" Miyake gestured across the moat at the towering structure looming above Tokyo, "—is enough to destroy a man's career. Tezuka will probably commit *seppuku* if he fails."

Aizawa felt a pang of sympathy for the Thought Policeman. However, Miyake had a point. The burden of such a case was a miserable way to start the new year.

"By the way, Inspector, any news from your little geisha spy?"

Aizawa wondered how Reiko was. They hadn't seen each other in almost a month since she'd gone undercover for this new assignment. But their next meeting was tomorrow, or rather, later today. Partly for a full report and partly to wish each other a Happy New Year.

"She's been attending parties with a certain movie director."

"Oh yes. Matsumoto, right?"

"Yes, sir. He had contact with Communists in the past but now claims to have cut ties with them. Given the recent crackdown, the Tokko requested we assist in unearthing every last Red in Tokyo."

"And he's still allowed to make movies?"

"Apparently so. He had been in Manchuria, making films with the Army. Trying to clean up his name, I suppose. It doesn't matter. Reiko can pry secrets out of any man, so we'll know if Matsumoto is a Red or not. He's throwing a party for the Hashizume Regiment tonight."

"Ah, the 2nd Cavalry! That's my son's unit!" Miyake glowed with pride before a dark cloud swept over him. "Nobody in the Tokko knows about the little geisha, right Inspector?"

A tightness gripped Aizawa's chest. "No sir."

The statement was true enough. Only the Superintendent-General of the Metropolitan Police and Miyake knew about Reiko Watanabe's double life as a spy in Aizawa's Special Investigations Unit. However, there was one other who'd discovered this secret arrangement and might complicate things in the future. No need to let Miyake know about *him* just yet.

"Superintendent Abe won't be happy until he has every Communist in a cell. They call him the 'Red Hunter,' you know?"

"A fitting title."

"Sugamo Prison is getting so full that we won't have anywhere to keep them."

"Perhaps Ueno Zoo?" Aizawa suggested.

"I wouldn't subject the animals to such cruelty."

As they approached the staff car, a *junsa* bolted out of the driver's seat and held the door open. Miyake climbed into the back, halted, then turned to Aizawa.

"Give you a ride, Inspector?"

Aizawa masked his surprise. Such kind-hearted gestures were unbecoming of his superior. Still, a cold breeze prompted him to accept.

"Thank you, sir," Aizawa said, entering through the other side. "I live in Ueno," he said to the driver.

The car roared to life and propelled forward. They rolled through Kasumigaseki, now a frosty ghost town. They soon passed a small *izakaya* bar, marked by a glowing red lantern, which housed the few Japanese without friends or families to drink with on New Year's. It was Aizawa's favorite spot to spend lonely holidays, drowning himself in Asahi beers and melancholy jazz records.

"You're not married, are you, Inspector?"

"No, sir. Not yet."

Leaning back in the car seat, Miyake continued. "No family either, right?"

"No, sir. My parents and little sister died during the Great Kanto Earthquake."

Miyake fell silent. No Tokyoite could forget that day in 1923 when the earth beneath the Kanto region roared and ripped itself asunder, reducing the Imperial capital to a smoldering wasteland. Thousands were devoured in a monstrous firestorm, including the entire Aizawa family. Since that day, Kenji Aizawa had fought to protect Tokyo from any threat, from coup d'états to organized drug rings.

"Why not attend your New Year's shrine visit with us?" Miyake said, shattering the brooding silence.

"You, sir?"

"My family. We always visit the Meiji Shrine on New Year's Day. You can join us and meet my daughter."

Aizawa took it all in. So that's what this was all about. Superiors often meddled with subordinates' love lives, sometimes out of altruism but other times for shrewd career purposes. The past year had been promising for Aizawa and Miyake wanted to exploit it. What better way than becoming his father-in-law? Still, to outright refuse a superior's suggestion was unthinkable. Aizawa would only have to endure his offspring for a day. Then he could find some placating excuse of why he wasn't good enough to join the Miyake family.

"Your daughter, sir?"

"Yes, she's one of those modern girls. What do you call them?"

"*Mogas*," Aizawa replied.

"Oh yes. *Mogas*," Miyake sneered. Contempt was so thick it almost dripped off his tongue. "Well, you like those *mogas*, don't you, Inspector?"

Aizawa coughed. An image of Reiko Watanabe, not in her geisha outfit, but in her best *moga* ensemble – cloche hat, skirt, gloves, high heels, and bobbed hair – warmed his mind.

"I…uh, like their…style, sir."

"Well, you'll like Minori then. She convinced my wife to let her attend a women's college." He scoffed. "My son serves in the Army while my daughter fritters her life away with books!"

Aizawa searched for a diplomatic answer. "I hope she can find a job in this depression."

"She can't find a job or a husband. What kind of man would want a woman who knows more than he does? Ridiculous! Maybe you can introduce her to an eligible bachelor with good career prospects." Miyake paused, then added, "If you know any."

The hint was clear – *'Meet my daughter, marry her, and advance in your career. Reject her and stay an inspector for the rest of your days.'*

"Of course, sir," Aizawa forced out. "I'd be honored."

Miyake leaned back in his seat, a man looking ahead to the future. Aizawa gazed out the window, a man longing to escape. He hoped Reiko was having a happier New Year than he was.

CHAPTER FIVE

Twanging *shamisen* music filled the Silkworm Tea House like a miniature concert. With all eyes on her, Reiko Watanabe strummed out a bouncy, carefree melody, perfect for ushering in the New Year. Rows of kneeling geisha in multi-colored kimonos clapped along with a dozen or so Army officers in dark brown uniforms. Each officer knelt in front of a small, low-lying table complete with sake or beer and attended to by a geisha who refilled their drinks, lit their Golden Bat cigarettes, and made them forget every worry. It was in this frivolous atmosphere that Reiko felt most relaxed, even if it was a party thrown for the Imperial Army.

There must have been thirty people crammed into the room, but it was big enough to include several wall scrolls of golden ginkgo trees, pink cherry blossoms, and dainty bamboo branches. Fitting, since geisha districts were nicknamed "flower towns." While in this tea house, each man was transported to heaven, without a care in the world.

Most of the men were Army officers, but three civilians gathered in the corner, ignored but still entertained. After all, they were filmmakers from Shochiku Kinema, men accustomed to working behind the scenes. Two wore evening kimonos – the lead cameraman and editor – while a third – Koichi Matsumoto, wore gray slacks and a cardigan, suitable attire for a movie director.

Reiko concluded her song, followed by a burst of applause. She bowed, then set the *shamisen* aside as conversation resumed. Gliding across the room, Reiko presented herself to the film crew with a little bow. The movie men smiled and drank her up with their eyes, especially Matsumoto.

She'd been seeing the director for the past month and had become accustomed to his lingering stares. Not that she minded. Even Reiko was still taken aback when she viewed herself as a geisha – white face paint and black kimono with an ornate cherry blossom design, topped off by a wig in traditional *shimada* hairstyle. Every time she donned this getup, she felt like an impostor putting on someone else's skin.

"Happy New Year, gentlemen," she cooed, nestling down beside them.

"Well, at least one of the geisha finally noticed us," Matsumoto said with a laugh. "After all, Shochiku Kinema is footing the bill for this party."

"Matsumoto-san, you can't expect us to ignore our fighting men." Reiko gestured to the rows of Army officers and geisha, who all shared an alcoholic flush that even white face paint couldn't hide. "Besides, haven't I shown you enough attention lately?"

"Harutora-san," Matsumoto began, using Reiko's geisha name, Spring Tiger, "one can never get enough attention from you."

Reiko giggled and waved her paper fan, feigning modesty. Geisha were supposed to flirt and boost a man's spirits, but compliments from Matsumoto always brightened her up. She couldn't suppress an infatuation for creative men. Writers, actors, painters, and especially film directors left her weak in the knees. Matsumoto's looks didn't hurt either – warm brown eyes behind thin spectacles, parted black hair, and full lips just above a strong chin. But she had to at least *play* coy.

"Lovely words, Matsumoto-san. Do you say that to all the girls who want roles in your movies?"

"Just the ones who have dialogue."

Reiko couldn't hold back a genuine laugh. Still, she couldn't forget tonight's purpose. She was a spy for the Metropolitan Police Department, and that – not Koichi Matsumoto – paid her bills. But try as she might, it was hard not to be charmed by him. Not that there was any real competition here.

Army officers were a boorish lot, particularly those in the infantry and artillery services. But green collar patches marked these soldiers as cavalrymen, which lent them some gallantry. But after countless rounds of sake and beer, the dashing officers of the 2nd Cavalry Regiment had degenerated into cackling fools.

Two second lieutenants crawled out on their hands and knees, each with a geisha atop their backs. Like horses, they bucked and whinnied, then crawled across the tatami mats to the other end of the tea house, racing back and forth. Their geisha riders squealed for them to go faster and faster, until one toppled over and lapsed into a fit of drunken giggling. The losing pair each took another shot of sake.

"The pride of the Imperial Army…" Reiko muttered.

"Hard to believe, I know. But you should have seen them in Manchuria. Brave as samurai and ferocious as demons," Matsumoto said, then gestured to an impassive officer at the far end of the tea house. "Especially their commander."

"That's right, you mentioned him before. Colonel…?"

"Colonel Riku Hashizume. He was just awarded the Order of the Golden Kite by the Emperor himself."

Across the room, a gleaming medal hung around the Colonel's uniform collar.

"Well, I do like jewelry," Reiko said.

Matsumoto checked his pocket watch, then turned to his colleagues. "It's time for us to set up the theater, gentlemen." He turned to Reiko. "Harutora, would you please keep Colonel Hashizume company? He loves geisha."

Reiko sighed. "I've had unpleasant experiences with military officers."

"Ah, but Hashizume is a warrior *and* a writer. They call him Colonel Haiku."

"Is that so?" Haiku was the traditional poetry of Japan, stuffy and formal, but at least the Colonel had something of an artistic soul. "All right, I'll do it so long as he writes one about me."

Matsumoto smiled and stood alongside the other filmmakers. They exited the room, and Reiko began her journey through the gauntlet of guffawing officers, squealing geisha, and drunken singing. Colonel Hashizume knelt, gripping a bottle of Yebisu beer. A young geisha had joined him, one Reiko recognized as Wakakichi, barely older than a *hangyoku* apprentice.

Despite her age, Wakakichi was a professional, who tittered and told jokes while the Colonel gave half-hearted laughs between sips of beer. Reiko knelt across from her, making her presence known.

"Pardon me, Wakakichi-san, but may I have a word with the Colonel?"

It was less a request than an order. Just like the Army, age and seniority commanded respect among geisha. Wakakichi forced a giggle, revealing her black-stained smile. Showing teeth was considered unfeminine, and when laughing, women covered their mouths with their hands, paper fans, and handkerchiefs. More traditional geisha still followed the practice of *ohaguro*, dyeing their teeth black to create the illusion of a demure smile. Perhaps the Colonel would appreciate a more modern geisha.

"Of course, Harutora-san," Wakakichi said with a bow, first to Reiko, then to Hashizume. After she'd shuffled away, Reiko took in the Colonel's features.

Riku Hashizume looked more like a weather-beaten statue than a man. His stern, squared face was rock hard, with skin like dried parchment, a result of the brutal Manchurian winters. Thick eyebrows hung over inscrutable eyes, a slash passed for his mouth, and gray strands had almost overtaken his close-cropped hair. Whereas most of the other officers had unbuttoned their collars, Colonel Hashizume still upheld uniform regulation, despite a reddish hue in his taut cheeks. Around his throat, the Order of the Golden Kite twinkled in the soft glow of paper lanterns.

Yellow rank tabs marked with three red stripes and three stars were fastened to his shoulders, indicating his rank as a full colonel. Twin brass ornaments on the Colonel's green collar patches each bore the number *2* – identifying the 2nd Cavalry Regiment. A starched, dark brown tunic seemed molded onto Hashizume, as if it were his own flesh.

"Greetings, Colonel. I'm Harutora," Reiko announced herself with a bow. "Matsumoto-san has told me much about you."

Hashizume regarded her with a detached curiosity. "Is that so? And what has he said?"

"Of your heroic service in the Manchurian Incident. The Hashizume Regiment was known for its daring raids against the enemy."

Reiko waited for the Colonel to take the bait. Most military men were vainglorious, despite a facade of modesty. Compliment their past glories and they melted into malleable clay. But Hashizume appeared unmoved.

"My men were more heroic than I was. All I did was my duty. Nothing more."

Reiko searched for another angle. "Oh, I see. Well, Matsumoto-san told me that you write haikus. How fascinating that a sentimental artist resides within a warrior's body!"

"It's just a silly hobby."

"Oh please, would you write some for me?"

The Colonel swigged his beer and said, "My haikus are…personal."

With that, the conversation was over, and Hashizume flicked his wrist, dismissing her. Reiko sat there open-mouthed for a moment, before realizing she might be showing teeth. Without a word, she stood and crossed the room, hoping the white paint concealed the anger boiling inside her.

CHAPTER SIX

Shame and humiliation rose in Reiko's throat like bile. How dare he! To be insulted by that boor? How stupid she was, to think a cultured Army officer could exist. What a miserable way to start the year!

Luckily, Matsumoto and the other movie men had returned and were busy setting up a film projector along with a small screen. Reiko plopped near them, still fuming but calmed a bit by their presence. Wakakichi returned to Hashizume's orbit, presenting him with a new beer. The Colonel smiled and nodded, a master pleased with his pet.

The pair of geisha remounted the two lieutenants, holding their sheathed sabers like jousting lances. Tromping across the tatami mats, the officers charged at each other, sabers jangling in the geisha's unsteady hands. As they collided, one of the geisha spun off her lieutenant's back and onto the floor. Hooting laughter filled the tea house as the losing team downed their punishment of sake.

When the cackling subsided, an older geisha – so old that she didn't even bother with white face paint anymore – stood in front of the raucous crowd and quieted them.

"May I have your attention, please? First off, we would like to thank Shochiku Kinema for organizing this New Year's party!"

Applause thundered from the cavalrymen and geisha. Still helping set up the miniature movie theater, Matsumoto gave an embarrassed bow.

"Secondly," the older geisha continued, "the Asakusa Geisha Guild wishes to bestow the strong warriors of the Hashizume Regiment with a gift!" She held up a certificate before the entire tea house. "An English thoroughbred, purchased by our guild, will be donated to the 2nd Cavalry Regiment. He is currently housed at the Shinjuku Army Stables, awaiting Colonel Hashizume's inspection."

The older geisha moved across the room, bowed, and presented the certificate to Hashizume with both hands. A small smile softened the Colonel's imperious face as he accepted.

"Thank you, all," he said, handing the paper off to the black-toothed geisha. "I'm sure he'll serve the 2nd Regiment well."

Reiko couldn't hide a frown. That was it? Even she had donated to this stupid fund. He could at least make a speech. Drafting animals into the Army sickened her, but she had to save face in front of her fellow geisha and kept quiet.

"I would like to thank the brave men of the Hashizume Regiment," Matsumoto said, stepping forward, "and especially their commanding officer."

The Colonel gave a pleased nod, a clear command to continue.

"They agreed to let us travel along with them in Manchuria to make a documentary film. These soldiers not only faced Chinese bombs and bullets, but also the punishing ice and snow of the Manchurian winter!"

The praise electrified the officers, sending a second lieutenant to his feet. "A toast," he bellowed, raising a beer bottle, "to our brave commander, Colonel Hashizume!"

"Kanpai!" the cavalrymen roared in unison. After they drank, Matsumoto regained control of the room.

"As a token of our appreciation, the 2nd Cavalry Regiment has the honor of being the first audience to see Shochiku Kinema's latest picture – *Bullets and Horses in Manchuria*!"

The other filmmakers snuffed out the paper lanterns, flooding the room with darkness. The projector whirred and shone a flickering light. Shochiku Kinema's logo appeared on the screen, followed by the title and credits. One name stood out – *Koichi Matsumoto, Director*. Reiko resisted the urge to applaud then and there.

Although there were intertitles, Matsumoto stood off to the side and narrated, like the *benshi* who provided commentary and acted out dialogue for silent films.

"In early November, Showa 6, we arrived at the 2nd Cavalry Regiment's encampment," Matsumoto said as the camera panned along soldiers tending to horses, "and met its dashing commander." Colonel Riku Hashizume appeared onscreen, mounted upon a magnificent steed.

"From there, we accompanied them on the most decisive battles of the Manchurian Incident."

The projector flashed a whirlwind of images. November 1931 – the Battle of Tsitsihar, when Japanese forces expelled the Chinese general Ma Chan-shan from North Manchuria. December 1931 – the advance on Chinchow and the inglorious retreat of Marshal Chang Hsueh-liang from his homeland. February 1932 – the capture of Harbin and the defeat of the last Chinese defender, General Ting Chao.

In every segment, the 2nd Cavalry Regiment was shown in wide angles advancing on enemy positions, outflanking Chinese troops, and pursuing a routed foe across snowy Manchurian plains. Some of the footage was obviously staged – Reiko had seen enough movies to spot the difference – but plenty more were genuine shots of Colonel Hashizume leading the charge, saber pointed straight at the enemy.

Reiko flashed an approving glance at Koichi Matsumoto, still providing narration like a good *benshi*. What a wizard of film this man was. So potent was his moviemaking, even she rooted for this boorish lot of Army officers. Cinema had that effect on her. If only she could crawl inside a screen and live in that celluloid world forever.

*****

It was half-past two when the party finally dispersed. Geisha and Army officers stumbled out of the Silkworm Tea House before collapsing into waiting rickshaws and taxis.

Snug in his winter overcoat, Matsumoto lingered outside, smoking a cigarette. Thanks to a few rounds of sake, Reiko wobbled in her *geta* clogs as she joined the director outside. The frosty air prickled her skin and set her teeth chattering. Matsumoto's smoldering cigarette seemed to be the only source of warmth.

"Mind if I have one?" Reiko asked. "I'm all out of Golden Bats."

Matsumoto chuckled and presented her with a pink pack labeled '*Cherry Cigarettes.*'

"Only if you promise never to smoke those tasteless sticks ever again. Cherry is the only Japanese brand worth a damn."

Reiko plucked out a smoke and lit up. Smooth tobacco filled her lungs, warming her. Golden Bats were rough on the throat, but she'd grown up smoking them. However, Cherry cigarettes were like a new world – gentle and sophisticated.

"Thank you, Matsumoto-san. I enjoyed your movie. Are you going to make documentaries from now on?"

"No, that was a special assignment for Shochiku Kinema…" Matsumoto trailed off as Colonel Hashizume exited the tea house. Wakakichi followed close behind, like a little lost puppy. A khaki cap, flaked with snow, was draped over Hashizume's broad shoulders, while a service cap's black leather visor shadowed his eyes. The hat's bright red band and brass star clashed with the somber brown of the rest of his uniform. As he approached, a heavy saber knocked at his side with a metallic rasp. Just how many Chinese had he felled with that blade?

"Matsumoto-san," Hashizume said, extending an open palm. "Thank you for the enjoyable evening."

The director snapped to attention and shook the Colonel's hand. "My pleasure. Thank you for everything, Colonel. And…Happy New Year."

"Good luck with the picture," Hashizume said. "I'm sure it will be a hit."

"Only because of you, Colonel."

The cavalry officer gave a taut smile, then glanced over at Reiko and offered a curt, yet polite, nod. With that, Hashizume turned and walked toward an awaiting sedan, Wakakichi close behind. Headlights flashed and the car sped off, leaving Reiko and Matsumoto alone at last.

"I'm surprised he gave me a farewell nod," Reiko said, blowing out a puff of cigarette smoke. "Considering how he dismissed me as if I were one of his soldiers."

"Colonel Hashizume is tough but sentimental," Matsumoto offered. "A true officer and a gentleman."

"Well, you weren't kidding. He does like geisha. Enough to take one home."

"I certainly wasn't implying that when I asked you to keep him company."

"We wouldn't be speaking if you had, Matsumoto-san," Reiko said with a little grin. After a few more drags, she tossed the Cherry cigarette into the wet snow, extinguishing it. "Thank you for the cigarette. I needed it after tonight." She extended the pack to Matsumoto.

"Keep it," he said. "On one condition."

Reiko lifted her eyebrows. "Oh? And what is that?"

"That we have a date…a Western-style date. Tomorrow."

"Tomorrow?"

"Sorry, I meant January 2nd. Nothing is open on New Year's Day except temples and shrines."

"Where would we go, Matsumoto-san?" Reiko mused. "Half of Tokyo stays closed until the 3rd. The other half even longer."

"The Rheingold is hosting a special dinner. Lots of foreign businessmen and diplomats have to eat."

"That's in Ginza. Does that mean you'd like me to dress as a *moga*?"

Matsumoto smiled. They'd met at a geisha party thrown for the executives and big shots of Shochiku Kinema. As part of the recent crackdown on Reds, Inspector Aizawa had secured a spot for Reiko at the party with orders to milk

Koichi Matsumoto – who'd recently returned from Manchuria – for any possible "dangerous thoughts." Instead, they'd bonded over movies, and quickly set up another meeting. He'd been enticed by her geisha act as Harutora, but became enamored by the progressive modern girl – the *moga* – Reiko Watanabe. Still, she couldn't be *too* available.

"I'm not sure, Matsumoto-san. What will we do after? All the movie theaters will be closed."

"Well, I have something special to offer you." The director gave a knowing grin, his eyes twinkling behind those spectacles. "But I can't tell you yet. It's a secret."

"I don't like secrets. Unless I'm the one keeping them."

"You'll like this one," Matsumoto said, undaunted. "I'm going to make your dream come true, Reiko Watanabe."

CHAPTER SEVEN

"To the death of Marquis Maeda and to the Japanese Revolution!" Utako toasted. "Kanpai!"

"Kanpai!" the Red Terror Society chorused, before downing their cups of sweet *amazake* rice wine.

Their spirits were high, despite the squalid surroundings. Copies of *The Red Flag* – the Japanese Communist Party's newspaper – and *The Soldier's Friend* – the propaganda literature aimed at the Army – lay piled on the wooden floors. Aside from four worn-out futons, a humming electric lamp and heater, and small heaps of personal clothes, there were no furnishings, adding to the proletarian lifestyle. Nagant revolvers lay off to the side, grim reminders of tonight's victory.

Below them, on the first floor, was a Morinaga Chocolate Shop – just one of its many branches throughout Tokyo – while apartments occupied the second and third floor. All were unaware that just above them on the fourth story was the hideout of the Red Terror Society. Many Japanese feared the number four, since it could also be read as *shi* – death. Another foolish superstition, but at least it meant their rent was cheaper than the others.

Down the street stood the towering department stores, foreign restaurants, and nightclubs of Ginza, the city's shopping district. A blinking neon light, advertising Morinaga Milk Chocolate, flooded through the window, painting their faces with a reddish-yellow glow.

Pak looked satiated, both from the *amazake* and from tonight's bloodletting. Saburo Genda's thick frame remained tight, ready for action. Wataru Izumi leaned forward, his chubby cheeks brightened by a combination of alcohol and the flickering outside lights. A strange creature, Utako thought as she examined him. Izumi's frame was rail thin, but his face was plump and round, like the full moon.

But Major Kuno – still in civilian clothes – was rigid and firm all over, toughened by campaigns in the field. His long face had a predatory quality, like a wolf on the hunt. Huge, powerful arms at his sides were like the claws of a wild bear. Thankfully, this human beast was on their side.

"Comrades, I'm proud of you all, especially you, Natsume-han," Kuno said, setting aside his cup. His thick Osakan accent was obvious, using *han* instead of *san*. "Tonight's mission was a complete success. Many more enemies of the people will die this year."

"We couldn't have done it without you, Major Kuno," Utako said, raising her cup again. "After all, we didn't even know how to fire a gun before you joined us. It was your training that transformed the Red Terror Society from a motley gang of dilettantes into the samurai sword of the working class!"

"And one which will plunge straight into the soft belly of the bourgeoisie," Izumi giggled, his flabby cheeks rippling like waves. "Who's our next target, Major? Prime Minister Saito?"

"Too risky," Genda snapped. "An industrialist or a banker will be less guarded."

"I don't care who we kill next," Pak said, "as long as they're Japanese."

The statement hung in the air like a foul odor. Not that Utako could fault Pak. After all, his native Korea had been a Japanese colony for over twenty years now. Hatred for Japan had consumed Pak, transforming him into a bomb ready to explode. But he was a Communist now and his bitterness could be focused for the Revolution.

"Whoever is next," Utako said, "we mustn't forget our strategy."

"Please remind us, oh glorious leader," Izumi said, holding his pale hands near the electric heater.

Ignoring the taunt, Utako set her cup aside, then drew herself up like a teacher addressing the classroom.

"Jokichi Kazama and the other fools who ran the Communist Party thought they could bring about the Revolution through strikes and protests. Led by who? Most of our comrades are rotting in Sugamo Prison! But we don't need strikes or protests, comrades."

"Why not?" Genda blubbered, simple and curious.

"Because," Utako went on, "the Communist Party never gained widespread support of the Japanese people. We understand this. The Red Terror Society is not a mass party, but a Marxist-Leninist vanguard. But Kazama was correct about one thing. He urged Party members to reach out, not only to factory workers, but to soldiers. It is in the Army where will find comrades. The Party's publication, *The Soldier's Friend*, has made headway into the Army. More and more troops now realize that the Manchurian Incident was a criminal imperialist war, started to line the pockets of the *zaibatsu*. The only possibility for Communism to triumph in Japan is if the Army turns Red. Don't forget, comrades, the Bolsheviks didn't take power in Russia through a mass revolution but a coup d'état!"

"The Army will seize power in a coup?" Genda piped up again. "Like the 5-15 Incident?"

"No," she snapped, "that was a fascist plot against the bourgeois government. The anarchists did the same thing, ten years ago, with their so-called Guillotine Society, killing military and business leaders. 'Propaganda of the deed,' they called it." Utako shook her head. "But incompetence was their downfall. Only the military can bring about real change in Japan. The anarchists and the fascists failed to bring the military over to their ideals. We won't make the same mistake. Thanks to our comrade," her eyes flicked over to Kuno, "we now know that many in the Army are turning to Communism, just like what happened in Russia before their revolution. Once enough elder statesmen are assassinated, we, along with our allies in Army will seize the apparatus of state power and establish the Japanese Soviet Republic in one fell swoop."

Her comrades nodded in submission. Even Izumi looked mesmerized. If politics was grand theater, who better than a former actress to shape it?

"Stirring words, but I'm not sure who the next target will be yet," Kuno said, his burly voice like an artillery shell.

"If there's going to be another hit, we could use some firecrackers," Izumi said.

"You mean grenades?" Kuno asked.

Izumi grinned mischievously.

"I need to consult with my comrades in the Army."

Utako couldn't hide her curiosity. "Who are these comrades, Major? Officers, like you?"

Izumi leaned forward, his plump face curious. "Any generals?"

"You'd be surprised how many sympathize with our cause, Izumi-han."

"Is that so?" Utako said, smiling. "How do we know you're not really a wolf in disguise? The Communist Party is riddled with informants like fleas on a dog."

"A wolf?" Kuno gave a throaty laugh. "Would a spy train a gang of Reds how to rob banks and kill aristocrats?"

A valid point, Utako conceded. Besides, the spies from the Metropolitan Police only collected information, then struck in pre-dawn raids like the 3-15 Incident. If Kuno was in league with the Police or *Kempeitai*, then they'd already have been strung up inside Sugamo Prison by now.

"You haven't told the central committee about me, have you?" Kuno asked.

Utako scoffed. "Of course not. I just said that the Party leadership is infested with spies. Anything we tell them would be passed along to the Tokko. At this point, the only contact we have with them is, once a month, we provide them with money for their coffers. In exchange, they give us propaganda material."

"Good. Keep it that way." Kuno gave a satisfied nod, his anxieties quelled.

"What changed, Major?" Izumi asked. "We've tried for years to recruit Army men, and for our trouble, they tried to use us for bayonet practice."

Major Kuno pointed to an issue of *The Soldier's Friend* next to Utako's futon.

"That, for one. Don't underestimate the discontent that this depression has caused throughout the Army. Many soldiers are peasants from the Tohoku region, now ravaged by famine. Men cannot concentrate on their duties while their families starve. Your magazine captured the despair and misery many soldiers feel."

Utako beamed. She'd contributed many articles to *The Soldier's Friend*, urging troops to desert, disobey orders, and shoot their commanders. All under military pseudonyms, of course. It was easy to assume different roles, even the guise of a disgruntled soldier.

"The second reason," Kuno went on, "is the Manchurian Incident. We were used as cannon fodder for an imperialist war. The soldiers there are beginning to realize the false reasons we invaded. There are whispers among units that the Chinese didn't bomb the South Manchurian Railway, but rather, it was a staged attack by a small clique of officers."

"It wouldn't surprise me," Utako sneered. "The Imperial Army and Navy are nothing more than mercenaries for the *zaibatsu*. They're the true rulers of Japan, not that near-sighted peacock atop a white horse."

Kuno nodded. "Yes, I realize that now. And I have you to thank, comrades. Had I not read *The Soldier's Friend*, I'd still be nothing more than a weapon, used by the ruling class to murder fellow workers and peasants in Manchuria."

"When we take power, comrades," she said, "they will all answer for their crimes. Including our so-called Emperor…"

Insulting the Emperor still left Utako with a bitter aftertaste, an unfortunate by-product of years of indoctrination. The idea that the Emperor was divine, the direct descendent of the sun goddess Amaterasu, was so ingrained in Japanese society, that even many Communists were ambiguous toward him. Although it had always called for the abolition of the monarchy, the Party's main adversary had traditionally been the *zaibatsu*, the powerful capitalist families. A few comrades were even content to let the Emperor remain as a figurehead during the transition between capitalism to socialism.

That all changed with the Japanese Communist Party's 1932 Thesis, reemphasizing that the main obstacle to revolution was the Emperor System. The *zaibatsu* and landlords were the other two pillars of oppression, but the Emperor's mere existence made the Japanese people resistant to any revolutionary change. The imperialist war in Manchuria would be transformed into civil war, which would topple the Chrysanthemum Throne. Just as Russia overthrew the Tsar, Japan would free itself of its false god, paving the way for the Japanese Soviet Republic under Moscow's protection. Taiwan, Korea, and Manchuria would be free from Japanese imperialism, and Communist revolutions would spread throughout Asia. For the Red Terror Society, the 1932 Thesis was a blueprint of the future. Except for one troubling detail.

"Moscow insists Japan is still tied to feudalism, unable to have a true proletarian revolution," Utako continued. "The 1932 Thesis says we must have a two-stage revolution, first a bourgeois democratic uprising followed by a true Communist revolution led by a vanguard party. But this is Russian chauvinism, comrades. Moscow is ignorant of Japanese history, unaware of our tendency to rise up and fight against injustice. More importantly, the Russians don't realize that the Imperial Army is close to open rebellion, thanks to men like Major Kuno. With his help, we will overthrow the Emperor System in a swift and merciless coup d'état, then establish a Soviet Japan without any help from the bourgeoisie."

Utako shared a smile with her comrades until a knock rattled at the door. Silent tension filled the apartment, interrupted only by the buzzing electric heater. The Police? Utako glanced over to the window, where a fire escape offered a way up to the rooftop. From there, they could make their way down to the alleyway, where Izumi's car was parked for just such an emergency.

"Open up in there," a tinny voice whined. "The rent is due!"

Utako expelled a relieved sigh, then covered the pile of pistols underneath her futon. She hopped up and slid the door ajar, just enough to see the landlady's dour face, corrugated with wrinkles.

"But *obasan*, it's New Year's Day," Utako asked, using the term for "grandmother," regardless of any blood relation. Anything to sweet-talk this withered crocodile.

"The other tenants paid me in advance *before* the banks closed for the holiday. And I agreed to turn a blind eye to an unmarried woman living with three," the landlady fumbled for a suitable term, "men, as long as you paid the rent on the first of every month."

Rudeness wouldn't work with this old crone. Instead, Utako needed to pull out whatever sympathy remained inside her shriveled little body.

"Please *obasan*," Utako pleaded, lip trembling and eyes watery with forced tears. "Just a little more time. Money is still tight because of the depression…"

Concern flickered across the landlady's face, like an actual *obasan* for her granddaughter. "Fine, a few more days. But I want it soon."

That meant January 4th at the latest when Tokyo awakened from its holiday slumber. Utako nodded, bowed her gratitude, and shut the door. After the landlady's shambling steps faded, she turned to her comrades.

"Landlords," Izumi grumbled, rubbing his thin hands. "When the Revolution comes, their lot will be up against a firing squad."

"Major Kuno," Utako said, rejoining them. "Loan us a few yen to shut that hag up."

Kuno scoffed. "I give you weapons, teach you how to kill, and now you want money?"

"Why not?" Genda grunted. "The Army has plenty of yen to spare! They steal it from the taxpayers to fund their imperialist war in Manchuria!"

Kuno shook his head. "Fool! Do you want me to be arrested by the *Kempeitai*?"

"Don't you get an allowance from your little boyfriend?" Izumi asked. "The movie director?"

Utako didn't reply but sank a venomous glare into him.

Kuno snorted. "What happened to the haul from that Yokohama bank?"

Frowning, Utako said, "A few days before our heist, a run had cleaned them out. We made off with pocket change and the Party took most of that for its coffers."

Kuno snorted. "Why not break with them completely?"

"I'm tempted, but they provide us with issues of *The Red Flag* and *The Soldier's Friend*. You did say how effective they are in bringing troops to our side."

"Yes, of course…so, why not rob another bank? Tokyo is full of them…"

Utako flashed a knowing smile to her comrades. First an assassination, and now a bank robbery. The Red Terror was coming to Tokyo at a rapid pace.

"As ordered, Major."

CHAPTER EIGHT

Even early in the morning, the Meiji Shrine was overcrowded, leaving Inspector Aizawa with a tightening sense of claustrophobia. Well, what did he expect on New Year's Day? *Hatsumode*, the first visit of the year to a Shinto shrine or Buddhist temple, was a time-honored tradition, and the Meiji Shrine was one of the most popular sites.

Dedicated to the deified spirits of the Meiji Emperor and Empress – grandparents of the current Emperor – the Shinto shrine was situated within the enormous Yoyogi Parade Ground, where the Imperial Army held their annual review. However sacred, the Meiji Shrine was located in western Tokyo, across town from Aizawa's home in Ueno, and a pain to get to.

Last October, the city had merged with the neighboring unincorporated areas, ballooning the number of wards from fifteen to thirty-five, and became "Greater Tokyo." Six million instead of three now inhabited the Imperial Capital, stretching the Metropolitan Police even thinner in their duties. Tokyo had grown from a dense, yet compact city, into a sprawling metropolis, devouring everything in its path.

Aizawa passed underneath a wooden *torii* gate, gateway to the spirit realm. Here, gods watched over the mortals who queued up to pray for their blessings. The Meiji Shrine's spacious courtyard swarmed with people, blotting out every inch of pavement. Last night's snow had melted but it hadn't warmed up any. Most of the visitors wore their fanciest winter kimonos, but Aizawa ignored tradition for comfort, opting for his usual black overcoat and fedora.

Despite the lines, there was no pushing, shoving, or cutting, since most Japanese were naturally obedient. Besides, to do so in their sacred space might upset the gods, a very risky thing so early in the year. Although Aizawa dreaded meeting any offspring of Superintendent Miyake, he found some comfort in the serene beauty of the Meiji Shrine. For a moment, his own parents and little sister appeared in his mind, visiting their local shrine for *hatsumode* as a family.

Aizawa retreated into his overcoat to escape the biting cold and those haunting memories. New Year's always made him feel the most alone, as if all Japan shunned him. Thankfully, a group of four approaching figures jerked him out of self-pity. Wearing a blue winter kimono and *haori* jacket, Superintendent Shinsaku Miyake looked strange out of uniform, a lizard who shed its last skin. Two women walked behind him, both in colorful winter kimonos, while a young Army officer traipsed alongside.

"Ah, Inspector, good to see you," Miyake said. "Allow me to introduce my wife, Mayumi."

Miyake's wife stepped forward, allowing for a better look. Gray-haired and with a face cut by two long wrinkles, Mayumi Miyake still retained a matronly beauty.

"And my daughter, Minori."

Mayumi Miyake's looks lived on in her daughter. Pale-skinned and graceful, Minori was a traditional Japanese maiden in a snug-fitting kimono. But her rouged cheeks, shadowed eyes, and black hair, rippling in a permanent wave, hinted at the *moga* lurking inside.

"And my son, Eisaku Miyake."

Careful not to linger, Aizawa shifted his eyes from Minori to her brother. Tall and lanky, Eisaku didn't wear a kimono, but rather the brown uniform and overcoat of the Imperial Army. Two rank insignia on his shoulders – two stars against a single yellow stripe and two red – along with brass "2" numerals against green collar patches – marked him as a first lieutenant in the 2nd Cavalry Regiment. Lest there be any doubt of his parentage, Superintendent Miyake's sharp, angular features were present in the Lieutenant's face.

"This is Inspector Kenji Aizawa," Miyake said.

"It's a pleasure to meet you all," Aizawa said with a bow. The Miyake family reciprocated, with the women bowing a little deeper. Stranger or not, Aizawa was still a man.

Following the Superintendent's lead, they all queued up before the *haiden* worship hall, where offerings and prayers were made to the gods. Luckily, the line kept moving and they advanced at a steady pace.

"It's only going to get worse as the day goes on," Miyake mused aloud. "Good thing we got here early."

Mayumi murmured her agreement, but their children kept quiet. The conversation stalled, and after moments of strained silence, Aizawa gestured to Eisaku's uniform.

"You served in the Hashizume Regiment, Lieutenant?"

"Yes, sir. You're familiar with us?"

"I read about Colonel Hashizume in the papers. Your unit is part of the Second Division, right?" Eisaku nodded. "You boys practically overran Manchuria by yourselves! By chance, you weren't at a geisha party last night, were you?"

Embarrassment colored Eisaku's young face. "No, sir. I spent New Year's Eve with my family."

"And we're better company than a bunch of painted-up geisha," Minori said with a grin. "Aren't we, big brother?"

Eisaku blushed a deeper shade of red but didn't reply.

"When did you return from Manchuria?" Aizawa asked.

"Just arrived last week, sir. First time we've been in the home islands since the fighting began."

That amounted to over fifteen months. The Manchurian Incident had erupted in September 1931, when Chinese units appeared to dynamite a portion of the South Manchurian Railway, lifeline of the Japanese Empire. Like an unstoppable typhoon, Japan's force in the region – the elite Kwantung Army – expelled Chinese forces out of Manchuria entirely, proclaiming the independent nation of Manchukuo shortly after.

"Welcome back," Aizawa said. "I know how queer the home islands can seem after being at the front. When I returned from Siberia, Tokyo was like a fantasy world, stranger than any fairy tale or movie."

"You were in the Siberian Expedition?" Eisaku said with a little smile.

Aizawa nodded, memories repeating in his mind. In the final year of the World War, Japan and other Allied nations rushed troops into Russia, now mired in civil war after the Bolshevik Revolution. Officially, the mission was to aid the Czech Legion, now stranded in Siberia, and safeguard stockpiles of weapons sent to Russia. But the hidden objective was to crush Bolshevism and aid the counterrevolutionary White forces.

Most foreign troops were dispatched to Siberia, with Japan sending far more than any other Allied nation. The Imperial Army seized large swaths of Siberian territory, intending to establish puppet state under some Cossack warlord, safeguarding Korea and the home islands from the Bolshevik threat.

But the Expedition devolved into an endless quagmire with no clear objective. Aizawa and his comrades didn't even fight the Red Army, but out-of-uniform Bolshevik partisans who blended into the endless forests and snow. In 1920, the rest of the Allied armies evacuated Siberia, but Japan remained, much to frustration of its own citizens.

Morale plummeted, with some soldiers becoming infected with the "dangerous thought" of Communism. The civilian government wanted to withdraw, but hardliners in the Army General Staff held out for years. After all, this was their best chance to neutralize the Russian Bear forever. A confusing guerrilla war between Bolshevik partisans and Japanese soldiers lasted until 1922, when the Japanese government finally pulled its troops out, rendering the entire Siberian Expedition a bewildering failure.

Eisaku spoke again, returning Aizawa to the present. "So, you know how cold it can get up there, don't you Inspector?"

Aizawa laughed. "Winter in Tokyo is balmy by comparison. I hope you don't have to go back for a while. The newspapers are full of stories of those so-called 'Volunteer Armies' prowling the Manchurian countryside with Soviet weapons."

"'Volunteer Armies?'" Eisaku gave a wry smile. "They're nothing more than anti-Japanese bandits. But they aren't equipped by the Russians. That's a line the generals put out to save face. The bandits' biggest supplier of arms is the Manchukuoan Army. Whenever they're ambushed, our Manchukuoan allies drop their weapons and turn tail."

"Is that so?" Aizawa remarked. He should have known the Army leadership would lie to save face, even if it blamed the Soviets to do so.

Sensing the awkward shift, Miyake stepped closer and announced, "Eisaku is being transferred to the Imperial Guard." Evident pride laced his words.

"The Imperial Guard? Congratulations, Lieutenant," Aizawa said. "Only the best of the Army qualify to become guardsmen."

Again, the Lieutenant reddened. "Thank you, sir. I am grateful they've accepted someone unworthy as me."

With a scoff, Minori stepped closer. "Eisaku-oniisan is too modest. Tell the Inspector about how you charged those Chinese troops at Tsitsihar!"

Eisaku coughed and replied, "Colonel Hashizume led that attack. I only followed orders."

Minori rolled her eyes. "My humble big brother won't admit to any positive attributes unless you torture it out of him, Inspector. The Army teaches that modesty and frugality are the only traits worth having."

"I take it you disagree?" Aizawa asked.

"There's nothing wrong with bragging, so long as it's true."

"Minori-chan," her mother hissed. "Stop talking like that. It's unladylike!"

"My apologies, Inspector," Minori said. "Ever since attending college, my brain has grown, but so has my mouth. I even read books for fun now. How unladylike!"

Minori's parents exchanged irritated glances.

"Do you have any hobbies, Inspector?" Minori asked.

The question took Aizawa aback. Women usually weren't so forward, but Miyake did warn that his daughter was a *moga* at heart.

"I'm afraid I don't have the time for hobbies, Minori-san," Aizawa replied, using her given name but with the respectful *san* attached. Enough to not offend anyone, but also enough to let her know he was interested.

Minori gave a long sigh. "That's the problem with Japanese men. Work consumes their entire life, so a hobby is like having some shameful vice or mistress."

"Minori-chan!" her mother snapped.

Minori put a hand to her mouth in mock embarrassment. Aizawa let out a chuckle.

"If you have any suggestions, please let me know," he said, just as they reached the front of the queue.

Along with the Miyake family, Aizawa approached the *haiden*, tossed a handful of coins into the offering box, bowed twice, clapped, and gave a silent prayer. What blessings should he ask the Shinto deities for? World peace? A male heir for the Empire? An end to this economic depression? Advancement in his career?

He cast a glance over at Minori, eyes closed in prayer, and found his answer. An end to his loneliness would suffice.

CHAPTER NINE

Reiko watched streams of people traipse in and out of the Senso-ji Temple's grounds, feeling a twinge of melancholy. Children stuffed into fancy silk kimonos followed their parents into the main prayer hall, reminding Reiko of the kimonos she used to wear for *hatsumode*, though hers were more threadbare.

The Watanabes had never seen the need to give their daughter nice clothes, since she'd just outgrow them. If only her parents could see her outfit now – a cloche hat, pea coat, beaded handbag, leather gloves, and pumps – probably costing more than they spent on clothing all year.

Reiko bit her lip, choking down past bitterness. Her childhood had few comforts, but the Senso-ji Buddhist Temple was one of them. The Watanabe family often visited Senso-ji, located in the heart of Asakusa, if only because it was close by. As a little girl, Reiko fell in love with the Senso-ji, from the purification fountain with stone dragon spouts, to the five-story pagoda adjacent to the main temple itself, painted a dazzling, auspicious red.

Her prayers concluded, Reiko contented herself with watching the crowds until Inspector Aizawa arrived. They usually rendezvoused at Ueno Park, but meeting him here would kill two birds with one stone. She could brief him on last night's events and also get her *hatsumode* out of the way.

A continuous current of people passed beneath the great Nio Gate, entryway to Senso-ji's inner grounds. Twin statues of *nio*, the fearsome spirit guardians of Buddha, flanked the sides while an enormous red paper lantern dangled beneath its arch. Most everyone in Asakusa would visit the Senso-ji today, along with Inspector Aizawa, who – wrapped in black clothing – stuck out in this sea of ornate kimonos.

Aizawa saw her too and made a beeline over.

"Happy New Year, Reiko-san," he said, with a bow. "Sorry I'm late. I just came from across town."

"Don't apologize. Happy New Year, Inspector," Reiko said, bowing.

They held each other in a soft stare for several moments. It had been almost a month since their last rendezvous, far too long. Without speaking, she led him over to the large stone pot, belching smoke and flame. Incense wafted out, soaking groups of people standing nearby. Reiko and Aizawa bathed themselves in it, waving the smoke toward them and into their coats, hats, and any exposed skin until their eyes watered with tears. Incense baths were a good way to purify oneself against illness and evil spirits, starting the New Year right.

They retreated toward the Nio Gate, where Aizawa presented an enveloped card with both hands.

Greeting cards were one of many New Year's customs, and tradition dictated that they be mailed several days prior. But Aizawa's conspiratorial mind didn't want any official link between the Metropolitan Police and her, even if Reiko was on their payroll as a spy. Not that she blamed him. In their world, dark plots and vast conspiracies swirled around them like thick fog.

On the card, rows of cartoon characters lined up with smiling faces. Mickey Mouse, Felix the Cat, and Betty Boop stood on the left, representing America. On the right were Japanese heroes – Norakuro, the stray black dog who joined the Imperial Army, Peach Boy Taro, the young warrior who fought an entire island of devils, and the Golden Bat, a yellow-skinned, skull-faced hero who took his name from the cigarette brand. Above them was the year – 1933: Showa 8 – and below read, "East meets West for a Peaceful New Year."

"Awww," Reiko cooed. "A man who understands my love of cartoons and world peace."

Inspector Aizawa scratched the back of his head in embarrassment. Reiko dug into her handbag and pulled out her own card.

Aizawa opened it with a grin. Chuckling, he flashed it over for her to see. Since 1933 was the year of the rooster, a proud cock crowed while sunrays shone in the background. Patriotic and timely.

"Sorry, there aren't any cartoons in yours," Reiko said. "Maybe next year."

Aizawa slid the card into his coat pocket, then removed another envelope, and pressed it into her gloved palm. Its thickness indicated that it was her monthly payment, and a subtle hint to begin the report.

"Not too much to say about Matsumoto-san," Reiko said, dropping the envelope into her handbag. "But he did say he was 'going to make my dream come true.' Oh, I hope he's not proposing." She smiled. "Not yet anyway. I think I'd make a better mistress than a wife. Don't you agree?"

Aizawa raised an eyebrow. "Why don't you start from the beginning?"

"As requested, I've been seeing Koichi Matsumoto for a month now. Last night he gave us a private screening of his latest film. A charming picture, if you're Genghis Khan."

"A war movie?"

Reiko nodded. "A documentary about the exploits of the 2nd Cavalry Regiment. I don't know why you think he's a Red. That picture was so patriotic, it might as well have been footage of a Rising Sun flag. But at least it was well made."

"Says the smitten schoolgirl."

Reiko felt her face redden. "Regardless, I've never heard Matsumoto voice any sympathy for Communism or—"

A large group of families drifted over to the Nio Gate, gawking, chattering, and taking photos. They seemed oblivious of their conversation but were still within earshot. Inspector Aizawa beckoned her to follow as they walked underneath the Nio Gate and out into the Nakamise market street. Stalls lined the sides, hawking everything from *mochi* rice cakes and chopsticks to red *daruma* dolls and full-sized samurai swords. Although passersby surrounded them, they never lingered for more than a few seconds before being carried along down the Nakamise.

"What did Matsumoto mean by 'make your dream come true?'" Inspector Aizawa asked as they walked.

"I have no idea. But he asked me out on a date tomorrow and promised to tell me then."

"Tomorrow? Most everything is still closed."

"Not the Rheingold. It's a German beer hall in Ginza. Ever heard of it?"

"Of course. Lots of foreigners go there. Fine. Let's meet after. January 3rd, perhaps? You can brief me then."

"Okay, but I still don't understand why you think Matsumoto's a Red. Like I said, that picture he made—"

Aizawa gave a silencing stare.

"Although he never joined the Party, your little crush used to associate with several Reds. With the recent arrests, the Communist Party has been dealt its death blow. Only a few stragglers remain," Inspector Aizawa sneered as if he were talking about a cockroach infestation. "But in their desperation, they've become more dangerous, sticking up banks for quick cash. If Matsumoto knows where any are hiding, that will put us one step closer to destroying the Communist plague once and for all."

Reiko nodded along but wondered if the Inspector might be more conservative than she had realized. Still, who was she to argue? The Metropolitan Police paid her bills and Aizawa was her *senpai*, her mentor. Besides, she had sworn to protect Tokyo from any threat, whether it be right-wing patriotic societies, drug-peddling yakuza gangs, or bank-robbing Communists.

CHAPTER TEN

Utako banged out a steady knock against the Takano Bank office's glass door. It was a small branch, located in the government district of Kasumigaseki, and just one of many that Takano Bank had in Tokyo. Perhaps this was the one branch in Tokyo that had truly been abandoned over the New Year holiday. The others sure weren't.

All throughout the city, banks were guarded by young, strapping men who would put up a fight. Up until a few months ago, most banks didn't even employ guards, since armed robbery was unthinkable in Japan. The Omori Bank Incident had put an end to that naivete.

She was about to knock for a final time, but the door creaked open. Standing in front of her was a watchman, or at least he wore a watchman's uniform. A maze of wrinkles on his shriveled face, along with sunken cheeks and small, deep-set eyes, gave the impression of a walking corpse rather than a bank guard.

"May I help you, young lady?"

Utako jumped into her new role, a flustered *moga.*

"Oh please, sir. I know it's New Year's Day, but I simply must make a withdrawal!"

The guard shook his head. "I'm afraid that is impossible, young lady. You see, the bank is closed until January 4th. You can make your withdrawal then."

Utako forced out a pitiful whimper and bit down on her gloved hand. "Is anyone from the bank here today?"

"Sorry, it's just me."

"Just you?"

He nodded. "Just me until nightfall. Then, two other guards come to relieve me. The bank wants two men for the night watch, given the recent robberies."

"Oh, I see. Well, I'm glad you don't have to work all by yourself tonight. Will you be here tomorrow?"

"Yes, ma'am. All day. But like I said, the bank won't reopen until the 4th. You can withdraw your money then."

Utako stifled another whimper. "I understand. Please stay safe. And Happy New Year, sir."

The elderly watchman bowed before closing the door. Utako turned and hurried down the steps. The sun was setting, and grandpa's relief would be here soon. But tomorrow, he'd be all alone, without any witnesses. Utako walked around the corner, her high heels clicking on the deserted sidewalk. Large, stately brick buildings towered around her, but almost all were empty. The Kasumigaseki district was home to the government bureaucracy, most of which would be off for the next few days. Except for the Metropolitan Police, whose headquarters loomed only blocks away, like a volcano ready to erupt. Still, this bank was just too tempting to pass over.

Izumi's Ford came into view, idling at the curb. Utako climbed through the side door and the car pulled out into the street.

"So?" Izumi asked. "What did you find?"

Utako grinned. "Payday."

*****

The small wooden home in the western outskirts of Tokyo looked humble enough in the dusky twilight, though somewhat out of place. West of the Imperial Palace was known as Yamanote – the high city, where *daimyo* lords had built their *yashiki* estates during the Tokugawa Era, which now housed Tokyo's affluent class. Eastern Tokyo was nicknamed Shitamachi, the low city. Aside from a few wealthier exceptions like Ginza, it contained working-class areas – Ueno, Asakusa, Honjo, and Mukojima, with its squalid slum of Tamanoi.

It was there that Major Junzo Kanemaru felt more at home. After all, he'd grown up in the Nishinari Ward of Osaka, full of dilapidated buildings, day laborers, unlicensed prostitutes, and petty criminals. That is, until the Imperial Army offered him a way out. It felt good to be back in uniform – his brown tunic, peaked service cap, and rank badges on each shoulder – two gold bars, one red stripe, and a single star – identified him as a *shosa*, a major. Not many from the Nishinari slums ever escaped, let alone climbed so high.

Shedding the persona of Major Taro Kuno was also freeing, but he was used to slipping in and out of where he didn't belong, shifting between multiple identities and behind enemy lines.

Kanemaru was not only a commissioned officer but also a member of the *Tokumu Kikan*, the Imperial Army's Special Service Agency. In contrast to the Army's more honorable services like the infantry and the cavalry, the *Tokumu Kikan* lurked in the shadows, responsible for espionage, sabotage, and all sorts of intrigue.

Miniature trees sprouted up in the garden, suggesting that its owner – Lieutenant-General Sadao Araki – was a cultured man as well as a soldier. Major Kanemaru slid open the front door, where a young maid padded up to him, then lowered herself in a supplicating bow. Tugging off his jackboots, he placed them alongside the others, sticking up like rows of stovepipes. Other Army officers must be here too. After donning a pair of slippers, the maid ushered him to a room at the far end of the hall. She knelt down, slid open the *shoji* door, and allowed Kanemaru to enter, closing it behind him.

It was a modest room, with a sofa that hosted three junior Army officers, their brown service uniforms clashing against its tiger-skin throw. Another subaltern admired a mounted suit of samurai armor, its helmet topped off with a golden dragon statuette. Ample evidence that Sadao Araki was of samurai lineage. At the other end of the room was a world map along with a painting of a tiger – ready to pounce

– which hung above a Western-style table and chairs, completing the furnishings.

Most wealthy Japanese had at least one room decorated with Western furniture and paintings, but someone as patriotic as Araki managed to make his appear part Japanese. Attired in a black silk kimono, the General sat at the Western-style table, conversing with a junior officer. Unlike Kanemaru, who couldn't hide his military bearing even out of uniform, only Araki's massive, neatly clipped handlebar mustache hinted at his Army background. A shaved head, pint-sized frame, and soft voice made him look more like a Buddhist monk than the Army Minister.

As Major Kanemaru made his presence known, Araki gave him a welcoming nod.

"I'm sorry, lads, but all lieutenants must leave," he said softly. Despite his hushed tone, the conversations around the room ceased and the officers began piling out. Each man expressed his gratitude and wished Araki a Happy New Year before leaving. As they passed, the lieutenants gave Kanemaru respectful bows, but without the admiration they showed toward Araki. The General was well-known for entertaining young junior officers on New Year's, a rarity among the stodgy upper ranks.

Only the officer seated next to General Araki remained. A quick inspection of his shoulder rank tabs showed three stars against a gold stripe, the rank of captain. He was older than the lieutenants and far more aristocratic-looking with coifed hair and owlish glasses perched on a thin nose that ran between plump cheeks and wide ears, above a weak chin. If Araki looked like a monk, this captain resembled a schoolteacher more than an Army officer.

But within seconds, the face took on a startling familiarity. Chichibu – Crown Prince of the Japanese Empire.

CHAPTER ELEVEN

Major Kanemaru froze, unable to speak. Instead, he sank into a deep bow, befitting a member of the Imperial Family. Prince Chichibu's service in the Imperial Army was well-known, but it was strange seeing the Emperor's younger brother in such a casual setting. Straightening up, Kanemaru tried speaking again, but the words stuck in his throat. Thankfully, General Araki intervened.

"Allow me to introduce Major Junzo Kanemaru. The Major served in Mukden at the beginning of the Manchurian Incident."

Incident – a sly word to describe anything from political unrest to full-scale war. The recent campaign in Manchuria was described as an incident, as if to fool the League of Nations. Manchuria was the lifeline of the Japanese Empire, essential for raw materials, but the region had been vulnerable to a Soviet invasion. Impotent politicians couldn't defend Manchuria, so Junzo Kanemaru joined a clique of like-minded officers, determined to act rather than talk.

Through guile and intrigue, they manufactured the phony bombing of the Japanese-owned South Manchurian Railway line, just outside the city of Mukden. The Kwantung Army had an excuse to invade, and now Manchuria, along with its limitless resources, was firmly within the Japanese sphere of influence. Kanemaru's scheming earned him a new nickname from his fellow officers – the God of Intrigue.

"Ah, yes," Prince Chichibu said, his voice authoritative, clashing with his bland face. "You served our nation well."

Kanemaru found his voice. "Thank you, Your Highness."

"Please, Major. You outrank me. Address me as 'captain.'"

"Of course, Captain."

Behind his glasses, Chichibu scrutinized Kanemaru. "We will need men of your courage and intelligence in the coming year, Major. Given what's happened tonight."

"Beg your pardon, Captain?"

Araki chuckled. "It's rare when Major Kanemaru is out of the loop. We've just received a telegram that the soldiers of the Kwantung Army have clashed with Chinese forces at Shanhaikwan."

The name was familiar, and Kanemaru lifted his eyes to the enormous world map hanging just above Araki's bald head. Located on the eastern coast, Shanhaikwan was where the Great Wall began. Nestled between Manchukuo and China, it was a strategic location for any future invasion. Kanemaru wondered if another *incident* was brewing.

"Japanese soldiers are invincible in battle," the Prince declared. "I'm sure they will prevail, no matter the odds." Chichibu checked his pocket watch. "I must be going." He rose, prompting General Araki to stand, and Major Kanemaru to snap to full attention.

As a mere captain, Chichibu offered a salute and a bow to both men. Kanemaru saluted back, unsure how low to bow to a captain who was also her to the Chrysanthemum Throne.

"Happy New Year, gentlemen. I know it will be a fateful one for the Japanese Empire."

With that, the Crown Prince slid open the *shoji* door and left. Only when the patter of his slippered feet faded away did Kanemaru exhale.

"You can relax now, Major," Araki said. "Please, have a seat."

Kanemaru removed his peaked service cap and placed it on the table, then sat where the Crown Prince had been. Prince Chichibu seemed so – human, despite how sacrilegious it was to think so. Every schoolchild knew that the Imperial Family was descended from the Sun Goddess Amaterasu. But despite his bland features, even Kanemaru had to admit that there was something authoritative in the

Prince's voice and piercing stare, the traits of a man you'd follow into battle.

"I never thought I would ever meet His Highness."

"Captain Chichibu is a remarkable officer, popular among the men." A gleam shone in Araki's eye. "He also supports the Imperial Way."

In the past few months, two factions had appeared and vied for command of the Imperial Army. The *Kodoha* – the Imperial Way – was comprised of radical young officers and led by hotheaded generals like Sadao Araki. Indeed, it was at a news conference, where Araki urged citizens to shed selfish individualism and follow the "Imperial Way," which gave the faction its name. Their end goal was the Showa Restoration, a violent overthrow of the status quo. It would redistribute vast fortunes to the poor, eliminate the civilian government, grant full power to the Emperor, and mold Japan into a militarist state, ready to face the northern threat of the Soviet Union.

Challenging them was a loose collection of officers called the *Toseiha* – the Control Faction. They were planners, schemers, and bureaucrats, who also desired a militarist state, but urged restraint. The next war would be a total one and victory required the assistance of the civilian bureaucracy along with the *zaibatsu's* heavy industry and finance. Both sides opposed liberals and Communists with equal rancor, but the struggle between the Imperial Way and the Control Faction had devolved into an unofficial war for supremacy.

Neither faction appealed to Junzo Kanemaru. For him, there was only one ideology that mattered – "the weak are meat for the strong." Whoever triumphed in this petty factionalism was right on the simple merit that they were stronger.

"Sir, about Shanhaikwan—"

"You will read about it in tomorrow's newspapers. But for now, what do you have to report, Major Kanemaru? Or should I call you Major Kuno?"

Kanemaru held his head high. "The mission was a complete success."

"Nobody saw you?"

"Two police officers, but they were disposed of."

Araki bristled. "Unfortunate, but such losses are acceptable, so long as our connection with those Reds isn't discovered."

"That is why I supplied them with Soviet pistols. Should the Police find any evidence, they'll think it's Moscow funding some terrorist group. However, they did ask for more powerful ammunition."

"Which is?"

"Grenades."

"Fine. We have some old Type 10s they can have. Do the Reds suspect anything?"

"They're delusional and desperate to believe someone is on their side. I tell them the Russians are supplying Red Army pistols to Manchurian guerillas, just to make their fantasy of a worldwide revolution more real. It's a good cover story since we captured so many Nagant revolvers during the Siberian Expedition. However…"

"However?"

"They were curious as to why Marquis Maeda was chosen. I tried to rationalize that he was a symbol of the aristocracy. Now they want to know who our next target will be."

"And they will know. In due time."

"But sir, even I don't know why Maeda was chosen. Perhaps if I knew more about this operation, I could control these Reds better and—"

"Enough!" Araki's voice rang out like a gong before subsiding into a monotone hum. "You will only know what is necessary. Understand?"

Kanemaru's head lowered. "Yes, sir. Forgive my impudence."

Rubbing his thick mustache, Araki said, "You have a long history of these types of operations. The 'God of Intrigue' must know that compartmentalization is vital to success."

"Yes, sir."

"Tell me, who is the best shot among them?"

Kanemaru thought back to the bloodbath from last night, specifically Natsume felling two police officers so gracefully. Still, Pak had the most experience out all of them.

"The Korean, followed by the actress."

The General said nothing but rose, then padded across the room to a file cabinet, partly hidden behind the samurai armor. He returned holding a small folder and slid it across the table. Kanemaru flipped through a report from the *Kempeitai*, accompanied by a few photographs of a stern-faced Army officer.

"Colonel Riku Hashizume," Araki said, sitting down again. "He commands the 2nd Cavalry Regiment. But not for much longer."

"Sir?"

"He will be placed on the reserve list in a few days, after the annual review at Yoyogi. The *Kempeitai* discovered several compromising haikus he wrote. He's politically unstable. A shame really. If soldiers lose their fighting spirit, what hope is there for the masses?"

When the Manchurian Incident began, the Japanese public had briefly become enamored with militarism. Araki played into that, creating new *gunshin*, military gods, out of recently fallen soldiers. After the brief but bloody Shanghai Incident, Araki lauded the Three Human Bombs who "voluntarily" blew themselves up to destroy a Chinese position.

More mythmaking occurred during the Shanghai Incident when Captain Noboro Kuga was taken prisoner. Though later released, his shame proved to be too great and he committed ritual suicide as atonement. Moved by his warrior code, Araki posthumously promoted Kuga to major and praised him as a national hero, a role model for all military men.

"Major Kuga has shown the Japanese solider that, whatever the circumstances," Araki told the press, "one cannot expect to live after being taken prisoner by the enemy."

The Imperial Army and Navy long considered surrender disgraceful, but after Kuga's suicide, it was utterly unthinkable. Perhaps Hashizume's war hero façade hid a shameful coward?

"Is this Hashizume our next target, sir?"

General Araki shook his head. "For now, I want you to observe the Colonel. Ever since his unit returned from Manchuria, he's been idling his nights away with geisha at the Silkworm Tea House."

The name struck Kanemaru like a bolt of lightning. It was last May, at the Silkworm Tea House where the Okamura Gang and his mistress – Chizuru – had hosted a lavish party. Those were better times, as he and Chizuru expanded their opium ring and were poised to rule Japan through bought-off politicians. That is, until Inspector Aizawa ruined everything.

Kanemaru masked his emotions and nodded.

"Go to the Silkworm and strike up a conversation with Hashizume. As Major Kuno, you will play the role of a disillusioned veteran from Manchuria. Report back to me afterward."

"Yes, sir."

Scanning through the report, Major Kanemaru struggled for a clear picture. But even the God of Intrigue was lost in this strange labyrinth, unable to find his way out.

CHAPTER TWELVE

Approaching the Takano Bank, Utako Natsume caught her reflection in the glass door. With bobbed hair, cloche hat, pea coat, handbag, and high heels, she looked like the quintessential *moga*. Of all her roles, Utako could play this part without effort. After all, she had been one of those empty-headed modern girls, once upon a time.

She knocked, then glanced back to ensure that everyone was in position. Parked a few yards down was the Ford, idling like a purring tiger. Wataru Izumi gripped the steering wheel, ready for a clean getaway. Pak and Genda waited in the back seat, trained animals waiting for Utako's signal to pounce.

"Oh please," she whined. "Please, sir, open up! I simply must get my money out today!"

The door swung open, revealing the elderly watchman's skeletal frame and blue uniform.

"You again? I'm sorry, young lady, but the bank is still closed—"

Utako's gloved hand plunged into her bag and retrieved the Nagant revolver. Without a word, she jammed it into the guard's ribs, silencing him. She jerked her head to the side, then pushed the watchman inside. Carrying two burlap bags, Genda and Pak burst out of the Ford and dashed into the bank behind her, slamming the glass door shut.

The bank office was even smaller inside, with just two teller booths, behind which stood a human-sized safe. Hands in the air, the watchman's bleary eyes goggled at them.

"The safe," Utako snapped. "Open it up."

The watchman shifted his gaze to the floor and kept quiet. Utako leveled the Nagant point-blank at his wrinkled face, wide with fear.

"I…I…"

"Stop wasting time!" Utako hissed, slapping the butt of the Nagant against his skull. "Hurry!"

The watchman's cap toppled off his head as he steadied himself against one of the teller booths. After a moment, he shambled over to the vault, his bottom lip quivering. With twitching fingers, he dialed the safe's combination, then opened the door. Utako pushed him out of the way and inspected the stacks of paper bills. It wasn't much, but this was a small bank.

"Get to work, boys," Utako ordered.

"What are you going to do with him?" Genda asked. His big brown eyes were pools of innocence.

A fair question. Their last heist in Yokohama had been bloodless since everyone had cooperated. It would be simple to just tie this guard up and leave him unharmed. Well, mostly unharmed.

"Kill him," Pak hissed, stuffing bills into his burlap sack. "The last thing we need is a witness."

"He's a fellow worker," Genda protested. "If we shoot him, we're no better than the bosses who exploit him."

Utako eyed the watchman, rubbing his wounded temple.

"What happened, *ojisan*?" she asked, using the friendly term for "grandfather." "Why's an old-timer like you working at your age?"

The watchman lifted his eyes from the floor before settling on the Nagant. "My…my son's business failed during the depression. I took this job to help him out of debt."

"How sweet," she said with some sincerity. Collective support was an admirable trait amongst the Japanese, one that Communism could harness.

"Comrade Stalin robbed banks in Siberia," Pak said, shoving another box into his sack. "Do you think he hesitated in killing guards?"

"You just want him dead because he's Japanese," Genda fired back.

"He has a point, Comrade," Utako said, studying the watchman's blue uniform, so similar to the outfits worn by those vicious wolves of the Metropolitan Police. "We cannot rely on the petite bourgeoisie. Their kind is who fills the ranks of the fascist patriotic societies and the Police."

"Does he look like a fascist?" Genda asked, gesturing to the whimpering guard. No, not a fascist, Utako conceded. Just an old man desperate for a few extra yen in this horrible depression. Sympathy let her pistol drop for a moment. The opening was all the watchman needed. He turned, then bounded toward the teller booths. In one quick motion, he crouched down and slapped a button on the counter, releasing a screeching ring throughout the entire bank.

*****

Sitting in his office, Aizawa handwrote his latest report. He took a swig of coffee and sighed. Most officers were out for the New Year's holiday, but here he was at Metropolitan Police Headquarters, catching up on paperwork. Still, he had to summarize Reiko's words from yesterday while they were fresh.

Yet, Minori's taunting voice rang out in his head – '*That's the problem with Japanese men. Work consumes their entire life, so a hobby is like having some shameful vice or mistress.*'

Aizawa sipped the coffee and let his mind wander. Maybe he should take up a hobby in what little spare time he had. Origami? No, his thick hands were too cumbersome. Baseball cards? His childhood collection had been burnt during the Great Kanto Earthquake, and restarting it seemed morbid. Archery? Better to spend time at the firing range with his Colt automatic.

Perhaps he could ask Minori for suggestions, if he saw her again. Outside, a furious knocking banged at his door and a young *junsa* stormed in.

"Inspector Aizawa," he cried out with a haphazard salute. "Our operators detected that an alarm has gone off at the Takano Bank in Kasumigaseki. It's being robbed!"

CHAPTER THIRTEEN

The alarm continued its hideous shriek. Dumbfounded, Pak and Genda froze and looked toward Utako. The watchman straightened up, a man prepared for his own execution. After a moment, Utako leveled the Nagant at his chest and raised her voice over the drawn-out screech.

"Why?"

"Because…" The watchman spread his weathered hands. "It is my duty."

At least he was honest. Utako squeezed off two rounds, tearing through the old man's scrawny chest. His body slumped over, blood splattering across the floor. So much for mercy.

"I told you to kill him," Pak yelled over the wailing alarm.

Utako swung the revolver around. "Shut up! We haven't much time!"

The implied threat was clear enough, prompting Pak and Genda back to work. Utako stepped over the watchman's prostrate corpse and over to the door. As she peered outside, her body tightened. A police officer approached from across the street. A *junsa* out walking his beat, investigating the commotion.

After tucking the pistol inside her coat sleeve, Utako opened the door and cried, "Help!"

The police officer drew his sword and rushed toward her. Japanese women were such frail waifs that one robbing a bank was almost unthinkable. Utako painted her face with a helpless, panicked expression, a perfect damsel in distress.

"What's going on here?" he bellowed.

"Oh please, sir, the bank's been robbed!" She pointed to Izumi's Ford, idling at the curb. "They're getting away!"

The *junsa* spun around and bellowed, "You in the car! Stop right—"

Sliding the revolver out, Utako jerked out a quick shot, burrowing straight into his gut. The blade clattered to the ground, followed by the *junsa's* body. He lay there, twisting in pain, panting like a wounded animal. Killing an elderly watchman was unfortunate, but necessary. Killing police officers filled Utako with a sadistic pleasure she couldn't hide. Watching blood leak from his mouth, Utako flashed the *junsa* a bright smile, hoping it was the last thing this wolf ever saw. Within seconds, the twitching ceased and a death rattle forced itself out through his compressed lips.

Over the incessant scream of the bank alarm, shrill, whining sirens waxed louder in the distance. Utako looked up as a sedan swerved around the corner, then cruised straight toward the bank.

"Hurry up, you two," she shouted. "The wolves are here!"

*****

Riding in the passenger seat of the Datsun patrol car, Inspector Aizawa weighed the odds. The New Year's holiday had stripped the Metropolitan Police down to a skeleton force of fresh-faced rookies. The Datsun was nominally a two-seater, a *junsa* – one of the few officers he could find – squeezed himself between Aizawa and the driver. A brown leather holster clashed against his sleek black uniform. Crime was low in Japan, and police officers were rarely armed with anything but a short sword. However, the economic depression had made everyone – especially the criminals – willing to take risks. Aizawa's own Colt automatic, snug in its shoulder holster, grazed his side.

The car raced deeper into Kasumigaseki. After turning a corner, the Takano Bank office came into view, accompanied by a piercing screech. A foreign automobile – a Ford – idled at the curb, probably the getaway car. The Datsun was one of the new Type 11 models, and although well-made, it paled in comparison to the power of an

American engine. Still, the Metropolitan Police owned few vehicles, so they'd have to make do.

A woman loomed over a crumpled mass at the bank's entrance. Drawing closer, the details of a police uniform became clear, along with the woman's features. Her slim frame wore a dark green pea coat and blue skirt, along with brown heels. Slender hands were gloved in brown leather, one of which brandished a revolver. A delicate, pretty face was cupped by a chic bob and a green cloche hat, like a *moga* straight out of a fashion magazine.

Her weapon whipped up and opened fire. A bullet smacked into the front window, but thanks to the reinforced glass, only cracked it. Startled, the driver wobbled and skidded the Datsun to a sudden stop on the sidewalk, several meters away from the bank office. Aizawa and the armed *junsa* drew their pistols and piled out of the car, only to be greeted with renewed gunfire. Crouching low, Aizawa peered through the door window.

The *moga* was now joined by two male comrades, each clutching a gun in one hand and a burlap sack, slung over their shoulders. One was a walking wall of flesh, huge and imposing. A beefy face and wide eyes bulged out from beneath a flat cap, like a sumo sizing up his opponent. The other man was tall and thin, with taut, sallow skin and sunken cheeks. Wrapped in a long black coat and fedora, he looked like death itself, a living skeleton.

The strange trio blasted out another volley. Bullets thwacked against the Datsun, cracking windows and twisting metal. Aizawa and the *junsa* probed for an opening, but the bank robbers soon dove into the idling Ford. Tires squealed and the car shot off away from the carnage.

"Go inside and search for any survivors," Aizawa ordered. The *junsa* dashed toward the shrill ringing from inside the bank. Aizawa heaved himself back into the passenger seat and barked, "Follow them!"

Gears clashed and the driver gunned the motor, propelling the Datsun forward through the Tokyo streets.

CHAPTER FOURTEEN

The Ford raced northward, weaving around what little traffic there was. Sitting in the passenger seat, Utako glanced at the rearview mirror, where the Police Datsun made rapid gains on them. Straight ahead, the bulk of the Imperial Palace came into view, and they whisked past the Sakurada Gate. Memories of Marquis Maeda's bloodied corpse flashed through Utako's mind.

"What the hell took so long?" Izumi snapped, his hands gripping the steering wheel like a vise.

"Someone lost her nerve," Pak taunted from the backseat.

Utako whipped around and lifted the revolver at Pak. The Korean's tawny face remained rigid, but alarm flashed in those narrow eyes.

"Want to see if I've lost my nerve?" Utako asked.

Pak didn't reply but shifted his gaze out the window. Anger still churned within Utako and needed an outlet. She rolled down the passenger window and leaned out. The Datsun was close now, she could see the wolves inside. The uniformed driver's features were distorted by a web of cracks in the window. But the passenger – probably a detective, judging by his black suit and fedora – glared back at her with a squared face harder than rock.

Utako aimed the pistol and hammered out a volley. Most of the shots missed, but some bullets pinged off the Datsun's hood with shrill whines, while another ricocheted against the front window, sending more cracks sprawling outward. The passenger heaved himself halfway out the side window and returned fire. Utako dove back inside for safety as the Ford swerved from side to side.

"What are you doing?" she shouted at Izumi.

"Trying to avoid his shots!" he snarled, whipping the steering wheel back and forth. The car rattled as Izumi changed gears, but any acceleration was minimal.

"Why aren't we going faster?" Utako shouted again.

Izumi shook his head and gritted out, "Damn contraption is overdue for a tune-up."

From the backseat, Genda said, "When was the last time you had the oil changed?"

"I haven't had the time or the money," Izumi said, his chubby cheeks quivering with rage. "In case you've forgotten, you hairless gorilla, we've been strapped for cash!"

Genda snorted. "Figures a spoiled brat like you wouldn't know how to repair your own car!"

"Genda-san," Izumi hissed, "we need to lose some weight. Why don't you jump out to give us some extra speed?"

Genda growled, but Utako cut him off.

"Shut up, both of you. We have to keep our wits. Izumi-san, turn right and head south."

"What?" Izumi's voice shot up. "Aren't we heading back to Ginza?"

"We can't outrun them," she said. "But we might lose them in a crowd."

Understanding glowed behind Izumi's glasses. The Ford swung around a corner and sped southward.

*****

"Turn right!" Aizawa ordered. The driver obeyed, jerking the steering wheel. Although bullets had reduced half of the front window to a jigsaw puzzle, Aizawa still had clear visibility on his side. As long as they stayed on the open road, they could keep up with these bank robbers.

The Ford was heading south now, trying to outrun them. Aizawa leaned forward and examined the vehicle, but there were few identifying marks. The robbers had removed its license plate and he didn't recognize this Ford sedan, meaning it was a recent model. The Colt automatic, firm in his hand, was reassuring, but what he really needed was a car radio. He'd read that Australian Police cruisers were outfitted with two-way radios, but such technology was rare among Japanese law enforcement. For now, no backup was on its way.

Up ahead, the Ford twisted around another intersection, heading east now.

"Turn left!"

The driver hooked the Datsun around the corner, roaring after them. Within moments, their destination became clear. Hibiya Park spread out before them, its frosted greenery teeming with crowds. The Ford plunged into the park, cruising down the main thoroughfare. The Datsun followed and Aizawa's heart sank. Although much smaller than Ueno Park, Hibiya was still a popular destination for families, couples, and anyone else enjoying the New Year's holiday. The bank robbers might not be able to outrun them, but enough civilians would serve as roadblocks.

"Slow down," Aizawa commanded, "we can't risk hitting anyone!"

Most people clustered to the side of the road or off onto the green, gawking in stunned silence. The Datsun's speed lowered but kept a steady trail on the Ford, until it bolted off the road and onto the grass. Couples admiring Kumogata Pond scattered out of the vehicle's path, fleeing pell-mell. After ensuring the civilians were out of the way, Aizawa ordered the driver to follow.

But within seconds, the Ford whipped around and charged straight at them, its engine howling. Closer and closer it rushed until Aizawa screamed at the driver to swerve. The Datsun's tires slithered across the grass, wet with patches of unmelted snow. Brakes wailed as the car skidded straight into a nearby tree with a loud crunch.

A jolt of pain jarred Aizawa out of his daze, regaining his senses. Nothing was broken, but he'd slammed against the passenger door, inflaming his shoulder wound, courtesy of the Okamura Gang last May. Other than that, nothing seemed broken. He glanced over to the driver who, although rattled, appeared unhurt as well.

Aizawa holstered his pistol, swung the door open, and drew a deep breath of frosty air, helping ease the burning pain in his shoulder. The driver joined him near the hood, wrapped against the tree trunk.

"Is it ruined?" Aizawa asked.

The driver shook his head. "No, sir. It's damaged but still drivable. Should I go after them?"

Aizawa looked up and saw a ring of civilians staring at them in dumb curiosity. In the distance, the Ford hurried away, deeper into Hibiya Park and out toward the open sea of Tokyo. Pride demanded pursuit, but public safety was more important. There would be another chance to redeem himself and the Metropolitan Police.

CHAPTER FIFTEEN

Cheerful music poured out of the scratchy gramophone, filling the Rheingold with German polka. Cutting into her schnitzel, Reiko couldn't help but tap her foot to the tune. Across the table, Koichi Matsumoto whistled along between bites of bratwurst. Smiling Japanese *fräuleins* in dirndls darted from table to table, passing out plates of sauerkraut and beer steins. This evening, the Rheingold was packed with Westerners. Foreign diplomats and businessmen chatted in a cacophonous mixture of languages, making Reiko feel like an outsider in her own city.

"I must say, I'm impressed at how well you use a knife and fork," Matsumoto said, raising his voice over the music. "You'd be surprised by how many Japanese claim to love Western food but try to eat schnitzel with chopsticks."

Reiko smiled. The quickest way to her heart was complimenting her worldliness, despite having never left Japan.

"I explore the world through movies and food."

Matsumoto laughed and whistled along to the polka.

"Love the music here," she said. "The Germans make such wonderful art. Especially their cinema."

Behind his glasses, Matsumoto's eyes lit up. "So true! *The Cabinet of Dr. Caligari*, *Dr. Mabuse*, *Metropolis* – all masterpieces. Speaking of which, did I ever tell you that I met Fritz Lang?"

"No, you didn't," Reiko cooed, leaning closer. "Tell me everything."

Matsumoto took a final bite of his bratwurst, then said, "It was a few years ago, just after the 3-15 Incident. The Tokko picked me up for my…associations but soon released me. However, even a whiff of suspicion from the Tokko can ruin a man's career, so Shochiku sent me on a year-long tour to study foreign cinema."

"Your boss must like you."

"He should. I directed one of Shochiku's most successful pictures. *Modern Girl of Ginza*. Ever seen it?"

"Oh, that was you?" Reiko feigned surprise. "I loved that movie. The *mogas* in it were a source of inspiration." She gestured to her bobbed hair and face, made up with eye shadow, lipstick, and rouge.

Matsumoto smiled. "Thanks. The Shochiku big shots liked the money it pulled in, so they decided to get me out of the country until the heat was off."

"Where did you go?"

"Hollywood, London, and finally Berlin. There I met Fritz Lang, who was busy filming *Woman in the Moon*."

"What was he like?"

"Practically a dictator, but he's a genius, so it's forgivable. He gave me some good advice. 'Ach, Herr Matsumoto,' he said, 'film is too important for self-indulgence. You must be responsible in the way that you use it!'"

"Sounds like he's talking about a gun."

"Cinema is a weapon, depending on who is using it. Take the picture I just made, for example. The militarist sentiment it might arouse is as lethal as any firearm."

Reiko swallowed the last of her schnitzel. "Oh, you noticed that too?"

Matsumoto blew out a chuckle. "Don't misunderstand me, I admire Colonel Hashizume, but I had to make that picture to rehabilitate myself. For the past few years, I've been working as a second unit director under an alias. Directing something patriotic convinced the big shots at Shochiku that I wasn't a Red. Now I can use my real name again."

"Oh, so you're not a Red? I'm so relieved."

Matsumoto's expression went cold. "No, never have been. I'm actually a member of the Social Mass Party."

A tension deep within Reiko evaporated. Koichi Matsumoto had never been a Communist, just a social democrat. Following a merger of the Social People's Party and all other social democratic groups, the Social Mass Party had become the largest center-left political organization in Japan. Inspector Aizawa might not be happy that he was a dead end, but it was the truth. Better to change the subject, lest Matsumoto get too suspicious.

"Matsumoto-san," she said, taking a swig of her gimlet. "You said you'd make my dreams come true. This has been a lovely evening, but it's short of what you promised."

Matsumoto twinkled behind his glasses. "Reiko Watanabe, would you like to be in my next movie?"

Reiko sat still, gimlet in hand, scrutinizing his face for any sarcasm, but there was only a genuine honesty that she found so charming.

"You're serious?"

He nodded. "It won't be a big part, but you'll be in a few scenes. I need an actual geisha to give the picture some authenticity."

"Of course, I accept!" Reiko squealed. "What's the picture about?"

A boyish grin spread across Matsumoto's lips. "It's a period film titled *The Poisoned Blade*. Set during the Tokugawa Era, it's about this masterless samurai – a *ronin* – who goes around killing corrupt merchants and court officials."

"Sounds like the world we live in."

"Exactly! It's a tendency film, you know, the ones that exhibit left-wing 'tendencies?' The Tokko has been cracking down on tendency films set in modern times, so we have to dress up any political messages in samurai costumes."

Reiko nodded along, trying to contain her glee. She gulped the rest of her gimlet to get a grip. Just then, the music faded out on the phonograph. A bulging white foreigner replaced the record, set the needle, and filled the Rheingold with a new bouncy song.

"Papa Ketel," Matsumoto said, gesturing to a nearby foreigner whose ruddy, jovial face was offset by white, tangled hair. Although crammed inside a suit and tie, *lederhosen* would have been more fitting.

"He was a German soldier at Tsingtao during the World War," Matsumoto went on. "When the Japanese Army took it over, Ketel was taken prisoner and fell in love with our country. Married a Japanese woman and stayed here."

Reiko shrugged. "At least one good thing came out of that war."

"We, the people of the world, need to make sure there isn't another one. Manchuria didn't widen into another world war, but the next incident might. Did you read the papers today?"

Reiko flushed with embarrassment. She consumed a steady diet of newspapers and magazines, but the past two days had been a little hectic.

"Japanese and Chinese troops clashed at Shanhaikwan. It might resolve itself, but it might lead to something else. Japan is already a pariah at the League of Nations. They're going to vote on whether to adopt the Lytton Report next month. Which way do you think they'll vote if Japanese troops are attacking North China?"

Reiko didn't answer. The Lytton Report was a full investigation into Japan's invasion of Manchuria, which declared it illegal and exposed the "independent" nation of Manchukuo as a hollow puppet state. The elaborate masquerade hadn't fooled anyone outside of Japan.

"We," he took her hand, "can use film as a weapon to awaken the Japanese people. About Manchuria. About the *zaibatsu*. About this entire corrupt system. Do I have your support?"

"Of course, Matsumoto-san…"

"Excellent. Shooting starts tomorrow."

"Tomorrow?"

"Most everything else in Tokyo is still closed, but I can't wait around any longer. I need to get back to work or I'll go mad."

"Ah, a Japanese Fritz Lang!" Reiko smiled.

"I'll take that as a compliment. So, be at the Shochiku studio lot bright and early tomorrow morning. You know where it is, right?"

"The Kamata Ward, in southern Tokyo, right?"

"Yes, you can take a taxi there, we'll reimburse you. You can't miss it, since Shochiku is the only movie studio still left in Tokyo."

"Yes, all the others relocated to Osaka after the Great Earthquake, didn't they?" Reiko gave a coy grin. "I read all about it in *Kinema Junpo*."

Chuckling, Matsumoto said, "I should have known you read that magazine."

"Read it? Hell, I have stacks of old issues underneath my bed. Helps me sleep at night."

Matsumoto smiled and began whistling along to the polka again, but Reiko's mind soon left the Rheingold, left Ginza, left Tokyo altogether and entered the dream world of cinema.

CHAPTER SIXTEEN

Back inside the Ginza apartment, Utako began counting the day's haul – just under six thousand yen. Given the holidays, it was fortunate the bank had that much liquid currency on hand. Not bad, but the robbers who'd pulled off the Omori Bank Incident made off with thirty-two thousand yen. Then again, those fools had gotten themselves caught.

Pak sat off in the corner smoking a cigarette, while Izumi and Genda gazed at the pile of money.

"Don't get too attached," Utako said. "This is going to our rent."

Izumi lifted his eyes with a defiant glare. "And to repair my car."

Genda snorted. "Why not buy a new one? Your driving almost landed us in Sugamo Prison."

"Why don't you walk next time, *Comrade*?" Izumi hissed.

Genda was about to respond when a loud knocking silenced him.

The landlady's shrill voice came from outside. "You have a visitor."

Utako gathered the appropriate amount for their rent, then shoved the rest of the bills underneath her futon. She padded across the apartment and answered. Standing next to the crone was Major Kuno, wearing civilian clothes and a galled expression, holding a small package.

"Good evening, *obasan*," Utako cooed. "Would you believe that we managed to scrape together our rent? Thank you for being so patient with us."

The landlady snatched the money and, after counting each bill, traipsed down the stairs.

"Major, please come in," Utako said. "Our operation today was successful, despite some interference."

Without removing his shoes, Kuno entered, and Utako shut the door. Izumi, Genda, and Pak assembled before the Major like schoolboys before a disappointed principal.

"Successful?" Kuno growled. "Is that what you'd call your little fiasco?"

"We got the money. See?" Utako lifted up her futon. "That's all that matters."

"It's not just a bank robbery anymore. You murdered a watchman and a police officer. The Metropolitan Police won't let one of their own remain unavenged. And what if they connect it to Marquis Maeda?"

"Natsume-san was too merciful," Izumi spoke up. "If I had been in charge, that security guard would have been dead the minute we entered the bank."

"But the central committee put *me* in charge of this cell," Utako countered.

"That may be true," Izumi said, "but women lack the strength to lead. Besides, how do we know you didn't screw those old farts for your position?"

In Japan, a woman's authority was brittle. Even inside the Communist Party, Utako's ideas were ridiculed and dismissed by sensible leaders like Jokichi Kazama. Instead, she kept quiet, wrote her articles, and fetched tea for the men. That is, until the arrogant fools got themselves arrested while on vacation. It was time for radical action, as she always had insisted upon. The few central committee members who escaped arrest at Atami finally recognized Utako Natsume's talent. While they rebuilt their ranks, they gave her command over an underground cell. But even now, jealous vipers sought to undermine her.

One nod to Genda was all it took. Lashing out a thick arm and beefy hand, he gripped Izumi by his collar and heaved him up against the wall. He thrashed back and forth, his feet treading air.

"Put me down, you oversized ape! Natsume…order him…to—"

Izumi's protests subsided into strangled gurgling as Genda tightened his grip, turning his plump cheeks a shade of brilliant red. Defiance needed to be ruthlessly crushed, just like in Russia. Comrade Stalin had the OGPU, Utako Natsume had Saburo Genda. On her orders, Genda had strangled two previous members, just in case they were informants. Still, the Red Terror Society needed all the manpower it could muster. But Wataru Izumi – and his car – still had a purpose.

"Genda-san," Utako cooed, laying a dainty hand on the brute's taut, flexed arm. "Please let him down. I'm sure Izumi-san didn't mean it."

Within moments, Genda dropped Izumi to the ground with a thud. Tearing off his crumpled bow tie, he sucked in short, panting gasps of air. Any rebellion was now tempered.

"We must stick together, comrades," Utako said. "Or else the wolves win."

Kuno scoffed. "If you were soldiers, I'd court-martial the lot of you. I'm not sure you deserve these."

He handed the package to Utako. Inside were nestled several small grenades, fresh firepower for the Revolution.

"Where did you put Izumi's car?" Kuno asked.

"In the…back alley," Izumi rasped, still on the floor.

"Make sure it's hidden. You changed the license plates, right?"

Utako answered for him. "Please, Major, it's not our first bank robbery."

"At least you're not complete fools. All that matters now is that we have proper funding."

"Who is our next target, Major?" she asked.

"That's not your concern now. For the time being, you all need to lay low. Don't leave this apartment unless it's absolutely necessary."

The thought of going stir-crazy in here tightened Utako's throat, but an order was an order.

"Natsume-han, give me three thousand yen."

Utako couldn't disguise her dismay. "What for?"

Anger sharpened the Major's features until Genda took a step forward. The two of them appeared equal in brute strength, but a smart man like Kuno knew when not to fight. However, the Major needed to know that Utako Natsume was his willing partner, not a docile puppet. Genda's huge, clenched fists made that message clear.

"We're going to need another hideout," Kuno explained. "Ginza is too conspicuous."

"Fine, then."

Setting the grenade box down, Utako walked over to the futon, counted the amount of bills, and pressed them into Kuno's palm.

"Look for a place in Tamanoi," she said. "The rents are cheaper there. I know from experience."

"Is that so?" Kuno smirked. "Then why did you hide out in Ginza?"

Utako didn't answer and drifted over to the window. She gazed out into the frosty night as blinking signs from nearby buildings bathed her in a neon warmth. On the streets below, *mobos* and *mogas* – modern boys and modern girls – scurried in and out of nightclubs, cafés, and department stores. The whole scene was painfully bourgeois, but it invoked a morose nostalgia within her.

"Because," she breathed a wistful sigh, "it reminds me of my past life."

CHAPTER SEVENTEEN

Aizawa approached Superintendent Miyake's office, bracing himself for the worst. It was early in the morning, but already he sensed that it was going to be a rough day. He'd left a written account of yesterday's bank robbery on Miyake's desk, however, this debacle demanded an explanation in person. Careers had been ruined by less, but hopefully, his previous successes would shield him. Drawing a steadying breath, Aizawa knocked and announced his presence.

"Enter, Inspector," Miyake called out.

Inside the office, Aizawa took in the surroundings – a glass case of service medals, calligraphy that proclaimed "Law and Order" in fanciful brushstrokes, and a mounted *jitte*, the sidearm that the Shogun's Police Force had used centuries ago. A fitting collection. Shinsaku Miyake was chief of the First Investigative Division, responsible for policing the most heinous crimes in Tokyo, a man with little tolerance for failure.

"Good morning, Inspector," Miyake said, sitting behind a desk. He was back in uniform, a samurai who'd found his misplaced armor. "What do you have to report?"

Aizawa searched his superior for any hostility but found only a cool regard.

"Sir, I'm here to brief you on the Takano Bank robbery."

"Oh yes, I read your report," Miyake said, tapping a file on his desk. "Unfortunate business, but we can thank the depression for this sort of foreign crime. I hear there's a bank robbery every day in America."

First early-morning pleasantries and now this? Perhaps Miyake's personality change was a New Year's resolution.

"The question is, Inspector," Miyake said, leaning forward, "what do you plan on doing about it?"

"Sir, the robbers used a Ford as their getaway vehicle, a recent model. I plan on obtaining a list of all import companies that brought Fords into Japan within the past few years."

"Sounds like looking for a needle in a pine field."

"It is, sir, but I had a good look at the suspects. With any luck, they already have a record."

Miyake gave a satisfied nod. "All right, Inspector. Get to work. The honor of the Metropolitan Police is on the line!"

Aizawa saluted, then turned toward the door before Miyake called him back.

"Sir?"

Miyake's cool demeanor cracked for a moment as he shifted in his chair. "Inspector, my daughter wanted to know if it would be…acceptable to visit your residence. She has a—" he coughed "—a gift for you."

Aizawa nodded and hid a smile. So that explained Miyake's sudden switch. Perhaps he'd made a better impression on Minori than he thought.

"Of course, sir. I would be delighted."

*****

The fourth floor of the Metropolitan Police Headquarters housed the Records Department. Rows of imposing file cabinets lined the walls, containing reports that stretched back to the dawn of the Meiji Era. After checking out female arrest records for the past five years, Aizawa got to work.

The files were filled with the dregs of Japanese womanhood – unlicensed prostitutes, housewives who'd poisoned their husbands, mothers who drowned their children, pickpockets, gamblers, and blackmailers. The recent bank robbery in Yokohama had featured a female accomplice, which meant the same gang was likely behind both crimes.

The woman's pretty face, bobbed hair, and chic cloche hat had etched themselves into Aizawa's mind.

Unfortunately, each year of files turned up empty. That is until he scanned the contents of 1928 – Showa 3 – and found the same woman staring back at him through a mugshot, stapled against a short report. Her dark eyes, sharp bob, and pouty lips hadn't changed much and her features didn't resemble a hardened criminal, rather a model playing dress-up.

He soon found out why. Utako Natsume had been an actress working for Shochiku Kinema since 1925. Most of her movies were apolitical, but she became romantically involved with a director – Ichiro Hayashi – and began making tendency films. According to the report, Hayashi and Natsume joined the underground Japanese Communist Party and were swooped up in the 3-15 Incident. Hayashi died in prison under "complications" – a euphemism for torture that went too far – while Natsume underwent *tenko* – turning.

Another codeword for shame, torture, and conditioning that transformed Communists into decent citizens. For confessing her past sins and renouncing her "dangerous thoughts," Utako Natsume was released in 1930, just as the depression hit Japan's shores. With her film career ruined, she was reduced to unlicensed prostitution. The Tokko had lost track of her but suspected she had maintained contacts with other Communists, meaning her *tenko* was just an act.

Aizawa assembled the facts in his mind. The Takano Bank robbery was a political matter now, complicating matters. Even more troubling were the high heel snow prints outside Tatsuo Maeda's car, meaning Utako Natsume was likely involved with the Red Terror Society and the Marquis' assassination as well. Superintendent Miyake would probably turn the entire case over to the Tokko, and Aizawa couldn't blame him. But an irritable curiosity arose. He'd seen forbidden information in previous cases and wondered if there were even uglier monsters crawling underneath the surface of this investigation.

For now, he could pursue the bank robbery as an entirely non-political crime. Reiko's meetings with that director – Matsumoto – might lead straight to Utako Natsume. Aizawa scanned the rest of the report for its author, but already had his suspicions. At the bottom of the page was a name in kanji along with a red stamp – Inspector Hiroshi Tezuka.

CHAPTER EIGHTEEN

"More sake, honorable sir?" Reiko asked, looking over the plump man kneeling beside her.

With his tailored kimono, greasy jowls, and *chonmage* top knot, he looked the part of a merchant from the Tokugawa Era – corrupt and greedy. The Shogun viewed them little better than parasites since they produced nothing of value, casting them down to the bottom wrung of Japanese society. But through bribery, some merchants had become almost as powerful as some *daimyo* lords and their samurai warriors. With ostentatious wealth, they threw themselves lavish geisha parties while common folk wallowed in grinding poverty.

"Yes, yes," the merchant crowed, holding out his cup. "More sake for everyone!"

Reiko giggled alongside two other geisha, their white-painted faces gleaming in the stage lights. Trying not to wince, she cast her eyes beyond the fourth wall. Several cameras captured Reiko Watanabe – or rather Harutora – transferring her to immortality. Wearing a blue cardigan and flat cap, Koichi Matsumoto surveyed the scene, a Japanese Fritz Lang crafting another masterpiece.

A frown from Matsumoto directed her attention back to the bloated merchant. She refilled his cup and waited for her cue. At the other end of the set, a *shoji* door whooshed open. A *ronin* – a masterless samurai – holding an enormous *katana* sword, stepped forward. Along with the other geisha, Reiko screamed in mortal terror, hoping the camera would catch every detail.

"You greedy dog," the *ronin* announced, raising his *katana* high, "prepare to meet divine punishment for your crimes!"

Dropping his cup, the merchant kowtowed in whimpering submission. "Mercy! I'll pay whatever you want!

I have connections with the Shogun!" He jerked his head up to plead more, but the movement ripped off his *chonmage* wig and sent it flying off.

"Cut!" Matsumoto shouted through a bullhorn. The whirring cameras hushed as an exasperated sigh filled the entire studio set. Rubbing his eyes, he announced, "Everyone, take a break. And could someone please fasten that damn thing on properly?"

The *ronin* helped the pudgy merchant to his feet while a production assistant trotted over to fetch the wig. The other two geisha stood and stretched their legs. Despite Reiko showing them how geisha properly sat, stood, and posed, these actresses could look the part for only a few minutes.

"Watanabe-san?" Matsumoto said. "May I have a word with you?"

Reiko rose and shuffled over to him. He tapped out a Cherry cigarette and offered her one.

"Thanks," she said, lighting up. "I never realized how hard it is to make a movie. So many takes of the same scene!"

"I like to get things perfect," Matsumoto said, taking a puff on his Cherry. "Which reminds me. Your line is 'More sake, *venerable* sir?'"

Reiko took a drag before responding. "Sorry, but isn't this a *silent* picture? Nobody will catch that."

"I will," Matsumoto said, blowing out a trail of smoke. Reiko kept quiet and took another puff. Matsumoto had made her cinema dreams come true and didn't need an ungrateful prima donna blowing her lines.

"You're free the rest of the week, right? I want to shoot the rest of your scenes soon."

Reiko nodded. The script had her character – an unnamed geisha – hosting several banquets and parties while the wily merchant bribed corrupt government officials. It seemed strange to film the climax on the first day of shooting, but who was she to second guess an artist at his craft?

Instead, she looked over the set and took in its sights and sounds. Gaffers fumbled with wires, the camera crew inspected the film reel, and actors relaxed over cigarettes. Not as glamorous as articles in *Kinema Junpo* presented it, but Reiko Watanabe felt at home.

At the far end, two uniformed figures appeared, cutting through the set like a black fog. They made a direct path toward Matsumoto and Reiko, allowing her to inspect them closer. Both were Army officers wearing mud-brown uniforms, peaked caps, and menacing sabers at their sides. Each sported a mustache – the younger officer's was a small, toothbrush-style above his slit-like mouth. The older man's mustache was a thick, handlebar kind, like something out of European royalty.

"Matsumoto-san?" the younger officer asked.

"Uh, yes," he said, stubbing the Cherry cigarette out. Reiko followed suit.

"This is Lieutenant-General Sadao Araki, the Army Minister," he clipped out, rigid and precise. "He wishes to speak with you."

The titles stiffened Matsumoto's frame and lowered him in a deep bow. Reiko followed, even deeper. The crew busied themselves, stealing curious glances.

"You directed *Bullets and Horses in Manchuria?*" the General asked, his voice wispy and soft.

"Yes, Excellency."

"I received an advance copy of it yesterday. A most stirring film." Araki extended a bony hand. "I offer my congratulations and the gratitude of the Imperial Army."

"Thank you, Excellency," Matsumoto said, shaking hands. "It's due to be released in theaters this week."

Behind the mustache, General Araki looked pleased.

"Films like that will mold the Japanese people," he said, drawing his small frame up. "We are in a time of *hijoji* – national crisis. The Manchurian Incident, the 5-15 Incident, and now this border skirmish at Shanhaikwan…Japan must face these challenges with a soul of steel."

The word *hijoji* rang out in Reiko's mind. Newspapers were filled with it these days – right-wing militarists like Araki used it to arouse patriotism, while liberals applied it to a creeping fear of fascism. *Hijoji* was vague enough to be applied to any situation.

"Yes, of course, Excellency," Matsumoto said, nodding. Reiko nodded too but kept quiet. After all, why would the Army Minister need the opinions of a mere woman?

"I'm dabbling in filmmaking myself," the General stated.

"You, Excellency?"

"Yes, that's why I'm here today. I'm to be the narrator of a new documentary titled *Crisis-Time Japan*," Araki went on. "It will highlight the unfortunate decadence that has corrupted our youth into these vulgar *mobos* and *mogas*." His hand lifted and balled into a fist. "But its main purpose will be to spiritually mobilize the Japanese people and lead them to the Imperial Way."

Reiko didn't like the sound of that. Regular mobilization meant war, but what did spiritual mobilization entail?

After a few moments, Matsumoto found his voice. "I look forward to seeing it, Excellency."

With a departing nod, General Araki and the other officer turned and walked off the set. Once out of earshot, Reiko drew herself closer to Matsumoto.

"Hey, you know what time it is?" she whispered. "It's national crisis time!"

It was an old joke, but Matsumoto burst out laughing anyway, then stifled it.

"Shhh, don't talk like that. The last thing I need is a visit from the Tokko."

"Sorry, but he can't be serious. The man looks like a cartoon."

"Dead serious. Araki is intent on making Japan a nation of samurai. Don't you remember all those speeches he gave, glorifying the suicide of Major Kuga? Or how after the 5-15 Incident, he defended the assassins of Prime Minister Inukai? Said they were 'pure and naïve' and how he was moved to 'unrestrainable tears' because of their actions. Pretty words for fascist gangsters."

Reiko fought back her discomfort. Last May, a group of Navy officers attempted a coup d'état, but only succeeded in murdering the prime minister. That awful day saw her stopping the assassination of Charlie Chaplin and ended with a hellish struggle against the Okamura Gang.

"I was a little busy during the 5-15 Incident."

"Well, he's one of the reasons the political parties are useless now. He and the Navy Minister refused to back any cabinet headed by a party politician."

Reiko shrugged. "Sorry, I can't vote, so I can't sympathize."

"Play dumb all you want, but I know there's a brain underneath that wig." Matsumoto tapped her *shimada* hairstyle with a grin. "All right, everyone," he boomed. "Let's take it from the top!"

CHAPTER NINETEEN

Inspector Aizawa dragged on a Golden Bat, scanning Ueno Park's few pedestrians for Reiko. He'd already gone through three cigarettes and still no sign of her. The sun began to sink, casting a shadowy gloom. Aizawa glanced up at the Great Buddha statue, their usual rendezvous spot.

Its enormous stone head lay at the Buddha's feet, serene and peaceful, despite being decapitated. The Great Kanto Earthquake had beheaded this ancient statue, like some cosmic executioner. A few visitors paid their respects to the Great Buddha, but Aizawa was otherwise alone. A frigid gust of wind reminded him why. Only a little snow still clung to the barren tree branches, but an unsettling chill hung in the air. He shivered inside his overcoat, keeping a manila folder tucked tight underneath his arm.

Aizawa warmed himself with another puff on his Golden Bat as he spotted Reiko Watanabe approaching in the distance. Wearing a blue pea coat, cloche hat, brown leather gloves, and heels, she was her usual attractive self, but for a brief moment, he pictured Minori's face instead of hers. All his life, he'd expected to marry a traditional Japanese woman of austere beauty and modest morals. But nowadays, all he could fantasize about were these decadent *mogas*.

"Good evening, Inspector," Reiko said with a bow. "Sorry I'm late."

Aizawa grumbled but dropped the issue. "Anything new to report?"

"You're looking at Shochiku Kinema's newest star!" she said, gloved hands on her hips.

"Please say you're joking."

Her face fell into a pout. "Well, it's only a bit role. Matsumoto-san wanted an actual geisha to make his picture more realistic."

"Is it another tendency film?"

"Yes, but I have some good news! Matsumoto-san isn't a Red. Never was."

Inhaling on his Golden Bat, Aizawa let his skepticism show. "Is that so?"

"He's actually a member of the Social Mass Party."

"We already knew that. Matsumoto himself doesn't really matter. He's a conduit—" Aizawa whipped out the manila folder under his arm "—for people like her."

Reiko took the folder and pored over it. Moments passed as she scrutinized the picture of Utako Natsume.

"I know her," she said, almost stunned. "She was a big star several years ago, at the beginning of the Showa Era."

Aizawa dropped the Golden Bat and smashed it with his heel. "Figured you'd know who she is. Well, Natsume doesn't make pictures anymore. She robs banks now."

"Robs banks?" Reiko handed the folder back. "It says she was arrested for being a Communist."

"That may be true, but she's now part of a gang called the Red Terror Society. They knocked over a bank in Yokohama last month and just hit one in Kasumigaseki yesterday."

"I see…so what does this have to do with Matsumoto-san?"

"He directed a film she starred in—" Aizawa flipped through the folder.

"*Modern Girl of Ginza*," Reiko answered for him. "Yes, I understand now. You think he knows where she is?"

"That's what I want you to find out," Aizawa said, tucking the file back under his arm. "He was friends with a Communist director named Ichiro Hayashi."

"Why don't you ask him where Natsume is?"

"I would, but he's dead," Aizawa said, reaching for his Golden Bats, but stopped when Reiko presented him with a pink cigarette pack.

"Try these. Once you taste Cherry, you'll never be satisfied by those sawdust sticks again."

Aizawa plucked a cigarette out and lit up. Smooth, but they lacked the punch that Golden Bats carried. "A gift from Matsumoto-san?"

"How'd you guess?" Reiko said, lighting a Cherry for herself.

"Your infatuation isn't subtle," Aizawa said, holding up a hand before she could protest. "Not that it matters. So long as he's not hiding Natsume and her gang, we're willing to overlook any tendency films he's making. All that matters is bringing them to justice."

Reiko blew out a wreath of smoke and asked, "Who's 'we?' You and the Tokko?"

Aizawa said nothing and took another drag.

"Since when are you a Thought Policeman? Inspector, you're not being straight with me. I get the feeling that this isn't just about a bank robbery."

Before Aizawa could answer, another rush of chilly air extinguished his Cherry cigarette. Fumbling for a lighter, he pondered how best to inform Reiko how complicated this case actually was. Still, they'd survived the past only by sticking together – he the *senpai*, the senior, and she the *kohai*, the junior. The Metropolitan Police was riddled with careerists and nationalists, who viewed Aizawa with jealousy and suspicion. Until recently, Superintendent Miyake had only tolerated him. Strange that a woman – a *moga* no less – was the only person he trusted anymore.

"You're right," Aizawa said, lighting the Cherry. "This is between you, me–" he pointed to the headless statue behind them "—and Buddha."

Reiko put a gloved finger over her lips.

"A few minutes after New Year's, Marquis Maeda was assassinated," Aizawa said. "The Tokko took over the investigation, but I suspect Utako Natsume was behind it."

"Assassinations and bank robberies? Natsume-san must be a busy woman," Reiko quipped, before tossing her cigarette to the ground. "Wait, who's Marquis Maeda?"

"A member of the Privy Council."

She let out a whistle. "One of the Emperor's advisers? Guess this *is* important."

"Very. Right now, we're just interested in Natsume's gang for the bank robbery. But I have a hunch it will lead to more."

"Why not let the Tokko handle this?"

"You know how incidents like this are covered up. We promised to protect Tokyo, no matter what."

Reiko released a fit of laughter. "Didn't you say the Japanese Communist Party is near death? They're now just a bogeyman for the Tokko to scare people into behaving like good citizens."

Aizawa took a final puff and tossed the Cherry aside. He glanced up at the Buddha, serene and comforting, even without a head. But it couldn't stave off a horde of hideous memories that came swarming out of his mind like hungry rats. Brutal marches across the Siberian wilderness, with snow, ice, and rain slashing against his skin. Ambushes by Communist partisans, who'd vanish into the woods like ghosts. And above all, that inhuman atrocity on the Amur.

"You're wrong," Aizawa said, shifting his gaze back to Reiko. "I saw what Communism did to Russia. In 1920, right after I arrived in Siberia, we were ordered to relieve a Japanese settlement called Nikolayevsk, along the Amur River. Bolshevik partisans had captured it, then butchered the inhabitants – Japanese civilians and Russian refugees – burned it to the ground, and then fled."

He sighed, full of sorrow. "The Reds were short on ammunition, so they resorted to more creative methods of execution. Bayoneting was common, but I saw Japanese children as young as three with smashed skulls, their brains oozing out like rice porridge. Others were shoved into the Amur River and left to freeze in the icy water. We cannot let *that* come to Japan."

Aizawa took in a gasp of frosty air, tempering his emotions. It wouldn't do to lose face in front of his *kohai.*

But there was no disgust on Reiko's pretty face, only a determined fortitude.

"It won't, Inspector. I promise."

CHAPTER TWENTY

Asakusa was lively at night, with an effervescent *ero guro nansensu* – erotic grotesque nonsense – which so typified the neighborhood. The narrow streets were a jigsaw of endless *nagaya* row houses and storefronts, illuminated by the soft glow of paper lanterns. Children darted in and out of stores, while savory smells wafted from food kiosks. Off-duty salarymen in blue suits stuffed themselves with fried *tempura*, baked sweet potatoes, and roasted chestnuts. Red-faced students from Tokyo Imperial University – identified by their black uniforms and caps – stumbled out of Kamiya Bar and bawled out a drunken song. Despite being in full uniform, Major Kanemaru felt almost inconspicuous in these heady crowds.

Asakusa was a playground compared to his childhood home, Osaka's slummy Nishinari Ward. Only Tokyo's Tamanoi neighborhood, across the Sumida River in the Mukojima Ward, was comparable. It was there where he'd already found another safe house for the Red Terror Society, by renting out one of the many restaurants that had closed during the depths of the depression. Despite the economy improving, recovery was still too slow for many in the cities, and even slower in the countryside.

Regardless, the Silkworm Tea House appeared full of patrons tonight as Kanemaru stepped inside. An elderly proprietress approached him, her face alit with recognition.

"Oh! Have we met before, Major…?"

"No, ma'am. I've never been here." He pressed a handful of paper yen into her bony hand. "My name is Kuno."

Understanding flashed across her eyes. Women like her understood discretion, provided they were paid for it. "Yes, of course, Major Kuno. Pleased to meet you! I'm afraid all our rooms are booked up for the moment."

"I would like to see a certain officer who has been coming here regularly. His name is Colonel Hashizume."

"Oh, I'm sorry, but the Colonel has rented out a private room and doesn't wish to be disturbed."

"Please," Kanemaru insisted with another wad of bills. In this depression, bribery was just good business sense. After a quick nod, she signaled Kanemaru to remove his boots, then follow her deeper into the tea house. The soft whisper of her slippered feet was soon smothered by bawdy singing and laughter from the main room. Only months ago, the birthday celebration for Boss Takahiro Okamura had been held there, where he and Chizuru…Kanemaru bit his lip and pushed those memories down into the abyss.

The proprietress halted in front of one of the private rooms, while Kanemaru stood off to the side. After kneeling, she slid open the *shoji* door and supplicated herself with a low kowtow.

"Oh, honorable Colonel," she said in the politest Japanese possible, "please forgive my unworthy self for interrupting, but a Major Kuno wishes to see you."

Without waiting for an answer, Kanemaru stood in the doorframe and bowed. A young geisha with black-stained teeth and ghostly white face gaped back, both frightened and irritated by this intruder. Colonel Hashizume, still wearing his service uniform and holding a bottle of Yebisu beer, flashed Kanemaru a scrutinizing stare.

"Forgive my rudeness," Kanemaru began, "but I couldn't leave without introducing myself to the great Colonel Hashizume." The Colonel's face remained impassive, until Kanemaru added, "You see, I'm also a Manchurian veteran."

That seemed to impress Hashizume. Flicking his wrist, he dismissed the elderly proprietress, then beckoned Kanemaru inside the private room.

"This is Wakakichi," Hashizume said. The geisha bowed, then offered Kanemaru a fresh Yebisu.

"A toast," Kanemaru said, raising the bottle. "To Colonel Hashizume!" Wakakichi opened a bottle for herself and joined them. Hashizume half raised his beer, then gulped the remainder. Although the night was still young, the Colonel's cheeks were already stained red. But this wasn't the drinking of a returning war hero, but a cynical man drowning in bitterness and regret.

Kanemaru took a swig, then lowered his voice. "Your heroics were the only good thing to come out of the Manchurian Incident."

A mischievous smile curled Hashizume's lips. "That's dangerous talk, Major Kuno. Should I report you to the *Kempeitai*?"

"Forgive me, Colonel, but I've been out in the field too long. At least *there* you could talk freely."

Hashizume gestured to Kanemaru's yellow aiguillette cords, fastened to his tunic. "Doesn't that little ribbon mean you're a staff officer now?"

"Yes, but my old unit was the 29th Infantry Regiment."

"So, you were stationed in Mukden right at the start of the Manchurian Incident?"

"Yes, we took the West Gate of the city before sunrise."

"I hope they gave you a medal."

"One or two, but I'd rather have the lives of my men back. Did you hear about Shanhaikwan?"

"Last thing I read the Kwantung Army and the Chinese are still fighting over it."

Kanemaru shook his head. "Thankfully, the Chinese retreated and a ceasefire has been declared. How much do you want to bet that this is the opening act to another *incident*?"

Hashizume didn't respond but motioned to Wakakichi. The geisha bowed, retrieved a *shamisen*, then began plucking out a morose folk song.

"The rain falls on the horse,
It's impossible to go further,
A bloody sword in my right hand."

Kanemaru recognized it as "Tabaruzaka," a mournful ballad about the Southwestern War of 1877. Back then, an army of samurai under Takamori Saigo – a former general – rebelled rather than see their warrior class abolished. The Imperial Army utterly annihilated them, but admiration for Saigo's pure ideals earned him a beloved statue in Ueno Park. Hashizume closed his eyes and swayed along with the music, hinting at the Colonel's own rebellious sympathies.

One beer turned into another as the hours bled together. The red in Hashizume's face deepened until he almost glowed. Even Kanemaru felt his brain sloshing inside his skull. Wakakichi, however, maintained her prim etiquette as she poured drinks, led games, and sang "The Moon Over a Ruined Castle," the weepiest of dirges.

"Moonlight shone on the unsheathed swords,

But where was the brightness of bygone days?"

As Wakakichi wailed out the lyrics, Hashizume and Kanemaru exchanged war stories – the Colonel's were gallant and dashing, while Kanemaru's were invented fiction. A 20th century samurai wouldn't appreciate the God of Intrigue's actual service record.

However different they were, the two officers bonded over endless alcohol and past suffering. Strumming away on the *shamisen*, Wakakichi continued her deluge of melancholy songs.

"Ah, the moon over a ruined castle!"

CHAPTER TWENTY-ONE

Reiko hovered at the edge of the set, waiting for her cue. Other actresses in geisha makeup stood beside her, silently mouthing their lines one last time, but Reiko was too focused on the drama playing out inside the tea house set to recite her own.

Two men knelt over a table, mired in conspiracy. The fat merchant, who she'd shared a scene with, was very much alive and now in the middle of bribing a distinguished-looking man. From his elegant kimono and embroidered crest, he fit the image of a government minister of the Tokugawa Shogunate.

"I hope we can come to a mutual understanding," the fat merchant said, sliding an envelope across the table.

The Tokugawa minister eyed the offering with an aloof poise. He swept a hand over it, swallowing it with his voluminous kimono sleeve.

"The government contracts are now yours," the minister said. "A pleasure doing business with you."

The merchant grinned and clapped, giving Reiko and the geisha their cue. They shuffled on-set in their multi-colored kimonos and white face paint, then kowtowed to both men.

"Have a good time tonight, Minister," the merchant chuckled. "Take your pick of geisha. My favorite is Harutora."

Reiko straightened up, but the brilliant glare from stage lights blinded her. Squinting, she tried to make out the merchant's plump face but soon settled on Matsumoto's irritated scowl.

"Cut!"

The stage crew and cast broke into a dozen hushed conversations.

"I think we should do another take, Matsumoto-san," the minister-actor said. "Maybe my character should smile more to illustrate his greedy nature."

"No, you were perfect. Play him stern-faced. But Watanabe-san, may I have a word with you?"

Reiko flushed like a schoolgirl about to be scolded. She joined Matsumoto in a corner, out of earshot from the others.

"Yes?"

"Try not to look directly at the stage lights, dear," he said, with a gentle smile.

"Sorry," was all Reiko could offer with a sheepish frown.

"Don't worry about it. You've done a remarkable job, given this is your first movie."

That pulled a small grin from her. "I owe it to your direction."

"Depending on how this picture does, I'd like to cast you in a few other movies."

Reiko almost squealed. "Really?"

"The studio big shots are talking about that geisha singer, Ichimaru. Well, I figure if a geisha singer is popular, what about a geisha actress?"

Struggling to keep calm, Reiko lowered herself into an ingratiating bow. "Thank you, Matsumoto-san. Thank you!"

"Keep in mind, nothing too big yet. We'll see how audiences like you first. Trust me, they're fickle creatures."

Her smile broadening, Reiko imagined future roles. First as just a geisha in period pieces, but then as a *moga* getting into all sorts of romantic escapades. An approaching woman pulled her out of such fantasies. Narrow eyes, pale skin, waved hair, and an elegant Western dress combined to form Kinuyo Tanaka, the sweetheart of Japanese cinema.

"Ah, Matsumoto-san," she cried, drawing close to the director. "I heard you were back from Manchuria!"

"Tanaka-san! Lovely to see you again!" Glancing over at Reiko, Matsumoto said, "May I introduce Watanabe-san? This is…"

"Kinuyo Tanaka-san!" Reiko blurted out with a bow. "I've seen all your movies. *I Graduated But…*, *The Army Advances*, *The Neighbor's Wife and Mine*. You were fantastic in that. The perfect casting for Japan's first talkie!"

Reiko realized she'd said too much, but Tanaka offered a gracious smile and thankful bow, before redirecting her attention back to Matsumoto.

"I'm shooting a gangster picture called *Dragnet Girl*. Have you heard of it?"

"Oh yes, that's Ozu-san's film, right? I'm sure it will be a big hit!"

"Thank you," Tanaka said between titters. "I hope we can collaborate in the future. I'd love to be in a Koichi Matsumoto picture!"

"I would be honored to direct you, Tanaka-san."

"One day, I hope to be a director half as good as you are."

A woman director? That seemed unlikely, but if anyone could make the jump, it was Kinuyo Tanaka.

Beaming, the actress turned back to Reiko. "Pay attention to everything Matsumoto-san tells you, dear. If he's taken you under his wing, it means you have real talent."

After another round of bows, Kinuyo Tanaka left the set, leaving Reiko flustered with a racing heartbeat. It wasn't every day she met one of her idols, if only for a moment. But Tanaka's appearance reminded Reiko of another Shochiku actress, Utako Natsume, and reinvigorated her duty to Aizawa-senpai.

"Hope I didn't make too big a fool of myself."

"Don't worry about it. Tanaka-san is used to dealing with fans."

"Tell me, Matsumoto-san, doesn't Tanaka-san remind you of Utako Natsume?"

"I don't see much of a resemblance…"

"Whatever happened to her? She was the Japanese It Girl and then poof! She vanished from the silver screen and

Tanaka-san became Shochiku Kinema's star! Maybe she has poor Natsume-san locked in a closet somewhere!"

Behind his glasses, Matsumoto's eyes screwed into slits. He scanned the crew and cast, all busy either rehearsing, checking equipment, or on cigarette breaks. Although well out of earshot, he lowered his voice to a conspiratorial whisper.

"I'm partly to blame."

"You?"

"After we finished *Modern Girl of Ginza*, I introduced Natsume-san to a friend of mine – Ichiro Hayashi. He was a director too, but made tendency films. Very avant-garde stuff about poverty, imperialism, and women's issues."

"What happened?" Reiko asked, feigning ignorance.

"Hayashi and Natsume-san really hit it off. They seemed so different, the left-wing intellectual and the painted up *moga*. But before I knew it, they were lovers and she'd even converted to his beliefs. I didn't know it at the time, but they'd joined the Communist Party in secret."

Reiko nodded along as if listening to a radio play.

"He even cast her in the lead role of his last movie, *Woman of the Streets*."

Reiko dug through past issues of *Kinema Junpo* in her mind but came up empty. "What was it about?"

"Natsume-san played the wife of a factory foreman who is killed in an accident. But it was determined to be his fault, so the company won't pay her compensation. Eventually, Natsume's character goes broke and has to whore herself out in Tamanoi, just to get a mouthful of rice. When her child dies of hunger, the movie ends with her walking up to the Imperial Palace and—" Matsumoto glanced around again, then leaned closer "–condemning the Emperor himself for allowing such a system to exist in Japan."

Reiko let her surprise show. A picture that condemned the Emperor wasn't just a mere tendency film, but tantamount to treason. Big business, politicians, even the military could all be criticized, but His Majesty was sacred.

"It doesn't sound familiar," was all Reiko could say.

"I'm not surprised. It premiered in March 1928, a few days before the 3-15 Incident, and was pulled from theaters immediately after."

"So, Hayashi-san and Natsume-san were arrested by the Tokko?"

Matsumoto gave a somber nod. "Not only had they joined the Communist Party, but the Tokko claimed *Woman of the Streets* was a direct attack on the Emperor himself. A Tokko inspector beat Hayashi to death because of it. A real brute named Tezuka. He picked me up too but soon discovered I wasn't a Red, just friends with them." He shook his head. "Natsume-san suffered much worse. She was eventually released, but no studio would hire her."

"Poor girl. Do you still see her?"

Matsumoto gave another suspicious sweep over the set. "From time to time, yes. Since I introduced her to Hayashi, I feel as if what happened to her is my fault, so I pass along some money each month. It's still hard for her to find work, especially in this depression."

Now was her chance. All she needed was Utako Natsume's whereabouts, then Reiko Watanabe and Koichi Matsumoto could make beautiful films together undisturbed.

"Oh, would you please introduce me! I would give anything to meet the Japanese It Girl in person!"

Rubbing his chin, Matsumoto furrowed his brow and gave another glance toward his crew. The smoke breaks had ended, the equipment was reset, and the cast looked ready for another take.

"All right then, I'll see if I can arrange it," Matsumoto said, a sudden darkness behind his glasses. "But you might not like what you see."

CHAPTER TWENTY-TWO

Superintendent Miyake had ordered Aizawa home early, a subtle hint that his daughter would arrive in the evening. After changing into a kimono, Aizawa set to work cleaning every inch of his *nagaya* row house. It was small, but homey, consisting of the main lounge, a den, and kitchen. Aizawa couldn't help but think of the annual "cleanliness inspections" conducted by the Metropolitan Police on every home in Tokyo and felt a twinge of sympathy.

Everything appeared to be in order. The den with its Western-style chair and bamboo desk was dusted, the bookshelf organized. In the main lounge, the low-lying *kotatsu* table was free of clutter, an incense stick burned at the Buddhist altar, and a New Year's double *mochi* rice cake, topped off with a bitter orange, stood on display. Outside, a melodious voice interrupted his last-minute cleaning.

"Aizawa-san? Are you home? It's Minori Miyake!"

He rushed over to the front door and slid it open. Carrying a small bag, Minori Miyake looked chic in her *moga* clothes – gray cloche hat, tweed coat, brown gloves and matching heels.

"Minori-san, please come in."

After she removed her shoes in the *genkan* vestibule, Aizawa took her coat and hat, hanging them in his den. With her waved hair, tight sweater, and pleated skirt, Minori exuded a serene, modern beauty.

"Please forgive me for pestering you," she said, rifling through her bag. "But I come bearing gifts."

She presented a New Year's card, emblazoned with a colorful portrait of the Seven Lucky Gods, soaring through the skies on their flying treasure ship, the *Takarabune*. A thoughtful gesture, since their blessing was essential for any successful year.

"I'm sorry, I don't have one for you…"

"Don't worry about it. I love giving gifts." Minori then pulled out a small plant, secure in a squared pot.

"A bonsai tree?"

"Yes, for your new hobby. Are you familiar with them?"

Out of all the hobbies to pick from, bonsai hadn't entered Aizawa's mind.

"Only in passing…"

"Well, you determine its shape by pruning." Minori reached back into the bag, removing a pair of clippers and a slim manual titled "Caring for Your Bonsai."

"Thank you," Aizawa said, hoping it sounded genuine. Still, it was a nice gesture.

"During the winter months is when you clear it of dead twigs and weeds," Minori said, clipping through the bonsai. "Would you like to try?"

Aizawa accepted the clippers and examined the tree, found an unsightly twig and snipped it off. Strangely enough, it was satisfying, like scratching an itch.

"Thank you," Aizawa repeated with more sincerity.

"Bonsai reminds me of you. Strong, yet gentle. It's a hobby that suits your personality."

Aizawa chuckled. He placed the tree next to the Buddhist altar. "I think it adds some color to the room, don't you?"

"Yes, the dual symbols of life," Minori pointed to the tree, "and death," she gestured at the altar, "are very poetic."

"Oh yes, that was intentional." Aizawa flashed her a wry grin, getting a laugh from her.

"Is that your family?" Minori asked, looking straight at the tattered photograph inside the altar.

It was the Aizawas's last family portrait, taken during a stroll in Ueno Park. Set against a backdrop of cherry blossoms, his mother and father looked blissful in their kimonos, his little sister Tokiko, adorable in her school sailor suit, and *junsa* Kenji Aizawa, stoic in a Metropolitan Police uniform and short sword. A statuette of the Buddha was perched above the photo, acting as guardian for the deceased.

"Yes, that's the only picture I still have of them. Everything else burned during the Great Kanto Earthquake."

"Oh, I'm sorry." Minori lowered her head. "We live out west in the Shinjuku Ward. The damage there wasn't as bad as it was in the eastern half of Tokyo."

Time to change the subject. Talking about the Great Kanto Earthquake for too long might bring back unpleasant memories and choke him with emotion.

"Tell me, what was it like growing up as the daughter of a police officer?"

"Miserable," Minori groaned. "My father expected me to be a model daughter, so whenever I misbehaved, no matter how minor, all the other kids would tattle on me. I felt like a prisoner."

"Is that why you went away to college? To get free?"

"I never thought of it that way, but you're right. That's why you're a detective, I suppose."

"A lucky guess. What did you study?"

"Literature. I'd like to be a writer, but work is still hard to come by for a woman, especially in this depression. You know that saying, 'I graduated, but…'?"

"Wasn't that the name of a movie?"

Minori's face lit up. "Yes! Kinuyo Tanaka starred in it. I'm impressed, Inspector. You're more modern than I thought."

Aizawa smiled, silently thanking Reiko for lecturing him about cinema. He couldn't pass up this opening.

"I haven't seen a picture in years. Perhaps we could go together?"

"That would be lovely," Minori said, bringing her hands together. "Oh, I almost forgot." She dove back into her bag and retrieved a small round doll, with no arms or legs but a bright red, bulbous body and blank eyes.

"A *daruma* doll?" Aizawa said, accepting the gift.

"Of course, it's a New Year's tradition. Have you ever used one?"

"Not since I was a boy."

"Well, in case you've forgotten how it works, you make a wish or a goal for the year, paint one eye, then once it's fulfilled, you fill in the other."

"If I remember, the head of the household is the one who paints the eyes."

Minori scoffed. "I didn't think you were so traditional, Inspector. Well, anyway, you're the head of the Aizawa family now."

Holding the little doll, Aizawa considered what would be an appropriate goal. He'd already asked the gods for a companion at the Meiji Shrine, so something more professional might be in order. The answer presented itself, but a problem still arose.

"I don't have any paintbrushes in my—"

Minori pulled out a small kit with a brush, paints, and oil, presenting it with both hands.

"You're prepared for anything, eh?" Aizawa said, accepting the kit.

"I didn't go to college for nothing, you know."

With delicate precision, Aizawa dabbed the brush in black paint, then colored the left eye with a pupil. The right would have to wait until the Red Terror Society had been brought to justice.

CHAPTER TWENTY-THREE

The Mitsukoshi Department Store in Ginza was more crowded than usual, thanks to the extended New Year's holiday. Men accompanied housewives browsing display cases full of jewelry and makeup counters selling Shiseido cosmetics. Mannequins showed off everything from ball gowns and opera gloves, to intricately embroidered *haori* jackets worn over kimonos. Walking alongside Matsumoto, Reiko fought off an urge to stop and browse. Shopping would have to wait.

Matsumoto led her to a semi-isolated spot between displays selling bars of Cow Toilet Soap and Moonstar Shoes. A nearby poster showed a little boy dressed up as an Army officer, leading a platoon of children with a trumpet. "Wherever you march, wear Moonstar Shoes!" it proclaimed. A group of boys and girls were more interested in the toy section, just across the aisle. Model tanks, dolls, kites, *menko* counting cards, and *sugoroku* board games attracted little attention, but the kids swarmed around a display case selling yo-yos.

High-pitched screams erupted as the salesgirl brought another dozen boxes out, ensuring there were enough yo-yos for everybody.

"The latest fad," Matsumoto snorted. "In a year, they won't be able to give those damn things away."

"What I would have given to have a yo-yo when I was a little girl. The most I got was a needle and thread."

Matsumoto grinned, then lowered his voice. "Utako Natsume should be here soon. She said she'd be near the Cow Toilet Soap display on the third floor."

"Is this where you usually meet?"

"No, it's different every time. She always contacts me at the beginning of the month and chooses a spot. You just got lucky because we'd already agreed on this place yesterday morning."

"She sounds paranoid."

"You would be too if you endured the same hell she has."

A fair point. But one thing still bothered her. "You don't know where she lives?"

"No, nor do I want to know," Matsumoto said, his tone dropping even further. "If the Police ever pick me up, then I might betray her by accident."

Reiko bit her lip. This was going to be more difficult than expected. But maybe by playing the dimwitted fan, she could uncover something useful. She searched the crowds of shoppers flowing around the many kiosks and displays like a fast-moving stream. There were many *mogas* about, some single, some with men, but none were the Japanese It Girl.

Over in the toy section, a young, skinny man in a blue overcoat, bow tie, and flat cap towered over the swarm of children. While the salesgirl divided her attention among eager boys and girls, the man palmed one of the yo-yos on display, then walked away without a second glance. Casually spinning the yo-yo up and down, he made his way over to the Cow Toilet Soap display. As he drew closer, Reiko inspected his features. Horn-rimmed glasses shielded cruel eyes that darted between her and Matsumoto. While his frame was almost skeletal, the man's plump cheeks lent him the appearance of a bulldog puppy.

"Natsume sent me," the man said.

"I see," Matsumoto said, then held out a hand. "You're Izumi, right? Utako has told me about you."

"Not so loud," Izumi snapped, jerking the yo-yo back into his palm. "The money."

Matsumoto nodded, pulled out a folded envelope, and handed it over. Pocketing the cash, Izumi cast a hostile glare at Reiko.

"Who's she?"

"Reiko Watanabe," Matsumoto answered for her. "An actress."

"I was hoping to meet Natsume-san," Reiko said, forcing a girlish smile. "I'm a huge fan."

"Fool," Izumi hissed at Matsumoto. "Who else did you tell?"

"Nobody! Just Watanabe-san!"

Turning back to Reiko, the scrutiny on Izumi's plump face melted into contempt. "Well, she's not coming, so put your little autograph book away."

"Is Utako-chan all right?" Matsumoto asked, a sweet sincerity lacing his voice.

"She's fine. But the heat's been on us lately, so she decided to lay low. Her pretty face is very recognizable, you know."

Matsumoto gulped. "What do you mean, 'the heat's been on?'"

"Don't worry about it. I wouldn't want to shatter your little bourgeois world," Izumi said, bouncing the yo-yo up and down. "For all her faults, Natsume-san is a revolutionary, unlike you two." He swung the yo-yo toward Reiko. "An empty-headed *moga* who's a plaything–" then over to Matsumoto "–for some liberal dilettante."

"That's enough," Matsumoto growled through clenched teeth. "You will not insult Watanabe-san like that."

Izumi whipped the yo-yo back up. "Sorry, I'm sure she's a *fine* actress."

Anger flushed Matsumoto's face, but he fought it down. "Can you please ask Utako-chan to meet us here?"

Spinning the yo-yo back and forth, Izumi let the request hang in the air for a while. The incessant chattering of customers filled the awkward silence, before he finally responded.

"You'll see her soon enough. All these vapid fools—" Izumi gestured around the entire Mitsukoshi Department Store "—will see all of us then. You heard about the Shirokiya fire, right?"

Reiko and Matsumoto nodded in unison. Less than a month ago, the Shirokiya Department Store had caught fire due to a malfunctioning Christmas light. Several women had let themselves be consumed by the flames rather than jump into a safety net on a street below. All wore kimonos without panties and couldn't live through the shame of exposing themselves to strangers below. Underwear sales had doubled since then.

"That blazing inferno is this city's future," Izumi went on. "Mitsukoshi, Hattori, Daimaru, Matsuya…all these temples of the bourgeoise will burn soon. Make sure that you're not inside when they ignite."

What more could be said? Reiko knew when to keep her mouth shut, and from Matsumoto's stupefied, flustered expression, he did too. Twirling the yo-yo, Izumi tipped his flat cap, then strode past the Cow Toilet Soap display and was carried away by a river of customers.

CHAPTER TWENTY-FOUR

Reiko watched as Izumi paused in front of a display case full of watches, then sneered in contempt. Too luxurious for a stodgy Communist? Or perhaps he was upset that he couldn't swipe a Rolex as easily as a yo-yo.

"Charming fellow," Reiko said. "Money must be tight for Natsume-san and her friends if they're stealing children's toys."

A grimace tightened Matsumoto's face. "I suppose my monthly 'allowance' hasn't been enough."

"Don't make excuses for them. You're doing more than most men would."

"Thanks, but I feel a tremendous *giri* toward Natsume-san, after all she's been through. I'm sure you understand."

Reiko did. *Giri* was duty, social obligation, and burden, all rolled into one. Her own *giri* was to the Metropolitan Police, but all Japanese were duty-bound to something, be it work, family, or society. Its main nemesis was *ninjo*, personal desires and emotions, fighting a never-ending war for control of the Japanese people. The conflict between the two was even blamed for the recent outbreak in love suicides.

Izumi had made his way past the display case and merged with a throng of shoppers outside the elevator. He was still the best lead to discover Natsume's whereabouts. But to tail him successfully, she'd need to cut Matsumoto loose.

"I think I'll call it a night. After all, tomorrow is my last day of shooting, right?"

"Yes, you'll just be in the background for a few shots." Matsumoto rubbed the back of his head, flaunting his embarrassment. "I'm sorry for this, Reiko-san. Please, accept my apology."

Reiko's eyes flashed over to the elevator, where Izumi was elbowing his way to the front of the line. She didn't have much longer.

"Don't worry about it. It's not every day I'm called a *moga* plaything by a Communist."

"Please, let me make it up to you." Matsumoto looked ready to weep. "Have you ever been to the Kamiya Bar?"

The elevator gates closed over Izumi's chubby, bespectacled face. There was no time to waste.

"Plenty of times, but I'd love to go again." Reiko gave a hasty bow. "You can buy me a drink!" With that, she turned and trotted over to the stairs, then waved a gloved hand. "See you tomorrow, Matsumoto-san!"

The director gave a little wave, unable to hide his confusion. She'd make it up to him later but now, she needed to focus. Racing down the escalators, her heels clacked out a drumbeat as she weaved past customers. Reaching the ground floor, she searched for Izumi. A thick stream of shoppers poured out of the main doors, but Izumi's yo-yo – bobbing up and down – was easy to spot.

Reiko kept a steady distance as she walked out of the Mitsukoshi Department Store and into Ginza, now a sea of sparkling lights. Off to her side crouched an enormous bronze lion, guardian of Mitsukoshi and an exact replica of the statues in Trafalgar Square. Across the street stood the curved facade of the Hattori Building, its neo-renaissance clock tower shimmering in the chilly night. Buildings in Tokyo were restricted to eight stories since no structure could be taller than the Imperial Palace, so the Ginza department stores were the closest thing to skyscrapers in Japan, and a source of pride to all Tokyoites. Reiko looked up at the clock tower – almost nine o'clock.

After waiting a few seconds, she advanced out onto the sidewalk. Izumi was walking south, now twirling his yo-yo back and forth. Cold wind whipped against Reiko's pea coat and stockinged legs, and she merged with a passing crowd for obscurity and warmth. Any moment now, Izumi might duck into one of the many taxicabs cruising down Ginza's main drag and speed off. But no, he kept sauntering southward like a *mobo* – a modern boy – out for an evening stroll.

Reiko kept walking, passing rows of boutique shops, nightclubs, and coffeehouses with exotic names like Mon Ami and Le Printemps. How she loved Ginza, but only second to Asakusa. If she didn't focus, the warm neon glow could swallow her up.

Izumi hung another corner, going south again. Reiko followed, maintaining a safe distance. Her heart sank when he and his yo-yo were nowhere to be found. This side street only had a few businesses open, mostly food stalls. But one – the Morinaga Chocolate Shop on the ground level of a four-story building – seemed the most promising. Despite it being closed, several lights dotted the windows, indicating that the top stories were residential. A neon sign flashed against it, proudly advertising Morinaga Milk Chocolate.

Reiko peered into the Morinaga Shop, selling chocolate bars, dry milk, and Marie biscuits. No sign of Izumi in there, so Reiko made her way to a door for the residential tenants and found it unlocked. With tepid steps, she entered, then glanced over at the mailboxes, scanning for anything labeled Utako Natsume.

A shadow fell over her, along with a sudden, squirming fear. Before Reiko could turn around, a hand slapped across her mouth while another grabbed her hands. She tried to scream, but a handkerchief was crammed between her lips while yo-yo string wrapped around her gloves like spider webs.

"Well, well," Izumi hissed into her ear. "Looks like I caught a little *moga*." He removed the hand from her mouth and began leading her forward with the yo-yo. "You wanted to meet Utako Natsume, did you? Well, she'll be the last thing you ever see."

CHAPTER TWENTY-FIVE

With a sharp tug, Izumi pulled Reiko out of the vestibule and began leading her upstairs. The hallways were dim and deserted. Reiko tried crying for help, but the gag strangled her protests into muffled gibberish. Humiliation and hopelessness burned through her. Like a dog on a leash, Izumi guided Reiko up to the fourth story, where only one apartment stood, then yanked her inside.

Shutting the door behind them, Izumi gripped her shoulder and pushed her down to the floor. Reiko knelt in submission, her bound hands close to her chest. The apartment was small, futons and an ashtray the only furniture. Outside, neon light flooded the room, allowing Reiko to make out three figures in the gloom.

A thin, narrow-eyed man with taut skin examined Reiko with a flinty stare. Meanwhile, a beefy man in a winter kimono and *haori* jacket looked back at her, sympathy welling in his big, brown eyes.

Only Utako Natsume, with bobbed hair and movie star features, was recognizable. Wearing a khaki sweater, blue skirt, and thick socks, she looked more like a *moga* mistress of some salaryman rather than a Communist bank robber. Her pretty face softened with a smile.

"Your date for tonight, Izumi-san?" she asked.

"Yeah, I stole her from that idiot Koichi Matsumoto."

"Matsumoto-kun?" Natsume's smile dropped.

"His latest 'movie star.' Guess he replaced you."

Natsume ignored the taunt and held out a hand. "The money."

Izumi pulled out the envelope and slapped it into Natsume's palm. "Feels a little light. Isn't he making pictures again? Stingy bastard can afford to pay more."

Flicking through the bills, Natsume counted, then crammed them back inside the envelope. "Matsumoto-kun does this out of the goodness of his heart. He has a strong sense of *giri.* A pampered playboy like you wouldn't understand."

"Well, he also brought this little *moga* along to meet you, Natsume-san. Even followed me all the way from Mitsukoshi. She must really want your autograph."

Natsume moved closer to Reiko. "If I remove the gag, promise not to scream?"

Reiko mumbled in agreement, the handkerchief moist and soggy inside her mouth. Natsume pulled the gag out and tossed it aside, allowing Reiko to work her jaw and stretch her tongue.

"Thank you…"

"What's your name?"

"Reiko Watanabe."

There was an imperious nature to all of Utako Natsume's gestures, as if she was still on a movie screen. "Well, Watanabe-san. Here I am. Why did you want to meet me?"

The question simmered in Reiko's mind. Anything close to the truth would be tantamount to a death sentence. Her only hope was to play the dimwitted *moga* again.

"You're the Japanese It Girl," Reiko squealed. "*Modern Girl of Ginza* changed my life. I modeled my whole look after you and—"

Natsume's palm slid over Reiko's mouth, silencing her again. "Flattery is overrated, Watanabe-san." She let her hand drop.

"Sorry," Reiko said with a timid giggle. "I'm a little nervous."

Natsume gave a commanding nod to the hulking brute beside her. "Genda-san, please untie the poor girl."

Genda grabbed the yo-yo string and ripped it apart with one tug. After rubbing her sore wrists, Reiko offered a thankful bow.

"We apologize for your poor treatment, dear. Any friend of Matsumoto-kun is a friend of mine."

The words were reassuring, and Reiko forced a wan smile.

"You're an actress?" Natsume asked.

"This is my first picture. I'm little more than an extra."

"But I assume you're a student of cinema?"

"Oh yes! I have a subscription to *Kinema Junpo* and I've seen all your films!"

"Is that so? Even *Woman of the Streets*?"

"Well, not that one."

"I'm not surprised. The Tokko banned it after the 3-15 Incident. They said it was 'an unforgivable insult to His Imperial Majesty.' I took it as a compliment! But alas, all known copies were burnt." Natsume huffed out a bitter sigh. "It was my finest performance too."

"Yes, Matsumoto-san told me about your tendency film. I'm sorry it was destroyed," Reiko said, surprised at the genuine sympathy in her voice.

That seemed to please Natsume. "Has Matsumoto-kun shown you any other tendency films?"

In that open-ended question, Reiko saw her salvation. "Oh, I've seen many before I even met Matsumoto-san. *Tokyo March*, *That Night's Wife*, *A Living Puppet*, and *What Made Her Do It?*, just to name a few…"

"Wonderful! You are quite the cinephile, Watanabe-san."

Time for the one-two punch. "Matsumoto-san is directing a tendency film of his own."

Scornful laughter burst out of Izumi. "Him? What a joke!"

The cynicism seemed contagious, and even Natsume gave a skeptical frown. "Matsumoto-kun is my friend, but he is not a comrade. He's like you, my dear. A liberal dilettante."

"But he's a member of the Social Mass Party!"

This time, the entire Red Terror Society broke out laughing. Embarrassment flooded through Reiko, like a bullied child.

"Social fascists," Izumi hissed with more venom than a snake.

Glancing around for a friendly face, Reiko mumbled, "Social…what?"

"Social fascism," Natsume said, straightening up like a schoolteacher. "My dear, social democracy is thinly disguised fascism. In the Social Mass Party's myopic program, it seeks to only reform capitalism, not abolish it. But fascism is the final form of capitalism, whether or not social democrats like Matsumoto-kun realize it."

"I understand," Reiko said, hoping she sounded convincing.

"I was once like you, my dear. A vacuous little doll that capitalist movie studios played dress-up with. *Modern Girl of Ginza* was only made to compete with that Clara Bow picture *It*. They even billed me as the 'Japanese It Girl!' I was nothing but a product, commodified and sold like a bottle of perfume or a pair of high heels."

"And Hayashi-san was different?"

The name widened Natsume's eyes, before they narrowed into pinpoints. "I see Matsumoto-kun has shared my life story with you."

"Just the highlights."

"Yes, Ichiro Hayashi was very different. A worldly *mobo*, but unlike Matsumoto-kun, he wasn't some soft liberal. You're a *moga*, so I'm sure you remember what newspapers and magazines used to call us? '*Mobos* and *mogas* are really just nicknames for *Marx Boys* and *Engels Girls*!'" She let out a mocking laugh. "Well, in our case, it was true. Hayashi showed me there was a world beyond makeup and clothes. Have you ever seen *Battleship Potemkin*?"

Reiko offered a tremulous grin. "I read about it in *Kinema Junpo*."

"It's a Soviet film, so the Tokko banned it. A shame too, since it's a brilliant portrayal of class struggle. But Ichiro obtained a copy and showed it to me. That picture opened my eyes to poverty, imperialism, and revolution. As decent as Matsumoto-kun is, he always had one foot in the bourgeois world."

Reiko nodded along as Natsume and Genda regarded her with soft eyes, like concerned parents. However, Izumi and the taut-skinned man fixed her with glares so contemptuous, she felt like an insect about to be stomped. If she was going to survive the night, Reiko needed to do a little acting of her own.

"Matsumoto-san has changed!" she cried. "That's why he's making this tendency film. So have I! This depression has shown me just how cruel capitalism is!"

Leaning back, Natsume said, "What do you say, boys? Should we let her go?"

"Watanabe-san reminds me of my little sister," Genda croaked, emotion straining his voice. "She didn't mean any harm."

Nodding, Natsume looked over her shoulder.

"Pak? What do you think?"

The taut-skinned man pulled his lips back against his teeth in transparent disdain. "I don't trust the Japanese bourgeoise. She could reveal our location to the Police."

Reiko's heart thudded against her ribcage as her gloved hands gripped a chunk of her skirt. The outside lights cast a reddish hue on their faces, lending them all a devilish appearance.

"Izumi-san? What do you say?" Natsume singsonged across the room.

Izumi just shrugged. "She's just a woman, and a stupid little *moga* at that. No threat to us. Besides, it would be a shame to fill that pretty face of hers full of holes."

Reiko couldn't suppress a nervous laugh, full of anxiety and relief. Utako Natsume leaned forward and examined her again, one actress to another.

"Looks like the votes are in your favor, Watanabe-san. You can leave, but only on one condition."

"Anything..."

Natsume padded across the room to the futons and rummaged about. Even in the darkness, a pile of pistols were visible, inert but threatening. After a moment, she pulled something out, then returned to Reiko's side.

"You must read this, cover to cover." Natsume handed her a slim book titled *Kanikosen – The Crab Cannery Ship* by Takiji Kobayashi. "Then, give it to Matsumoto-kun with my compliments."

"A novel?" Reiko asked, flipping pages.

"Also banned by the Tokko. It's the best example of proletarian writing in Japan. If it doesn't convince you and Matsumoto-kun to become comrades, *true* comrades in Communism, then nothing will."

Clutching the novel, Reiko realized it was her life raft. "I'll start reading tonight. Thank you, Natsume-san. Thank you!"

Forcing herself up on trembling legs, she stood and made her way to the door.

"Watanabe-san, not a word of this to anyone beside Matsumoto-kun," Natsume said. "Or we *will* find you."

Swallowing her fear, Reiko bowed and stalked out, thankful for all those tendency films she'd watched over the years.

CHAPTER TWENTY-SIX

A furious knocking stirred Aizawa awake from underneath his warm futon. Fumbling for a light, he clicked on the lamp and checked a nearby alarm clock. Almost eleven o'clock. At least it wasn't *too* late. After a deep yawn, he shambled to the front door and slid it open. Reiko Watanabe faced him, her brown eyes alight in the frosty darkness.

After kicking off her heels in the *genkan* vestibule, Reiko followed Aizawa deeper into the *nagaya* row house. Although wrapped in a peacoat and cloche hat, her teeth chattered, but Aizawa suspected it wasn't entirely because of the cold.

"Want some tea?"

"N-no thanks."

Instead, she pulled out a pack of Cherry cigarettes and lit up. After a deep intake, she exhaled a breath of smoke which wafted over to the bonsai tree, nestled beside the *daruma* doll.

"Who gave you those?"

"How do you know I didn't buy them?"

"Because they're not practical."

The detective instinct was strong in his *kohai*, Aizawa conceded. He was almost proud of her but didn't want to reveal his matchmaking troubles with the Miyake family.

"Why are you here? I'm assuming it must be important, since you didn't bother to telephone me."

Reiko took another puff before answering. "I found out where those Red gangsters are hiding out."

"Where?"

"On the fourth floor of a building in Ginza. A Morinaga Chocolate Shop is on the ground level."

"Excellent work, Reiko-san! I taught you well."

A flustered look distorted her pretty features. "Well, that's the thing, Inspector. They caught me."

"What do you mean?"

"Let's start from the beginning. You were right, Inspector. Koichi Matsumoto is still in contact with Utako Natsume. Apparently, he gives her a hundred or so yen every month."

"Why?"

"Out of the goodness of his heart. He blames himself for her getting blacklisted by the movie studios. After all, he introduced her to Hayashi."

"Go on."

"So, this month's rendezvous was the Mitsukoshi Department Store in Ginza. But Natsume-san wasn't there. Instead, she sent one of her underlings, a real pompous ass named Izumi."

Aizawa withdrew into his study, then returned with a pencil and notebook. "Continue."

"Well, I followed Izumi back to his hideout in Ginza."

"Did he see you?"

Taking a drag, Reiko considered how best to answer. True she had been careless, but quick thinking saved her skin.

"Yes, but I played a vapid *moga* and they bought it. Turns out I'm a hell of an actress."

A grunt announced that the Inspector wasn't pleased, but he moved on. "Was it just Izumi and Natsume there?"

"No, there was a big guy named Genda. The simple and sweet type. Said I reminded him of his little sister, so he urged them to let me go. But the other, some man named Pak, looked like the Grim Reaper." She paused, dragging on her cigarette. "Pak…that's a Korean name, right?"

"Some Koreans have joined the Japanese Communist Party. They think that by overthrowing our government, their own country will be liberated," Aizawa said, jotting down more notes. "I'm pretty sure I met Genda and Pak. They were robbing a bank with Natsume."

"Explains the pistols I saw underneath her futon."

"Any other weapons?"

"It was dark in their apartment..."

Another discontented grunt. "All right, I have what I need. I'll need to muster a raiding party tonight."

Reiko spat out a cloud of smoke. "Tonight?"

"Even if the Red Terror Society let you go, the fact that you discovered their location might spook them. We have to strike before they abandon that hideout."

"That makes sense," Reiko said, drawing again on her Cherry.

"Good work. I figured Matsumoto would prove useful." Aizawa flipped the notebook closed and rose to his feet.

Shame hit Reiko like a slap. What if Matsumoto was rounded up in the dragnet? Hadn't she just admitted that he provided financial aid to those Red gangsters? No, she'd never forgive herself if a good man like Koichi Matsumoto rotted away in Sugamo Prison. Stubbing out her cigarette in an ashtray, she reached over and gripped Aizawa's wrist, squeezing it tight.

"Inspector, promise me that Matsumoto-san won't be involved."

The Inspector nodded, a patient *senpai* comforting his *kohai*.

"You have my word of honor. Matsumoto will be none the wiser of what's about to happen."

The simple, firm statement banished any shame and worry. Men like Inspector Aizawa were honor personified. Reiko let out a relieved sigh, embarrassed for ever doubting him.

"Thank you, Inspector."

He retreated into his study again. The telephone receiver clicked, followed by the Inspector's voice. "Yes, Miyake residence please." A brief pause before, "Hello? Minori-san? I apologize for calling so late. Yes, I would love to see you again too. Would you please put your father on?" More moments passed. "Superintendent? Yes, sir, we've found the lair of the Red Terror Society…"

*****

Utako sipped her coffee, noticing a twitch in her fingers. Well, she was on her third cup. After letting that stupid *moga* leave, she'd stalked out to one of the many all-night cafés in Ginza. The Mon Ami was a rendezvous spot where Major Kuno would call her if he was unable to meet in person. After that bank heist, laying low would have been the sensible course of action, but she would be damned sending Izumi in her stead. Collecting money from Matsumoto-kun was one thing, but any contact with Major Kuno needed her strict supervision. Especially when he would be calling with the location of their new hideout.

At half-past midnight, Mon Ami was almost deserted. A few waitresses in kimonos and white aprons lounged around the counter, while a group of university students discussed the literary merits of *ero guro nansensu*. Utako once considered recruiting these types to fill her ranks, but they were little more than dilettantes, more willing to talk about revolution than fight for it.

A shrill ring cut through Mon Ami. One of the waitresses answered the telephone, then set the receiver down, and shuffled over to Utako.

"Are you Oguchi-san?"

Utako nodded. Oguchi was one of her many aliases, the name of her character in *Woman of the Streets* and a pseudonym she used in *The Soldier's Friend.*

"There's a call for you."

Utako followed the waitress back to the counter and took the receiver.

"*Moshi moshi*?"

"I've found a place in the Mukojima Ward. Tamanoi to be specific. Thanks for the suggestion," Major Kuno's gravelly voice said. "It's an *izakaya* that went out of business. Leave that apartment in Ginza tonight."

"Tonight?"

"There's no time to waste, Natsume-han. Ginza is too conspicuous. The Police will find you eventually."

A valid point, she conceded. Too bad, since they'd just paid the rent. Utako jotted down the address on a notepad, then hung up. She sauntered back to her coffee, drained the cup, and walked out of Mon Ami, into Ginza's neon sparkle. She'd miss this place, but Kuno was right. They needed to set up headquarters in a more inconspicuous neighborhood fast. From there they could strike their next target and retreat into anonymity. Walking through the Ginza streets, she wondered who it would be.

Killing a high-ranking police officer would be ideal, especially if it were a member of the Tokko – like that bastard Tezuka. For the time being, Utako banished such fantasies from her mind and concentrated on the present. Rousing the boys from their sleep would cause a lot of grumbling, but it was necessary to evade the Emperor's wolves. As she neared the Morinaga Chocolate Shop, headlights flooded the street.

Squinting into the distance, Metropolitan Police markings were visible on several cars and motorcycles, all rumbling toward her. Fear and instinct tightened her muscles as she gripped the doorknob and ducked inside the building. Only two options were available now: escape or death. They might have to make a last stand, but the Red Terror Society would never surrender.

CHAPTER TWENTY-SEVEN

Aizawa stepped out of the Datsun patrol car and surveyed the target. Apart from the Morinaga Shop on the bottom, it was a nondescript four-story building, almost a photographic print of the other structures it was sandwiched between. Patting his chest, he felt the bulletproof vest, snug underneath his overcoat. Aizawa had led many raids before, against the Okamura Gang's gambling house, then against their opium den, but these Red gangsters were something different. More like a miniature army than common criminals.

The squad of a dozen *junsas* mustered at attention, all wearing bulletproof vests. Even more, each man carried a pistol instead of his standard-issue short sword. Such protection was a rarity for the Metropolitan Police since private firearms were illegal in Japan. But as leader of this raid, Aizawa would be damned if he'd charge into the enemy's lair without *some* protection. A youthful sergeant stood at attention along with his men and greeted Aizawa with a sharp salute.

"Sergeant Daisuke Fujita, at your service," he said. An imposing bulletproof vest was draped over the Sergeant's black uniform. But his peaked cap still presented an enticing target. Should he have ordered every man to wear a helmet? Before Aizawa could think further, the purring hum of crimson motorcycles demanded his attention. A pair of *junsas* from the Red Bike Force pulled up alongside and awaited instruction.

"You're to be on the lookout for a blue four-door sedan, a supercharged Ford Model 18," Aizawa said, raising his voice over the droning engine noise. "It should be somewhere nearby in Ginza. If you find it, don't let it out of your sight. Be careful though. These suspects are armed to the teeth."

The motorcycle *junsas* saluted, then shot forward into the night. Sergeant Fujita drew up beside Aizawa.

"Has there been any activity, sir?"

"I saw a woman enter, just as we were pulling up," Aizawa said, his breath frosting the cold night air. "I don't know if it was Utako Natsume, but let's assume it was."

"What if they try to escape?"

"We'll cover the exits on all sides but we must strike quickly."

Fujita saluted, confidence shining underneath his peaked cap, but dread raced through Aizawa. As the most senior man, he'd have to shoulder the blame if something went wrong, even if it was a subordinate's fault. Japanese society believed in the merits of group punishment. He drew himself up and faced the wall of *junsas*.

"We are about to raid the hideout of a gang of bank robbers. They are armed and extremely dangerous. Each man should try to take these criminals alive, but you are to defend yourself with lethal force if attacked."

Aizawa turned to Fujita and nodded, a silent order to commence operations. Drawing his Colt automatic pistol, Aizawa spun around and strode toward the building, Sergeant Fujita close behind. He muttered a quick prayer to the gods, hoping they'd be with him once again.

*****

Utako's footsteps pounded up the stairs and echoed off the thin walls. There was no point in being discreet anymore. She wouldn't let the Police take her as they had during the 3-15 Incident – groggy, confused, and wearing only a nightgown. No, if they were all going to die tonight, they'd take some of the Emperor's wolves down with them.

She reached the fourth floor and tore open the door, locking it behind her. Though the apartment was completely dark, the neon sign outside gave enough light to distinguish her comrades asleep inside their futons, like cocooned caterpillars. Utako took in a deep breath and began slapping her gloved hands together.

"Wake up! The Police are here!"

Pak and Genda stirred, then shot upright. Their bleary eyes and fatigued faces sharpened. Without question, they reached underneath the futons and grabbed their pistols. Armed, they rushed over to her like dogs greeting their master. Squinting into the darkness, Izumi donned his glasses, then began clumsily dressing himself.

"What are you doing?" Utako snapped.

"We need to escape," he replied, buttoning up his shirt, "and it's too cold to run around Tokyo without a coat."

Pak scoffed. "Escape? You won't get far."

"All we need to do is get to my car," Izumi said, tugging on his coat. "Then we'll run circles around the wolves."

Drawing herself away from Pak and Genda, Utako stomped across the apartment and gazed out the window. Underneath the fire escape, the blinking Morinaga neon sign illuminated a pair of police officers on the street below, waiting to pounce on their prey.

"We can escape by rooftop," Utako said aloud, turning back to face them. "Then Izumi-san can guide us to where he stashed the car."

Genda and Izumi nodded in agreement, but Pak shook his head.

"You won't get far, unless someone holds them at bay." Holding his Nagant revolver up, a grim fatalism shadowed Pak's skull-like face. "I'll stay behind and fight them off as long as I can."

Genda couldn't hide his shock. "But what if you're taken prisoner?"

"They'll never take me alive. And I'll kill twenty of those bastards before I go. Ten for my wife, ten for my daughter."

Utako drew closer to him. Pak Sang-hoon had always been an enigma to her – cold, aloof, and brutal. But his wife and daughter had been murdered by a Japanese mob during the Great Kanto Earthquake, so his bitterness was understandable. True, he had joined the Communist Party primarily to free his homeland, but she'd never doubted his convictions. But Utako wondered now if he was staying behind for the Japanese Revolution, or to satiate his own bloodlust.

"Comrade Pak," she murmured, "thank you."

Near the window, Izumi and Genda donned their flat caps, ready for the frigid temperature outside.

"Izumi, give Pak your gun," Utako ordered.

Impudent anger crinkled Izumi's plump face. "Why?"

"What use is a gun to a getaway driver? Pak will need all the firepower he can get. Genda-san, bring those grenades over."

Lumbering across the apartment, Genda heaved the box up to his chest and brought it closer to Pak. She'd have to thank Major Kuno again, if they lived long enough.

"Take some for yourself," Pak said, accepting Izumi's Nagant.

Utako swiped two grenades and handed them to Izumi, who pocketed them inside his overcoat.

"Let's give a banzai cheer for our brave comrade, Pak Sang-hoon," Utako said, a rising theatricality in her voice.

"Don't bother," Pak said, holding both pistols up. "I give my life for the Japanese Revolution. Just be sure to carry it out."

CHAPTER TWENTY-EIGHT

Aizawa entered the vestibule, followed by a parade of *junsas*. He and Sergeant Fujita slammed against the door, cracking open the lock and depositing them into the main lobby. Pallid electric lightbulbs cast a dim glow throughout the building. The first floor contained a side entrance to the Morinaga Chocolate Shop, but a sprawling staircase in the center, flanked by tall banisters, led up to the residential apartments.

Trailed by Sergeant Fujita and the *junsas*, Aizawa ascended the stairs with creeping steps. Doubt and concern gnawed at him like swarming ants. Should they have evacuated the other apartments? But then he remembered the 3-15 Incident, which had been so surgical in netting Communists. As long as they struck hard and swift, there wouldn't be a possibility of failure.

They plodded up to the third floor and looked up. A lone apartment stood on the fourth floor, the lair of those Red gangsters. High guard rails spread out, providing ample cover to anyone with the high ground. Within moments, the door swung open and a dark object hurtled out, slamming against the staircase below.

"Grenade!" Aizawa cried.

The *junsas* scattered and retreated down the steps, leaving Sergeant Fujita and him stranded behind a banister, caught in limbo between the third and fourth stories. They slammed against the floor, just before a vicious explosion ripped through the building like a small earthquake. Shrapnel spat against the banister, but the thick wooden structure provided just enough protection.

Aizawa peered below, seeing a huge chunk of staircase ripped asunder, cutting the rest of the *junsas* off from them. He looked up, just as a figure rushed out of the upstairs apartment with a pair of revolvers. Aizawa recognized that grim, parched face as one of the bank robbers – Pak. The Korean opened fire, sending a hail of bullets downward.

Sergeant Fujita and Aizawa crouched below the banister, their makeshift shield. Lead smashed against the wood, splashing splinters across their faces. For a brief moment, the firing ceased, and through the mist of wood pulp wafting upward, Pak had let his guard down reloading his revolvers. Aizawa jerked his own pistol up and snapped out quick shots.

Pak's left arm exploded in a cloud of blood, but his face remained rigid, like a block of concrete. Somehow, he continued to reload, though fluttering eyelids betrayed what agony the Korean must be suffering. No matter. That taut-skinned face made for a perfect target as Aizawa leveled the barrel of his Colt for the killing shot. On the third floor, a door swung open, jarring his aim. A stunned middle-aged woman with red-rimmed eyes and baggy kimono goggled at them.

"Police!" she screamed. "Someone! Call the Police!"

"Fool! We are the Police!" Sergeant Fujita snarled.

"Go inside and don't come out!" Aizawa said.

The woman slammed the door and thudded back into her apartment. The brief respite was all Pak needed. He swung the revolvers back and blasted away. Aizawa sank behind the banister with Fujita as a renewed storm of bullets rained down.

"We can rush him," Fujita said, raising his voice over the roar of gunfire. "One of us is bound to get through."

A definite possibility, but that horror show in Siberia had shattered any beauty in sacrificing your life for the mission.

"Leave suicidal charges to the Army," Aizawa said over the blasting pistols. "The Metropolitan Police uses its head."

The shots ceased, giving them a brief opening.

"Pak!" Aizawa shouted, still crouching beneath the banister. "This whole building is surrounded. Surrender now and we can make a deal with you."

A burst of slow, taunting laughter rippled throughout the hallways, smothered by a renewed blast of gunshots.

*****

Gunfire rumbled out in the hallway. There was no time to waste. Utako and Genda rushed over to the window and, with one heave, pushed it open. A rush of cold air gusted over them, sending Utako's teeth chattering. She bit her lip and gripped her pistol, steeling herself for the coming battle. On the street below, the police officers below jerked their guns up and opened fire. Bullets pinged and ricocheted off the sides of the fire escape.

Crouching down, Utako and Genda angled for a clear shot, but the metal frame outside provided the *junsas* below with an ample shield. Luckily, they'd brought heavy artillery to this gunfight.

"Genda-san," Utako said, "bomb them!"

Murderous glee lit up Genda's thick face as he grabbed one of the grenades from his kimono, pulled the pin, and hurled it down into the alley. The police officers ceased firing just long enough to scatter. A tremendous burst went off, spraying shrapnel in all directions. One of the *junsas* keeled over, shrieking in agony. His comrade, apparently unhurt, rushed to his aid, still keeping a bead on the window above with his pistol.

No matter, now was their chance to escape. Utako pulled herself through and out onto the fire escape. Her gloved fingers gripped the ladder, frigid and moist. Climbing the steps, she kept an eye out on the police officers below. Although they were vulnerable, the *junsa* seemed more concerned with dragging his comrade to safety.

Hoisting herself onto the rooftop, Ginza spread out before her, shining like a massive swarm of fireflies. The glow from the neon lights looked warm and inviting on this cold, black night, and for a brief moment, she remembered her old life. She was the Japanese It Girl, strolling through department stores, modeling the latest chic outfits, reading scripts at cafes, and dancing at nightclubs without a care. Now, how many of these people would even remember who Utako Natsume was?

Shame almost choked her. To wallow in such decadent memories was bourgeois. None of those insipid films were of any importance. Only the Japanese Revolution mattered now. Still, she would miss Ginza, if only for its dazzling lights and their hypnotic beauty.

A pair of strained grunts accompanied Genda and Izumi hauling themselves to the rooftop. Another volley of gunfire punctured the eerie silence, grim evidence that Pak was still fighting. If he could hold them off just a little longer, then perhaps the Red Terror Society would live long enough to fight another day. Utako turned and followed Izumi and Genda into the night.

CHAPTER TWENTY-NINE

Bullets blasted over Aizawa and Sergeant Fujita, sunk low behind the banister. Up above, Pak was too well-situated, making a direct shot impossible. Perhaps retreat was their only option? But the damaged stairs below presented a clear opening for Pak and a certain death trap. On the third floor, a door swung open and the woman from earlier, along with her two children and husband, rushed out, escorted to safety by the *junsas* stranded below.

"Pak!" Aizawa cried over the gunshots. "There are innocent civilians here! Give us ten minutes to evacuate them! Does the Red Terror Society value the lives of women and children?"

A haunting silence filled the hallways, broken by a contemptuous scoff.

"A Japanese police officer pleads for the lives of women and children? Where were you when my wife and daughter were lynched by angry mobs?"

Aizawa bit his lip. In the aftermath of the Great Kanto Earthquake, as Tokyo lay a smoldering ruin, vile rumors spread that Koreans had been poisoning wells in order to overthrow the Emperor. Whipped into a frenzy by right-wing patriotic societies, Japanese vigilantes prowled what remained of the city, hunting down anyone who even resembled a Korean. Days passed before order was restored.

Aizawa was about to speak up again, anything to keep this madman talking, when a fresh volley from Pak stifled him. Gunshots smashed against the banister, revealing just how flimsy their makeshift shield was. A few more bullets would shred it to oblivion. The staccato blasts brought back memories of Siberia, blurring his senses.

It was April 1922, but snow still blanketed the forests. The Reds had launched an offensive on Vladivostok and

Aizawa's platoon had been rushed to the front. An enemy machine gun crew opened fire, pinning them down. The Bolshevik partisans were well-entrenched, but his lieutenant had a plan. While he drew their fury, Aizawa and other soldiers flanked the Reds, completely unguarded on the left. Only when they caught their own reflections in the gleam of Japanese bayonets did the Bolsheviks realize their mistake.

"I'll draw his fire, Sergeant. Then you flank him on the left."

Fujita shook his head. "You're a better shot than me, sir. I'll stay behind."

"No, I outrank you. I should be the one to—"

Without waiting, Sergeant Fujita stood and pumped out gunshots, pinning Pak down. Aizawa muttered a curse at such disobedience but took the opening anyway. Crouching low, he stalked out of the safety of the banister and dashed up the stairs. Sergeant Fujita continued to blaze away until a deafening click-clack sounded. Out of ammunition.

Pak sprang up, flung out his revolvers, and blew out a burst of gunfire, hammering Sergeant Fujita backward. Aizawa swung around the banister, raised the Colt automatic, and fired off a round of bullets. Pak jerked and twitched as chunks of gore and splatters of blood were ripped out of him, like a puppet pulled by a hundred strings at once. Within moments, the Korean twirled around before slamming face-first to the floor. The two pistols fell out of his loosened hands with an impotent thud, but more concerning was another grenade that rolled out of Pak's kimono.

With bloodied, feeble fingers, the Korean reached for it in one futile grasp. Stopping it with his shoe, Aizawa bent down and picked the explosive up. He'd inspect it later. For now, he pocketed the two revolvers lying harmlessly on the floor, just in case Pak caught a second wind. Leaning over the banister, he saw Sergeant Fujita struggle to his feet and breathing in pained groans.

"How are you feeling, Sergeant?"

"My lungs feel like they're black-and-blue, but this armored apron—" Fujita patted the bulletproof vest "—did its duty."

"I'm sure it'll receive a commendation from Superintendent Miyake," Aizawa said, cracking a smile. A strained gasp from Pak announced there wasn't much time for an interrogation. Looking at the grenade, Aizawa recognized it as a Type 10, issued to Japanese soldiers during the last year of the Siberian Expedition. Sergeant Fujita soon joined him on the fourth floor and helped lean Pak up against the wall. Frothy blood bubbled at the Korean's lips as his glazed eyes looked up with a truculent glare.

"Where did you get all of these toys?" Aizawa asked, holding up the grenade.

Pak hacked out a gory cough. "From…our comrade in the Imperial Army…"

"The Imperial Army?" Aizawa asked, pocketing the grenade. "Some disgruntled private?"

Pak shook his head, sending droplets of blood spraying out. "An officer…who has joined our cause. Your vaunted Imperial Army rotting from within."

"Such impudence," Sergeant Fujita growled.

"It's true," Pak said, his breath coming out in jerking rasps. "Japanese soldiers are flocking to our ranks. The Army is on the verge of mutiny. Soldiers now realize that they were used as cannon fodder so the *zaibatsu* could build factories in Manchuria."

"Who is this officer?" Aizawa asked.

"You'll know soon enough…when he leads the Japanese People's Army to overthrow your precious—" a bubbling cough rose from Pak's throat "–Emperor. Maybe he'll end up like the Tsar. Rat-tat-tat!"

Aizawa looked over to Fujita, who boiled with rage. Any insult to the Emperor strained a police officer's patience. However, the Sergeant kept his poise but sank a hateful stare into Pak's broken form, as if he were a crushed cockroach.

"Yes, a fitting trade. My wife and daughter for the Japanese Empire," Pak said, blood leaking out of his mouth like a faucet. There was no time to waste.

"Why did you kill Marquis Maeda?" Aizawa asked.

Pak's head lolled back and forth, his eyes dazed and dimming. "It doesn't matter why…all that matters is that the Revolution…"

"Revolution?"

Pak's head bobbed up and down. "It will set Japan aflame and free my beloved Korea…Communists in the Army will lead the way and the people will follow…it will begin soon…and then you wolves will all swing from the cherry blossom trees…"

A gurgling hiss smothered Pak's words and his swollen, bloodied lips spread back in a ghoulish smile. With a wheezing rattle, the rest of the Korean's face hardened into a death mask, defiant and mocking. Aizawa wondered what secrets Pak took with him.

CHAPTER THIRTY

As Izumi led the way, Genda and Utako raced across another rooftop. They dared not stop, lest they lose the momentum to leap across to the next building. They'd crossed six so far, no easy feat despite most structures in Ginza being clustered together. Aside from the towering department stores in the distance, most of the surrounding buildings were only four stories high.

"Last one," Izumi called out.

A good thing, since fatigue strained Utako's entire body. With a bounding leap, Izumi launched himself across the alleyway and onto the neighboring building. Genda followed, his *geta* clogs stomping louder as he gained speed, then hurled his heavy frame into the air, landing with a loud smack. Utako dashed across the remainder of the rooftop, then jumped, sticking out her feet for landing.

As her high heels slapped across the roof, exhaustion seized Utako's legs, knocking her off balance. Wobbling back and forth, she flailed out for anything to steady her, but the Nagant was still pressed firmly into her gloved hand. She stumbled backward, the narrow gap between buildings opened up, threatening to swallow her. Weightlessness enveloped her as she fell back, but only for a brief moment.

Genda's hand yanked her forward, away from the pit below. Regaining her balance, she flashed him a thankful smile, then turned back toward Izumi, already stumbling down the fire escape. Would that bastard have even bothered to stay behind and help her? At least she'd always have Saburo Genda, simple and loyal.

They followed Izumi down the metal ladder, depositing them into an alleyway. Genda jumped down first, his *geta* clomped against the pavement. He looked back up, held out his arms, and caught Utako as she dropped below. Genda set her down and they both took in long, quivering gasps of chilly air.

"Don't just stand there!" Izumi snapped at the end of the alley, near the supercharged Ford. Thankfully, the wolves hadn't sniffed it out yet. "Let's go!"

They piled into the car, Genda in the back, Utako in the front, and Izumi behind the steering wheel. The engine rumbled to life, first with a buzzing hum, then a ferocious snarl as they sped toward the mouth of the alleyway.

"Don't go too fast," Utako said between pants. "We can't draw attention to ourselves."

Izumi nodded as he turned out of the alley. "I'll use the back streets for now."

"Head north. Major Kuno gave me the address for our new hideout in Tamanoi."

With its headlights off, the Ford threaded through a maze of narrow alleys and side streets, deserted at such a late hour. Even far away from the main drag, Ginza's lights provided some illumination as they crept northward. In the passenger seat, Utako stewed in a pool of bitterness and hate. She'd avenge Pak, just as she'd avenge Ichiro Hayashi, and all the other comrades.

The Ford pulled out onto another side street when the flash of a headlight stabbed through the murky darkness. A purring motorcycle passed them, its body a brilliant red. Only too late did the driver become visible, clad in the black uniform of the Metropolitan Police, his eyes hidden behind a pair of insect-like goggles.

The motorcycle swung around, and Izumi flicked on the headlights, then gunned the engine. Gears clanged as the car shot forward. There was no point in hiding now. Izumi swerved around a corner, then skidded out onto Ginza's main thoroughfare, still basking in a neon glow. The red motorcycle swung out behind them, gaining speed.

The Hattori and Mitsukoshi Department Stores whooshed by in a flickering blur of lights. There wasn't much traffic out, but the Ford snaked in and around what few cars and rickshaws were still on the road. A futile attempt, since the motorcycle's slim frame followed with ease, its siren now wailing.

"Get him off me," Izumi said.

"I thought this little toy of yours was fast," Genda sneered.

"Motorcycles weigh less than cars, you overgrown fool."

"Stop arguing," Utako said, lifting her Nagant. "Comrade Genda, we'll have to get that wolf off our scent."

Genda drew his own revolver, rolled down the window, and opened fire. The motorcycle wove back and forth, impossible to draw a bead on it. Even worse, another red motorcycle of the Metropolitan Police approached from behind with rapid speed.

Utako and Genda leaned out the window and began shooting – he from the right, she from the left. Caught between the murderous volleys, the police officer wobbled and swerved. The motorcycle's tires whined, and the vehicle gave way with a piercing shriek, rocking over and skidding out all over the street. The other red motorcycle driver lurched past his wounded comrade, then continued the chase. Even more troubling, the driver whipped out a pistol of his own and aimed, without even slowing down.

The crack of a gunshot rang out, whipping past Utako's face. The next wouldn't miss. The motorcycle continued speeding forward, coming close enough that she could see the officer's bug-eyed goggles. Utako raised her revolver, but hesitated. Something more powerful was needed.

She pulled out the grenade, yanked the pin, then tossed it low onto the passing stream of pavement. It bounced up and down like a basketball, shrinking into the distance. The driver whooshed the motorcycle to the side, trying to escape, but it was too late. A thunderous explosion ripped his back tire asunder, sending twisted hunks of metal, shrapnel, and rubber twirling upward.

The shredded vehicle spun out of control, tossing the driver off like a weightless rag doll. He slammed against a parked automobile before crumpling onto the hard pavement. The motorcycle continued lurching forward, propelled by speed but fatally wounded. It flipped up, then smashed against a neon sign advertising Calpis Soda, sending a torrent of sparks showering down.

"*Yatta*!" Genda cheered. "You did it!"

Utako slid back inside the Ford, cold wind slapping against her face. Police sirens screamed in the distance until they faded into a mournful whimper, far away.

CHAPTER THIRTY-ONE

Aizawa puffed on a calming Golden Bat as he took in the apartment. It was small and drafty, but large enough to hold four rumpled futons, along with a stack of magazines and newspapers. Underneath the sheets was a stash of paper yen, the Red Terror Society's haul from the Takano Bank robbery, or at least what remained of it.

Taking a lungful of smoke, Aizawa wondered what his punishment would be. Not only had the Red Terror Society escaped, but their sole witness was now dead. Added to that were at least three casualties, that he knew of. Past triumphs offered no protection when faced with such a fiasco.

Aizawa shifted his focus to the stack of literature, thumbing through past issues of *The Red Flag*, the official newspaper of the Japanese Communist Party. Long since banned under the Peace Preservation Law, *The Red Flag* continued to be mimeographed in underground cellars and left on subways, strewn across park benches, and stuffed into mailboxes. Thankfully, most Japanese wouldn't touch such rags lest they be contaminated with "dangerous thoughts," but some headlines were lurid enough to pique Aizawa's curiosity.

"THE SHOWA DEPRESSION IS THE DEATH KNELL OF CAPITALISM!"

Below it was a cartoon, showing a factory worker and a rice farmer, ready to pummel a *zaibatsu* capitalist, decked out in a frock coat and top hat. Aizawa tossed *The Red Flag* issues aside, then pored over another stack of newspapers labeled *The Soldier's Friend.* Similar in tone, every article had apparently been written by actual Army personnel. Most lambasted the Manchurian Incident, decrying it as an "imperialist war" to further enrich the *zaibatsu* and Marunouchi stock traders.

On the front page, an editorial cartoon practically screamed for attention – a giant skeleton, wearing an Army peaked cap and waving a military saber, danced over a map of Manchuria. A nearby article written by a Superior Private Oguchi, urged his fellow soldiers to stop fighting brother Chinese workers and turn their weapons on their true enemy – the *zaibatsu*. Aizawa scanned a few other columns, but certain similarities resonated. The cadence, sentence structure, and word choice suggested most articles possessed a single author.

Pak's words came to mind – *'Japanese soldiers are flocking to our ranks. The Army is on the verge of mutiny…'* Such boasts sounded hollow since membership in the Japanese Communist Party was never more than a few thousand. Still, where had the Red Terror Society obtained such firepower? Even in the underworld, guns were uncommon, and grenades suggested some credibility to Pak's statement.

"Inspector Aizawa," a voice called out from the open window. Aizawa folded *The Soldier's Friend* and looked over as Sergeant Fujita climbed in off the fire escape. After him, a figure in a black overcoat and fedora slithered into the apartment like a living shadow. Straightening up, Inspector Hiroshi Tezuka revealed himself.

Aizawa snapped a salute and bowed. "Inspector, I'm honored to see you again."

A nod was Tezuka's only response.

"I took the liberty of informing Inspector Tezuka," Fujita said, stiff at attention. "Since the suspects are Reds, the Tokko should be involved."

Aizawa drew on the Golden Bat and held the smoke in his lungs, soothing his nerves. Now that the case had a political dimension, it would be turned over to the Special Higher Police. He and his men did the bleeding, and Inspector Tezuka would receive the credit. Still, the last thing he could do was lose face in front of both a senior and a subordinate.

"Excellent work, Sergeant," he said, blowing out a trail of smoke. "Are all the civilians back inside?"

"Yes, sir, but that grenade damaged the stairs, so we'll have to enter and exit through the fire escape."

"I see. Did you interview the landlady?"

"Yes, sir." Sergeant Fujita flipped open a notepad. "She began renting this place to them in December. She even said they were a few days late with the rent this month."

"That was *before* their withdrawal. Did she have anything else to say?"

"Just that she'll never rent to men and women who aren't married anymore."

"So, nothing useful." Aizawa tossed the Golden Bat on the floor and ground it underneath his heel. "What about our wounded?"

"Two were taken to the hospital but are expected to survive. A motorcycle driver was seriously wounded and is in critical condition."

Aizawa let the news settle in his mind. Casualties were a grim reality for any commanding officer, but the honor of the Metropolitan Police had been dealt a severe blow.

"Thank you, Sergeant. Would you please leave us?"

Fujita nodded, saluted, then crawled out the window, his footsteps clanging against the fire escape ladder as he descended. An ominous silence engulfed the apartment.

"Where's the Korean?" Tezuka finally asked, his gruff voice like a pistol shot.

Aizawa led him out into the hallway, where Pak's mangled corpse lay propped up against the wall. Leaning over, Tezuka tilted the dead man's face up.

"Pak Sang-hoon."

"You know him, sir?"

"The Tokko keeps records of all Koreans living in Japan. Especially Communists. Pak-san joined the Party in 1927 and we picked him up in 1928. Before his trial, he escaped and went underground. He freelanced as a hitman for a few yakuza gangs to make ends meet, but always remained loyal to the Communists. Even donated most of his blood money to the Party's coffers."

"I'm impressed, sir. You must have a file cabinet in your brain."

A smile cracked underneath Tezuka's thick mustache. "I've been studying these people so long, they're almost like family now."

"Family or not, Pak Sang-hoon and his gang robbed a Takano Bank office just a few days ago. That's why we were after them."

Nodding, Tezuka added, "They also killed Marquis Maeda. But I'm sure you figured that out long ago."

Japanese police officers enjoyed testing their subordinates, but the Tokko added a more sinister weight to such mind games. Still, playing dumb might backfire, inflaming Tezuka's suspicions even further. Trying to match wits with a Thought Policeman was like a fly escaping a spider's web.

"Yes, I recognized Utako Natsume and found her arrest record."

"Oh? And what did you find out, Inspector?"

No point in being coy. "That you tortured her boyfriend, Ichiro Hayashi, to death."

"Those artsy types are all soft. They can't take any pain." Tezuka shook his head. "It's a shame too."

There was actual sincerity in that deep voice.

"'A shame,' sir?"

"Yes, that I couldn't reform him. Each Japanese lost to dangerous thoughts is like losing a man to cancer."

"Forgive me, sir, but that's not how I imagined you'd feel toward Reds."

Tezuka gave an annoyed grimace. "Would you hate a leper just because of his disease, Inspector? Communists are sick, contaminated with dangerous thoughts and foreign ideologies. The Special Higher Police is concerned with rehabilitation, not punishment. Yes, our methods can be severe, but only the Tokko can turn these invalids back into respectable Japanese. Unfortunately, there are times when the infection is too great and the patient cannot be saved."

"What about Utako Natsume?"

"My most disappointing failure. I thought I'd turned her, but it was all a charade. Serves me right for being fooled by an actress."

"And the other two?"

"Saburo Genda and Wataru Izumi? The former is a dimwitted brute. Two years ago, he worked at the Senju Wool Mill, making uniforms for the Army, but the fool was caught passing out Communist pamphlets to coworkers during his shift."

"And the latter?"

"A spoiled rich kid from Nagoya. He was attending Tokyo Imperial University but was expelled after getting involved with some Reds on campus. All of them joined the Communist Party and after our raid at the Atami Hot Springs, they were assigned to a cell under Natsume's command."

"Why did they give a woman command of a cell?"

"I suppose the central committee trusts the others even less. But they're all extremists, just like her."

"Pak mentioned the 'Japanese Revolution.' Is that what they're planning?"

"In their own mind, I suppose. They're a tiny group, but far more dangerous than any yakuza gang. The old guard of the Party was too tame for them. Their old leader, Jokichi Kazama, tried to expand membership by curbing the radical elements who wanted to arm themselves. But since our crackdown began, the central committee is so weak, it has virtually no authority over Natsume's group. It seems that the only contact they have with the Party leadership is when they receive propaganda material. In exchange for money stolen from banks, that is. Natsume believes that only terror can bring about revolution."

Aizawa imagined what a Japanese Revolution would resemble. Probably Nikolayevsk, but a thousand times over.

Brutal memories of Siberia reminded him of the Type 10 grenade, snug in his overcoat pocket.

"They had a few of these," Aizawa said, pulling the explosive out. Tezuka examined it with growing concern. "Along with Russian pistols, Nagants. I saw a lot of them up close while serving in Siberia. The weapon of choice for Bolshevik commissars. Do you think the Soviets might be supplying them?"

Tezuka shook his head.

"That was my initial thought too, but I've had the Soviet Embassy under surveillance for months now and haven't seen any connection to the Red Terror Society. Besides, their officials rarely speak to our Communists. Too risky for them. They're scared the Kwantung Army will use Manchukuo to invade Siberia. While they'd love to see a Soviet Japan, any fool can see that the Communist Party here is near death. Stalin is too busy with that famine in the Ukraine and doesn't want to risk antagonizing us for the lost cause of Japanese Communism."

Aizawa thought back to Pak's boasts about the Imperial Army being on the verge of mutiny. They didn't sound so hollow anymore.

"Pak mentioned a contact in the Army, who furnished the weapons. The Russian pistols and Japanese grenades could be supplied by a soldier who served in Manchuria. But, I'm doubtful..."

"And why is that?"

"The newspapers claim that the Volunteer Armies in Manchuria operate with Soviet weapons. It's possible that a Communist in the Army provided weapons, captured from Manchurian guerillas. But I recently talked to an Army officer who told me something very different. Apparently, the Volunteer Armies fight with weapons captured from defeated Manchukuoan troops."

"And what does that mean, Inspector?"

"Whoever supplied the weapons to the Red Terror Society wants to appear as a Manchurian veteran. Defeats of our Manchukuoan allies have been censored, so the Army blames the Soviets for supplying the guerillas. The Red Terror Society would likely be fooled by this, as they read Japanese newspapers too."

An ominous look gathered over Tezuka's face. "Unfortunately, you may be right, Inspector."

Aizawa pocketed the grenade again before glancing over at the shredded body of Pak, then up to Inspector Tezuka, glaring back in the darkness. How many secrets hid in that brain of his? Still, there was one nagging question that demanded to be answered.

"Why was Marquis Maeda assassinated?"

"I don't know, Inspector. Yet." Tezuka drew in a long breath. "There are some matters I need to attend to first, so I'd like you to continue your investigation."

"You mean, this is still my case?"

"Yes, but since it involves Communists, keep me informed."

"Certainly, sir. I'll submit a report to your office—"

Tezuka held up a gloved hand. "Actually Inspector, I would like to keep this just between us. For now."

Aizawa gave a thankful bow, then produced his *meishi* card with both hands. Tezuka offered his own as a formality, but tradition dictated that the senior call upon the junior at his leisure.

"Thank you, Inspector, I'll be in touch."

They walked out of the hallway and toward the open window, leaking gusts of cold air inside. "And Inspector, not a word to anyone about our meeting." He put a finger up to his lips, then gestured out the window, into the gloomy night, suffused with a neon glow. "There are evil things lurking in the shadows of this city. If you let your guard down, they'll emerge and devour you."

With that, Inspector Tezuka climbed out the window, leaving Aizawa with a chill colder than the wintery air.

CHAPTER THIRTY-TWO

The Ford wove through the crooked streets of the Mukojima Ward, its headlights throwing blobs of bright yellow against rows of closed businesses. Most had just shut down for the night, but many others were closed and shuttered for good. Despite the government's assurances of economic recovery, the Showa Depression still festered in the worst slum of Tokyo – Mukojima's Tamanoi neighborhood.

Most of the streets were deserted, but looking out the passenger window, Utako saw a few eerie silhouettes scurry in and out of alleyways like rats. Probably streetwalkers, since Tamanoi was the center of unlicensed prostitution in Tokyo. A far cry from the resplendent brothels of Yoshiwara, Tamanoi whores screwed behind trash cans and noodle stalls. Utako had joined their ranks years ago, right after her release from prison. Blacklisted by every movie studio, the Japanese It Girl had survived through back-alley peep shows and playing men's flutes for a bowl of rice.

How fitting, since the same fate had befallen her character in *Woman of the Streets*, her finest work. Well, if Ginza was the first act of Utako Natsume's life, then Tamanoi would make for a fitting climax. Izumi hooked the car right, pulling into a cramped alleyway with a dead end.

"You're sure this is the place?"

"It's the address Major Kuno gave me."

The Ford crept deeper into the alley, then halted in front of a darkened, one-story building. Izumi killed the headlights but kept the car running, just in case they needed to back out quick. Someone stirred inside the building, then slid open a *shoji* door and peered out. Although a veil of darkness hung over him, Major Kuno's broad shoulders and tall frame were easy to make out. Utako rolled down the window and leaned out.

"We need to hide the car," she said in a hushed tone. Kuno nodded, then pushed the *shoji* door open even more, revealing a sizable entrance. The Ford crept inside, scraping the door frame against its side mirrors. After Kuno shut the door, Utako, Genda, and Izumi piled out. The Major lit a paper lantern, painting their surroundings in a warm, reddish glow.

The building was moderately-sized, with a large, unfurnished main area, big enough for the Ford and maybe even a few futons. Off to the side was a curved counter, evidence of a bar. They were in an abandoned *izakaya*, the working-class drinking establishments that honeycombed Tokyo. Most were small, cramped spaces, but this *izakaya* was twice as large as usual, indicating that it catered to the Tamanoi masses. Well, at least it used to, until falling victim to the Showa Depression.

"What took you so long?" Kuno asked.

"The Police raided us," Izumi said.

"The Police? I told you Ginza was too conspicuous! What happened?"

"Pak sacrificed himself so we could escape," Utako said. "A revolutionary to the end."

"Natsume-san was a true leader," Genda piped up. "Thanks to her, we outsmarted the wolves."

Utako threw back a thankful smile. She needed her pet more than ever now.

"How did the Police discover your whereabouts?" Kuno demanded.

Izumi was about to answer, but a piercing glare from Utako silenced him. The last thing she needed was a lecture about letting that dimwitted *moga* go.

"As you said, Major, Ginza was *too* conspicuous," Utako replied.

Kuno grumbled in the red-tinted shadows, but the answer seemed to placate him.

"What about the money? Did you at least recover that?"

Izumi pulled a wad of bills from his coat pocket. Snickering, he said, "What we could manage."

In the hazy reddish light, Kuno's face was an inferno of rage. "And left the rest for the Police? You fools!"

A desire to defend herself and her comrades rose inside Utako, to explain to this arrogant soldier what hell they'd endured tonight. But the coffee from earlier had long since worn off, and her body sagged with fatigue. She sauntered past him and over to the bar. A drink would hit the spot, but everything was cleared out, leaving only a glaze of dust on the floor. Behind the bar, outlines of two cellar doors were visible despite the dust. Probably where the extra bottles of sake were kept. She creaked both open, but they were empty except for a wafting, musty stench.

"Major, we lost a comrade tonight and barely escaped with our lives," Utako said, straightening up. "If you want to berate us, then please, do it in the morning."

Izumi and Genda chuckled, whereas Kuno looked ready to burst like a volcano. Biting his lip, the Major whipped open the door and stalked out. He'd cool off in a few hours, but for now, she needed rest. Climbing atop the bar, Utako curled into herself for warmth and let sleep bury her.

*****

Superintendent Miyake scrutinized the report, filling Aizawa with a clawing dread. He'd gotten little rest last night, catching what sleep he could at his desk. When morning came, he wrote a quick report, taking full responsibility for the raid's failures, and downplaying any success. Although his punishment might be severe, humility was still an essential trait for the Metropolitan Police.

"So, according to this," Miyake began, lowering the report, "the Red Terror Society was armed with both Soviet pistols and Japanese Army grenades?"

"Yes, sir. They've all been submitted to the Records Department as evidence."

"Is that so? Well, it's a wonder you didn't have more casualties."

"Sir?"

Miyake tossed the report on his desk and tented his hands. "The Superintendent-General was furious that three *junsas* were injured. He demanded that the lead officer on duty be punished severely."

That meant loss of pay, suspension from duty, and maybe even demotion. Swallowing hard, Aizawa braced himself.

"But I explained to him that given how well-armed these Red gangsters are, it's unreasonable not to expect casualties. Luckily, the three *junsas* are expected to survive. What's more, I suggested that to punish the man who'd been awarded the Order of the Rising Sun from the Emperor himself might create a firestorm in the press."

Perhaps past glories were a shield after all. He'd earned that medal for his role in the Kusanagi Society Incident, over a year ago, and it still carried some clout.

"Sir, I apologize for my failure," Aizawa said, lowering himself in a sincere bow.

"Regardless, the Superintendent-General saw my reasoning and ordered that I only reprimand you verbally. So, consider yourself punished."

Aizawa fought back a grateful smile.

"Unfortunately, now that we know that the Takano Bank robbers and the assassins of Marquis Maeda are one and the same, you'll have to work closely with Inspector Tezuka."

"Yes, sir, I spoke to him last night," Aizawa said, careful not to add more.

"Good. Keep me informed Inspector, but let Tezuka take the lead on this. I don't want to step on the Tokko's territory."

"Understood, sir. Perhaps we can enlist the press' cooperation? We can distribute mugshots of Utako Natsume and her cohorts to the newspapers. Somebody is bound to tip us off as to their whereabouts."

A deep frown carved itself onto Miyake's tight face. "The last thing we want is the press learning that three of these criminals slipped through our fingers. It would mean a severe loss of face to the Metropolitan Police…and to you."

Aizawa swallowed his shame. "Yes, sir."

"We cannot hide this from the press much longer, so we expect results soon," Miyake said, leaning back in his chair. "By the way Inspector, Minori told me you promised to take her to a movie? Given last night's events, I understand if you want to cancel."

Now it made sense. Miyake had stuck his neck out for his potential son-in-law. Well, at least Aizawa had someone looking out for him against the top brass. But Miyake's suggestion doubled as a veiled warning not to break an engagement with his daughter.

"That's quite all right, sir. I'm looking forward to seeing Minori-san again."

Miyake's sharp face softened into what resembled a smile. "Excellent. I'll tell her the good news. You can take off early to get some rest, Inspector."

Aizawa nodded, saluted, and smiled on the way back to his office.

CHAPTER THIRTY-THREE

Secure in his uniform, Major Kanemaru scanned the morning edition of the *Yomiuri Shimbun.* The tramcar trundled westward, toward the Kasumigaseki district, the nerve center of the Japanese government. He didn't venture there much anymore, but given last night's debacle, General Araki had summoned him for an in-person report. Kasumigaseki literally meant the "Gate of Mist," fitting for all the intrigue that went on here. Although the tram was almost empty, Kanemaru pulled the leather visor on his peaked cap down further and busied himself with the newspaper.

The *Yomiuri's* headline screamed "LATE NIGHT RAID IN GINZA" detailing how the Metropolitan Police – led by Inspector Kenji Aizawa – had raided the hideout of a gang of bank robbers, killing one, a Korean Communist with a sordid criminal past. No further details were given since it would be a loss of face to admit that three out of four suspects had escaped.

Scouring the newspaper further turned up a few distractions. Peace had returned to North China after the Kwantung Army's capture of Shanhaikwan, though Chinese troops in the neighboring Nekka province remained on high alert. An article blasted the recent findings of the Lytton Report for suggesting that Manchukuo was a Japanese protectorate and not a genuine case of self-determination. It even demanded that Japan withdraw from the League of Nations, should the report be adopted by its assembly. Another editorial lamented that Her Majesty, the Empress, had still not produced a male heir to the Japanese Empire.

The tramcar rounded the moat that ringed the Imperial Palace, passed Metropolitan Police Headquarters on the left, then screeched to a jerking halt inside Kasumigaseki. Tossing the *Yomiuri Shimbun* on the seat, Major Kanemaru stepped out of the tram and strode across the street toward the bulky structure of the Army Ministry. The weather was cold but sunny, warming Kanemaru slightly underneath his khaki uniform cape. Few people were out in the mid-afternoon, but one man – underneath a lamppost, smoking a cigarette – caught his attention.

Draped in a long overcoat and fedora, he practically screamed "plainclothes detective." Fear caught in Kanemaru's throat and his mind buzzed with conjecture. Inspector Aizawa? Here? Impossible! But the plainclothesman was older, probably early fifties, and a thick mustache stamped his wide face. Well, what did he expect? Kasumigaseki and neighboring Nagatacho swarmed with government workers, especially police officers. The mustached detective glanced over at Kanemaru, then continued smoking his cigarette, uninterested.

Striding inside the Army Ministry, a sentry, standing ramrod stiff in the lobby, saluted him with his rifle. Returning the gesture with a nod, Kanemaru ascended the massive center staircase, his heavy footsteps and clanking saber booming off the walls with deep echoes. He turned the corner and saw a procession of Army officers coming the other way. Their uniforms were similar to his, save for one detail. They all wore black collar patches, the insignia of the *Kempeitai*, the Police of the Imperial Army.

Most of the officers were nondescript, aloof men, but one – wearing oval glasses over a tight, slit-like mouth – was instantly recognizable as Takumi Hatsu, bringing back a swarm of memories.

Last May, as the Okamura Gang's ship sunk to the bottom of Tokyo Bay, Kanemaru had found himself fished out of the murky waters and saved by a *Kempeitai* squad, led by Hatsu. Placed under arrest, he was driven to the Army Ministry and brought before General Araki himself. Handcuffed and humiliated, Kanemaru sat in silence as Hatsu demanded his court-martial for smuggling opium into Tokyo, dishonoring the Imperial Army.

General Araki had listened, thanked Hatsu for his service, ordered Kanemaru uncuffed, then dismissed the *kempei* officer. He conceded that for the unforgivable crime of peddling drugs in the Imperial Capital, death was a justified punishment. But Araki had heard of Junzo Kanemaru's role in the Siberian Expedition and the Mukden Incident. He still had use for the God of Intrigue.

It made sense, Kanemaru figured. Araki had served in Siberia too, as the *Tokumu Kikan* chief in Vladivostok. This polished, stiff-necked general had once been a shadow soldier in the dark world of espionage and double-dealing. They were like kindred spirits in conspiracy. In exchange for dropping the charges, Major Kanemaru became General Araki's private spy, sent out on missions too unsavory for more honorable men.

The *kempei* officers pounded down the steps, passing him without acknowledgment. Even Hatsu stared ahead unconcerned. Kanemaru stalked up the staircase and strode down the hallway to the office of the Army Minister. Rapping on the door, he heard a soft voice announce, "Enter."

Inside, Sadao Araki sat at his desk, armored in a brown tunic, festooned with service ribbons. Like all generals, his stiff collar lacked colored patches that denoted service branch, but the Order of the Rising Sun glinted at his throat. Badges gleamed on his shoulders, solid gold with two stars each, the rank insignia of a *chujo*, a lieutenant-general.

The office was far sparser than Araki's house, with a portrait of the Emperor and a Rising Sun flag the only furnishing. Several staff officers swarmed around the General, worker bees fawning over their queen. After a dismissive gesture, the other officers saluted, then walked out, leaving them both alone.

"Yes, Major?" Araki said, summoning him closer. "What do you have to report?"

"I assume you saw the morning papers, sir," Kanemaru said, drawing up beside the General. His eyes shifted to the window, casting a glance outside. Across the street, the plainclothes detective was no longer there, releasing an unconscious tension from Kanemaru's gut.

"Apparently, the Police raided our nest of Reds," Araki said, tugging at his handlebar mustache.

"Only the Korean was killed, sir. The others escaped."

"How unfortunate. The Korean was the best shot, right?"

"Yes, sir."

"But the actress is unharmed, right?"

"Yes, sir."

"She'll have to do. The Police are becoming troublesome."

"Yes, sir. That man, Inspector Aizawa, led the raid last night."

Contempt flickered in Araki's eyes. "The same Inspector Aizawa?"

"Yes, sir. The same."

"Forestall any personal plans of vengeance, Major. But if this Inspector Aizawa, or any other police officer, should get too close, do not hesitate in your duty."

Kanemaru clicked his heels, understanding the implicit order to kill anyone who interfered. The soul of his little viper, Chizuru Okamura, could not rest until Aizawa was sent straight to hell. But attacking him directly might backfire, and Araki might rescind his offer of clemency. For all the Inspector knew, Major Kanemaru had drowned in Tokyo Bay. Besides, there would be time for revenge later.

"And what about Colonel Hashizume?" Araki asked, ripping Kanemaru from his thoughts.

"I had a few drinks with him at the Silkworm Tea House. As you stated, he enjoys geisha, but also wallowing in self-pity."

"What of his political beliefs?"

Kanemaru related every detail, from the geisha playing the song "Tabaruzaka," to disparaging comments about the Manchurian Incident.

"What is your assessment?"

"Colonel Hashizume is an anachronism, sir. An honorable samurai unaccustomed to fighting in dishonorable times. A man who harbors dangerous grudges against superiors."

The General remained placid, but satisfaction rustled behind his mustache. "Good. I've been thinking, Major. It took too many bullets to fell Marquis Maeda. Since the Korean is dead, I want you to train that Red rabble how to shoot better. The actress especially. She must learn how to shoot a target with only one bullet." He held up a single finger. "One bullet. And it must be a fatal shot."

"Yes, sir. May I ask who the next target will be?"

Araki's eyes narrowed into pinpoints. "You will find out only when you are given orders, Major. But know this, we must tread carefully. The Control Faction surrounds us, scheming to discredit me and the Imperial Way. Those bureaucratic weaklings care nothing for the poor and will put the Imperial Army into the claws of high finance and big business. The fate of the Japanese Empire is at stake, Major."

Kanemaru nodded but was overwhelmed by a wave of confusion. Perhaps Colonel Hashizume was to be the next victim of the Red Terror Society, but why not just say it? The ultimate goal of this mission remained elusive, a ghost fading in and out of the darkness. But a soldier obeyed orders, whether or not he understood them.

"Yes, sir."

CHAPTER THIRTY-FOUR

Exiting from the tramcar, Major Kanemaru began to relax a little. It was dark now and streetlamps flickered to life, illuminating the Tsukiji neighborhood. A blustery wind blew off the banks of the Sumida River, glistening in the neon lights from nearby Ginza. The frigid air bit into his cheeks, and Kanemaru wrapped himself in his khaki uniform cape, flapping in the breeze. The Tsukiji Fish Market swarmed with Tokyoites stocking up on tuna, eel, and squid. Anything cold and slimy was nauseating on a night like this, and his thoughts drifted to steaming bowls of ramen, spicy curry rice, and *shabu shabu* hotpot. Turning the corner, his *machiya* townhouse came into view. Although Kanemaru rented only the top floor, this dwelling was the closest thing to a home since arriving in Tokyo a year ago.

As he approached, headlights flashed through the darkness and a red sedan rolled up. The meter in the front window identified it as a one-yen taxi, transporting passengers anywhere in Tokyo for a single yen. The engine still puttered as the plainclothes detective from earlier stepped out, his gloved hands gripping a pair of binoculars. No wonder he'd disappeared from view. After Kanemaru had stepped inside the Army Ministry, this crafty plainclothesman must have retreated to a taxicab and monitored his movements from afar.

"Good evening, Major Kuno," the man said, chilled breath leaking from his lips. "I'm Inspector Hiroshi Tezuka of the Tokko."

Being tailed by a member of the Thought Police lessened the humiliation. Had it been a common policeman, ritual suicide might have been in order.

"Pleased to meet you, Inspector. What can I do for you?"

"I just have a few questions."

"I'll do my best to answer since I know you Thought Policemen can read minds."

A hollow chuckling spread between them, two serpents looking for the best angle to strike. Inviting him inside, Kanemaru led Tezuka up the creaking stairs and into his room. A low-lying *kotatsu* table, stove, and a few extra kimonos were the only furnishings, lest he had to vacate on a moment's notice. Neither man bothered to remove his footwear, and Kanemaru left his peaked cap on and kept his saber at his side, a soldier ready for battle.

"My apologies for not offering you any tea or food, Inspector," Kanemaru said, as they knelt at the *kotatsu*. "But as you can see, I enjoy few luxuries."

"Quite all right, Major. It was rude of me to come so late. But unfortunately, duty waits for no man."

"Too true! What can I assist you with?"

Inspector Tezuka set his binoculars down on the *kotatsu* and leaned forward, an interrogator at work. "Forgive me, Major, but I've seen you before."

"Is that so?"

"On New Year's Day. I was parked a few yards away from General Araki's house and using these—" he tapped the binoculars – "I spotted you at his house. And soon after you entered, all the other officers left in a hurry, including His Highness, Prince Chichibu."

Kanemaru cracked a grin. "General Araki wanted to share his New Year's *mochi* with me only."

"Well, I figured you must be an important officer, so I asked some of the officers there. Most knew you only as 'Major Kuno.' Informally, they knew you as 'General Araki's pet dog.' Their words, not mine."

"All soldiers are dogs, Inspector. We're loyal and bite when ordered."

"Very true. Forgive me, Major, but Tokko inspectors are always curious. I called the *Kempeitai* to inquire about you."

"And?"

"They refused to provide anything detailed, other than 'Major Kuno is unknown to us.' So, my question is, who are you really?"

"You heard correctly. Araki's pet dog. Woof woof."

"Perhaps I should provide more information about myself. You see, I'm assigned the Tokko's First Department, Special Police Work."

"Meaning…?"

"We investigate and uncover all subversive ideologies – fascism, anarchism, but mostly Communism."

"I heard you netted all the remaining Reds at Atami."

"Most of the leaders. Unfortunately, there's still a few underground cells out there, chewing away at our national foundation like termites. In November, I discovered that one of these cells started calling itself the Red Terror Society."

"Well, Communists do love their theatrics."

"Regardless, I took a special interest in this group. Some government officials were concerned about the recent crackdown on Reds, and wanted detailed reports – General Sadao Araki and Marquis Tatsuo Maeda."

Kanemaru forced himself to remain placid, while his brain spread in a thousand directions. How much did this Thought Policeman know? Too much, that was for certain. Let the fly keep talking while the God of Intrigue spun his web.

"Marquis Maeda?"

"He was a member of the Privy Council. A very conservative man, obsessed with protecting the Emperor System at all costs. You don't understand how terrified the aristocracy is of Communism, Major, even when it teeters on extinction in Japan."

"Well, isn't Communism like a cancer? You must cut it out completely or else it'll grow back."

"Too true! And we Tokko are the surgeons! Marquis Maeda and General Araki ordered weekly reports about this group, but just as I closed in on them–" Tezuka opened his gloved hands, creaking the leather "—they would always escape. Like magic."

Kanemaru thought back to November when Araki had ordered him to infiltrate the Red Terror Society. He'd even given him a list of areas where they could be hiding out. He found them in an Asakusa flophouse, full of ideas but no strategy. After supplying them with pistols and target practice, they were ready for their first assignment. December's bank robbery in Yokohama went well and they'd moved out of Asakusa and into their new hideout in Ginza, slipping right through Tezuka's fingers.

"I see, and how can I be of help, Inspector?"

A smile formed underneath Tezuka's mustache. "You can help me understand why Marquis Maeda was assassinated."

CHAPTER THIRTY-FIVE

Laughter pushed out of Kanemaru's throat, tight with tension. "I wish I knew."

"Well, I have some theories," Tezuka said, leaning back off the *kotatsu*. "Just before his assassination, the Marquis informed me about his suspicions."

"Suspicions?"

Kanemaru bent closer, his left hand planted on the table. Drawing his saber would be too difficult, leaving the binoculars as the only viable weapon.

Above the mustache, Tezuka glowered. "He told me there were unsettling rumors haunting the Imperial Palace like ghosts. Rumors involving General Araki."

Lunging forward, Kanemaru grabbed the binoculars and swung them around. The metal smacked against Inspector Tezuka's skull with a loud crack, sending him to the floor. Kanemaru bolted upright, knocking over the *kotatsu*, and drew his saber, filling the room with a metallic rasp. He heaved it back, ready to sink steel deep into the Tokko inspector's exposed throat.

The saber thrust downward, but Tezuka rolled out of the way. His gloved hand reached out and grabbed Kanemaru by the wrist. Twisting it, Tezuka sent the sword clattering to the floor, but Kanemaru still gripped the binoculars. Another gloved hand reached up and crashed into Kanemaru's chest, toppling him over.

Panting, Tezuka fumbled inside his coat. Kanemaru lurched forward, grabbed the saber, and considered another charge. Too late. Inspector Tezuka had regained his balance and drew a pistol, aiming for a clear shot. Spinning on his heel, Kanemaru rushed toward the sliding door, burst through it, and pounded down the stairs, his cape whipping up behind him.

"Stop!" Tezuka bellowed as the loud clap of a pistol shot burst behind him. A chunk was ripped out of the paper wall just in front of him, but Kanemaru didn't slow his pace. He tore out of the *machiya* where the one-yen taxi still idled.

Bundling into the cab, Kanemaru roared, "Drive! Now!"

The driver opened his mouth to protest, but the glinting saber silenced him. Putting the taxi into gear, he shot off, just as Tezuka ran outside, his pistol hanging impotently beside him. Sheathing his sword, Kanemaru realized he still held Tezuka's binoculars. He almost laughed, but instead, he sank into the backseat with a trembling sigh, as the Fish Market, Tsukiji, and soon all of Tokyo molded into an amorphous blur.

*****

The Rokku – Asakusa's Sixth District – was a mass of twinkling lights and banners fluttering in the chilly night. Names of Hollywood films and stars, alongside their equally popular Japanese counterparts, shimmered in a maze of electric bulbs. Hordes of people filtered in and out of the movie theaters packed inside the Rokku. If there was still a depression on, the cinema didn't seem to notice.

Aizawa and Minori Miyake stepped out of the Denkikan Theater where Tarzan greeted them. A smiling cardboard cutout of Johnny Weissmuller, wearing only a loincloth, stood at the entrance, below a poster showing Tarzan in a life-or-death battle with a vicious lion. The movie *Tarzan* wasn't nearly as exciting, but it was foreign, and Aizawa wanted to show this *moga* just how worldly he was.

"How'd you like the picture?" Aizawa asked.

Minori smiled as she donned her gloves and pulled her cloche hat tighter. "I've seen better, but the ending with all the elephants sure was something."

Aizawa chuckled and they began walking. The Denkikan – the Electric House – was Japan's oldest movie theater, but just one of many in the Rokku. Chattering crowds swarmed around other theaters, blazing with lights. *Love Linked to Heaven*, a story dramatizing the recent epidemic of love suicides, brought in droves of schoolboys and schoolgirls, probably for inspiration. *Bullets and Horses in Manchuria* attracted paltry crowds, a sign that perhaps the Japanese people's romance with militarism was beginning to wane. Most popular though was *Chushingura: The Story of the Forty-Seven Ronin*, proudly advertised as the best sound film of the year.

"Another talkie?" Aizawa commented. "They'll put the *benshis* out of business at this pace."

"Not fast enough," Minori scoffed. "Most Western pictures are all talkies now. Japan hasn't caught up since we love hearing *benshis* read movies to us. If I want to read, I'll open a book."

"Reading is a luxury for me. Duty takes up too much time, so movies are a good substitute. I used to take my little sister here before the Great Earthquake. We'd see samurai pictures starring Eyeballs Matsu. Remember him?"

"Oh yeah, the actor with the big peepers?" Minori popped her eyes wide.

"You look just like him."

The suffocating crowds thinned as they made their way out of the Rokku and into Asakusa's snakelike streets and alleys.

"What *was* the last book you read, Inspector?"

"Do newspapers count?"

"No."

Thinking back, only one title stood out. "I read *Botchan*."

"Every schoolchild has read *Botchan*! What about *I Am a Cat* or anything by Edogawa Ranpo?"

"Edogawa who?"

"Ranpo. He writes those Detective Akechi stories. Ring a bell?"

"Unfortunately, no. But I've read enough Police reports to count as a mystery novel."

"I'd love your professional opinion about his writing. I own a complete volume of his works. Perhaps I can loan it to you?"

The suggestion was another opening for a date. But why end the night so early?

"I'd like that," Aizawa said as a cold wind moaned. "But for now, how about we warm up over a drink?"

CHAPTER THIRTY-SIX

Kamiya Bar was filled with the soft murmurs of conversation, clinking glasses, and an air of *ero guro nansensu* that typified Asakusa. As one of the oldest Western-style bars in Tokyo, Kamiya had a sense of *haikara* – high-collar class – that those cramped *izakayas* lacked. Outside a red neon sign buzzed its name in bold, Western letters, luring patrons into its seductive atmosphere. Most were *mobos* and *mogas* out on dates, like Reiko and Koichi Matsumoto.

"Kanpai!" Matsumoto toasted, raising his Asahi beer. "To the new goddess of cinema, Reiko Watanabe!"

Tittering, Reiko lifted her *denki bran* and sipped. Sweet, flowery notes filled her mouth as the thick liquid went down. Although a devotee of gimlets, the *denki bran* – electric brandy – was Kamiya Bar's specialty and drinking anything else here was akin to screwing in a Shinto shrine.

"Another toast," Reiko offered, "to the success of *Bullets and Horses in Manchuria*."

"It needs all the help it can get. Before coming here, I passed by the Rokku. They've barely sold any tickets since it premiered. It'll probably be pulled from theaters by the end of the month."

"Oh, that's too bad. I hate war movies and even I liked it."

"The public is a fickle beast," Matsumoto said, lowering his voice. Tables in Kamiya Bar were all communal, making privacy difficult. "A year ago, putting out a war picture was like printing money, but not anymore. Too much time has passed since our victory in Manchuria."

"Japan is falling out of love with militarism," Reiko whispered. "That deserves a toast."

"Yes and no," Matsumoto said, his voice still strained. "It wasn't the Army, the government, or the press that whipped up that war fever when the Manchurian Incident began. It was the Japanese people themselves. The *Asahi Shimbun* was against the invasion, but when its competitors began printing pro-war editorials, there was a spike in sales, so they followed suit."

"Anything for a few extra yen." Reiko sipped her *denki bran*. "Can't blame them in this depression, I suppose."

"What worries me is something else might reawaken this militarist monster. Shanhaikwan is over, but there might be future *incidents* in North China."

"We are a nation of samurai, after all."

"Nonsense." Matsumoto swigged his beer, as if to wash out a bitter taste. "The people were disillusioned by the depression. The politicians in the Diet squabbled like children, but the Kwantung Army took bold, decisive action. In troubled times, people look to be led."

Reiko offered a teasing smile. "Sounds like something a militarist would say, not a member of the Social Mass Party."

"I'm just stating the obvious. But now that the economy's improving, albeit slowly, the people are distracted by other things. All these 'love suicides' in the press, for instance. We need to raise their class consciousness and promote liberalism before the next *incident* erupts."

Raising her *denki bran,* Reiko said, "Well, let's hope your next film does just that."

"If it does, it'll only be because the audience is so enraptured by a certain geisha's beauty."

Reiko took another sip to hide the blush flooding her cheeks. "Oh, that reminds me." After setting the glass down, she opened her handbag and pulled out *The Crab Cannery Ship*. Glancing around, she slid it across the table as if it was a top-secret document.

"Maybe this can give you some inspiration for future tendency films. I read it in one sitting. It's about the inhumane conditions workers endure when they're out at sea, catching all the fish and crabs we eat here in the cities. It'd make a hell of a picture."

Matsumoto glowed with childlike glee. "Where did you get this?" he asked, dropping his voice lower still. "I've always wanted to read it, but it's been banned for years."

Revealing the novel's source might spoil this romantic night. Especially after she'd tipped the Metropolitan Police off to Utako Natsume's hideout.

"Please, Matsumoto-san, I'm not completely bourgeois. I have my sources too."

That seemed to placate Matsumoto, who shoved the novel inside his overcoat, a smuggler stowing away contraband. Such boyish eagerness was endearing, and she suppressed an urge to kiss him then and there. Despite being a *mobo* and a *moga*, such public displays of affection would probably earn shameful stares, even in Asakusa. Instead, she shifted her eyes toward the door, where a new couple just entered.

The woman was a pale-skinned beauty with alluring eyes and, when she whipped off her cloche hat, a headful of waved, black hair – stylish and modern. More than just modern, she was the epitome of *haikara* class. The man with her had a rock-solid face and a square jaw, flanked by a pair of sideburns, dotted with a pair of brooding eyes – Inspector Kenji Aizawa. Reiko's gaze followed them as they sat at the far end of the table.

A date? Here? It didn't make sense. Her *senpai* was the type who'd marry a traditional woman, wrapped up tight in a kimono and tittering behind a paper fan. A strange jealousy gripped her. This *moga* was *haikara*, and what was Reiko Watanabe? An actress at best, a mere pretender at worst.

Matsumoto glanced over at Aizawa. "Handsome fellow. You know him?"

The words tore Reiko from her shock. "No, no, I thought maybe I'd seen him before. My mistake." After polishing off the rest of the *denki bran*, she said, "Let's go. This place is getting a bit too crowded."

"Oh, yes, how about a picture at the Rokku? Or maybe a show at *Casino Follies*?"

"Anything sounds lovely," she said, standing up. As they donned their hats, Reiko stole a final glance at Aizawa and his little *moga*. Neither had even noticed they'd left the table.

*****

A banging outside yanked Utako out of the hazy murk and back into consciousness. She rubbed her eyes and slid off the *izakaya's* counter, still her makeshift bed. Genda and Izumi stirred awake and joined her near the back door. They shared tense, conspiratorial looks until a familiar voice rasped from the other side.

"Open up, it's Major Kuno."

The *shoji* door whooshed and Kuno stepped inside, looking gallant in his brown tunic and peaked cap, binoculars dangling from his neck.

"I found our next target. A Tokko agent who raided my quarters," Kuno said, pacing back and forth. "He must die before he can alert the *Kempeitai* about my sympathies."

Utako looked over to her comrades, now fully awake with bloodlust. "Who?"

"Inspector Hiroshi Tezuka."

A warmth gripped Utako's heart. Religion might be the opiate of the masses, but this was a sign that the gods had answered her prayers at last.

CHAPTER THIRTY-SEVEN

Over a cup of morning coffee, Aizawa reviewed the latest reports at his desk. Saburo Genda's siblings – two older brothers and one little sister – claimed not to have seen him in over a year and didn't know where he'd be. Furthermore, the *junsa* assigned to monitor their cramped *nagaya* row house in the Honjo Ward had reported no suspicious activity yet.

Wataru Izumi hailed from Nagoya. A long-distance call was made to his father – the wealthy owner of a chemical plant; it turned out that Father Izumi had disowned his impudent son after learning he'd been expelled from Tokyo University for Communist activities. Unfortunately, he had no clue where the brat might be, but if the Police found him, he asked, would they mind returning the Ford? Utako Natsume had no family left, all killed in the Great Kanto Earthquake, so that was a dead end.

Most residents in Tokyo were registered with the Metropolitan Police, but given Natsume's penchant for aliases, finding her might be more difficult than the average criminal.

Draining his coffee, Aizawa drifted back to last night, spent with Minori Miyake. They'd agreed to meet again, this time at Café Lion for dinner. At this rate, they'd be engaged by spring, and he'd have a *moga* to call his own.

After a quick knock, his office door swung open and Inspector Tezuka entered. A swollen face and black eye were enough evidence that he had important information to share. Aizawa bolted upright and offered a bow.

"Morning Inspector. Have time for a chat?"

"Yes, sir. Would you like to read our latest reports about the Red Terror Society?"

Tezuka waved his hand, swatting the suggestion away. "There's nothing in those that I don't already know. But there's plenty to share with you." Tezuka's dark eyes shifted around the cramped little office, strewn with clutter. Shameful yes, but Aizawa was too busy to clean these days. "Away from here. Too many listening ears."

Well, Tokko inspectors were a naturally paranoid bunch. "Certainly, sir. Where do you suggest?"

Tezuka pointed to Aizawa's empty coffee mug. "Want another cup? I know a place in Ginza."

*****

Peering through binoculars, Utako surveyed Police Headquarters for any signs of Tezuka. She'd seen him enter over twenty minutes ago but hadn't had the chance to open fire. Secure in Izumi's Ford, several blocks away, they would just have to wait until that Thought Policeman slithered out again. Major Kuno was right, this was a cunning trick. Outside the entrance, a *junsa* stood guard with a *keijo* stick, like a samurai guarding his lord's *yashiki* mansion.

She remembered going through those doors during the 3-15 Incident. The torture by Inspector Tezuka was still raw in her mind – beatings with bamboo swords, tied upside down for hours, and left naked in unheated cells during winter. But that pain was trivial compared to the agony that seized her upon viewing Ichiro Hayashi's corpse. His once handsome face was a maze of bruises and swollen to the size of a basketball.

Inspector Tezuka apologized, not for the endless beatings, but for not being able to save Hayashi-san from "dangerous thoughts." Utako stewed in bitter memories until two figures in black overcoats and fedoras alighted from the entrance. Even far away, she recognized Tezuka's mustache. The detective with him also looked familiar. Of course, that plainclothesman who'd chased them days before in Kasumigaseki! Out on the street, they both hailed a taxicab and piled into it.

"What do you see?" Izumi asked, leaning over the steering wheel.

Utako motioned for him to follow and replied, "Payback."

*****

The Mon Ami café was a charming little place on Ginza's main thoroughfare with a mishmash of foreign trinkets and Japanese knickknacks inside. An Eiffel Tower poster hung above a *maneki-neko* – a beckoning cat statuette – perched atop the counter. Teenaged waitresses in kimonos and white aprons brought trays of coffee over to groups of long-haired young men in university uniforms. These types of cafés were *kissatens* – tea rooms, literally – but ironically only coffee was served here. For a few sen, college intellectuals could sip coffee, flirt with waitresses, and discuss Marx for hours. Off to the side, a coin-operated phonograph blared out a tropical tune, clashing with the European aesthetic.

"My lover is the chief's daughter. She has black skin, but she is a beautiful woman in the South Pacific. In the Marshall Islands, a country just below the equator, people dance under palm trees."

Aizawa recognized the song as "The Chief's Daughter," perfect music for the dead of winter. A glass counter was crammed full of pastries – Napoleons, *Baumkuchen*, and American-style doughnuts. Cans of fresh Kimura coffee beans were available for purchase next to a cheeky sign – "In this time of national crisis, our death-defying waitresses are trained to serve you!"

But there was stiff competition. Aizawa glanced out the window where one enterprising young man had attached a vat of coffee to his back, dispensing it out in paper cups with a spigot. An advertisement on the vat proclaimed "Modern Coffee! Only 5 sen!"

Well, one had to make a living in these tough times. But inside was warm and inviting, and a waitress led Aizawa and

Tezuka to a booth table. Tezuka faced the entrance, a man weary of having his back turned.

"Two cups of Kimura coffee and doughnuts, please," Tezuka ordered. The waitress bowed and within moments, returned with two steaming cups and doughnuts. "The proper way to eat a doughnut is to dunk them first," Tezuka instructed, plunking his into the coffee cup. "Just like the Americans."

Aizawa followed and took a bite. "Tastes good. To be honest, sir, I'm surprised you picked this spot. It's a little *foreign*."

Tezuka chuckled. "We in the Tokko are immune to all sorts of foreign influences. Besides, these *kissatens* are good for leads." He gestured to the table full of university students, who'd moved on from Marx and were now debating the political situation in Germany. "I'd say they're all budding writers, judging by their long hair. Proletarian writers love long hair. It's a sign of rebellion." Tezuka chuckled and took a sip of coffee. "I'm sure I'll see them again soon."

The words were more of a promise than a threat. Aizawa drank his coffee in silence.

"Also, after your raid, I asked around and discovered our little actress was here the same night calling herself Oguchi."

"I see," Aizawa said, burning with humiliation. So much had happened, he hadn't even thought of asking the Ginza cafés for any leads.

"But I doubt she'll be back here again. I just wanted to try their doughnuts, so here we are."

"Sir, what did you want to speak to me about?"

A darkness fell over Tezuka's face. "A plot of high treason. And we are running out of time to stop it."

CHAPTER THIRTY-EIGHT

Aizawa took another sip of coffee to hide any surprise. Not that he should be since treasonous plots and attempted coup d'états were becoming an annual event in Japan. But the ominous tones in Tezuka's voice hinted that he wasn't referring to just another right-wing assassination plot.

"What do you mean, sir?"

Darkness remained in Tezuka's face like a gathering storm. "Before I proceed, you must swear that this conversation will not be repeated. Not even to Superintendent Miyake."

He'd used discretion around Miyake for months now, so that would be nothing new. "Of course, sir."

"I reviewed your file, Inspector. An impressive career, tackling yakuza and patriotic societies with equal fervor. You're not some ideologue like your old superior, Joji Shimura. You're a law-and-order man, like me."

The comparison was supposed to be a compliment, but it left him uneasy. Was he looking into the face of his future? Still, better to appear modest than worried.

"Thank you, sir. I'm not worthy of such praise coming from an accomplished detective like you."

Tezuka swallowed another bite of the doughnut, then said, "Unfortunately, I'm not much of a detective these days. I know that this insidious plot exists, but when I reach out to grab it, it evaporates in my palm."

"Sounds like you're hunting evil spirits, sir."

"Very true, Inspector. Very true." Tezuka fell silent for a moment, a man haunted by phantoms. "Let me start at the beginning."

The Thought Policeman slurped the remainder of his coffee and leaned back; a storyteller ready to spin a fantastic yarn.

"Ever since the 3-15 Incident, the Communist Party has been on the decline. But there were attempts at rebuilding it. In 1930, right when the Showa Depression began, they entered their so-called 'armed' period, instigating strikes and riots, which were thankfully crushed by the Metropolitan Police."

Aizawa remembered those turbulent months, when it seemed he and every other police officer doubled as strikebreakers. Almost a thousand labor disturbances occurred in 1930 alone. Communists tried to seize control every protest and strike, and turn them into anti-police riots, arming people with swords, pistols, and bamboo spears. The unrest climaxed on May Day, 1930, when massive throngs gathered at Tokyo's Hibiya Park and attempted a "march on the Diet." These agitations were dispersed by the resolve of the Metropolitan Police, aided by a new invention – tear gas.

"Moscow was furious at these failures and installed Jokichi Kazama as Party boss. He put an end to the violence and took the organization deep underground to increase membership. However, last October, we arrested him and most of the Party leaders at the Atami Hot Springs. The head of the Communist worm was severed, but the segmented body kept squirming. The Party survives now as small, decentralized cells, one of which is the Red Terror Society, but it might as well be an independent group at this point. Since I handled Utako Natsume's *tenko*, I felt responsible for her activities and decided to bring her to justice once and for all. A member of the Privy Council, Marquis Tatsuo Maeda, took a personal interest in my investigation and summoned me to the Imperial Palace for private briefings."

That name again. Like a vapor, Marquis Maeda's spirit permeated every facet of this case. Aizawa sipped his coffee and kept quiet. Off to the side, the melody from "The Chief's Daughter" dwindled and the phonograph went still. "The Marquis was a remarkable man, a staunch conservative," Tezuka continued. "Did you know that before he joined the Privy Council, Maeda used to be a Dietman and supported the Peace Preservation Law?"

Aizawa didn't know, but it explained why Tezuka liked him. Any law that banned "dangerous thoughts" made a lot of friends in the Tokko.

"Maeda wanted constant updates concerning the remaining Communists in Tokyo," Tezuka went on, "In particular, the Red Terror Society alarmed him. I tried to explain despite the theatrical name, the Red Terror Society was just one cell, and a small one at that. Besides, the Japanese Communist Party was fatally wounded and its demise was inevitable. But the Marquis insisted that so long as one Communist remained free, it was a threat to the Emperor System and the reign of His Majesty."

Mention of the Emperor deserved respect, and both men held their tongues for a moment.

"A wise man, sir. I saw what the Bolsheviks did at Nikolayevsk."

Tezuka stayed expressionless behind his mustache. "Yes, that was in your file as well. Regardless, my search for Natsume-san and her comrades proved fruitless. I had the sneaking suspicion that my efforts were being thwarted by some invisible hand. It was around this time that General Sadao Araki began attending these briefings."

"The Army Minister?"

Tezuka nodded. "The same. It's not surprising, since both men are aristocrats and despise Communism. Did you know that Araki served in Siberia too?"

"It doesn't surprise me, sir."

"Apparently, it left the General with a lifelong hatred of Bolshevism. But Araki and Maeda were worried about different things," Tezuka said, rubbing his mustache. "Marquis Maeda was terrified the Reds would overthrow the Emperor, like what happened in Russia, and all aristocrats would be machine-gunned into a ditch."

"Not a baseless fear."

"Quite right, Inspector. General Araki agreed to an extent, but his main concern wasn't our homegrown Reds, rather, the threat that the Soviet Union posed. He believes that since our troops are now in Manchuria, a great confrontation with the Soviets will occur by 1936."

"That's a specific date."

"Who understands these semi-mystics? They look for signs in everything. Regardless, Araki is convinced we'll be at war by 1936 and sees the softness in our people as a sure sign of defeat."

"The conquerors of Manchuria have gone 'soft?'"

"Araki thinks so, and I tend to agree with him. You'd be surprised how susceptible our people are to dangerous foreign thoughts. Our victory in Manchuria has receded into memory, replaced by frivolous nonsense. I'll show you."

Tezuka sauntered over to the phonograph, plugged in a sen coin, then rejoined the table. The martial strands of "The Manchuria March" seeped out, filling Mon Ami with bombastic lyrics.

"When my gun, sword, gun barrel, and horse's hooves froze in the extreme cold, thirty below zero, we saw the shadow of the approaching enemy."

Angry jeers burst from the college intellectuals.

"Turn that militarist noise off!"

"Put something on that we can dance to! Play 'The Speed Age!'"

His point made, a knowing smugness spread underneath Tezuka's mustache. "See? A year ago that song was on every citizen's lips. Without constant struggle, people are lulled into a decadent stupor by dangerous thoughts."

"And a war with Russia will help cure us of these dangerous thoughts?"

"No, Inspector. Like I said, General Araki doesn't think we're ready yet. Instead, he wants to harden the Japanese people, like a formless metal being molded into a bayonet."

"What did Marquis Maeda think?"

"He had a certain—" Tezuka searched for the word "–distaste for Araki. Maeda was a strict conservative, after all. Like us, he supported law and order. He viewed General Araki as too radical. His constant talk of *hijoji* – national crisis – stressed the need to alter society, which offended Maeda."

"I see," Aizawa said, before swigging the last of his coffee. He remembered last night's pitiful showing for *Bullets and Horses in Manchuria.* Added to that was Mon Ami's sardonic sign mocking the entire concept of the *hijoji.* Perhaps this militarist fever had broken. A waitress appeared with a fresh pot and refilled their cups without a word, then scurried off. Once she was out of earshot, Aizawa asked, "Sir, you mentioned high treason…"

"As I said, Araki was more concerned about Russia, but he took a peculiar interest in the Red Terror Society. He wanted to know their whereabouts and if they were funded by Moscow."

"What did you tell him?"

"I shared some possible leads on their hideouts, but was skeptical about Soviet involvement. They were amateurs at best. Strangely though, when I went to investigate those hideouts, they were empty, as if Natsume and her comrades had been warned in advance. What's more, the bodies of two known Communists were found in the Sumida River, their windpipes crushed. I suspect that brute Genda killed them with his bare hands."

"Why?"

"Probably suspected them of being informants. Neither was, but paranoia runs deep among Communists. They usually turn on themselves and implode from the inside. I suspected that would happen to the Red Terror Society. But then, in December, they knocked over a bank in Yokohama like some elite military unit, armed to the teeth with pistols. Soviet pistols. As mentioned, the Tokko has the Soviet Embassy under constant surveillance, so it seems that the pistols were an attempt to frame the Russians. Then that

Korean Pak claims they have contacts within the Imperial Army itself, some disillusioned Manchurian veteran."

Aizawa poured cream and stirred his refilled coffee. "But you don't sound convinced, do you, sir?"

Tezuka nodded, a teacher pleased with his pupil. "Correct, Inspector. And I located this alleged 'Manchurian veteran.'"

The coffee cup rattled in Aizawa's hand. "Who?"

"I don't know his real identity, but he goes by the alias 'Major Kuno.' After Marquis Maeda was assassinated, I staked out General Araki's home and saw him enter and exit. After asking around, Kuno is a man without a past. But everyone referred to him as Araki's 'pet dog.'"

"Could you describe him, sir?"

"Tall, broad-shouldered. Long face, thick eyebrows. Speaks with an Osakan accent."

The description echoed inside Aizawa's mind, filling him with a frightful chill. Major Junzo Kanemaru possessed those attributes, but then again, hundreds of other officers did too. Besides, Kanemaru was dead, no doubt locked in a watery embrace with that venomous Snake Queen – Chizuru Okamura – at the bottom of Tokyo Bay. Aizawa concentrated on solid facts and assembled them into a coherent theory.

"Sir, may I be blunt?"

Tezuka chuckled. "Another trait mentioned in your file. Go ahead, Inspector."

Lowering his voice, Aizawa said, "Are you suggesting that General Araki is controlling the Red Terror Society through this Major Kuno?"

Pride glittered in Tezuka's dark eyes, soon shadowed by an ominous dread. "It goes much further than that, Inspector. Just before Marquis Maeda was assassinated, he asked me to look into a few…whispers."

"Whispers, sir?"

"Whispers of a far-flung plot strangling our nation…" Tezuka coughed, as if the words clogged in his throat. "It's difficult for me to repeat his words, but you should know…"

Tezuka trailed off, distracted by something at the entrance of Mon Ami. His narrowed eyes widened in shock. A jingling bell at the door announced another customer, but the sound was smothered by the sharp crack of a gunshot. Tezuka tried to stand, but his face exploded like a bloody firecracker, showering the table with flecks of gore and mustache hairs. His body slumped forth, spilling the coffee cup.

Flicking out his Colt automatic, Aizawa hunched down into the booth and stole a quick glance out. Utako Natsume stood near the door, her bobbed hair peeking out beneath her cloche hat, her gloved hands brandishing a Nagant revolver. Across the café, "The Manchuria March's" foreboding tune spilled out from the phonograph.

"For the peace of East Asia, we don't regret if we die. Manchuria is Japan's lifeline! Protect Manchuria with ninety million lives!"

CHAPTER THIRTY-NINE

Panic filled the Mon Ami café as Utako Natsume stepped deeper inside. Waitresses and customers scattered, blocking any chance for Aizawa to get a clean shot. Natsume blasted away, bullets thwacking into the booth's wooden frame.

"Inspector Aizawa, is it?" she called out, her voice theatrical and mocking. "Well, here's your chance to take down the leader of the Red Terror Society and give the audience a new twist in the story!"

Another volley crashed out, shredding the booth table even further. Keeping low, Aizawa looked over to Tezuka's corpse, his butchered face lying in a puddle of blood and coffee. Somehow, Aizawa's own refilled mug remained intact, trails of steam billowing from it.

The morning had taken such a bizarre turn, he considered the possibility that they were in one of Utako Natsume's movies. Through the booth's many jagged holes, he surveyed the carnage. Waitresses crouched in fear, the lucky ones hiding behind the pastry glass. The college intellectuals sat trembling at their table, raising supplicating hands. "The Manchuria March" had faded out, but a woman wailed in terror until her fainting left the café with an echoing silence. There were still too many civilians around to get a clear shot, made even worse by Natsume shifting herself over to the table of intellectuals.

"It's you I want, Inspector, but I'm prepared to shoot everyone here until you show yourself."

The Nagant leveled straight at one student's head, who chewed his trembling lip. Any bullet would slice through him as well, and that was one embarrassment the Metropolitan Police couldn't afford. Aizawa glanced back at the coffee mug, still steaming. He gripped the cup, bolted upright, and hurled it straight at her.

Hot coffee flung outward, sprinkling the college students, but dousing Utako Natsume completely. She stumbled back and forth, her Nagant wobbling up and down. It was the only opening Aizawa would get. He whipped his gun into position but a searing pain exploded from his old shoulder wound, distorting his aim. Of all the times to flare up again!

The pain soon subsided, but it was too late. Even with coffee dripping from her cloche hat and the tips of her bob, Natsume had managed to grab one of the college students, hoist him to his feet, and dig the pistol into his throat. The young intellectual was a head taller, completely shielding Natsume from any line of fire.

"A good trick, Inspector," she rasped from behind, guiding them both toward the entrance. "I won't underestimate you again. Until next time!"

A forceful push sent the college student stumbling forward into Aizawa's arms. Steadying him upright, he saw Natsume duck out the entrance and dash into the street. After a quick inspection to ensure nobody else was hurt, he followed her outside where he almost collided with the Modern Coffee salesman.

"Hey, no need for that," he said, pointing at Aizawa's automatic. "You can have all the coffee you want, sir!"

He began filling a paper cup when a low-throated roar rose from down the street. A Ford sedan lunged forward, barreling toward them, its supercharged engine screaming. Careening off the street and onto the sidewalk, the car rushed closer and closer. Behind its windshield, the driver was visible, fat-faced with murderous sadism blazing behind thick glasses – Wataru Izumi. Utako Natsume sat beside him, frazzled but grinning in triumph.

The Ford hurtled toward them like a screaming mortar. The only way to survive such an attack was to get out of the way and hit the ground. Aizawa flung the full weight of his body against the Modern Coffee salesman, sending them both out into the street. Unable to shift the attack, the Ford continued on the sidewalk and shot past Mon Ami for several more blocks, before skidding back onto the street and merging into the rest of the traffic. The roar of its engine dwindled into Ginza's background noises, and Aizawa could finally hear his thumping heart and panting gasps.

Glancing around, it was miraculous that nobody was hurt, although the vat of coffee strapped to the salesman's back was fatally wounded. Steaming coffee poured from a gash on its side and the salesman fixed him with an accusing stare.

All Aizawa could do was offer an apologetic bow, and say, "Sorry, it's been a rough morning."

*****

After a squad of *junsas* cleaned up at Mon Ami, Aizawa dodged questions from reporters and retreated to Metropolitan Police Headquarters, presenting himself to Superintendent Miyake. Anger pinched his superior's already tight face to the breaking point.

"Unforgivable," Miyake shouted, pounding a fist for emphasis. "To assassinate a Tokko inspector, a member of the Metropolitan Police, in broad daylight! This shame must be avenged!"

"Yes, sir. We're following up on every lead we have. We know their identities, and it's only a matter of time before the Red Terror Society is apprehended."

"Inspector, the Emperor will attend the Imperial Army's annual review in mere days. We cannot have Communist bandits prowling throughout Tokyo!"

Aizawa swallowed and conceded that point. Whenever the Emperor left the Imperial Palace, local riff-raff and hoodlums were rounded up as not to sully him with their presence. Even ordinary citizens were ordered to the ground floor of every building since no subject was allowed to look down upon the Emperor as he passed.

Shortly after the Showa Depression began in 1930, an unemployed factory worker had climbed a chimney to protest labor conditions. The press dubbed him "Chimney Man" and reminded readers that the Emperor was scheduled to pass by in a few days. The Police had to swallow their pride and negotiate to prevent such an unworthy person from gazing down on His Majesty. A shameful incident, yes, but far less humiliating than a gang of bank-robbing Communists running amok.

"Of course, sir."

Tension drained from Miyake's taut face. "Good. With Inspector Tezuka dead, you will lead this case now. But you have my complete support and the resources of the entire First Investigative Division at your disposal."

Aizawa saluted, turned on his heel, and pushed back a smile. Last night's date with Minori must have gone better than he thought if the Superintendent was this supportive. Exiting Miyake's office, a *junsa* pounded up and stiffened to attention.

"Sir, an officer from the *Kempeitai* is here to see you."

"*Kempeitai*?"

"I believe his name is Hatsu, sir. We escorted him to your office."

Aizawa nodded and turned down the hall. Exchange one secret policeman for another.

CHAPTER FORTY

Takumi Hatsu hadn't changed much since Aizawa had last seen him in May – horn-rimmed glasses shielded slitted eyes in a clean-shaven head sitting atop a bullish neck. Aizawa's office was small, cramped, and a bit cluttered, no doubt offending an officer who adhered to strict regulations in everything.

"Welcome, Major Hatsu," Aizawa said, closing the door behind him and moving behind his desk. "And Happy New Year."

"Happy New Year, Inspector. But it's actually Lieutenant-Colonel Hatsu now." He indicated the rank tabs on his shoulders – three red stripes, two yellow, and two stars. The rest of his uniform was the same. A dark brown tunic and a stiff collar with black patches indicating his membership in the *Kempeitai*. Officially the Police Force for the Imperial Army, the *Kempeitai* functioned more as an espionage and counterespionage agency. Their powers were supposed to apply only to military personnel but *kempei* were known to spy on civilians sometimes, encroaching on the Tokko's turf.

"Congratulations, Lieutenant-Colonel," Aizawa said, taking a seat. "Let me guess. For your services during the 5-15 Incident?"

Hatsu allowed a grin. That day was still a nightmarish blur, ending with Aizawa – bleeding like a stuck animal – and Reiko almost drowning in Tokyo Bay. Although they'd been saved by Hatsu's *kempei*, the connection between Reiko Watanabe and the Metropolitan Police had been revealed. For months, Aizawa had wondered when that lit fuse would finally blow.

"Yes, Army Minister Araki was so pleased that the Okamura Gang's opium supply was intercepted, he personally promoted me the next day."

Aizawa tapped out two Golden Bats and lit them, passing one over to Hatsu. They puffed away for a few moments, the long tendrils of cigarette smoke drifting up toward the ceiling like vaporous snakes. The confiscated drugs were no doubt shipped back to Manchukuo and sold in *Kempeitai* run opium dens, but better not to bring up such ugly details.

"Well, I do appreciate your assistance that day," Aizawa said before dragging the cigarette.

"That's what I'd like to talk to you about, Inspector." Smoke poured through Hatsu's teeth. "I would like to borrow your geisha spy."

"Is that so?"

"As General Araki says, we're still in a time of national crisis. The *Kempeitai* and Metropolitan Police must cooperate for the good of the country."

Tucking the Golden Bat between his lips, Hatsu pulled out a piece of paper from his tunic pocket, and slid it across Aizawa's desk. Opening it revealed a haiku, traditional poems consisting of three short lines evoking a general theme.

"Endless bloody fields
Sunset over Pingdingshan
The swamp swallows me"

"I thought haikus were supposed to be subtle," Aizawa said, taking another puff. "What's Pingdingshan?"

Hatsu snatched the paper back, stuffing it back into his tunic. "That's classified. Regardless, the haiku's political statements are apparent. We don't want this type of anti-war claptrap promulgating within the Army."

"May I know who the author is?"

After a deep drag, Hatsu answered. "Colonel Riku Hashizume."

"The war hero?"

Hatsu waved his hand, leaving a pattern of cigarette smoke drifting through the air. "Only in the public eye! The image of a dashing cavalry officer is artificial, created by that insipid film *Bullets and Horses in Manchuria.* His nickname is Colonel Haiku, for obvious reasons. When my men secretly searched his quarters, they discovered a dozen poems, all similar to that one. Unbeknownst to him, we made copies for evidence."

"Evidence?"

"When Colonel Hashizume returned from Manchukuo, he was summoned to an audience with the Emperor. I am not at liberty to give details, but we believe he's been contaminated with dangerous thoughts."

"That sounds like the Tokko's line of work."

"Perhaps, but the *Kempeitai* handles all discipline within the Imperial Army."

"If that's the case, why do you need the Metropolitan Police's assistance?"

"Since his return, Colonel Hashizume has spent every night at the Silkworm Tea House in the arms of a geisha. I'd like to see how many dangerous thoughts are inside Hashizume's brain, and if he's infected any other Army officers. He might spill everything he knows to a loving geisha. After all, aren't they supposed to take secrets to the grave?"

"Unless they report to me."

Aizawa took a last drag and mashed out the Golden Bat. The idea of trading Reiko off like some bugging device was shameful, but Lieutenant-Colonel Hatsu could be as useful an ally as deadly an enemy. After what Inspector Tezuka shared, insight into the *Kempeitai's* files about this Major Kuno and General Araki might answer many riddles.

"Perhaps I could arrange that, Lieutenant-Colonel, but I would ask for something in return."

Hatsu chuckled. "Do you need help catching that gang of Reds?"

The loss of face was humiliating, but the last thing he wanted was *Kempeitai* assistance on this case. "The Metropolitan Police can handle the Red Terror Society. But I would like information on certain Army officers. Major Kuno, in particular."

Smoking his Golden Bat, Hatsu remained placid. "That's classified information, Inspector. But I am willing to cooperate, so long as you loan us your little geisha."

Although it was akin to selling his soul, Aizawa couldn't resist.

*****

Lounging inside her apartment, Reiko thumbed through the latest *Kinema Junpo* issue. The magazine covered the world of cinema through a Japanese lens, and she'd saved every single issue dating back to 1927. Some people kept scrapbooks, but Reiko Watanabe understood history through what movies had been playing at the time. The issue's main feature was a review of *Bullets and Horses in Manchuria.*

"A fine war picture," the reviewer declared, "and one that chronicles the struggles of our soldiers during the Manchurian Incident." But, it added, "While we're sure *Bullets and Horses in Manchuria* will find an audience, the upsurge in love suicides and romance pictures suggest Japanese moviegoers have lost their appetite for war films."

Reiko couldn't agree more. Hopefully, Koichi Matsumoto's second career was just beginning, one that would land her several more roles. Even if it didn't, she'd settle for his company. Their last date – Kamiya Bar, a late-night show at *Casino Follies*, coming back to her apartment – left her with a sweet aftertaste. Only the sight of Aizawa and that *moga* blemished it. How silly. To be jealous over the Inspector?

The telephone rattled and she leaned over to answer it. Aizawa's clipped voice came through.

"Reiko-san?"

"*Senpai*, I was just thinking about you. It's still working hours. I thought you weren't supposed to call me from your office since it could be bugged."

"I'm in a phonebooth."

"A wise choice."

"Listen, I have a new assignment for you, Reiko-san."

"You're the boss, *senpai*."

"Lieutenant-Colonel Hatsu has requested your geisha talents tonight at the Silkworm Tea House."

Reiko felt her nose scrunch. "That *kempei* lizard? I knew he would try something eventually."

"Unfortunately. However, he's offered to help in certain areas that only the *Kempeitai* can reach. Reiko-san, I am expected to settle this incident before the Emperor attends the Army's review. Please."

She could almost see him bowing inside the phonebooth. Every lead to those Red gangsters had been followed up, and the last thing she wanted was to bring Matsumoto-san back into this. Swallowing her distaste, she said, "I'll do it for you, *senpai*, not Hatsu. But only on one condition."

"Name it."

"Who was that *moga* you were with at Kamiya Bar?"

Awkward silence ticked by until the Inspector replied, "She's…Minori Miyake. The Superintendent's daughter."

Everything aligned with clarity. Poor Aizawa, to have Superintendent Miyake as a matchmaker. Still, that *moga's* pretty face, and chic outfit inflamed her jealousy again. A pretty girl from a good family would make a suitable wife for Kenji Aizawa. Even more, her being a *moga* would quench a thirst that a traditional housewife could never slake. But someone as low-class as Reiko Watanabe would always be cast as a mistress to men like Koichi Matsumoto. It was a role she'd come to expect.

"All right, Inspector, what's the job?"

CHAPTER FORTY-ONE

Major Kanemaru made his way from the tram stop to the Araki residence, his eyes sweeping over the nearby brush for any signs of Inspector Tezuka. Allowing himself to be observed was an amateurish mistake, unbefitting the God of Intrigue. Hopefully, Utako Natsume had already avenged his honor. As he entered the *genkan*, he pulled off his boots, and handed his service cap and cape to a waiting servant. Kanemaru was led to the General's study, where he entered with a sharp salute and stiff bow.

"Leave us," Araki said, dismissing the servant, who slid the *shoji* door behind him. The General sat stiffly at the table beneath the world map and tiger painting, like a schoolteacher impatient for class to begin. He was in full uniform, hinting that this was no informal chat he'd summoned Kanemaru to.

Araki beckoned him forward. Kanemaru strode through the study, past the mounted samurai armor, looming off to the side, and took a seat across from the General who remained silent for several moments before checking a pocket watch.

"Top of the hour," Araki muttered, then clicked on a nearby radio. After a warbling screech, an announcer's crisp voice broke through.

"Good morning, ladies and gentlemen, here are the top stories of the day so far. Tensions continue to boil between Chinese and Japanese troops over Shanhaikwan. There has been a ceasefire in effect, but questions abound as to whether any future fighting will erupt. In local news, a police detective was shot today at a Ginza café. The assailants escaped and are considered armed and dangerous. If you have any information, please contact the Tokyo Metropolitan Police Depa—"

Araki snapped the radio off and glanced back at Kanemaru.

"That's been on every news report this morning. Your work, I assume?"

"It had to be done. Inspector Tezuka discovered my boarding house and—"

"How much did he know?"

Kanemaru cleared his throat. "He didn't know my real name, but he knew of our connection."

A coldness hung on Araki's face, before it broke with a sneer. "No matter. Both he and Marquis Maeda are dead. They can't interfere any longer. You trained that Red rabble well, Major. Who did the shooting today?"

"I assume the actress did."

"That's what I thought too," Araki said, rubbing his thick mustache. "Yes, she will be put to good use soon enough."

The General's sly words and coy tone had kept Kanemaru lost deep inside this labyrinth, fumbling for an exit. But not anymore. Tezuka had illuminated it partially, and Kanemaru would banish this black fog at last.

"Excellency, Tezuka shared something very interesting with me."

"Is that so?"

"Yes, namely that he was providing you and Marquis Maeda with briefings about the Red Terror Society. Is that why you ordered Marquis Maeda assassinated? To prevent him from revealing too much?"

Araki radiated a calm, zen-like impassivity until a smirk shone beneath his mustache.

"Not exactly. Maeda died for three reasons. The first was to give the Reds an actual target to shoot before their real assignment. If Maeda hadn't been chosen, I would have sent them to kill some liberal in the Minsei or Social Mass Party for target practice. Japan has enough of them as it is. Two, he favored the Control Faction."

"And the third reason?"

Araki's eyes fell over to the door, to the shadowy samurai armor, and then back to Kanemaru. His soft voice dropped to a hushed murmur. "This conversation never happened. That is an order. Understand?"

A nod was enough confirmation as anticipation rippled across Kanemaru's muscles. Answers lay before him as if he were the first man about to solve the riddle of the Sphinx.

"Good," Araki continued, piping up slightly. His posture resumed a rigidity, a commander ready to deliver orders. Instead, he shifted over to the world map and palmed the region between Manchukuo and North China. "Tell me, Major. What do you know about the Nekka Province?"

Answer a riddle with a riddle. Still, better to play the old man's game when he was so close.

"That's just what we call it. To the Chinese, it's Jehol or Rehe," Kanemaru said. "It lies just between Manchuria and the Great Wall, right above Peking. Or Peiping as the Nationalist Government calls it now."

"Correct," Araki said, withdrawing his hand from the map. "It will be your next assignment, Major."

"Sir?"

"After your work in Tokyo is completed, that is. Nekka is rich in opium, something you're familiar with. We'll need a man of your talents harvesting and distributing it throughout Manchukuo."

Kanemaru nodded again as memories flooded back. Even before the Manchurian Incident began, he had run several opium dens in Mukden, funneling the money back to the *Tokumu Kikan* for the benefit of the entire Kwantung Army. His involvement in the Okamura Gang's opium racket had nearly cost him his life, so it seemed ironic it would also be his salvation.

"But sir, we've only taken Shanhaikwan. Is the Nekka Province to be annexed?"

"Shanhaikwan was only the appetizer, Major. We needed that town to secure our eastern flank. Japan's economy has not fully recovered from the depression. The occupation of

Manchuria drains us financially. But Nekka will soon become a province of Manchukuo, and its opium production will boost the economy tenfold. Arrangements are being made to bring the warlord who currently rules Nekka into our orbit. He's nominally loyal to Nanking but might succumb to a hefty bribe. Should this fail, a military option will be implemented."

"You mean, invasion?"

"Yes, invasion. The Kwantung Army leadership has already decided. In two weeks, the League of Nations will convene its so-called 'Committee of Nineteen' to discuss the Manchurian issue. It might take weeks but eventually the League will vote on whether or not to adopt that damnable Lytton Report."

"It is all but certain they will, sir."

"Unfortunately, you're probably right. If the world condemns our righteous mission in Manchuria, then we might as well expand into Nekka. Military actions are estimated to begin in late February. We at the Army Ministry and our counterparts in the General Staff, will provide support."

Kanemaru almost laughed. The Kwantung Army was almost a rogue force, but at least this time they bothered to inform Tokyo of their plans.

"Yes, sir. How will we provide support?"

"We must persuade the Emperor to give his approval for such an enormous operation. His Majesty is very cautious and concerned about upsetting the League of Nations further. I'm confident we can convince him now, but I am more concerned about future military operations. You see, the annexation of Nekka is part of a long-term strategy. Are you familiar with the Crisis of 1936?"

Anybody close to General Araki was aware of his apocalyptic vision for the future, but that didn't stop him from quizzing his students from time to time.

"Yes, sir. As I understand it, since the Soviet Union's five-year plan has strengthened their industry and the Red Army, they're bound to attack us by 1936."

Satisfaction beamed from behind Araki's mustache.

"Not only Russia, but America too. The Navy is convinced that 1936 will be a decisive year for them as well. But the Soviet Union is our greatest threat!" He slapped a hand on the world map, spreading bony fingers across Siberia. "There have already been several border incidents between Manchukuo and Russia. They send spies, airplanes, and troops into Manchuria, testing the Kwantung Army's resolve. If the Soviet Union continues to annoy us, then I shall be forced to purge Siberia, as one cleans a room of flies. Later this year, I will present a plan to the Army senior leadership, detailing a future war with Russia.

"If it is adopted, then within two years we will have stockpiled sufficient ammunition, built enough fortifications, and improved Manchurian railways for a final showdown with the Russians. But we must hurry. Soviet factories churn out tanks, artillery, and planes every day! Nekka's opium fields will provide us with much-needed revenue, but our industry still languishes, mired in the muck of the depression. The longer we wait, the weaker Japan will be when that fateful day arrives. We cannot listen to dithering fools…"

Most Army officers realized a showdown between the Japanese Empire and the Soviet Union was inevitable. Lessons learned from the Russo-Japanese War and the Siberian Expedition had birthed the *Hokushin-ron*, the Northern Advance, which dominated Army strategy and planning ever since. But many officers balked at the idea of attacking in 1936, unless radical change was implemented.

"You mean, the Control Faction, sir?"

Araki nodded. "The Control Faction feels that any war with Russia should be postponed until we 'modernize' our industry. The fools. That could take an entire decade. Don't they realize that Stalin already has a five-year head start? If we do not take action soon, then we've already lost and

Japan will become Bolshevized." Araki shook his head. "It was a colossal mistake to evacuate our troops from Siberia, all those years ago. Now, the gluttonous Red Bear looks eastward for its next meal. 1936 will be the pivotal year, Major. We must strike first or be devoured."

A bold move, Kanemaru admitted, similar to the decisive action he and his fellow officers took back in 1931.

"Besides," Araki said, "we do not need the Control Faction's obsession with bureaucracy and industrialization to achieve victory. Not when every Japanese solider has the inviable Yamato Spirit within him and the will to die, like the noble Major Kuga. But our civilian population is lacking in fortitude. Stalin is molding the Russians into a martial race, unafraid of war.

"In contrast, look at our own people," Araki continued, his voice measured but masking an inner fury. "The Japanese cheered the Manchurian Incident, but even during this time of national crisis, they've lapsed back into selfish liberalism. Hollywood movies, jazz music, and dance halls have infected Japan with the disease of frivolity. Every week, the newspapers are filled with new stories of our vapid youth committing love suicides. Our people are distracted by nonsense, unaware that it's only a four-hour flight from Vladivostok to Tokyo. Must we wait until swarms of Soviet bombers blot out the Rising Sun and burn our cities to ash? No, we'll drill the populace for air raid preparation and harden them for the coming battle ahead."

"If only we had a Japanese Stalin," Kanemaru said, then added, "But one who isn't a Communist."

"A good idea, Major, but there have been several attempts at a coup d'état." Araki shook his head. "All failures. It must go deeper than that."

"Deeper, sir?"

"During the 5-15 Incident, it's rumored that Prince Chichibu stood firm behind the young officers. He even urged the Emperor to support the uprising, abolish the civilian government, and suspend the Constitution. Regrettably, it caused a rift between them."

Rumors that Kanemaru had heard as well. The Crown Prince and His Majesty argued so loudly, even the Emperor's aide-de-camp overheard it.

Araki leaned back in his chair, a dreamy smile on his face. "Athletic, virile, and a born leader! Why, Prince Chichibu is one of the most popular company commanders in the entire Army. He knows the dangers our nation is facing and agrees with the Crisis of 1936. What's more, he is a firm supporter of the Imperial Way Faction."

The General sounded like a schoolgirl blubbering about a crush. Playing it safe, Kanemaru offered, "Yes, I've heard many positive reports about Captain Chichibu."

"His Majesty has many fine qualities too. He's a quiet, studious man, fascinated by marine biology and very concerned with international diplomacy." Araki's voice fell to a strained whisper, his eyes screwed into suspicious slits. "It's a shame he does not have a male heir yet. Only daughters. Don't you agree, Major?"

The words exploded like dynamite inside Junzo Kanemaru. The dark maze he'd wandered through was at last illuminated, the last puzzle piece snapped into place. The plotters of those past coup d'états had been so close, but there had been a fatal flaw in all of their plans. They'd all sought to overthrow the government and install a dictator of their own choosing. But Japan didn't need a new government or a dictator.

Japan needed a new emperor.

CHAPTER FORTY-TWO

Kanemaru felt as if he were inside a waking dream. Assassinating the Emperor was so unthinkable that it bordered on insanity. His Majesty was descended from Amaterasu, the sun goddess herself. How could mere mortals kill a living god? Not that it hadn't been attempted before.

No Japanese could forget the Great Treason Incident of 1910, when anarchists plotted to assassinate the Meiji Emperor with a bomb. Their plan failed, but it led to the creation of the Tokko in order to root out individuals with similar "dangerous thoughts." Nor could anyone forget when, shortly after the Great Kanto Earthquake, a Communist youth took aim with a pistol and shot at the Emperor's car – who was the Crown Prince at the time – but only succeeded in cracking the windshield. Or last year even, when a Korean nationalist hurled a bomb at the Emperor just outside the Sakurada Gate.

It was an intriguing prospect though. Japan would benefit from the strong hand of Prince Chichibu, but even someone as cynical as the God of Intrigue found the idea of *lese majeste* so shameful, he almost wretched.

"General…is Prince Chichibu aware of the…the…" Kanemaru said, the words stuck inside his throat, unable to vocalize such treason.

General Araki's hard eyes held him tight. "That is not your concern, Major."

Rebellion rose within Kanemaru like a firestorm. The God of Intrigue was not some puppet to be led around, blind, deaf, and dumb.

"It is my concern, sir," Kanemaru said, drawing his broad shoulders back. "I've lived in the intelligence world for years now. My first assignment in the *Tokumu Kikan* was during the Siberian Expedition, in the Trans-Baikal region, trying to convince Buryat tribes to secede from Russia. I also provided intelligence to that Cossack ataman, Grigori Semenov, for his struggle against the Bolsheviks. After that, I ran opium dens and spy networks in Manchuria all throughout the reign of the warlord Chang Tso-lin and his brat, Chang Hsueh-liang. And as you know, I had a hand in the *incident* along the South Manchurian Railway. But never have I encountered a plot with so many shadows as this."

Rage flickered across Araki's face, but it was soon extinguished. "I know all about your past record, Major, which is why I saved you from the firing squad. Are you aware of mine?"

Kanemaru figured Araki didn't mean his stint as army minister. "I've heard you served in the Siberian Expedition, sir."

"Yes, and like you, I also carried out some…unsavory missions there as head of the *Tokumu Kikan* in Vladivostok. Being a soldier is not all parades and glorious calvary charges. Sometimes, we must do what's for the greater good, what strengthens Japan, no matter how shameful it might seem."

"But sir—"

"To answer your question, no, the Crown Prince is unaware of these," the General paused, searching for a suitable euphemism, "machinations. The important thing is that he is sympathetic to the goals of the Imperial Way."

So, even Prince Chichibu would be a puppet. He wouldn't be the only one in Japanese history. There were plenty of past emperors and shoguns who'd been installed by cliques of intriguers to serve one purpose or another. Kanemaru braved another question.

"Who else knows about this?"

A steely glower was enough of an answer from General Araki. No doubt there were other conspirators, but they would remain forever obscured.

"What about Marquis Maeda?" Kanemaru asked, retreating to safer ground. "And Inspector Tezuka?"

"As I said, the Marquis began to look into certain rumors. It's well-known how popular the Crown Prince is with the Army. In addition to hunting the Red Terror Society, he ordered Tezuka to ascertain whether such insidious rumors held any merit."

"How close did he get to the truth?"

"Your Reds dealt with them both before they could put all the pieces together." General Araki shook his head like a disappointed father. "Marquis Maeda was too conservative, unable to accept any change. He refused to understand how serious the Crisis of 1936 is. Like the Control Faction, all he cared about was maintaining the status quo. But the war – the real war – is fast approaching. It will ignite and consume the whole world, and Japan will burn if our people do not ready themselves. Unless we change our national character, the Russian Bear will slaughter us."

Although ranting, Araki's voice was calm, measured, as if he were explaining modern science to a classroom of simpletons. But there was also a religious intonation to his words, ominous echoes of the distant past. In the 13th century, the Buddhist monk Nichiren had warned against spiritual decadence and urged the people to prepare for war, just before the Mongol hordes invaded. Back then, the *kamikaze* – the divine wind – had saved Japan from subjugation, smashing the Mongol fleet while the samurai mopped up the remains. But today, only the Imperial Army and Navy, under the command of a strong-willed emperor, could save the nation from Bolshevik slavery. A dark thought crept into Kanemaru's mind.

"Sir, last year at Sakurada Gate…was that—"

Araki's hand went up. "No, Major, that was not our doing. But it did serve as inspiration."

"Sir, will we…recreate the Sakurada Gate Incident?"

"No, it failed for a reason," Araki clipped out, as if the question was beneath contempt. "Your Reds will abduct a certain Army officer tonight."

"Who?"

"Colonel Hashizume."

The name struck a thunderbolt down Kanemaru's spine, straightening him up. The broken pieces continued falling into place.

"Sir, why Hashizume? Isn't he a war hero?"

Araki let his displeasure show, a venomous scowl behind his mustache. "He has been contaminated with dangerous thoughts. When Hashizume returned from Manchuria in December, the Emperor personally awarded him the Order of the Golden Kite. But the audacious fool brought up an alleged 'atrocity' that occurred in Pingdingshan."

"Pingdingshan?"

"Some insignificant Manchurian village," Araki scoffed. "The fool even begged the Emperor to punish the soldiers responsible for this 'massacre.' Such impudence! To sully His Majesty's radiant presence with salacious stories about worthless Chinese peasants!"

There was a mirthless humor in caring about the Emperor's honor while also plotting his assassination. Well, to some Japanese, face was more important than human life.

"After that reprehensible performance," the General went on, "I ordered the *Kempeitai* to secretly search Colonel Hashizume's quarters. They found a dozen haikus like this one."

Araki pulled out a piece of paper and read aloud.

"The father is weak,
Our family is ashamed,
Screams will not be heard."

Araki set the haiku aside and said, "The *Kempeitai* also informed me that he lost a son, a Second Lieutenant Yasuo Hashizume, during the first month of the Manchurian Incident. Together with this Pingdingshan affair, Hashizume is a tinder box, ready to be ignited. We must choose where and when he explodes."

Kanemaru nodded, recollecting his night with the Colonel. Presenting himself as a disillusioned Manchurian veteran must have gained Hashizume's trust. The plot smacked of insanity but peeling back its layers revealed a very real possibility rooted inside the most common of all human emotions – grievance.

"So, Hashizume will carry out this," again the thought strangled Kanemaru until he coughed up a suitable euphemism, "incident?"

Again, Araki gave a disappointed glare. "No, he is only a means to an end. Your Reds will abduct him tonight, at the Silkworm Tea House. Ever since returning from Manchuria, Hashizume has spent every night drinking himself sick with geisha, disgracing his uniform even further."

Kanemaru flashed a confused expression. "And then?"

"Then you, Major, will persuade him to avenge the dead in Manchuria, including his own son, along with those massacred at Pingdingshan. That actress will be useful. Have her play the role of a grieving war widow or the little sister of a dead soldier."

"The actress?"

"She will play another role, an officer attached to Hashizume's regiment. I've been informed that the Asakusa Geisha Guild donated a horse to the 2nd Cavalry as a New Year's gift." Araki's mustache drooped. "She can ride, can't she?"

The question conjured up memories of that Utako Natsume picture from years before, *Modern Girl of Ginza.* They'd even shown it in Mukden, a taste of home for the Japanese soldiers stationed there to defend the South Manchuria Railway. Natsume played an equestrian *moga*, alternating between riding horses and dating eligible bachelors.

"Yes, sir, she learned for a film. I imagine it's like riding a bicycle."

"Good. She'll accompany Colonel Hashizume to the Imperial Army's review at the Yoyogi Parade Ground." Araki smiled, an architect satisfied with the sturdy foundation he'd laid. "During the review, she will only have one shot. Only *one* shot. The little actress and Hashizume will be cut down by the Imperial Guard, and you will dispose of those other Reds before reporting to your new assignment."

Kanemaru nodded, taken by the plot's sheer audacity. It was bold, daring, and treasonous, but the Great Japanese Empire was at stake. What did the life of an individual, even a god, matter when compared to that? But there was a confusing detail in this intrigue.

"Why Hashizume, sir? Can't we just use the Reds?"

Araki cast a disappointed frown. "Don't you see, Major? After the Sakurada Gate Incident, His Majesty's security has been increased tenfold. A military parade is the only opportunity we have. Furthermore, there must be an Army officer involved. This will provide me with the perfect reason to purge our ranks of the Control Faction."

"I see. Is Hashizume a sympathizer?"

"It does not matter whether he is or isn't," Araki hissed. "If we say Hashizume is part of the Control Faction, then he is. What matters is they'll tied to Communist traitors and discredited. The Imperial Way will be ascendant."

As long as this ridiculous factionalism ended, it was worth it. The Army needed to be united – under the Imperial Way or the Control Faction – if it was to achieve victory over the Soviet Bear. Not only the Army, but the entire nation needed to be led by a strong emperor when the real war began. An emperor like Chichibu.

Kanemaru would return to Manchuria to serve the nation there, but only after he had settled the score with Inspector Aizawa. Across worlds, Chizuru Okamura's tortured soul screamed for vengeance. The plot could work, but another flaw pestered him.

"Sir, what if Colonel Hashizume refuses to help?"

Araki's eyes drifted upward, to the painting of the tiger, crouched low and ready to pounce. With a soft breath, he said, "Then they all must vanish, Major. Everyone. The Colonel, the little actress…everyone. Understood?"

A grim comprehension seized Kanemaru, realizing just how paltry he was. He was only a mere mortal. Lieutenant-General Sadao Araki was the true God of Intrigue.

CHAPTER FORTY-THREE

Back at the gutted *izakaya* hideout, Utako and her comrades savored bowls of steamed rice, seasoned with *furikake* seaweed, washed down with cheap sake. It wasn't much, but it sufficed for a victory meal. Inspector Tezuka's shattered face lingered in her mind, making each mouthful taste sweeter. Wherever Ichiro Hayashi rested, his soul was satisfied. But Tezuka's assassination hadn't merely satisfied Utako, but reinvigorated her, prickling her entire body with sensations that had long been numbed.

"This tastes like paper," Izumi groaned, staring into his rice bowl. "Even the *furikake* doesn't help."

Genda grunted. "Spoiled brat. If you don't like it, then go hungry, rich boy."

"We have to be frugal and stretch out what little money we have left," Utako said.

"Unless we rob another bank," Izumi suggested with a snicker.

Utako glanced over to the supercharged Ford, parked inside the *izakaya* for safekeeping. Bullet holes pockmarked its body like battle scars. The Police must have alerted every mechanic in Tokyo to be on the lookout for it. There would still be some use for Wataru Izumi's little toy, but a mercy killing was fast approaching.

"Don't be stupid," Utako snapped. "Every bank will be on alert now."

Izumi looked ready to protest when a gruff voice called from outside.

"Open up. It's Major Kuno."

Genda lumbered to his feet and slid open the *shoji* door, letting Kuno inside. The Major was as dashing as ever in his uniform, a commander ready to bark orders.

"Welcome, Major," Utako said. "Why don't you join us?"

"No thanks. I already ate. Besides, we have work to do."

Izumi's plump cheeks puffed out further. "Perhaps you didn't hear, Major, but it's been a busy day. We plugged that weasel detective who's been stalking you."

"So I heard," Kuno said, kneeling beside them. "Who shot Tezuka?"

"I did," Utako answered. "With a single bullet."

"You're improving. Run into any trouble?"

Utako swallowed a heap of rice before replying. "That other detective, but we got away clean."

Worry shrouded Kuno's features. "Was it Inspector Aizawa?"

"I suppose so," Utako said, scraping the last bit of rice from her bowl. "The same wolf we saw at the Takano Bank."

"What happened? Did you kill him too?"

"Unfortunately, no. And he was so close to becoming a hood ornament on my darling," Izumi giggled, patting the side of the Ford. "Do you know him?"

"Let's just say I have a history with Aizawa-han. But the important thing is that Inspector Tezuka is out of the way. A good thing too, since those Tokko weasels are as tenacious as the OGPU."

The statement released disapproving hisses from Izumi.

"Don't compare the OGPU with the Tokko, Major. The former is the hammer of the Revolution, smashing capitalists, wreckers, and counter-revolutionaries, while the latter are mercenary bloodhounds for the *zaibatsu*, the true rulers of this feudal country."

A grin split Kuno's lips. "My mistake, Izumi-han. But we'd do best not to underestimate those Thought Policemen, now that the Japanese Revolution is imminent."

"Does that mean we've found our next target?" Genda asked.

"Not exactly. But my comrades within the Army have identified a potential ally." Kuno took a breath, drawing out the suspense. "Colonel Riku Hashizume. Apparently, he's been accused of writing his 'dangerous thoughts' down in haikus. We need to act before the *Kempeitai* arrests him."

"Is that so?" Izumi asked. "Is he a sympathizer as well?"

"Unfortunately not. But he's seen the truth regarding the Manchurian Incident. He'll be in some geisha's arms tonight over at the Silkworm Tea House. You'll abduct him tonight and bring him back here. He'll no doubt balk at assisting Reds, but thankfully, we have Japan's finest actress to convince him."

Utako leaned back with a sigh. "And how will I do that?"

Kuno gave a knowing smile. "All of us will. We'll adopt new identities, more palatable to Colonel Hashizume's politics."

"Isn't it a little risky to kidnap an Army officer?" Utako asked. "How about we meet him for coffee instead?"

"Three wanted bank robbers strolling into a Ginza café? Fool! Besides, if Hashizume refuses to help, he might report us. But if he's our prisoner, we can…dispose of him much more quietly."

"Why don't we try to convert this Colonel Hashizume to our cause?" Izumi asked.

Shaking his head, Kuno said, "Hashizume is a conservative man, born from samurai stock. Communism is tantamount to treason to him. But rebellion isn't. The Boshin and Southwestern Wars were both led by disaffected samurai. After he serves his purpose, the Communists who have honeycombed the Imperial Army will rise up and establish the Soviet Republic of Japan."

Utako leaned forward, hoping her skepticism shone. "Why don't we enlist one of these true Communists in the Army to help us?"

Kuno was undaunted. "Like me, they're mostly staff officers. And none of them leads a unit that will participate in the annual review at Yoyogi Park."

It was insane, almost laughable, but the signs pointed to one target.

"Major, what are you saying?" she asked.

Kuno braced his wide shoulders and raised his head high. "Have you forgotten? The 1932 Thesis has already identified the main component to Japanese feudalism. We cannot waste time and bullets on men like Marquis Tatsuo Maeda any longer. The Emperor System is the main thread that holds this tangled spider web of oppression together. Remove it, and the entire rotten structure will collapse."

An ominous hush swept through the *izakaya* like some freezing wind. The Emperor himself. Utako bit her lip and thanked the gods for letting her live to see this day.

CHAPTER FORTY-FOUR

Reiko's *geta* clogs clacked against the winding streets as she walked deeper into Asakusa. Dozens of dimly lit lamps illuminated the way, attached to storefronts that lined the neighborhood. But Reiko had been to the Silkworm Tea House so many times that she could sleepwalk there if needed. It was there where she'd first encountered the Okamura Gang and its poisonous daughter, Chizuru.

Pushing those thoughts aside, Reiko concentrated on the present. Although she'd foregone white face paint, her outfit put her in the right mood for the task ahead. Decked out in a sleek purple kimono, decorated with a bamboo, pine, and plum blossom motif – the three friends of winter – and topped off with a *shimada* wig, she had fully transformed into Harutora. She'd undergone this metamorphosis hundreds of times, but here lately, she wondered which identity was her face and which was the mask?

Not only her, but who Inspector Aizawa was these days. An errand boy for the *Kempeitai*? No, her *senpai* wasn't a fascist brute like that bespectacled reptile, Lieutenant-Colonel Hatsu. But this mission left her uneasy. Report anything seditious Colonel Hashizume might say? She felt like a Thought Policeman rifling through someone's dirty laundry.

Up ahead, the Silkworm Tea House beamed with paper lanterns. Geisha filtered in and out like a colorful river. Many dismounted from rickshaws, while others were followed by supplicating men, their *hakoya*. More traditional geisha never carried their own musical instruments, since it might spoil their graceful movements. Instead, their *hakoya* trailed behind holding disassembled *shamisens* in cloth pouches, to not blemish the geisha's dainty gait. Reiko didn't bring a *hakoya* or a *shamisen*. Her personality was entertainment enough.

She pushed through the *noren* curtain at the entrance and was greeted by the proprietress, a tiny *obasan*. After removing her *geta*, the proprietress led Reiko past rooms overflowing with excited, cackling voices. They stopped at a side *shoji* door and knelt. Geisha always entered after the client, and never through the same door. Reiko and the proprietress both bowed low, before the *obasan* slid the *shoji* screen open.

"Oh, honorable Colonel, this evening's geisha has arrived," the old lady croaked.

"Greetings, Colonel, I am Harutora, here for your entertainment."

Straightening up, Reiko shuffled inside, as the *shoji* shut behind her. Low lighting crafted a seductive atmosphere, offset by a wall scroll of a red-crowned crane, the national bird of Japan. Under it was Colonel Riku Hashizume, stooping over a low-lying table, beer in one hand and a sheathed saber in the other. But his unbuttoned collar – below which hung the prestigious Order of the Golden Kite – and red flush suggested the sword was more to keep his balance than anything.

"Harutora…Harutora," the Colonel said, then bit his lip. "Oh, yes, we met at the Shochiku party."

"Yes, and I hope not to disappoint you again."

"What happened to Wakakichi?"

"She was busy tonight, so the *okiya* sent me."

Tea houses usually relied on *okiya* geisha houses to provide geisha, Aizawa and Hatsu had arranged this night's party.

"I see. Well, I was getting tired of her anyway. She's a fine singer but makes for lousy conversation." Hashizume swigged his beer. "Do you still live at the *okiya*?"

"No, I moved out long ago. But a geisha will always retain ties to the *okiya* where she trained."

Hashizume took another gulp. "You live on your own? I didn't know geisha could afford that."

True, debts from kimonos, food, and training usually followed geisha for a lifetime, but Reiko had managed to pay hers off by moonlighting as a *moga* mistress. Most geisha still relied on their *okiya* for contacts but Reiko, ever independent, freelanced on her own, making her an outlier in the flower and willow world.

"The gods of fortune smiled upon me," Reiko said, before adding, "Not to mention a few men with cash to burn."

That pulled a laugh out of Colonel Hashizume, loud and brusque, but good-natured.

"Geisha always cheer me up! They're like dolls and clowns rolled into one."

"Clowns? Sorry, I didn't wear my makeup tonight."

Hashizume laughed again, almost slumping over. The coldhearted warrior from New Year's had been replaced by a jovial drunk, making her job much easier.

"Well, good thing for you that I love geisha. My wife doesn't though."

"Most wives hate us. With good reason."

Another laugh and Hashizume threw back his beer, draining the remnants. He fumbled for cigarettes, but Reiko cut him off by presenting a lit Cherry. Drawing the smoke in, Hashizume leaned back and examined her. His eyes were suspicious and penetrating, flashes of the stern officer from earlier. Time to use the geisha's most formidable weapon – flattery.

"You were so gallant in Matsumoto-san's film, Colonel."

Blowing out a plume of smoke, Hashizume snorted. "That's all movie magic. There was very little gallantry in Manchuria."

"I know something about movie magic. Matsumoto-san cast me in his next film, you know."

"Oh?" Hashizume took another deep drag. "What's it about?"

Wagging a finger, Reiko said, "Tut-tut, Colonel. I can't give away such treasured secrets. Unless you share something in return."

"And that is?"

Under normal circumstances, the best way to obtain information would be over a round of drinks. But this fish had already swallowed the bait and was chewing on the line. "Well, Matsumoto-san's picture inflamed a real curiosity within me. What was Manchuria like? The real Manchuria, not those war stories we read in newspapers."

Another scrutinizing look from Hashizume as he smoked his Cherry. Did he suspect something? No, that razor-sharp stare was standard issue for Army officers. After a moment, he held up the bottle of Yebisu and said, "If we're going back to Manchuria, then I need another beer."

Reiko darted off and retrieved two Yebisus. Perhaps the direct approach was a little strong, even for a geisha. Better to camouflage it in party tricks. Handing a bottle to Hashizume, she suggested, "How about a game? Rock paper scissors. Whoever loses has to take a drink and answer a question."

"Fine by me, Harutora-san."

They threw their weapons – Reiko paper, Hashizume scissors. Groaning, Reiko gulped her beer and braced herself. "All right, so you want to know about Matsumoto-san's new movie?"

"Not really," the Colonel began after another cigarette puff, "I'd like to know how you became a geisha, Harutora-san. Did your parents sell you?"

An abrasive question, but geisha parties were known for outrageous talk, providing it all remained within the walls of the tea house. Times like these made Reiko sympathize with tightrope walkers, jugglers, and fire eaters.

"Nothing so romantic. The Great Kanto Earthquake took my parents and left me homeless. A geisha named Haruhana found me in the wreckage and adopted me as her apprentice, probably since the more qualified applicants were all dead."

More booming laughter. "Underneath that pretty kimono is a cynical soul." Hashizume sucked in a drag. "A fine quality in a woman."

"I'm glad you noticed, Colonel."

They dueled again; Reiko throwing rock, scissors for Hashizume.

"Haha, victory! Now, Colonel, please tell me the worst thing about Manchuria, and the best thing there."

After a drink, Hashizume frowned. "That's two questions."

"Oh, don't be that way!"

Waving his smoldering Cherry back and forth, Hashizume said, "Fine, fine. The worst thing was the cold. Our rice rations would freeze solid and we'd have to lick them like ice cream. Spit would turn to ice as soon as it left our mouth. During winter, we only had to fight the Chinese sporadically, but the cold was our constant, unrelenting enemy."

"And the best?"

A dreamy smile spread over Hashizume's reddened face. "Ah, it's a cavalryman's natural battleground! Manchuria is so vast, we used Naval tactics to fight the enemy. It reminded me of the Russo-Japanese War when we fought a worthy foe."

Reiko nodded along, then prompted another round. She threw rock again, Hashizume paper.

"Ask away, Colonel," Reiko said before swigging her Yebisu. The icy scrutiny returned to Hashizume's face, banishing the fun-loving drunk.

"Tell me, Harutora-san…are you a spy?"

CHAPTER FORTY-FIVE

The accusation quickened Reiko's pulse, but she fought back an encroaching panic. Feigning ignorance might arouse deeper suspicion, but a full confession was unthinkable. Such tactlessness was unusual in Japanese society, but Colonel Hashizume was practically soaked in alcohol. The question would wound any geisha's pride, meaning the only acceptable behavior was righteous indignation.

Reiko swept her open palm, slapping Hashizume hard against his cheek. The Yebisu beer clattered to the floor, leaking over the tatami mats. Surprise appeared on the Colonel's crimson face, before giving way to amusement. Still, the deception wouldn't work unless she was willing to carry it through.

"Good night, Colonel," Reiko huffed, standing up.

"Wait," he cried, waving his hand. "My apologies if I offended you, Harutora-san. But please understand, I have reasons to be suspicious."

After another round of huffing, Reiko knelt back down. Ever the dutiful geisha, she retrieved the beer bottle and placed it back on the low-lying table. Leaning back, Hashizume examined her with bleary eyes.

"What do you mean by that, Colonel?"

"I'm not certain, but I believe the *Kempeitai* has me under surveillance."

She'd hooked him, but a good fisherman knew that reeling one in was a slow and delicate process.

"I don't understand, Colonel."

"To be honest, Harutora-san, I don't really care if you work for the *Kempeitai* or not. They don't scare me anymore."

Reiko let her confusion show.

"The Army is getting rid of me, understand? Early retirement. I've become an embarrassment to them. Well, good riddance. I'm still deciding on the best way to repent for my crimes. What do you think, Harutora-san? Should I shave my head and become a Buddhist monk, chanting sutras for the rest of my life?" He patted the sheathed saber like an obedient dog. "Or is *seppuku* the only way out for me?"

This conversation was like walking through a dark forest, unsure if the rustling noises behind a bush belonged to a rabbit or a bear. Best to play it safe with a sympathetic, bemused look.

"What crimes? You've been awarded the Order of the Golden Kite, the highest honor the Emperor can give."

"This trinket?" He flicked the medal, swishing it back and forth beneath his throat. "I wonder what my father would say, if he saw this stupid thing."

"I'm sure he would glow with pride at the hero his son became."

"You didn't know my father. He was a stoic, humorless samurai, a man of deep conviction and loyalty. You see, the Hashizume Clan is from Niigata, and my father fought on the side of the Tokugawa Shogunate against the Meiji Restoration. While the Tokugawa Family accepted defeat, my father and others carried on the fight in Hokkaido."

Reiko nodded along as lessons from history class returned. The Boshin War had ended in victory for the Emperor's forces, but a small band of diehards declared Hokkaido an independent "Republic of Ezo," and fought on for months before the Meiji government finally crushed them in battle.

"Despite surrendering and submitting to Imperial rule, my father was forever stained. So, what did his foolish son do? He tried to bring honor to the Hashizume Clan by joining the Imperial Army himself!"

Gruff laughter poured through Hashizume's gritted teeth.

"But I failed, of course. You see, the Army back then was run by the Choshu Clan, the samurai who'd spearheaded the Meiji Restoration. They accepted me into the Army, even commissioned me as a cavalry lieutenant. During the Russo-Japanese War, I led my platoon into countless charges and saber duels with hordes of ferocious Cossacks!"

Did he expect praise for such bloodstained laurels? Well, best not to let the fish get away so quickly.

"I'm sure your father was proud of his warrior son."

"When I returned home, he called me an idiot and died shortly after, probably from shame. Later, I realized how right he was."

"How so, Honorable Colonel?"

"I should be a general by now, but the Choshu Clan delayed my promotions. They've since faded from senior positions in the Army, but dishonor still soils my family name."

"And that's why you are being retired?"

Another deep-throated laugh, thick with cynicism. "No, little Harutora, if only it were that simple." He leaned closer again. "Tell me, how much do you know about the Manchurian Incident?"

From Inspector Aizawa, she knew more than most. But the fantasy about a Chinese bomb planted on the South Manchurian Railway was the official story, so it was best to stick with that.

"Only that Manchuria is the lifeline of the Japanese Empire. We need the raw materials there and the Chinese tried to vanquish us. Luckily, brave soldiers of the Kwantung Army—" she gestured to Hashizume "—struck back and now Manchukuo is a vital ally."

The Colonel's upper lip tugged into a sneer. "My son was in Mukden when the fighting began and didn't survive. One of only two Japanese casualties that night! The Army sent me a telegram, congratulating me that my son had died for the Emperor. In front of my men, I gave him a banzai cheer, but that night I went to bed sobbing."

His already-bleary eyes swarmed with tears, until they were beaten back by bitterness. Empathy spread over Reiko. She too, had long ago learned that there was no glory in death, despite that insufferable propaganda about slain soldiers becoming "military gods" at the Yasukuni Shrine.

"My wife blames me for his death. She's right too. I was the one who pressured him into joining, even though he'd have made a better university student. How stupid. I wanted to erase the 'stain' from the Hashizume Clan, but instead, I doomed it to extinction! After me, there will be nobody left to carry on the family name…"

The Cherry cigarette smoldered between Hashizume's fingers, collecting ash in large clumps. The curls of smoke looked like lit incense for all the dead of Manchuria.

"Regardless of my personal feelings, I had a duty to carry out there," the Colonel said, mashing out the cigarette.

"Oh yes, I remember those scenes from Matsumoto-san's picture."

Hashizume laughed again, more good-natured this time. "But the conflict didn't stop after Manchukuo was founded. The remnants of Marshal Chang Hsueh-liang's Army formed the Volunteer Armies and fought on as guerillas."

Time to play the uninformed civilian again. "Oh, but aren't they just bandits? I read in the newspapers that the Russians funnel weapons to them in order to harass the Kwantung Army."

Another contemptuous sneer. "Lies. Matsumoto-san's camera caught many enemy stockpiles we captured, filled not with Soviet equipment, but Manchukuoan! But that didn't make it into *Bullets and Horses in Manchuria*…"

"Oh, but aren't they our allies?"

"Allies to our faces, enemies behind our backs. Like the rest of that miserable puppet state, the Manchukuoan Army is rotting from corruption. Their officers are all opium addicts and the soldiers are only concerned with filling their rice bowls. Whenever the Volunteer Armies attack, they're annihilated, or they just drop their weapons and run away!"

His reddened face hardened.

"Even worse, some Manchukuoan Army units desert and join the guerillas, bringing along the uniforms, guns, and equipment that we supplied them with. And to think my son died for this despicable farce. So, you see, my father was right all along…"

Without much to add, Reiko nodded along. Geisha were part entertainer, part therapist. Tight-lipped salarymen could blubber away to a sympathetic geisha, provided they were lubricated by alcohol. Reiko opened another Yebisu, a prompt to continue.

"Thank you," he said, before gulping the beer. "Tell me, have you ever heard of a place called Pingdingshan?"

"Is it in Manchuria?"

"It *was* in Manchuria." Hashizume let the statement hang in the air before saying, "In September 1932, my regiment was out on patrol when a nearby garrison requested help. They'd been attacked by a guerilla group called the Red Spear Militia, which took refuge in some dumpy village named Pingdingshan. By the time we rode back to assist the local garrison, it was too late. The Red Spear Militia had long since fled, but the garrison had already taken their revenge."

That empty, vacant stare flickered across Hashizume's face again as he gazed across the room. Reiko suspected the Colonel could see past the Sea of Japan, into Manchuria, and across time. Minutes elapsed in silence until the Colonel's raspy voice began again.

"I wrote many haikus about it." He leaned back, eyes closed like a monk in meditation. "Here's one. '*Machine guns and fire, screams are forever silenced, weep for Pingdingshan.*'"

Reiko was no judge of poetry, especially poems pertaining to atrocities. Still, her curiosity had been piqued, terrified yet eager to know what evil monsters slithered in secret.

"There was a massacre at Pingdingshan? Did Matsumoto-san film it?"

"No. There weren't any civilians around that day. You see, all eight hundred villagers were machine-gunned, bayoneted, or incinerated in their mud huts. By the time my regiment arrived, all we could do was gawk at the mass graves full of old men, women, and children, and listen to the cries of those still burning alive. Within an hour, the entire village was nothing but ash and bones. Ah, the brave Kwantung Army! We didn't crush the Red Spear Militia, but Pingdingshan will trouble us no more!"

Images from Inspector Aizawa's tale of Nikolayevsk flashed across Reiko's mind, mocking and taunting. Nikolayevsk and Pingdingshan, two reminders that brutality knew no national boundary.

"But Colonel, how are these your sins? You didn't order that atrocity!"

"Sweet child…because I was the highest-ranking officer on duty, even though I arrived after the crime had been committed. In the Army, you are always responsible for subordinates, regardless if they obey you or not. I could have shot the officer who gave the order, but instead, I filled out a complaint with my superior, who buried it. My father was right…I was a fool, believing in justice!"

"Nobody was punished?"

"No, and nobody will be either. Except me, perhaps. You see, in December my regiment returned to Tokyo and I attended an audience with His Majesty. He thanked me for my service in Manchuria and awarded me the Order of the Golden Kite. To think! The son of Tokugawa loyalists congratulated by the Emperor of Japan! I almost broke down right there."

"What happened?"

Hashizume shook his head, regrets and bitterness chewing away like termites.

"I don't know what came over me. Maybe I was possessed by my son's spirit, or the hundreds dead at Pingdingshan. But I asked the Emperor to punish those responsible for the massacre. The Emperor looked confused, like an innocent schoolboy and said, '*Shikata ga nai.*' It sent a chill down my spine."

Shikata ga nai – it cannot be helped. Whenever an earthquake or tsunami struck, these impotent words were muttered. It was the only way Japanese could cope with horrors beyond their control, reducing them to puny insects scurrying for safety. But for the Emperor, the direct descendent of the sun goddess Amaterasu, to utter such a phrase showed how deep fatalism was ingrained in Japanese society.

After a sigh, Hashizume resumed. "I was ushered out of the throne room by General Araki, who said my behavior had shamed the entire Army. I'm certain he sent the *Kempeitai* to search my quarters. But I don't care anymore. All that matters is that the Emperor could punish those responsible for Pingdingshan but chose not to. Japan is a giant ship headed for an iceberg, but the captain does not want to issue orders since they might offend someone."

The condemnation of His Majesty made even Reiko's cynical heart burn. Adulation and respect for the Emperor System had been indoctrinated since birth, as natural as breathing. She herself felt no ill will toward him, only the bloodthirsty generals, admirals, and right-wingers who killed, tortured, and brutalized in his name. Still, the idea of sharing all these dangerous thoughts with Lieutenant-Colonel Hatsu filled her with shame.

"Someone has to take responsibility for Pingdingshan," Hashizume announced, in between sips of beer. "I cannot leak the story to the press, since the Tokko will censor it. Instead, I'll lead my regiment for the annual review, after which I shall retire from active duty. After talking to you, Harutora, I have decided to sacrifice myself for the crime of Pingdingshan." His eyes slid over to the saber.

What to say to that? Soon, Colonel Hashizume would be dead, Hatsu would be satisfied, and the Imperial Army would lose one of the few decent men it had left. Reiko wanted to cry, for Hashizume, for Pingdingshan, and for the future.

"Now, now, aren't geisha supposed to cheer their clients up? If these are my last days, I want to spend them in the arms of pretty geisha with a song in my heart!"

"Yes, how stupid of me," Reiko said, blinking her tears away.

She trotted out and fetched a spare *shamisen*, then began strumming out a potpourri of folk songs, each bouncier than the last. The Colonel sang along, drank his beer, and even managed a smile. Reiko began another song when heavy footsteps pounded closer and closer until the *shoji* door was ripped asunder. The elderly proprietress stood in the frame, frozen in fear while two figures pointing revolvers loomed over her – Saburo Genda and Utako Natsume.

CHAPTER FORTY-SIX

Reiko clutched the *shamisen* while her eyes searched for some escape. But Genda, a *haori* jacket and kimono draped over his wide frame, blocked the way. Utako Natsume, in a sweater, skirt, and cloche hat, stood beside him, like Reiko Watanabe's evil twin. Standing in front, the elderly proprietress raised her bony hand at Colonel Hashizume.

"That's him," she croaked.

Hashizume sprang to his feet, although alcohol wobbled his stance. "Who are you?"

"Forgive us Colonel, but you must come with us," Utako said. Her tone was surprisingly measured and she even performed a respectful bow.

"Get the hell out of here."

"I'm afraid that isn't possible, Colonel. You are coming with us."

The saber slid from its sheath and Hashizume struck out in a slow, jerking slash. Endless beers had dulled any expertise with a blade. Genda rushed forward and clamped his hand around the Colonel's wrist, blocking the sword. With the butt of the pistol, he hammered out a shattering blow across Hashizume's face, reeling him backward. The Colonel crashed into the mound of empty Yebisu bottles, a groan hissing out of his open mouth, before his fluttering eyes shut.

Instinct seized Reiko as she jumped up, leveled the *shamisen* like a baseball bat, and swung it hard over Genda's bulky torso. The instrument splintered into pulp, but Genda's only response was an annoyed grunt. Off to the side, the little old proprietress wheezed out a moan before spilling onto the floor. Genda refocused his attention back to Reiko, a shark who'd caught a whiff of blood. The demure geisha act wouldn't work now.

A glinting flash of metal lashed forward and slapped Reiko across the cheek. She sprawled onto the tatami mats, blood dribbling from her throbbing lip. Lifting her head sent the *shimada* wig tumbling off, and brought Utako Natsume's pretty face into view, scowling down at her. Her contempt soon broke as recognition set in, blazing with a sadistic glee.

"Hello again, Watanabe-san."

*****

Pacing back and forth in the empty *izakaya*, Major Kanemaru tried to calm himself. Buddhist monks achieved zen through endless repetition of sutras, but he'd never been a religious man. Outside, a low rumbling and sharp headlights announced the return of the Red Terror Society. Kanemaru slid open the *shoji* and the Ford crept inside, parked, then cut its lights and engine. The doors flung open and Genda plopped out, carrying an unconscious Riku Hashizume over his shoulder. Although the Colonel was completely inert, his hands were tied behind as an added precaution.

"In the cellar," Kanemaru ordered pointing around the bar counter. Genda lumbered forth and disappeared underground, but another prisoner demanded Kanemaru's attention. Although bound and gagged, Izumi and Natsume struggled to restrain her. The ornate purple kimono lent a traditional dignity that clashed with her modern, bobbed hair and furious, strangled protests. Despite the darkness and a cloth gag wrapped around half of her face, Reiko Watanabe was unmistakable.

"You know her?" Natsume asked, still clinging to Watanabe's wiggling frame.

Perhaps Chizuru Okamura's soul had reached out from the great beyond with this gift. His geisha lackey was more than suitable bait to lure Inspector Aizawa to an ignominious death. So long as these Communist fools didn't suspect the truth.

"Yes," Kanemaru said. "She's a spy for the Metropolitan Police."

"I suspected as much," Natsume hissed. "This bitch led the wolves straight back to our front door. She must have used Matsumoto-kun to get to us."

"Let me borrow your saber, Major Kuno, and give me an hour alone with her," Izumi said, lips hardening into a cruel smirk. "Once she loses a few centimeters of skin, she'll confess everything."

Fear and fury flickered across Watanabe, who poured out another round of gagged curses.

"Shut up," Natsume said, slapping her. "Major, Izumi-san is right. Drain her for everything she knows and then a bullet will silence her for good."

Even with a swelled, reddened cheek, Watanabe glowered back.

Killing his bait so early might spoil any possibility at revenge. "Not yet," Kanemaru said. "She might be good leverage against Aizawa."

"Aizawa? The detective who raided us?" Natsume looked ready to boil. "Is he Tokko?"

"No, just a regular inspector," Kanemaru said, "but don't underestimate him. He's far craftier than any Thought Policeman."

Izumi frowned. "Still, I say we rip whatever we can out of his little whore."

Torture might bring up uncomfortable secrets. Better to keep her out of sight and let these puppets wallow in ignorant darkness. Across the room, Genda plodded up the steps.

"All you'll get out of her is lies. For now, toss her in the cellar and don't believe a word she says."

Izumi shrugged and tossed her to Genda, who grasped the squirming Watanabe in a steady grip. Hoisting her up, he carried her to the second, still empty cellar.

Izumi stepped forward, puffing his chest out. "Major, there's a political matter I'd like to discuss with you."

"Is that so?"

"Yes, you mentioned that several other Army officers are sympathetic to our cause. However, we'd like you to lead the newly formed Japanese Red Army."

"I didn't know there was one."

Izumi adjusted his glasses. "There will be. Feudalism is too entrenched in Japan, and our actions will inevitably lead to civil war. Just like in Russia, there will be a counter-revolutionary White Army in Japan, still loyal to the Emperor, even a dead one. When that happens, you should lead the Red Army, a Japanese People's Army, to victory!"

Kanemaru forced down a grin. This arrogant bastard was ready to hand out medals, despite looking like some coffee shop dilettante. Still, he couldn't resist toying with the pompous fool.

"I'm honored in your trust, Izumi-han. I'm certain we'll crush the White counter-revolutionaries, but I must rely on you."

"Me, Major?"

"Yes." Kanemaru gripped his arm. "You'll have a vital role to play as well. The people and the Red Army will need to be fed. We must ensure that there will be plenty of rice to go around and avoid a famine like in the Tohoku region…or the one that's been ravaging the Ukraine."

Izumi's chubby face puckered in rage. "Capitalist lies. Don't believe such fantasies printed in the *Asahi* or the *Nichi Nichi*. There is plenty to eat in the Soviet Union!"

Kanemaru couldn't push the mockery any further but allowed himself a taunting grin. "Ah, that's wonderful to hear, Izumi-han! I was worried about those poor Ukrainians!"

The cellar door snapped shut, smothering Watanabe's muffled shouts even further. Genda rejoined them, his thick face distorted with worry.

"What's wrong, Genda-san?" Natsume cooed.

The giant shifted in place. "She just reminds me of my little sister. If we have to kill her, please make it quick."

Mercy seemed poisonous to Izumi, who scrunched his nose and looked ready to vomit. Natsume shook her head, disappointed that her guard dog had lost its bite. Still, such sentimentality could be useful in the coming play they were about to rehearse.

"Gather around, comrades," Kanemaru said. "We need to prepare for our new roles."

CHAPTER FORTY-SEVEN

After a cup of green tea and some breathing space, the Silkworm's proprietress was finally ready to answer Aizawa's questions. It was shameful to put this tiny *obasan* through any more stress, but the discarded pack of Cherry cigarettes and *shimada* wig, along with a smashed *shamisen* on the tatami mats, were grim reminders that time was essential if they were going to find Reiko Watanabe alive.

"Please *obasan*, start from the beginning."

"It was just after eight o'clock, when a couple walked in, a man and a woman," she said, her voice brittle.

Aizawa jotted everything down in a notebook. "Describe them, please."

"The man was huge, maybe a sumo. His *haori* jacket and kimono looked ready to split at their seams." She pouted. "He didn't even bother removing those *geta* clogs of his."

The description was identical to what Reiko had given for Saburo Genda. Aizawa knew who his companion was but asked anyway.

"A young *moga*…pretty thing," she answered, "like she'd come straight from Ginza."

Izumi was probably idling outside, but he needed to be thorough. "Anyone else?"

The *obasan* shook her head. "They drew their guns and told me to be quiet. I almost fainted right there. The woman said, 'We won't hurt you, just show us where Colonel Hashizume is.' I led them back to the Colonel's private room. He was being entertained by a geisha."

Fighting to keep an impassive face, Aizawa offered a silent apology to Reiko. He continued jotting down the rest of her story. None of it was very surprising, especially Reiko shattering a *shamisen* over Genda's back. Harutora – Spring Tiger – had very sharp claws. After that, there was little else, since the proprietress had fainted, only to be revived by Aizawa once he'd arrived on the scene. The other clients and geisha weren't much help either, since they'd called the Police only after finding the tiny *obasan* passed out. Geisha parties were often loud enough to muffle an erupting volcano.

A *junsa* appeared in the doorway of the private room.

"Sir, a Lieutenant-Colonel Hatsu is here to see you."

Aizawa nodded, flipped his notebook shut, then turned to the *obasan.*

"Thank you for all your help."

The proprietress bowed, then shuffled over to the *junsa* as they both went back into the hallway. Hatsu entered, resplendent in his uniform.

"Take a good look, Lieutenant-Colonel." Aizawa fingered the *shimada* wig and *shamisen* pieces. "This assignment got Reiko Watanabe kidnapped along with Riku Hashizume."

Hatsu remained blank-faced but shook his head. "Most regrettable. When I was stationed in Manchuria, I lost many informants myself to that brutal warlord, Marshal Chang. A reliable spy is more valuable than a division of troops."

Gritting his teeth, Aizawa pushed back the anger. Erupting at Hatsu would only lose face, for himself and for the Metropolitan Police. Instead, he lit himself a Golden Bat and drew the calming smoke deep into his lungs. If Hatsu was perturbed that he hadn't been offered one, the *kempei* didn't let on.

"Any suspects, Inspector?"

"The Red Terror Society," Aizawa answered, a plume of smoke pouring from his lips.

Surprise flickered behind Hatsu's thick glasses. "Those bank robbers? What interest do they have in Colonel Hashizume?"

"I was hoping you could tell me that."

"Well, I know about as much as you do. But I wouldn't put anything past Communists. They hold the Imperial Army in contempt because of the Manchurian Incident. To them, the whole campaign was some scheme to further enrich the *zaibatsu*. Those fools even tried to indoctrinate troops with their idiotic rag *The Soldier's Friend*."

"Any success?"

A scornful scoff. "A paltry few. The vast majority of soldiers are proud Japanese, averse to Bolshevism. But a few simple-minded fools are taken in with that claptrap."

As Aizawa sucked on his cigarette, Inspector Tezuka's words swirled in his brain like a ghost story. What was this plot of high treason he hinted at? Some terrible disaster was approaching Tokyo, like some monstrous tsunami. Creeping suspicion whispered the involvement of an old enemy.

"Lieutenant-Colonel, I'm in the dark about certain matters." Aizawa took another drag, then added, "Army matters."

"What do you mean?"

"Major Kanemaru. General Araki. What is their connection to all this?"

A cold impassivity remained ironed onto Hatsu's face, but his eyes slitted with hostility, like a snake drawing back its fangs.

"What are you implying, Inspector?"

"Inspector Tezuka was investigating a tall Army officer with an Osakan accent going by the name 'Kuno,' and working for General Araki. Only there is no Kuno. But Tezuka suspected that whoever he is had some involvement in Marquis Maeda's death."

"I have no idea, Inspector. Besides, I am not at liberty to discuss any private information regarding a superior officer, and one who is the Army Minister, no less."

"And what about Major Kanemaru? Did he really drown in Tokyo Bay? Or was he reincarnated as Major Kuno?"

Such directness must have galled a stickler for the chain of command, but Hatsu remained composed. However, a frown rippled across his lips, betraying his aloofness.

"I see…" After another puff on his Golden Bat, Aizawa went on. "Why wasn't Kanemaru prosecuted? Are the Army's officers made up of drug dealers?"

"Not in the home islands, at least. Inspector, I don't know why Kanemaru was pardoned. It is my duty to obey orders, not question them. The *Kempeitai* is part of the Army, after all. But since this is partly my responsibility, Inspector, I will assist you in any way I can."

That was the least Hatsu could offer. Still, Aizawa gave a thankful nod as he shot out a trail of smoke. The empty *shimada* wig and *shamisen* splinters offered little clues as to where Kanemaru and his Reds were likely hiding. But the Cherry cigarettes reminded him that there was one person who might know where to find his old friend Utako Natsume. The promise he made to Reiko no longer stood, since her life was on the line. Walking out into the hallway, he called over the *junsa.*

"Put out an all-points bulletin," Aizawa ordered, "for Koichi Matsumoto."

CHAPTER FORTY-EIGHT

Major Kanemaru examined Utako Natsume, Saburo Genda, and Wataru Izumi, who'd transformed from bank-robbing Communists to liberal pacifists in only a few hours. What's more, they had absorbed details regarding Hashizume's "dangerous thoughts" and the atrocity of Pingdingshan in stunned silence. No matter, since they would soon be silenced forever. The important thing is that a stalwart samurai like Colonel Hashizume would balk at assisting Red traitors, but his sympathies for Takamori Saigo and insipid haikus suggested he was more rebellious than that stoic mask let on. Of course, the melodrama would have to be convincing. Hopefully, Natsume hadn't lost any of her acting talent.

Genda opened the cellar and beckoned Hashizume upward. The Colonel ascended the small staircase, his head held high in a dignified pose, despite hands bound behind him. His eyes darted around, inspecting his surroundings. But his taut face loosened in surprise as he gaped at Kanemaru.

"You're…Major Kuno!"

"Yes, I apologize for your treatment, Colonel, but you would not have come any other way." Kanemaru and the others gave an apologetic bow in unison, deep and respectful, befitting such a proud warrior. "We all share something in common with you."

Colonel Hashizume's face hardened to stone. "What's that?"

"We have all suffered because of the Manchurian Incident," Kanemaru replied.

After scrutinizing them up and down, Hashizume hissed out a contemptuous scoff. "A soldier's personal feelings are meaningless. Our only duty is to obey orders. You should know that, Major."

The stubborn old fool. But such resistance was to be expected. Walking relics like Hashizume still clung to loyalty and duty like life preservers. Luckily, such lofty ideals were convenient tools for manipulation.

"See?" Kanemaru said. "If we had politely asked, then you would have reported us to the *Kempeitai*!"

Concern wrinkled Hashizume's brow. "How do I know you're not really working for the *Kempeitai*?"

"What are you worried about? Your haikus?"

Shock stretched Hashizume's rigid features. "You know about them?"

"Yes, Colonel," Kanemaru said. "The Army Ministry knows all about your poetry, thanks to the *Kempeitai*."

Surprise gave way to anger. "I knew they searched my quarters! Those snooping cowards!"

"That's how we know you're sympathetic to our cause, Colonel. Ask yourself, if we were *kempei*, wouldn't we have arrested you for those haikus alone?"

Hashizume remained still, but his tension began to dissipate, a clear sign he was receptive.

"Colonel, remember what I told you the other night at the Silkworm? I didn't reveal everything. During the Manchurian Incident, my battalion lost a third of its manpower. But my superior officer ordered me to underreport casualties in order not to damage morale."

Kanemaru gestured to Utako Natsume who stepped forward.

"Honorable Colonel, my name is Utako Oguchi. My husband was in Major Kuno's battalion and died during the occupation of Manchuria. He and I were going to start a family when he…" she stifled a sob "…came back home."

Hashizume kept quiet but turned to face her. Genda was up next.

"Colonel-san," he blubbered, wringing his flat cap, "my kid brother also served under Major Kuno. We're both poor boys from Honjo. He and I worked in the Senju Wool Mill until we were laid off when the depression hit."

Kanemaru nodded, a subtle hint for Genda to hurry it along.

"You see, we both have to look after our elderly parents and our little sister. My brother died in Manchuria, and although we received compensation from the Army, it isn't enough. I can't provide for all three of them!"

The performance wasn't as emotional as Natsume's, but it would have to suffice.

"I am sorry for your losses, I truly am. I too lost a son. But a soldier's life is not his own. He must be willing to sacrifice his life at any moment. Take solace in knowing that they've become military gods, enshrined at Yasukuni."

There was something forced and mechanical about the Colonel's words, a duty-bound officer following regulations. Another nod from Kanemaru brought Izumi forth.

"I was a newspaper reporter in Manchuria when the Incident began. There were several troubling details that I was assigned to investigate. But my editors in Tokyo didn't like what I found."

Hashizume's gray eyebrow raised. "And that was?"

Izumi feigned a pensive demeanor, then continued. "That the Kwantung Army's reasons for invading were nothing but a farce. There are several troubling rumors, Colonel. Rumors that suggest it was our own soldiers who planted that bomb along the South Manchurian Railway and blamed the Chinese."

Pained clarity settled into Hashizume's features, like a child accepting that his favorite fairy tale was just make-believe.

"I haven't read anything about that."

"That's not surprising, Colonel," Izumi went on, "since my editors fired me before the article could go to print. They even reported me to Tokko, who locked me in an unheated cell last winter until I underwent *tenko*."

The story was convincing because so many journalists had fallen afoul of the Thought Police, but Hashizume's dour, hesitant expression suggested he needed a little more prodding.

"It's true, Colonel," Kanemaru said. "It was an open secret in Mukden. Whispers said the Kwantung Army was behind everything. I even overheard a Japanese officer, a Lieutenant Kawamoto, boasting that he was the one who planted the dynamite on those railroad tracks."

The harsh truth cracked Hashizume like glass. The foreign press wasn't fooled, but most Japanese – civilian and military – believed the official story. In Japan, conformity was regarded above all, even mass delusion.

"If what you say is true," Hashizume began with a quivering lip, "does the Emperor know?"

Kanemaru answered with a slow nod. "He knows and did nothing to stop it. Even now, new intriguers are plotting further conquest in the Nekka Province."

"The Nekka Province?"

"Yes, Shanhaikwan was just the beginning. The Kwantung Army plans to invade next month."

Hashizume's wide eyes and compressed lips hinted at anger, but also a horrified acceptance. Anyone who had served in the overseas force knew the Kwantung Army's appetite for land was voracious.

"After a similar 'incident' to justify it?" Hashizume asked, with a cynical chuckle.

"It wouldn't be surprising," Kanemaru said. "Colonel, someone must pay for the crimes of the past and for the future."

"What are you suggesting, Major?"

Kanemaru braced himself. Araki's entire plot hinged on every inflection, tone, and word that came next.

"It poisons my tongue to say this, but His Majesty is made of bamboo and will bend to whatever the militarists demand. Nekka could lead to a wider war with China or

Russia. We need an Emperor harder than steel to save the nation."

Alarm flashed across the Colonel's stern face. "What you're suggesting…is treason."

"But loyalty to Japan," Kanemaru insisted. "If the militarists see that their actions are punished, they'll think twice about manufacturing another *incident*."

"How do you know the Crown Prince will rein them in? Isn't he popular among their circles?"

Waving his hand, Kanemaru said, "All lies. Prince Chichibu is an Army man, beloved by his men and brother officers. He must obey his duty, but he doesn't indulge in warlike dreams. I know for a fact that he *opposed* the Manchurian Incident. If Chichibu had sat on the Chrysanthemum Throne, he would have stood firm against the militarists."

Eyes narrowing, Hashizume asked, "And how do you know about all of this, Major Kuno?"

Perhaps the truth would be best. "I'm attached to the Army Ministry, the hive of intrigue. But inside, there are sympathetic officers who use me as a conduit."

"Liberals in the Army," Hashizume shook his head, almost laughing. "What you say isn't untrue. But such talk is treason…do you expect me to carry out this insidious deed?"

"No," Kanemaru gestured to Natsume, "she will. All we need is for you to get her into the Yoyogi Parade Ground."

"Traitors…all of you…traitors," Hashizume growled. Still the loyal samurai, even to a cause he didn't believe in. Such devotion to duty was admirable, but foolish. Kanemaru's hand drifted toward his saber. If the plot was doomed to failure, better to hack through all of them now rather than delay the inevitable.

"Colonel," Natsume said, drawing close to him. "My husband, your son, they died for a lie. If we don't act, how many more will die in another *incident*?"

Hashizume's hands twisted against their bonds. "Young lady, it is the duty of a soldier to die."

"And what about the people of Pingdingshan?"

"Young lady…I…"

Eyes watering, she gripped the Colonel's tunic. "Someone must pay for these crimes! Who shoulders the responsibility? The one at the top! The dead cry out for justice, Colonel! Have you no shame?"

Despite his tight skin and rigid poise, Hashizume's face was a battlefield of emotions. Humiliation, confusion, grief, and anger warred with each other for supremacy but left the Colonel with a washed-out, vacant expression.

"Please," he murmured, shifting his gaze back and forth, "let me pray about this."

Well, it was better than an outright refusal. After Kanemaru nodded his acceptance, he gestured to Genda and said, "Untie him."

Gratitude shone on Hashizume's face as Genda's thick fingers snapped the rope as if it were twine. A token to build trust.

"Thank you," the Colonel said, rubbing his chafed wrists. "One last thing, Major. What happened to the geisha I was drinking with?"

Kanemaru glanced over to the other cellar and fought off a grin. The wooden door and gag had muffled any protests into oblivion.

"She's fine and will be released shortly." Kanemaru brought his heels together. "On my honor as a brother officer."

That seemed to satisfy Hashizume, who nodded, then marched back behind the bar counter and down the cellar steps. Genda traipsed behind and snapped the door shut, locking it. Moments passed before a relieved sigh cut the tension.

"Excellent performance," Kanemaru said. "Especially you, Natsume-san."

She grinned. "What now, Major?"

"Now we wait. Maybe we should pray ourselves."

CHAPTER FORTY-NINE

Koichi Matsumoto stared back as Aizawa and Lieutenant-Colonel Hatsu entered the interrogation room, like a deer greeting a pair of tigers. Fidgeting in his chair, Matsumoto's puffy, sleep-swollen face and unkempt clothes were almost pitiable. Hauling suspects out of bed was a crude but effective way to keep them disoriented and malleable. Aizawa felt like a potter about to work on a fresh batch of clay.

"Hello, Matsumoto-san," Aizawa began, sitting at the table across from him. "Cigarette?"

He slid the pink Cherry pack and a matchbook across to him. Eyeing it for several moments, Matsumoto reached inside and lit himself a smoke. He inhaled a long soothing puff, but trembling fingers hinted at how deep his fear was. Oval glasses were balanced between large eyes, squinting as he examined first Aizawa, then Hatsu, lingering behind him like an ominous shadow. Matsumoto then shifted his gaze to a portrait of the Emperor, hanging on the far side of the room, a child pleading for help. Many prisoners couldn't stand the shame of disappointing His Majesty, but as Matsumoto brought his eyes back to Aizawa, a variety of worries clouded his soft features.

"Thank you, Inspector…?"

"Aizawa."

"Oh yes, I've seen you before. At Kamiya Bar!"

"Good memory. Do you know why you're here?"

"I assume he's a *kempei*." Matsumoto gestured to Hatsu with his smoldering Cherry. "And you're with the Tokko."

A sigh leaked from Aizawa. "No, but I'm beginning to feel like a Thought Policeman. Rest assured, Matsumoto-san, I'm with the regular Police."

The announcement released some tension from Matsumoto, who took another drag.

"What's this about then?"

Aizawa tapped the pack of Cherry cigarettes. "Reiko Watanabe. She's been kidnapped."

Matsumoto's red-rimmed eyes bulged. "Kidnapped? By who?"

"Your friend Utako Natsume."

The nervous tremble reappeared, shaking Matsumoto's entire frame. "I…I don't know anything about this! Why would Natsume-san kidnap her?"

"That's what I want to find out." Aizawa whipped out his notebook and pen, then slid them next to the Cherry cigarettes. "Write down every date and location where you met with Utako Natsume."

"What are you talking about?"

"There's no time to play dumb. If you care about Watanabe-san, then cooperate."

"I don't know what you're talking about…I haven't seen Natsume-san in years."

"Don't lie. We know you met Wataru Izumi at the Mitsukoshi Department Store. You've been giving money to Natsume for months now."

"How…how do you know all this?"

Aizawa pulled out a copy of *The Crab Cannery Ship* and laid it on the table, the *coup de grâce.* Realization set in and paled Matsumoto's skin to a sickly white.

"We know everything about you, Matsumoto-san. You were arrested before, during the 3-15 Incident, weren't you? And now my men find banned literature in your apartment? Your connections with Communism are enough for me to turn you back over to the Tokko. You're familiar with their methods, right?"

The director almost flinched.

"But I'm not interested in that. You were a loyal friend of Ichiro Hayashi and looked out for his girlfriend. Very misguided, but honorable. You didn't know about her criminal activities. But if you don't tell us everything you know, then your previous stay here will look like a trip to the hot springs."

"Watanabe-san gave that novel to me," Matsumoto muttered in between puffs. "She set me up…she set me up…"

"Names. Dates. Locations. Now."

"I don't…remember…"

Aizawa glanced at his wristwatch – two in the morning. If Matsumoto kept retreating into himself, it'd take all night to drag him back out. Reiko couldn't wait that long. Distasteful as it was, alternative methods would have to be used.

"Stop these games! Watanabe-san's life is at stake! What kind of man are you that you'd sacrifice a woman?"

"She's working for you, isn't she? You ordered her to set me up! You know I'm shooting a tendency film, so you did this to sabotage me!"

Anger seized control of Aizawa as he gripped Matsumoto's hand, slid the pen between his slender fingers, and squeezed. Pain warped the director's face, his eyes looked ready to pop behind his glasses. The Cherry cigarette dropped to the floor, still burning. Minutes slogged by but Aizawa maintained the pressure, twisting and grinding Matsumoto's fingers, hand, and wrist into a grotesque contortion, ready to snap with an ounce more of strength.

"Please…please stop!" Matsumoto wailed. His skin flushed from a nervous white into an agonized crimson.

Aizawa released his grip. Gasping for air, Matsumoto sank over the table, his twisted hand laying impotently on the notebook.

"Since I didn't break anything, you can still write down everything you know."

"It won't help you! We always met in a public place. She arranged everything! I just showed up with the money. I swear, I don't know where she is!"

Hatsu stepped forward, a dog who'd ripped its chain off. "You're being too soft on him, Inspector. Cockroaches cannot be coddled, only crushed."

Fear flooded back over Matsumoto, leaving him with a sallow hue. The *Kempeitai* didn't have lofty goals like the Tokko. They weren't concerned with *tenko* or cleansing Communists of dangerous thoughts. As part of the Imperial Army, they thought only in terms of complete annihilation of an enemy.

But both organizations implemented torture so brutal that it would have made Genghis Khan squirm. Methods like constant beating and bamboo slivers underneath fingernails were not only barbaric, but totally ineffective. The Tokugawa Police Force had extracted confessions from people who claimed to be shapeshifting fox spirits, sent to assassinate the Shogun. However, Aizawa's preferred method of shaming the suspect into confession wouldn't work now. Not when time was working against them.

Aizawa gave Hatsu a nod, then braced himself. The *kempei* swept the chair from underneath Matsumoto, sending the director crashing onto the floor. Lifting his tall, black jackboot up, he smashed it down on Matsumoto's face with a sickening crunch. Blood squirted from his nose. The oval spectacles cracked and splintered. A pathetic whimper seeped out his lips.

Hatsu swung his leg again, landing a heavy blow straight into Matsumoto's groin, popping him like a balloon. Another kick followed, smashing into his crotch, his back, his chest, and everywhere else. Shrill wails reverberated throughout the interrogation room like a hideous symphony. Lighting a Cherry cigarette for himself, Aizawa shifted his gaze to the Emperor's portrait, staring back like a disappointed father.

CHAPTER FIFTY

The cellar was cold and dim, blanketing Colonel Riku Hashizume in darkness. After murmuring a litany of prayers, any answers from the gods were still vague. To join the plot was treason, but the same could be said about the Meiji Restoration and Saigo's rebellion. Thoughts, fears, and the alcohol from earlier swirled in his brain, manifesting as a merciless headache. He ached for sleep and, thankfully, his heavy-lidded eyes fluttered and consciousness soon dimmed.

Hashizume stepped out onto a field, expanding into infinity. The endless expanse was unmistakable as the Manchurian wilderness. Gazing into the horizon, a figure marched forward out of the morning sun, wearing a brown uniform, peaked cap, and a familiar face.

"Hello, Father," Lieutenant Yasuo Hashizume said with a salute.

"Good to see you, Yasuo, even if it's just a dream."

Yasuo shook his head. "This isn't a dream, Father. It's a warning."

The horizon became electrified with activity, units of Japanese soldiers advancing, columns of Rising Sun flags flapping in the Manchurian wind. Airplanes swept overhead in a droning swarm. In the far distance was the enormous, mechanical maw of battle, bursting with flesh and flame.

"This is a vision of the future, Father. Yesterday it was Manchuria, tomorrow it'll be Nekka, then Siberia, China, and the whole world."

The approaching horror turned Hashizume's insides to a soggy puddle. Mass suicide was Japan's future.

"*Shikata ga nai…*"

"Don't say that!" Yasuo barked. "You can stop the conflagration, save Japan from my fate!"

The words stung Hashizume with a bitter shame. Although he'd long suspected, he needed the truth about his son's true fate.

"Yasuo…have you become a military god? I visited the Yasukuni Shrine to pray for you, but your presence…wasn't there."

Gesturing to his tunic, now spotted with blood, Yasuo hissed, "All nonsense. There are no military gods or other fantasies. I am nothing but ash, all because of a lie. But you are flesh and blood, Father."

Hashizume stared into the distance. The mass of armies convulsed into one, amorphous blur, vomiting smoke and fire.

"This plot of theirs…it's treason…how can I face my ancestors after such a crime?"

A new figure joined them. His father hadn't changed since his death, still stern and disapproving, but even more imposing in full samurai armor and horned helmet.

"Riku, your first loyalty is to your family," his father boomed. "But now, we have been robbed of an heir to the Hashizume Clan. I have never regretted fighting for the Tokugawa Shogunate. You, however, have been plagued with doubt all your life. You must make a decision, Riku. Your family or your emperor."

Another storm of thoughts raged inside Hashizume. Betray the Emperor or his family? Save the nation from another war or perform his duty as a soldier? Avenge his son or salvage what honor remained of the Hashizume Clan? Anger, regret, and doubt coalesced into a bitter cocktail he almost choked on.

From the horizon, a new mass shambled toward him. Their sallow faces weren't soldiers, but they were dead nonetheless. Dark, otherworldly eyes held Hashizume in an accusatory grasp. Their peasant clothes were shredded rags, punctured by bayonets and bullet holes. His father and son vanished as the dead of Pingdingshan drew closer and closer.

In the far beyond, the great mechanical maw erupted in one continuous, swallowing explosion.

*****

Endless minutes ticked by as Reiko strained against the ropes biting into her wrists. The silken gag was damp from a steady stream of curses. That bastard Kanemaru! If only he'd drowned like his wretched mistress. Instead, he'd been resurrected as some vengeful spirit, the puppet master behind those Red gangsters. But what was his end goal? And more importantly, what did he have planned for her?

The cellar door creaked open, spilling a dull light on her. Heavy footsteps clomped against the steps and Genda came into view. Sympathy was painted on his wide face while his bulky hands held a small bowl. She wiggled and mumbled into her gag.

"If I take it off, you have to promise not to scream."

Reiko nodded and Genda yanked off the cloth, allowing her to work her jaw. Taking a deep breath filled her nostrils with the sweet smell of miso soup, garnished with tofu and seaweed, steaming from the bowl.

"For me?"

A sheepish smile stretched across Genda as he held the bowl to her lips. Reiko sucked it down with thirsty gulps, pausing only to chew the seaweed. After a satiated sigh, she leaned back and examined Genda in what little light trickled into the gloom. Such a change of scenery than from when they'd last seen each other, back at that Ginza apartment. What was it he'd said about her? Oh yes – '*Watanabe-san reminds me of my little sister. She didn't mean any harm.*' It wasn't much, but it was the only lifeline she had.

"Genda-san, please listen to me."

The giant edged closer.

"That man Kuno is not who you think he is. His real name is Major Junzo Kanemaru, an officer in Army Intelligence."

Genda pulled back, eyes shifting back and forth.

"Major Kuno already warned us about you. He told us that you're a spy for the Metropolitan Police."

Another stream of curses came bubbling up, but Reiko bit her lip to stifle them. Genda seemed like the type of simple ox who believed whatever he heard first, but maybe a little more sweet talk from his surrogate little sister would persuade him.

"Genda-san, listen to me. Major Kanemaru ran an opium den right here in Tokyo! He's using you!"

"Major Kuno told us you'd say that."

"Oh hell, think about it! How do I know his real name? Ask yourself that!"

"I don't know…but Major Kuno said he uses aliases to throw off the *Kempeitai.* He's part of a clique of Communists operating within the Army, you know."

"Fool! There are probably only a few hundred Communists in the entire country! A Red would have been weeded out of the Army years ago!"

Concern and doubt flickered across Genda, but any turmoil was soon fought off.

"Major Kuno told us that the Manchurian Incident has caused discontent within the Army. He's been our comrade ever since November. I believe him over a spy."

There was no point. Someone as thick-headed as Genda had already had his mind made up for him, untroubled by logic and inconsistencies. The only hope now was to gather some information about what Kanemaru and his puppets were plotting. That would require some reconnaissance.

"Genda-san, could you please let me get some air? It's so dank down here."

Apprehension was apparent on Genda, until Reiko made her eyes huge.

"All right, but I have to gag you again…or else Natsume-san will be angry."

CHAPTER FIFTY-ONE

Utako leveled the Nambu automatic straight at the Emperor, but his cold, impassive expression sent her hand trembling. Was she having regrets? Even if it was only a picture taped on the far end of the *izakaya*, taking aim at His Majesty filled her with such shame she almost gagged. The years of indoctrination had done their job well. Schoolchildren bowed before the Emperor's portrait before class, and teachers wore gloves when handling his sacred image. During the Great Kanto Earthquake, a school principal had stayed behind in a burning classroom to ensure His Majesty's portrait was safe, only for flames to swallow them both.

But a bitter procession traipsed across her mind's eye – the dead in Manchuria, the oppressed workers in factories and mills, and Ichiro Hayashi's corpse, bloated, beaten, and broken. The Nambu held steady as she squeezed the trigger. A hollow click rang out, followed by Major Kuno's gruff voice.

"Again! And don't hesitate this time. This isn't a game of golf, so you can't afford to choke on the swing."

Shame went through her again, but he was right. There'd only be one chance, one opportunity to cut the Emperor down. This mission would kill her, but she would live forever as the woman who freed Japan from this despicable Emperor System. The pistol rose again to His Majesty's thin spectacles and Utako snapped off another shot.

"How am I supposed to practice without a clip?" she asked. "Can't I use a Nagant?"

Scorn creased Kuno's long face. "Fool. A Russian revolver at the Army's grand review? You'll be arrested by the *Kempeitai* before the parade even begins. Be grateful I was able to supply a Nambu on such short notice. Either learn to shoot with it or the mission is doomed."

Bleating laughter poured from Izumi, leaning against the parked Ford. "Major, why not send me or Genda? They'll spot a woman before she even enters the parade ground."

Shaking his head, Kuno rasped, "Without those bottles on your face, you can't see two feet in front of you. And Genda's so big he'd tear any uniform we stuff him into. Unlike you two, Natsume-san can play any role given to her." Major Kuno flashed her a glance of pride. "Besides, now that Pak is dead, she's the best shot. The way she plugged Tezuka took genuine talent. This is just to get her used to the idea. After all, not everyone can kill a god."

Izumi crossed his arms, ready to protest, when a creaking cellar door cut him off. Genda lumbered upstairs, carrying Reiko Watanabe, still trussed up and gagged. Good, the last thing Utako could tolerate was another round of her lies. Genda set her atop the counter, an enormous child careful not to break his favorite doll. Watanabe didn't move, but her eyes were like searchlights, beaming around the *izakaya* before settling on the Emperor's photograph.

"Figured it out, huh?" Utako taunted, tickling her chin. "Well, you're a smart little cherry blossom, so I figured you would eventually. Don't worry about him though…you're going to have a much worse finale."

A low growl puffed into Watanabe's gag, her eyes burning.

"Sorry, Natsume-san," Genda blubbered. "She needed some fresh air…"

Utako shook her head, then returned her attention to Watanabe, fixating on her bobbed hair, clashing against that silk kimono. Without thinking, she twirled her own bob. "Poor Matsumoto-kun…infatuated with a cheap tramp like you. Every *moga* in Tokyo wants to be the Japanese It Girl! But there's only one Utako Natsume."

She giggled as Watanabe fumed in humiliated silence. A knocking from the other cellar door cut her off.

"Stuff her back in," Utako ordered. Genda obeyed and bundled Watanabe back underground, then released

Hashizume. The Colonel strode up the steps, surveying the *izakaya* with a cold stare. Major Kuno strode forward with a respectful salute.

"Yes, Colonel? Have you reached a decision?"

Hashizume let a silence spread before answering. "The gods have shown me the way. I would rather die a traitor to an inglorious cause than continue to live in such shame. You have my cooperation."

Utako couldn't hide her joy, presenting the Colonel with a low, gracious bow. Unconcerned, Hashizume focused back on Kuno and asked, "What comes next in your plan, Major?"

"It's very simple, sir. I will procure a uniform for Oguchi-san," Kuno nodded in Utako's direction, "and she will accompany you to the Army review at the Yoyogi Parade Ground."

Incredulity rippled across Colonel Hashizume's features. "You? Playing a soldier?"

A half-truth would fare better than a full lie. "I used to be an actress with the Takarazuka Revue," she offered, invoking the all-female dance troupe famous for also playing male roles. The explanation seemed to placate Hashizume, who returned his attention to Kuno.

"Your regiment is scheduled to pass by the Emperor's reviewing stand and that is when Oguchi-san will…" Kuno trailed off, as if even saying the deed aloud choked him.

For his part, Hashizume bit his lip and weathered the news like a stoic soldier, accustomed to unpleasant truths and hardship.

"Why don't *you* take the shot, Major?" the Colonel asked.

A shrug from Kuno, then, "As a staff officer, I have no unit to lead. Unlike you, sir, I can only watch from the sidelines, far away from His Majesty."

"There's no other choice," the Colonel murmured, gazing across the room at the Emperor's photo. "But what about the *Kempeitai*? They will be looking for me at the Army review."

Kuno smiled, full of secrets. "We have a few allies in the Army Ministry…the *Kempeitai* will be kept off the trail."

"Well, those are lovely words, but how do we ensure he won't betray us?" Izumi said with a dismissive frown.

Hashizume held the whelp in a knife-like stare. "You doubt the words of a samurai?"

"Anyone can lie. Samurai or peasant," Izumi sneered.

A valid point, and there was nothing to stop him from spilling everything to the Metropolitan Police once they released him. Colonel Hashizume drew himself up, tight enough to snap apart, but Major Kuno stepped between them.

"Please understand our predicament, Colonel. We must ask you to stay here."

"Am I your partner or prisoner?"

Kuno's hands went up. "I understand your frustration, Colonel, but it's only one more day until the parade. This way, we have no chance of failure. The Police have ways of detecting the truth from even the paltriest of details."

After a frustrated mutter, Hashizume gave a tepid nod. "Fine. But I demand a shave and a bath before the parade." He breathed deeply, then added, "And a fresh uniform."

"Of course, Colonel," Kuno said with an ingratiating bow. Satisfied his orders were to be obeyed, Hashizume knelt on the floor, closed his eyes, and lapsed into a deep meditation, a man bracing for the end.

No time to waste then. Utako would need all the practice she could before the grand finale. Flicking up her hand, she steadied her aim at the Emperor's photo and fired an empty shot. This time, there was no hesitation at all.

CHAPTER FIFTY-TWO

After a brief nap in his office, Aizawa and Lieutenant-Colonel Hatsu sat around his desk, sucking downs round of coffee and Golden Bats. They provided a nice jolt to stay awake, but a dull fog still hovered over Aizawa's brain. Matsumoto's all-night interrogation yielded little and the reports regarding Genda's family were just as useless. Instead, he and Hatsu pored over building records, looking for any semblance of a clue.

Criminals found it hard to hide in Tokyo, since all residents had to register with the Police after moving in. However, the depression had given way to hordes of squatters, drifters, and vagrants, passing through flophouses and abandoned buildings using nicknames and aliases. Aizawa and Hatsu scanned every report for abnormalities, along with any reference to a Major Kuno, Natsume, Izumi, Pak, or Genda.

The problem was that ever since the October merger, Tokyo had grown almost too big to police. Hundreds of Kunos, Natsumes, Izumis, Gendas, and Kanemarus lived in the city, assuming that the Red Terror Society still remained in Tokyo. A massive dragnet could widen the search, but with the Army review tomorrow, every *junsa* was busy rounding up the usual riff-raff, radicals, or anyone else who might sully His Majesty's presence. Meanwhile, those Red gangsters hid with impunity, like hornets rebuilding their hive.

"Lieutenant-Colonel Hatsu," Aizawa said, "does the *Kempeitai* have men to spare?"

Looking up from a report, Hatsu's bald head furrowed. "Probably not, what with the parade tomorrow. But this is a rather unusual situation."

Aizawa offered a thankful little bow as Hatsu reached for the candlestick phone on his desk.

"The Army Ministry, please," Hatsu clipped out, looking parade ready even after a rough night. Not as rough as Matsumoto's though.

Aizawa pushed the thought from his mind and looked out the window as streaks of morning sunlight filtered in. Tokyo let out a yawn as salarymen, government workers, and police officers passed by on the streets below, eager to begin the day. Stubble prickled Aizawa's skin, a reminder that he needed to shave before his date with Minori Miyake tonight. Reiko's safety demanded working through the night but canceling meant losing face with the Superintendent. Such were the perils of career growth.

"Good morning, General Araki," Hatsu spoke up again. "This is Lieutenant-Colonel Takumi Hatsu. I must request additional *kempei* for a case in cooperation with the Metropolitan Police." A pause, then, after a curious look, "Yes, sir, it *is* about Colonel Hashizume. I see, sir. Well, that is good news to hear." Hatsu kept quiet but nodded along, indicating that General Araki was far from finished. "Yes, sir…it is Inspector Aizawa who I was cooperating with. Yes, sir, he's right here."

Presenting the telephone to Aizawa, Hatsu's rigid posture broke with a bewildered expression. Aizawa grasped the receiver, wondering what strange mysteries he was about to hear.

"Inspector Aizawa speaking."

"Lieutenant-General Araki, Minister of the Army." The voice was wispy and soft, like a disembodied spirit. "Colonel Hashizume is safe."

"That is good to hear, General. May we speak to him?"

"No, he is in a safe location. Apparently, two gangsters attempted to kidnap him last night. He escaped their clutches and was picked up by a *kempei* patrol. Apparently, these criminals read about him in the newspapers and hoped to ransom him. This depression has made thieves of our people."

The story was thinner than cheap miso soup, but Aizawa just chewed his lip in silence. To outright accuse the Army Minister of orchestrating a kidnapping was tantamount to disemboweling one's own career.

"Unfortunately, they worked him over a bit, so he is recuperating. The good news is that he will be able to attend the parade at Yoyogi tomorrow."

"That *is* good news, General."

"Since we don't want copycats targeting our war heroes, I'd prefer it if this incident was kept out of the press. But there is no further need for you or Lieutenant-Colonel Hatsu to investigate any further."

"I completely understand, General. Thank you for your assistance. However, there is still the matter of the geisha."

A tense silence followed. "What geisha?"

"She was entertaining Colonel Hashizume. Do you know if she's all right?"

"I know of no such geisha."

"Ah, I understand. She must not have been able to escape like Colonel Hashizume."

"Yes, I see. Well, you must continue your investigation, Inspector. Unfortunately, Colonel Hashizume will be indisposed for the moment. I can arrange for him to speak to you tomorrow."

There was no point in pressing the matter, lest Araki lose face even further. Enough clues were available to stitch a coherent theory together.

"Thank you, General."

Aizawa hung up and turned to Hatsu, who'd resumed his stiff-necked, aloof posture.

"Something will happen tomorrow at the parade."

Hatsu gave no hint of alarm. "What makes you say that, Inspector?"

"The fact that I'll be able to speak to Hashizume afterward. General Araki wouldn't take that risk unless it's after whatever he has planned."

"And what is that?"

Aizawa offered a helpless shrug. "Isn't Hashizume infected with 'dangerous thoughts?' Perhaps Araki and Kanemaru have some use for that."

The *kempei's* pupils shrank. "You infer that the Army Minister, a descendent of samurai, is going to harm the Emperor?"

It did sound ridiculous when said aloud, despite how many scandalous haikus the Colonel wrote. Besides, His Majesty had the entire Imperial Guard for protection.

"Perhaps you have some idea then? After all, you were the one investigating him."

"On General Araki's order."

"And whose idea was it to involve Watanabe-san?"

Something approaching shame crossed Hatsu's bespectacled face. "That was mine. Again, I sincerely apologize for this, Inspector. But I cannot disobey a direct order."

"What do you mean?"

"General Araki ordered me off the case," Hatsu said, standing up. "I am to assist with crowd control tomorrow."

Rage ignited inside Aizawa and he slammed his fist on the desk. "Damn it! Araki's behind all this!"

"It wouldn't surprise me. He used to command the Vladivostok *Tokumu Kikan* during the Siberian Expedition. Old habits die hard, I suppose."

"Well, even if you don't care about Watanabe-san's life, you must care about what he's plotting!"

"Yes, I do. But you were in the Army, Inspector. You know that an order is to be obeyed, despite your personal feelings."

Giri versus *ninjo*, the curse of Japanese society. No matter how hard he struggled, Aizawa could never break free of their unending battle for Japan's soul.

"Do not despair, Inspector," Hatsu added, with a triumphant grin. "General Araki will get what he deserves soon enough."

"What's that mean?"

Stooping forward like a buzzard, Hatsu said, "There are many factions within the Army, all vying for power."

Another spider web of deceit, double-dealing, and intrigue. Aizawa felt as if he were swimming in a swamp.

"What factions?"

"General Araki's followers, for instance. They refer to themselves as the Imperial Way."

"Sounds like a religion."

"Practically! Almost all of them are radical junior officers, obsessed with mystical virtues. Most importantly, they want to abolish the *zaibatsu* and any form of civilian government, having the Emperor command the nation directly, just like the old shoguns used to do."

"And what faction do you belong to?"

A contemptuous frown from Hatsu, then, "Araki's sycophants would claim I'm part of the Control Faction, but no such formal group exists. We are only united by our opposition to hotheads like Araki."

"Is that so? I didn't know there were moderate voices in the Army."

"Bah! I'm not some soft-hearted liberal, Inspector. But the Emperor directly commanding the nation? Ridiculous! His radiant glory should not be concerned with trivial, day-to-day matters. And in a future war, we will need the factories and money of the *zaibatsu*. Victory cannot be achieved by belief alone."

Aizawa rubbed his eyes, taking in this added intrigue. Hatsu's words portended another oncoming catastrophe, but all that mattered now was finding Reiko, his *kohai*. "So, you won't help? Even if it discredits Araki's faction?"

Hatsu offered a stiff, apologetic bow, like a cinder block breaking in half. "While I do not support the current Army Minister or the Imperial Way, I must obey him. Orders are orders. We'll deal with Araki and whatever scheme he has planned, in due time. Goodbye, Inspector."

Aizawa boiled in anger, partly at Hatsu, but mostly at himself. What did he expect from a *kempei*? Now, he was truly alone. Aizawa could only muster an irritated hiss before waving Hatsu out. Alone, he lit another Golden Bat and stared at the long strands of smoke, stretching toward the ceiling.

CHAPTER FIFTY-THREE

The Army Ministry buzzed with activity as staff officers met in briefing rooms, strode down hallways, and clustered in groups. Passing them, Major Kanemaru picked out a few conversations pertaining to tomorrow's parade, but most referenced the upcoming Nekka operation. Shanhaikwan had been swallowed easily, but how could they plan a full-scale invasion in little over a month? That old man Araki must have lost his mind…

Kanemaru approached the Army Minister's office and knocked.

"Enter," ordered Araki's soft voice.

The General stood at his desk, gazing out the window. He turned around and pointed at a suitcase, leaning against his chair. Striding across the sparse office, Kanemaru gathered up the suitcase and popped it open on the desk. Two complete service uniforms were stuffed inside – peaked service caps, riding boots, sabers, and two brown tunics with green collar patches – one for a full colonel and the other for a second lieutenant.

"Are they sufficient?"

"Yes, sir." Kanemaru shut the suitcase and bowed. "Thank you for procuring these on such short notice. Particularly for Hashizume. He wants a clean uniform to wear tomorrow, since the one he's wearing now is soaked in booze."

"Make sure he sobers up before tomorrow."

"You were right about him, sir. It took a little prodding, but he came around."

Araki lifted his head high. "Of course, I was. Do you know why?"

"His haikus?"

"No, but they certainly reinforced my initial suspicion. When I was in Siberia, we captured a Bolshevik partisan. He was no older than seventeen, but the boy glared at me with murderous hatred. If given the chance, he'd have killed every Japanese soldier occupying his native land. That look was burned into my mind forever."

Kanemaru knew that look. It would be the last thing Inspector Aizawa saw just before he died.

"That day when Hashizume met the Emperor…the same bloodlust blazed in his eyes. It was only for an instant, but I recognized it at once. The gods were kind enough to grant us a suitable weapon to…" Araki trailed off, as if the word 'assassination' had gummed his mouth. "To save Japan."

"Sir, Colonel Hashizume is becoming restless. It is possible the *Kempeitai* will locate him before—"

"Don't worry about the *Kempeitai*. I have ordered Lieutenant-Colonel Hatsu to drop the case." Araki's mustached face adopted a suspicious glare. "But there is still the matter of the Metropolitan Police."

"The Police, sir?"

"Yes, this Inspector Aizawa told me that a geisha was abducted along with Hashizume. Why?"

Swallowing hard, Kanemaru searched for an excuse. Personal revenge was nothing more than selfish individualism, unbefitting an Imperial Army officer. But Chizuru Okamura's angry spirit would haunt him forever should he leave Japan without avenging her.

"Those idiots took her by mistake," Kanemaru offered. "They thought she was his mistress."

Frowning, Araki gave an understanding nod. "After Hashizume and that little actress leave tomorrow morning, dispose of them all. The geisha and those other Red fools." He rummaged through his desk and presented Kanemaru with a passenger ticket. "The *Fuji Maru* sets sail for Manchukuo tomorrow evening. You'll take it to your new assignment in Nekka."

Reviewing the ticket, Kanemaru beamed with admiration. A civilian ship further kept him off the books, omitting an official paper trail from this infamous *Tokumu Kikan* officer to the respectable Army Minister.

"But before you leave, make sure you silence any remaining witnesses."

"Of course, General. May I ask what will happen after the…incident?"

Araki's tone remained calm, but religious zeal gleamed in his eyes. "The Control Faction will be crushed, its sympathizers purged, the civilian government will be eliminated, the *zaibatsu's* assets will be confiscated, and we will achieve complete harmony between ruler and ruled," Araki said, like a Buddhist monk rattling off sutras. "But most importantly, we will march back into Siberia soon, reversing that dishonorable mistake made by weaklings in the Diet. After the…*incident* occurs, it will be apparent that the Russians aided that dishonorable gang of Red assassins. The Japanese people, numbed by frivolous decadence, will finally awake and howl for revenge against the Soviet Union. Of course, all this will be easier to achieve if we have…support from the throne."

An ominous realization crawled into Kanemaru's brain. Was this all some elaborate scheme to avenge Japan's inglorious evacuation of Siberia a decade prior? Well, personal vengeance was shameful, but national vengeance was a matter of honor. But men like General Araki wouldn't understand his predicament. They were too governed by ideology to appreciate the depths a man would sink for the woman he loved. Junzo Kanemaru would avenge his little viper, then fade away into the shadows forever.

CHAPTER FIFTY-FOUR

It was strange to be back in Ginza, given everything that had happened in the past few days. As Aizawa walked down its illuminated streets, the Red Terror Society's escape replayed in his mind's eye. Still, the hypnotic glitter of neon lights soothed his mood, pushing past failures from his thoughts. He hooked a corner and Café Lion appeared across the street. Entering, he was greeted by a chorus of polka music and Minori Miyake's pretty face. Lingering anxieties were banished, at least for the moment.

After exchanging 'good evenings,' a hostess led them out of the lobby. Café Lion was like a layered cake – the first floor held a modern salon, the second floor was the dining hall, and the third was a Renaissance lavatory boasting both Japanese *and* Western toilets. They reached the second story, furnished with wooden chairs and tables and low-hanging light fixtures. On the far wall was a mural of peasants harvesting grain and fruit above a tiled bar. Waitresses in dirndls busied about while a band in lederhosen poured out more polka. The entire atmosphere was a cheap facsimile of a German beer hall, but it still radiated a cosmopolitan allure.

Aizawa and Minori took a seat and ordered Asahi beer, and the dirndled waitress soon returned with two enormous steins.

"Kanpai," Aizawa cheered.

"Or *prost*, as the Germans say," Minori offered. They clinked their steins and drank. Aizawa glanced at the menu, a mishmash of German and Japanese food, but he already knew exactly what he wanted. Café Lion was famous for Western-style beefsteaks, costing only fifty sen. They both ordered the steak, and as the waitress trotted off, Aizawa found himself thumbing his beer stein.

"Something on your mind?" Minori asked.

"Police work…it's nothing," Aizawa said, forcing a smile. Best to change the subject. "Analyzing my gestures? Are you training to become a detective?"

"Oh no, a woman detective? It's a bit like a male geisha, don't you agree?"

The image conjured up Reiko along with a wave of shame.

"But, I must ask you, Inspector…"

"Call me Kenji, please."

"Kenji-san, what is your attitude about a woman working?"

The question bordered on tactless, but what did he expect from a *moga*? Hell, such directness lent Minori an allure reserved for Western women. Still, it required some consideration. Luckily, the waitress soon reappeared with their dinner. They dug in, and after a few bites, Aizawa settled on an answer.

"Well, I have no problem with working women, so long as they're not mothers."

After all, a mother's first duty was in the home, but that shouldn't stop women without children from supporting themselves. Traditionalists declared that women were fit only for marrying and breeding, but Aizawa was a modern Japanese man, in work and in leisure.

"That's wonderful to hear, Kenji-san," Minori cooed, bringing her hands together. "I've actually applied to a few publications. Living at home has been insufferable as of late. I write all the time, in my diary, short stories, so I figure I might as well get paid for it."

"Where?"

"The *Asahi Shimbun*, the *Nichi Nichi*, the *Yomiuri*, *Friend of the Housewife*, though I don't think they're interested in what unmarried women have to say." After sharing a laugh, Minori pulled a book from her bag. "While we are on the subject of detectives and writing…"

Aizawa accepted the book with both hands and examined it – *The Complete Works of Edogawa Ranpo.*

"Oh yes, that mystery novelist."

Minori leaned forward, her smile stretched wide. "It includes all of his Detective Akechi stories. New ones are still being published, so they'll probably release a second volume."

Aizawa flipped through the lurid titles – *Murder on D. Hill*, *Stalker in the Attic*, and *The Dwarf*. "Looks thrilling."

"And educational. Detective Akechi always solves the crime through deductive logic and reasoning."

"Like a Japanese Sherlock Holmes," Aizawa said, then finished the last of his beefsteak.

"Even better! Akechi is a modern detective, whereas Sherlock Holmes still had one foot in the last century." She took another bite of beef before saying, "My father told me that you are quite the Akechi yourself."

"What do you mean?"

"The Okamura Gang's gambling den."

Nostalgia overtook Aizawa for a moment, reminding him of simpler times. It happened in Showa 5 – 1930 – just before some right-wing assassin shot Prime Minister Hamaguchi, kicking off a wave of political violence that still rippled across the country. The Showa Depression had hit Japan's economy hard, hurting even yakuza gambling dens.

"It was nothing really. You see, gambling is illegal, but we tend to look the other way as long as yakuza gangs offer…" he trailed off, unsure of a suitable euphemism for bribery.

"Oh, don't worry, Inspector. I'm not naïve. As the daughter of a police officer, I know there's an ugly side to law enforcement. Let's call them 'donations.'"

Aizawa released a flustered smile. Low-level corruption was dishonorable, but Japanese society needed grease to stay lubricated. Compared to organized crime in other countries, the yakuza and Japanese Police maintained a live and let live attitude. Providing the former didn't engage in outlandish crimes, like opium smuggling or renege on protection payments.

"Well, the Okamura Gang's monthly 'donations' had decreased by half, but none of the other yakuza's had. I wanted to see how bad they were actually hurting, so I kept watch outside their gambling den for about a week, counting the number of gamblers that entered. Then when they exited, I had them picked up, questioned them about how much money they entered with versus how much they won or lost, then calculated the total. The Okamura Gang's real earnings were three times as many."

"Sounds like they got greedy."

"Apparently, the depression spooked Boss Okamura so badly, he decided to hoard everything he could. I convinced my superior, and we raided the den ourselves. We found entire sacks of cash hidden underneath their tatami mats."

"Amazing! Detective Akechi would be proud."

Aizawa smiled again, leaving out the part where the raid had inadvertently created two spiteful enemies in the form of Chizuru Okamura and her lover, Major Kanemaru.

"I wouldn't go that far. It did earn me a promotion and private office, small as it is. Still, it didn't take a lot of skill, just luck."

"You're so modest, Inspector. Just like my big brother! You're a real-life Detective Akechi!"

It hit him then. Her words explained just why a *moga* like Minori Miyake had taken such a fancy to Kenji Aizawa – he was her literary crush in the flesh. A brief sadness tugged at his heart, but it soon vanished. After all, hadn't he used her as a substitute for his own lust? Her waved hair, her Western clothes, and modern attitude were all just a stand-in for Reiko Watanabe. But Minori wasn't just any *moga*, she was educated, from a good family, and most importantly, the daughter of his superior. Far better than anything he could hope for in a wife.

And the same for her. Although such immodest thoughts shamed him, he was probably the best she could manage. Most marriages were still arranged, and Superintendent Miyake would select a potential husband from the

Metropolitan Police, just to keep an eye on them. Compared to sadistic brutes like Hiroshi Tezuka, Aizawa was a cosmopolitan poet.

"Thank you for the book," he said, setting it aside.

"Hopefully, they make a movie out of those stories. They'd beat anything Hollywood has to offer."

The mention of movies offered a tantalizing clue. What was that Utako Natsume picture Reiko had mentioned? That's right, *Modern Girl of Ginza*. Everything about Natsume seemed to be an elaborate performance, as if all of Tokyo was her theater. If her hideout had been in Ginza, then perhaps another film of hers could point to where she was now. And Reiko's treasured collection of *Kinema Junpo* magazines could help.

Aizawa bolted upright and gave a deep bow. "Please forgive me, Minori-san, but I just realized something important to this case." He pulled out a wad of yen bills and placed it on the table, followed by another bow, arms stiff at his sides. Ending a date early and leaving a woman to pay shattered any face he had left. But his *kohai's* life was on the line, face or no face.

Instead of irritation, Minori's face softened. "Like I said, Kenji-san. I'm the daughter of a policeman. Duty comes first."

"Thank you, Minori-san. I promise I'll make it up to you."

She tapped the Ranpo book and said, "How about I bring this over to your place tomorrow evening? Then you can make it up to me. And I can see how well you've treated your bonsai plant."

Flustered, Aizawa gave a final, supplicating bow, then rushed out of Café Lion.

CHAPTER FIFTY-FIVE

Stillness hung throughout Asakusa, as if it were in mourning. The tawdry *izakayas*, tea houses, and theaters were all quiet tonight. *Junsas* had ordered residents to clean every centimeter in preparation for the Emperor's review tomorrow. It didn't matter if he didn't intend to pass through Asakusa, the very idea of His Majesty setting foot in a dirty city was unthinkable.

Aizawa entered Reiko's Western-style apartment building and bounded up the steps to the fourth floor. Right after her kidnapping, he searched the place for any clues but turned up nothing. Those stacks of *Kinema Junpos* hadn't even crossed his mind, but now they were Reiko's only lifeline. Using his spare key, he pushed the door open and drew his Colt automatic. A bit much, but with Major Kanemaru involved, such preparations meant the difference between life and death. Two posters hung on the wall – Anna May Wong in *Piccadilly* and Louise Brooks in *Pandora's Box*. Poor Reiko might never join their ranks if he didn't find a clue in here.

After a thorough search of the apartment proved its emptiness, Aizawa holstered his pistol, sank to his knees, and searched under the bedframe. Piles of *Kinema Junpo* magazines lay in rows organized by year. Since Utako Natsume hadn't had much of a career as of late, Aizawa selected 1927 and 1928. Most issues offered nothing, but the cover of the late April 1927 edition showed a smiling Utako Natsume decked out in *moga* attire. Aizawa thumbed through the magazine until he found a two-page spread for *Modern Girl of Ginza* with various scenes from the film. Utako Natsume dressed as an equestrian – jodhpurs, riding boots, and helmet – along with her as the Japanese It Girl, gallivanting around Ginza with several different love interests.

"America can keep Clara Bow, Japan has Utako Natsume!" a headline proclaimed.

The rest of 1927 had only two other Utako Natsume pictures, also set in Ginza and the most modern areas of Tokyo. Aizawa moved onto the 1928 pile, most of which held nothing, until he found a brief article in the early March issue. Utako Natsume starred in her newest picture titled *Woman of the Streets*, a scandalous tendency film. The accompanying photo showed a different Natsume – poor, destitute, and angry. A brief synopsis listed off the plot – the wife of a dead factory worker being reduced to unlicensed prostitution in the Tamanoi slum.

A long shot, but it was the only clue he had that reduced the scope of his search. If everything was a theatrical performance for Utako Natsume, she might be reprising her most famous roles. Her hideout in Ginza was the opener, and Tamanoi might be the final curtain.

*****

Utako gazed into the parked Ford's side mirror, examining her transformation into a lieutenant of the 2nd Cavalry Regiment. The brown uniform was a snug fit, clinging to Utako's curves. She had done everything she could to obscure any feminine features – binding her breasts, padding the tunic's shoulders, stripping away any makeup, and mustering the deepest voice she could. Still, the saber at her side weighed her down like a shackle, and the boots squeezed her feet like a vise. Thankfully, the peaked service cap's leather visor shadowed half her face. Besides, all she needed was to pass for only a few minutes before…

"You still walk like a woman," Major Kuno said from behind. "This isn't a movie premiere, you know."

"Any suggestions?"

Thrusting back his shoulders, Kuno spun around and, cocking his head up, marched across the *izakaya* with such rigidity, he resembled a machine. But there was still some gracefulness in that mechanical walk. From the way he gripped the saber to prevent it from rattling, to the way his legs thrust out like pistons in perfect harmony. Clutching her sword, Utako squared her shoulders and strode over to him, a flawless imitation.

"It's a start. Keep practicing. But the most important thing is that you can still ride a horse. Make sure your spine is a steel rod the entire time. Cavalrymen only slouch when they're dead."

Utako nodded and resumed her march, back and forth, back and forth. Across the *izakaya*, Genda and Izumi tended to Colonel Hashizume, who'd sobered up after a final binge on Yebisu beer. They provided him with a fresh, starched uniform, tinkling with rows of medals. Snapping on his service cap completed the image of a Japanese war hero. Even Utako felt a brief moment of awe.

His uniform donned, the Colonel joined Major Kuno in scrutinizing Utako.

"She'll never pass," Hashizume growled. "Her features are too soft, like a cherry blossom pretending to be a bed of thorns."

Utako spun around, steeled herself, and fixed them both with the most menacing stare she could summon. The Army officers shared a laugh.

"Perhaps you're right, Colonel," Kuno said. "But luckily, I prepared for such a contingency." He rummaged into his tunic pocket and pulled out a small box containing a white gauze mask, the type used to safeguard against colds. Utako took it and hooked it around her ears, covering the bottom half of her face.

"I once knew a Navy officer who wore one of these for…different reasons," Kuno said.

"Ridiculous," Hashizume muttered. "But it will have to do. Oguchi-san, no Imperial solider is permitted to march past His Majesty wearing a mask. That disguise will throw off suspicion as we enter the parade ground, but you'll have to remove it once we move into the procession."

Underneath the mask, Utako beamed. She would give her finest performance without any inhibitions. Kuno stepped over to Izumi and Genda.

"We're leaving for the Shinjuku stables. You two stay here until I return with new orders." He pointed at the photograph of the Emperor. "Get rid of that."

Grinning, Izumi snatched the photo, held it beneath his lighter, and fired up. Flames quickly consumed His Imperial Majesty, just as they would the entire Japanese Empire.

CHAPTER FIFTY-SIX

A cool mist slunk through the Shinjuku Army Stables, soaking into Major Kanemaru's khaki cape and tunic. Darkness still hung over Tokyo, slumbering in its last peaceful dream, adding to the biting chill. No matter, Nekka would be much colder, so he had better reacclimate himself to such frigid temperatures fast. The frosty air didn't bother Colonel Hashizume, who led the way, stiff and commanding, as if he were still in Manchuria. Utako Natsume trailed behind as a dutiful second lieutenant, trying her best to maintain military posture.

Officers and men of the 2nd Cavalry Regiment busied themselves, saddling and prepping their horses, pausing only to salute their commander. A moon-faced *joto-hei* – superior private – the orderly in charge of supplies, snapped to and presented himself to Hashizume.

"Good morning, Colonel."

"Private, I want you to outfit Second Lieutenant Oguchi," he nodded in Natsume's direction, "with the horse donated by the Asakusa Geisha Guild."

"Second Lieutenant Oguchi?"

"He's a last-minute transfer to our regiment."

The superior private examined Natsume in her costume – from her spurred boots and peaked service cap tucked tight on her head, she looked the part of an Army officer. Her stylish bob has been shorn clean off and a white gauze mask obscured any telltale womanly features, but last-minute transfers before such an important review were rare. Still, orders from officers were not up for scrutiny from callow superior privates. It was this unhesitating obedience from subordinates that made the Imperial Army unstoppable.

After a quick salute, the private shot off to a nearby stable. Several minutes passed before he led out a strutting brown thoroughbred, saddled and parade ready. Natsume stepped forward and mounted the horse with minimal difficulty. If the orderly had doubts, his round face hid them.

"Take him out for a ride, Lieutenant," Hashizume said, "just to get a feel."

Natsume walked the animal out into the stable grounds, then broke into a steady trot. It was an awkward sight at first, with her dainty body bouncing up and down, but within moments, she steeled herself into a rigid poise, as if she actually were a cavalryman.

"Well, at least she can ride," Hashizume muttered under his breath.

"And she can shoot," Kanemaru said, once the orderly was out of earshot.

"Hopefully, the Imperial Guard are good shots also. I want my end to be quick. Or else," he jangled the saber at his side, "I'll have to perform a poor man's *seppuku* right on the spot."

As long as they both died, that was the important thing. It was going to be a busy day for Junzo Kanemaru, since he'd have to double back to the *izakaya* and dispose of those two fools, then prepare for a final reckoning with Aizawa.

"What will you do, Major Kuno?"

"Surrender myself to the *Kempeitai*."

"You would bear the shame of a trial?"

"Someone has to argue our motives. Otherwise, Japan will never understand."

An admiring warmth melted Hashizume's glacial expression. "Please Major…tell the court why I did what I did. I bear the Emperor no malice, but my honor forced me. For my son…for Pingdingshan…for the nation's future." The Colonel swallowed his sorrow, then said, "A man's life, any man, is worth nothing when compared to his honor. Please stay alive long enough to tell Japan that."

Across the stable grounds, Natsume slowed the horse back into a casual walk, still erect as steel. Up above, a splotch of dawn poked through the darkness and lit the sky.

"Yes, Colonel," Kanemaru said. "If there's one thing I am, it's a survivor."

*****

Stifling a yawn, Aizawa took another sip of coffee and scanned through the next round of building records for Tamanoi. Most were obvious dead ends, but he'd earmarked a few possible leads to call when the real estate companies opened for work. Thanks to the Showa Depression, the neighborhood had become blemished with abandoned structures and squatters. An unthinkable crime because of the shame it carried, squatting had become commonplace in recent years. Rubbing bleary eyes, Aizawa looked up and out his office window. The morning sun streaked between the structures of Kasumigaseki, another day that Reiko Watanabe had to wait for rescue, assuming she was still alive.

He checked his wristwatch – 0800. Japanese businesses were punctual right down to the second, and Aizawa began ringing up the list of property owners. Most provided meticulous notes about whether or not their properties had any new tenants, along with names, dates, and descriptions. None matched Major Kanemaru or the Red Terror Society. But one shuttered *izakaya* offered a tantalizing lead.

"Yes, that was rented a few days ago," the real estate officer said over the line.

"By whom?"

"A…uhhh…" the rustling of papers was audible "…a Taro Sato…"

Aizawa gripped the receiver. Taro Sato was an almost *too* common name. It also echoed a familiar face, the young peasant girl, Yuki Sato, who he'd freed from the Okamura Gang's brothel. Maybe it was Kanemaru's sick joke?

"Can you describe this 'Taro Sato?'"

"Please hold." The line went silent for several minutes, until finally, "I spoke to the representative. He can't remember much about the tenant, but he did mention an Osakan accent. Kept saying 'han' instead of 'san.'"

Aizawa jumped to his feet. "An Osakan accent? That's very helpful, thank you." He hung up and tore out of his office. Police Headquarters was abuzz with activity, and the First Investigative Division was its epicenter. Apart from the usual vagrants and riff-raff, last night's dragnet had netted a few possible political troublemakers. A surly detective questioned a university student at his desk. Fear had drained any color from the student's face but Aizawa recognized him as one of the dilettantes at Mon Ami from the other day.

The door was open at Superintendent Miyake's office, crammed wall to wall with a squad of *junsas*, led by Sergeant Daisuke Fujita. The Superintendent stood at his desk, a commander addressing his troops before battle.

"The Emperor's entourage will exit the Imperial Palace from Sakurada Gate, precisely at 0900 hours, and then proceed west along *Uchibori Dori.* Hundreds of *junsas* will guard the route, and a platoon of *kempei* is stationed around the Sakurada Gate. For added security, you all will accompany them. Any suspicious person must be arrested immediately. A repeat of what happened last year will stain our organization with such shame, it'll carry over to your grandchildren. Understand?"

"*Hai*!" was the thunderous reply.

"The Army review will take place between 1000 and 1200, after which, His Majesty will be driven back to the Palace. Remember, the honor of the Metropolitan Police Department is on the line!"

With a nod, Miyake dismissed Sergeant Fujita's squad. They began filing out, faces tight and steadfast beneath their peaked caps. Fujita offered Aizawa a respectful salute, before leading his squad down the hallway to the elevator. Stepping inside the deflated office, Aizawa presented his superior with a bow.

"Yes, Inspector?"

"Sir, I've discovered the hideout for the Red Terror Society."

"Is that so?"

"It's at an abandoned *izakaya* in Tamanoi."

"At least the rats are staying in the sewer this time. Very well. As soon as the Emperor's excursion is complete, I'll send Sergeant Fujita's squad to accompany you on a raid."

"But sir, they're holding Reiko Watanabe and Colonel Hashizume hostage."

"General Araki telephoned me, saying the Colonel was picked up by the *Kempeitai* and is quite safe."

"Sir…" A deep-seated resentment loosened Aizawa's tongue. "Did you believe him?"

"Not particularly, but I don't wish to cross swords with the Imperial Army. As for your little geisha, how do you know she's still alive?"

The possibility of his *kohai's* death wrapped Aizawa's stomach into knots. Still, any doubt might lose face, and Miyake was skeptical enough when it came to Reiko. Better to use shame to his advantage.

"Sir, the assassins of both Marquis Maeda and Inspector Tezuka are within our grasp! The longer we wait, the risk grows that they could slip into the alleyways of Tokyo again."

Miyake's sharp face tensed, a man weighing his options.

"Sir, think of the loss of face the Metropolitan Police might suffer should those Red gangsters, the murderers of a Tokko inspector, evade us yet again?"

The bombardment was working, but Miyake remained hesitant. "I cannot pull Sergeant Fujita's squad from their posting. The Emperor's safety is more important, Inspector. You, me, and your geisha spy, exist as tools to serve him."

Spoken like a good citizen, but in that loyalty lay an opportunity to exploit.

"Sir, Major Kanemaru, the same man from the Okamura Gang Incident, is controlling the Red Terror Society."

Miyake's silver eyebrows jumped.

"I'm not sure what, but I suspect they are plotting some unspeakable act against the Imperial Throne."

Nodding along, Miyake said, "Perhaps you're right, Inspector. We shouldn't wait."

"Thank you, sir. Will you recall some of Sergeant Fujita's men for backup?"

"No," Miyake said, puffing up. "I will be your backup, Inspector. Let's go."

CHAPTER FIFTY-SEVEN

Swarms of soldiers were fed into the Yoyogi Parade Ground, halted only briefly at a few chokepoints for inspections. Armed Imperial Guardsmen patrolled the perimeter, while their officers paused each unit, inspected the commanders, and let them pass after a few minutes. But officers unattached to units, like Major Kanemaru, entered through a different post with far more scrutiny.

"Papers, please," a young second lieutenant demanded.

Kanemaru presented his forged credentials, but for added emphasis, he said, "Major Kuno. Staff officer attached to Army Minister Araki."

Yellow aiguillettes looped around on Kanemaru's left shoulder and chest were sufficient proof of his status as a staff officer, but the mention of General Araki was more persuasive. Convinced, the Lieutenant waved Kanemaru through. The rest of Yoyogi opened up, showing off the full glory of the Imperial Japanese Army.

Across the field, rows of tanks, tankettes, and armored cars trundled into formation, the mechanical vanguard of the Japanese Empire. Nearby were heavy and light artillery guns, pulled along by rumbling tractors. But filling out the parade ground were columns of soldiers, stiff at attention, rifles and bayonets gleaming in the morning sunlight. The expanse of brown uniforms resembled a vast, muddy sea. Here were the conquerors of Manchuria in all their power, and soon, they would march again to glory in Nekka.

But even in the enormous crowd, the 2nd Cavalry Regiment was still visible, as were Colonel Hashizume and Utako Natsume atop their horses. From this distance, the little actress passed for a real soldier. Nearby, an infantry captain stood at the front of his company, an unsheathed saber glued into his white-gloved hand. His face was bland

and impassive, but underneath his peaked cap and behind those round glasses, Kanemaru recognized Captain Chichibu.

A glint of sunlight flashed against the Crown Prince's glasses as he turned toward Kanemaru and sank a brief, but lasting glare into him. Within seconds he resumed his rigid, aloof gaze toward the open field, but Chichibu's stare filled Kanemaru with strange questions. How much did the Crown Prince suspect? Would he actually agree to a war with Soviet Russia? Or had this dark plot been birthed from his brain all along? A breeze of crisp wind swept over the parade ground, chilling Kanemaru to the bone. It didn't matter. History would be made here, and like that fateful night on September 18th, 1931, Junzo Kanemaru had helped bring it about.

*****

As Aizawa pulled the Datsun out of the motor pool and onto the street, strange memories engulfed him. He was pulled back to Siberia, driving supply trucks for the Army. But only in Vladivostok where there was some semblance of civilization and paved roads. Along Siberia's many dirt trails, supplies had to be carried by man and horse, through endless dark forests where Bolshevik partisans lurked. The same dread lingered now, refusing to lift.

"We should head north," Superintendent Miyake said, sitting in the passenger seat. "It's the shortest route to Tamanoi."

True, but that also passed by Sakurada Gate at such an inopportune time. Aizawa checked his wristwatch – five till nine. Maybe he could make it before the Emperor exited. He pressed the Datsun northward and found huge throngs of citizens wearing their best suits and kimonos, Rising Sun flags fluttering in their hands. *Kempei* and *junsas* lined the streets, but the crowd controlled themselves for the most part.

Aizawa began turning right on *Uchibori Dori* but braked when, across the street, the Imperial Guard sentries rose their rifles in salute. A sedan shot out from the Palace grounds, followed by a motorcycle sidecar, manned by Imperial Guard officers. A few moments passed before another sedan, this one maroon-colored, drove out of Sakurada Gate, turning west on *Uchibori Dori*.

Although the windows were tinted, there was no mistaking the Emperor's official car. No other automobile in the entire Japanese Empire could be maroon-colored, just as no other Japanese could ride a white horse. Small details that every citizen knew and accepted. As if hypnotized, the throngs began bowing to His Majesty in unison. Aizawa cut the engine and stepped out of the Datsun along with Miyake.

They removed their hats and offered deep, solemn bows as the Emperor's entourage rumbled by. Moments passed before Aizawa felt clear-headed enough to duck back inside and start the engine again. The Datsun jerked forward, but a squad of *kempei* blocked their way. But within moments, Sergeant Fujita drew himself near and peered inside, recognizing both Aizawa and Miyake. Fujita had a few words with his Army counterpart and the *kempei* soon parted, allowing Aizawa to launch forth.

Pressing the gas, Aizawa begged Reiko to hang on for just a little longer.

*****

Reiko mumbled into her gag, but it remained locked in place. No matter, anything to work her jaw and fight off atrophy. When she got out of here, she'd talk nonstop for a week. If she got out of here, that is. She might just die of hunger, since Genda hadn't been down with her daily miso soup this morning. At least she thought it was morning. Traces of light seeped through the cellar door, but almost all conversation was effectively silenced.

Not that she needed to hear what the Red Terror Society was planning. That photograph of the Emperor said enough – assassination. But what was the Emperor to her? Colonel Hashizume's woes had made it clear that the ruler of the Japanese Empire was a weakling, intimidated by the militarists who stormed into Manchuria like a pack of ravenous dogs. All it would take was one command for the Son of Heaven, and the Imperial Army would be duty-bound to obey.

But the thought of someone assassinating the Emperor of Japan was so disgraceful, she almost wretched into her gag. An attack on him was an attack on the nation and every man, woman, and child. Maybe under her *moga* shell, beat the heart of a traditional Japanese maiden.

A loud, yet still muffled, pop exploded overhead. Reiko glanced up and the bursts continued in a steady cadence. Gunshots! There was no way the Reds would risk attracting that kind of attention, so it must be coming from outside! Reiko wiggled against the lashing ropes, but nothing loosened. She'd have cried, if she weren't so infuriated.

Just then, the cellar door creaked open and Genda's large head stooped over her. Above, she heard Izumi's voice, harsh and cruel.

"Get her out of there, Genda! We're going to need a shield to beat back the Emperor's wolves!"

CHAPTER FIFTY-EIGHT

The Datsun coasted through the run-down streets of Tamanoi, pockmarked with shuttered businesses and derelict homes. Tamanoi had always been an unsightly slum, but the depression had plunged the neighborhood into even lower depths of squalor. On normal days, the streets would be clogged with petty merchants, freelance laborers, pickpockets, and beggars, a rare sight in Japan due to the shame it carried. But today Tamanoi was deserted, thanks to a Police order for its residents to stay inside during the Emperor's visit. Wealthier neighborhoods could turn out and greet His Majesty, but for the slums, seclusion was the only honorable choice.

The abandoned *izakaya* spread out before them, dark and gloomy. Aizawa slowed the Datsun to a crawl and scanned for any hint of activity. He turned the corner, leading to a narrow alleyway running along the back. Two entrances, two potential avenues of escape for the Red Terror Society. Aizawa threw the car into reverse, backtracking toward the *izakaya's* front.

"Both entrances need to be covered," Miyake said. "I'll try and bluff them out, while you sneak through the alley."

There was an implicit understanding that Miyake would draw their fire, since superiors were expected to put themselves at risk before subordinates. However, the subordinate was expected to volunteer, going through the motions before finally relenting to the superior's wise advice. Maybe under normal circumstances, but time wasn't on their side. Instead, Aizawa nodded and cut the engine.

"Give me three minutes," he said, before hopping out. Miyake drew his pistol and took a defensive position behind the Datsun as Aizawa doubled back to the alleyway. Whipping out his Colt automatic, he gave thanks that no civilians were around to be consumed in the upcoming firefight. Creeping deeper into the alleyway, he reached the back of the *izakaya*, and crouched behind the sliding door, his muscles taut, his throat tight, and his gun locked.

"Attention, this is the Metropolitan Police," Miyake's sharp voice cut through the crisp morning air. "You are completely surrounded. Come out with your hands up."

Silence, followed by a frantic rustling mingled with stomping feet inside the *izakaya.* Then, an eruption of gunfire answered back. No time to waste now. Aizawa sprang up, ripped open the *shoji* door, and pointed his automatic into the murky darkness. To his immediate left was that supercharged Ford, dinged and battered, but still drivable. Across the *izakaya*, two figures pumped shots through the front door, blasting chunks through the wooden frame. Morning sunlight poured in through the bullet holes, illuminating the backsides of Saburo Genda and Wataru Izumi. Strangely, the rest of the structure appeared to be empty.

Aizawa took aim and snapped off a shot, exploding Genda's shoulder in a bloody burst. Gasping, the giant fell to his knees, but Izumi whirled around, an automatic in one hand and – more alarming – a bound and gagged Reiko in the other, effectively shielding him. Unable to draw a bead, Aizawa crouched down as Izumi blazed away, the dark *izakaya* brightened by flaming spurts.

Worse still, Genda renewed his volley, blood still oozing from his mangled shoulder. Aizawa searched for a shot, but Reiko's fearful face blocked any attempt. Instead, he rolled out the back exit, hopped to his feet, and began backtracking out of the alleyway, covering the gaping doorway with the Colt automatic. He whipped his head from side to side, just in case he was walking into an ambush. Instead, a group of goggle-eyed civilians gawked out a nearby *nagaya* row house. Even for Tamanoi, this was a strange sight.

"Police! Go back inside!" Aizawa barked.

A strange, detached stare was their immediate answer. Tamanoi was more rebellious than the rest of Tokyo, its people had less to lose. But there was one type of police officer that all Japanese – rich or poor – feared.

"This is a Tokko investigation," Aizawa said. "If you don't go inside now, you'll all be charged with thought crimes!"

The threat carried enough weight, and the shabby onlookers disappeared back inside the *nagaya*. For a moment, Aizawa felt the spirit of Inspector Tezuka pass through him, but he dismissed such fantasies. What disturbed him more was how easy the Japanese people could be cowed into obedience, and the dark temptation it offered any policeman, Tokko or not.

Crashing gunfire brought Aizawa back to the present. There were more pressing matters to deal with. The Reds were shooting back at Miyake, hopefully safe behind the Datsun. There was little else he could do but try to storm the *izakaya* again. But in that strategy, Reiko would be the first casualty. He thought back to previous standoffs and settled on that cold day back in December 1931. Lieutenant Nakajima had rigged the Marunouchi Building to explode, and it was shame, not force, that had drawn him out. Perhaps the same tactic could achieve victory here. What was it that Reiko had said? Ah yes, for some reason, she reminded Saburo Genda of his little sister.

Gunshots continued blasting as Aizawa crept closer, his Colt locked in place. Drawing close to the back door, he called out, "Izumi! Genda! You have no escape!"

A hateful snarl came from Izumi, then, "Neither does your little whore! Toss us your gun or I'll plaster the walls with her brains!"

"What kind of men torment a defenseless woman? Genda-san, what if your little sister could see you now?"

The firing stopped, followed by a stifling silence, punctured by labored gasps. Somehow, that sturdy ox was still alive. With any luck, he would be Reiko's salvation.

CHAPTER FIFTY-NINE

Reiko squirmed against Izumi's grip as he dragged her toward the parked Ford. Genda lumbered beside them, his pistol hanging limply beside him and clutching his gory shoulder, panting deep gasps. Despite his agony, he fixed her with a worried, sympathetic look. Outside, Aizawa's taunts continued.

"You still have a choice, Genda! Surrender like a man or die behind a woman, like a coward!"

"Perhaps he's right," Genda blubbered out, "we can't escape. They have the place surrounded."

Izumi spun around and hissed, "They're bluffing, you fool! It's just the two of them!"

The realization didn't diminish Genda's concern. Worry furrowed his brow as color continued draining from his skin. At this rate, he'd pass out from lack of blood. But Aizawa had the right idea. Anything to prey on this brute's sentimentality. Reiko widened her eyes and mumbled into her gag. From outside came another round of mockery from Aizawa.

"Genda-san! Your little sister begged us to take you alive! What will you tell her when she learns that you murdered an innocent woman? Think of the shame it'll cause her!"

Turmoil pulled at Genda as his eyes darted between the open back door and Reiko's bound figure.

"No spy is innocent," Izumi said. "Don't you remember what happened the last time we released her?"

Genda shook his huge head. "She's still a woman."

"Idiot! We're wasting precious time to escape. Get in the car and we can outrun these two wolves."

"Only if you leave her here."

"I'm not giving up my bulletproof vest just yet." Izumi swung Reiko around to the car and stuffed her into the backseat, where she wiggled like a giant caterpillar. Izumi watched her with a sadistic chuckle, not noticing Genda's enormous frame looming over him. Genda removed his beefy hand from the bloodied shoulder, gripped Izumi, and spun him around. A blinding flash burst out from Izumi's revolver, sending Genda writhing to the floor.

"Sorry Genda-san, but in the game of *go*, some pieces are meant to be sacrificed."

Izumi released another cruel snicker, then hopped into the driver's seat and revved the engine. Throwing the car into gear, he began turning toward the front exit just as Genda's bulky frame leaped forward, hitting the hood with a wet slap. Blood oozed everywhere as the giant clawed at the front window, like a vengeful ghost. Reiko screamed into her gag and Izumi slammed the accelerator, sucking Genda's brutalized body underneath the car. Two nauseating crunches reverberated throughout its interior, along with a strangled death rattle.

Gaining speed, the Ford smashed through the wooden door and skidded out into the street, narrowly missing a police car parked outside. A grizzled officer stared back, his pistol locked. Although Reiko had never seen Superintendent Miyake in person, he looked as how Aizawa had always described him – a taut face atop a scrawny frame, stuffed into a gaudy uniform. No doubt he recognized her also – even bound and gagged – and held his fire.

Izumi swung around and rocketed down the street, unencumbered by any more obstacles.

"*Yatta*!" he cried, "I did it! Thanks to you, my dear…" Izumi looked back with a taunting grin. "We'll need a place to hide out until the Revolution begins. Any suggestions?"

Reiko mumbled a barrage of insults, amusing him further. He turned back, and swung around a corner, down another street lined with shuttered businesses and telephone booths. Aizawa could never catch up now. There was only one way to stop him. Reiko rolled onto the car floor, lifted her legs up and, summoning every ounce of strength, she reached back and kicked Izumi's side.

The steering wheel jerked out of his hands. In his profile, Reiko could see terror contort Izumi's plump face. The car shook and wobbled, spinning completely out of control. Looking up, a telephone booth rushed toward them until an explosion of glittering glass filled the car's interior, followed by a violent, convulsing jerk.

*****

Screeching tires drew Aizawa out from his hiding spot and he pounded down the alleyway. Turning into the *izakaya*, he swept the room with his Colt, but only found the grisly remains of Saburo Genda. Wet, sticky blood still flooded from the man's shoulder and now from his torso. Worse was his head, now resembling an exploded melon. Tire tracks caked with gore led out to an enormous hole that punctured the *izakaya's* front entrance. Apparently, there was no loyalty among thieves *or* Communists.

Aizawa stepped through the front hole and back onto the main street. Superintendent Miyake was already behind the Datsun's wheel and flung open the passenger door.

"Get in! We can still catch them!"

Such confidence was doubtful, but who was he to argue with a superior's order? Aizawa hopped inside and the Datsun surged forward. There was little hope now, especially after seeing what that supercharged engine was capable of, but they had to try. He owed his *kohai* that much. As Miyake hugged a corner, squealing brakes rang out, followed by a grinding crash. A few blocks up ahead, the Ford lay smashed into a telephone pole, which had toppled over and flattened half the vehicle's frame. No, she couldn't be dead! Not after all this! His *kohai*, his *moga*, his friend, his…his…

The Datsun rolled up beside the pulverized Ford, its hood scrunched up like an accordion. Aizawa hopped out and peered inside. Wataru Izumi was visible, his head twisted around the steering wheel in a grotesque embrace. Through cracked glasses, he gazed back, but threads of blood dribbled from his nostrils and an agape mouth. Shards of silvery glass had gouged his chubby cheeks, forehead, and throat, like a thousand jagged knives. A fitting end for this Red gangster.

A muffled groan jerked Aizawa's attention to the backseat. Reiko stirred on the floor, her eyelids fluttering. He yanked open the back door and heaved her dainty frame out. After checking her pulse, he laid her gently on the ground, tore away the gag, and cradled her in his arms. Unable to speak, he sat there, stroking her beautiful bobbed hair, begging the gods for a final word with her. A crowd of onlookers had manifested, drawn out by the crash. Superintendent Miyake stood by, transfixed by the scene. Tears misted Aizawa's eyes, but thankfully, after a few torturous moments, Reiko opened hers.

"Inspector…"

"Yes, Reiko-san. You're all right."

Her eyes dimmed but she remained lucid. "The Emperor…you have to stop them."

"What do you mean?"

"The Emperor…they're going to assassinate…the Emperor…"

Of course! That's where Natsume and Kanemaru must be now! Aizawa checked his wristwatch. 0940. The Army review was scheduled to go on until 1100 hours, but time was still not on his side. The Yoyogi Parade Ground was on the other side of the city, but given the lockdown orders, traffic wouldn't be a problem for once.

"Thank you, Reiko-san…for everything." He flashed a reassuring smile, before hoisting her up into Miyake's arms.

"Sir, please take Watanabe-san back to Headquarters for a full examination. I'll catch a taxicab over to the Yoyogi Parade Ground and—"

"Nonsense!" Miyake roared. "You heard what she said! The Emperor is in danger! Take the Datsun and go!"

Aizawa nodded, saluted, and jumped back behind the steering wheel. The onlooking crowd parted to the sides, allowing him to drive forth unimpeded. But before he took off, he caught a wistful smile from Reiko, imparting him with all the confidence he needed for the battle ahead.

CHAPTER SIXTY

The horse stirred underneath Utako, its anxiety contagious. Added to that was a brass band's steady drone of the "Imperial Army March," martial and foreboding. They were far away from the reviewing stand, but she could make out the Emperor sitting atop his elegant steed – *Shirayuki* – White Snow. No other horse in the entire Japanese Empire could be white, lest they offend His Majesty, but *Shirayuki* was an impressive beast. Much more so than the Emperor himself, a bland, bookish little man with a thin mustache and thinner spectacles. Even the brown service uniform of an Army general hanging off his skinny frame didn't lend him much authority.

And this puny runt was supposed to be descended from Amaterasu, the sun goddess? What a farce! Utako remembered seeing a *kabuki* performance as a child, transfixed by an actress's stunning beauty. Then, after the play, seeing the woman's makeup stripped away to reveal a middle-aged man, shook little Utako Natsume to her very core. The same feeling engulfed her once again.

Off to the Emperor's side, his entourage sat mounted atop their own steeds, a veritable who's who of the Imperial Army. Grim-faced generals reviewed the parade, saluting a formation of tanks rumbling by. Imperial Guardsmen maintained a wide perimeter but kept their Arisaka rifles at the ready. A mounted officer bearing the Imperial standard – a flag with the golden Chrysanthemum insignia – sat next to another general, his mustached face strangely familiar.

Ah yes, Lieutenant-General Sadao Araki, the Army Minister. The worst of the militarist warmongers, he'd been agitating war against the Soviet Union for months now. Hopefully, he'd be the first to die in the Red Terror that would sweep Japan of any Imperial vestiges. But how many of these other officers were sympathizers like Major Kuno? The Russian Army had been riddled with Communists before their revolution. Entire divisions of the Chinese Nationalist Army had defected to the Kiangsi Soviet Republic. Japan's time had come.

A few feet from Utako, Colonel Hashizume sat rigid atop his own horse, stern and inscrutable. What a fine ally he would have made if only they'd had a little more time to convert him! But for now, he would serve his purpose in blissful ignorance. Glancing behind her, the troopers of the 2nd Cavalry Regiment stared forward, their ashen faces evidence of harsh campaigning in Manchuria. Surely these men would realize they'd been used as cannon fodder for bloodthirsty imperialists and *zaibatsu* capitalists!

But she would never truly know, since a volley from those Arisaka rifles would slice through her. No matter, at least she would die knowing that Ichiro Hayashi's death had been repaid. And that she – in her greatest performance – had slain the Japanese Empire.

*****

Aizawa pushed the thumping Datsun to its limit as it sped through the near-empty streets of Tokyo. The drab slums of Tamanoi bled into the working-class Honjo Ward, then into Asakusa, bursting with color and frivolity despite its emptiness, then, turning south, into the steel and brick financial towers of Marunouchi. The Imperial Palace loomed on his right, a reminder of what was at stake. Japan would be thrown into such turmoil, that even the entire Metropolitan Police Department might not be able to handle the disorder. What's more, the only suitable response for allowing the assassination of the Emperor would be ritual suicide, just to save what little face remained.

Aizawa swerved the Datsun westward, shooting through Kasumigaseki and Nagatacho and past Sakurada Gate, still thronged with *junsas* and *kempei*. He pressed the accelerator down to the floor and soon, Yamanote, the western 'High City' spread out before him. Speeding through the affluent Akasaka Ward, grandiose *yashiki* manors and Western-style buildings whooshed by in a spectacular blur. Minutes ticked by, but mercifully, the Meiji Shrine appeared in the distance, the northern tip of the Yoyogi Parade Ground.

Swinging the car south, Aizawa cruised along Yoyogi's perimeter, patrolled by squads of Imperial Guardsmen. Added to the security were certain chokepoints, manned by officers and sentries armed to the teeth. With any luck, they had already unmasked Utako Natsume but it was doubtful. A general calmness permeated the area, suggesting that any assassination hadn't happened just yet.

After parking the Datsun, Aizawa rushed toward the sentry station, his black overcoat flapping behind him. Two Imperial Guardsmen swung their rifles forward, not aimed directly at Aizawa but well within range in case of any trouble. A second lieutenant with familiar features stood between them.

"Lieutenant Endo?" Aizawa asked, drawing closer.

Endo confirmed with a nod, then held out a hand. "Your credentials, please."

"It's me, Inspector Aizawa, from the other night at Sakurada Gate. When Marquis Maeda was murdered."

The refresher had little impact on Lieutenant Endo, who held him in a cold stare.

"I must see your credentials, Inspector, to ensure you are permitted to attend the parade."

"There's no time for that. The Emperor's in danger!"

A hint of surprise crept across Endo. "The Emperor?"

"Yes, a woman named Utako Natsume has infiltrated the parade. She's going to assassinate him!"

"A woman?" Endo scoffed. "I'm quite certain we would remember a woman, Inspector."

"She's wearing an Army uniform. I'm certain she's with the Hashizume Regiment. Send someone to check!"

Creeping doubt flickered on Endo's face, settling there for several moments. He excused himself, then turned and disappeared into the parade ground. The two Imperial Guardsmen lowered their rifles slightly but maintained an intimidating posture. Masking his fear, Aizawa glanced at his wristwatch, half-expecting the crack of gunshots to ring out. Twenty minutes after ten. How could he face his ancestors knowing he had allowed the most monstrous of crimes to happen?

Ever since that day inside Isamu Takano's office, Kenji Aizawa wrestled with the Emperor's true identity. Was he a god or a mere mortal? In the end, it didn't matter. His Majesty was the symbol of Japan, the nation he loved and the land he had sworn to protect.

Lieutenant Endo reappeared, trailed by another Army officer. Their uniforms were almost identical – dark brown tunics, and peaked caps with crimson bands, ornamented with wreathed stars, the insignia of the Imperial Guard, but Aizawa recognized the second face as well – First Lieutenant Eisaku Miyake.

"Ah, Inspector Aizawa," Eisaku said. "Second Lieutenant Endo says you have some troubling news."

"Yes, the Emperor is in danger. There's an assassin in the Hashizume Regiment."

Eisaku's eyes goggled. "My old unit?"

"Yes, we must act now. There's not a second to lose!"

Glancing over to Endo, then to the two Guardsmen, Eisaku seemed to consider his predicament. In general, Japanese rarely troubled their superiors, but even the hint of assassination escalated up the chain of command quickly. However, if the entire plot was bogus, Eisaku would undoubtedly lose face in front of his subordinates, perhaps even being officially reprimanded.

After a few moments of weighing his options, a stern fortitude possessed Eisaku Miyake.

"It's all right, Lieutenant Endo. Inspector Aizawa serves under my father. I will vouch for his character."

Endo nodded and the two Guardsmen shouldered their rifles, allowing Aizawa to pass. Eisaku led the way, Aizawa quickening his pace into a full-blown sprint.

CHAPTER SIXTY-ONE

Aizawa followed Eisaku Miyake into the Yoyogi Parade Ground, his eyes questing about for Utako Natsume, Kanemaru, Hashizume, or anything remotely suspicious. Civilian spectators lined the perimeter, decked out in elegant kimonos and three-piece Western suits. Their taxes helped pay for all this, so why shouldn't they get to watch? Aizawa focused on the marching troops, where the assassin would likely be. The endless columns of brown uniformed soldiers were overwhelming, as if he were drowning in a bottomless pit of mud. Nearby, a stand contained dozens of foreign military attachés, their colorful tunics and caps clashing with the drab brown of the Japanese Army. Next to them, the Imperial entourage sat mounted on ceremonial steeds, but front and center, riding atop *Shirayuki*, was the Emperor of Japan.

An urge to bow, inculcated over years of education, almost overwhelmed Aizawa, but he fought it off and kept searching the parade ground. Streams of soldiers marched by, not on horseback thankfully, meaning they still had time.

"The Hashizume Regiment is scheduled toward the end of the parade," Eisaku said, gesturing Aizawa to follow. Was being placed toward the back punishment for all those haikus Colonel Hashizume had written? And, more importantly, had he lost so much face that he was actually willing to commit treason?

They moved through the grounds, weaving around the units of soldiers at attention. A few dirty glares trailed them, but the presence of an Imperial Guard officer silenced any protests. They pressed on, toward the back of the enormous, snake-like column, mostly foot soldiers at first but giving way to mounted cavalry troopers. Aizawa glanced at their green collar patches, but none bore a brass "2" numeral insignia.

The procession continued lurching forward, feeding the never-ending parade. Aizawa and Eisaku paused and scanned the ranks. A new unit appeared in the near distance, led by a stoic officer, silhouetted by the rising sun. Aizawa couldn't discern any distinguishing features, but it didn't matter. The officer riding next to him wore a white gauze mask and a lieutenant's uniform, but they couldn't hide the eyes of Utako Natsume.

*****

Utako gripped the horse's reins, twisting them to hide her anxiety. Within minutes, she would pass by the Emperor and secure her place in history. The Nambu pistol lay holstered at her side, but if the shot missed, she could always draw her saber and hack His Majesty to pieces. Overhead, a squadron of biplanes buzzed by, demonstrating the power of the Army Air Force. How many Chinese workers had her countrymen murdered when they dropped bombs on Chinchow and Shanghai? Soon, the Emperor would pay for all their crimes.

Up ahead, the 3rd Infantry Regiment marched past their supreme commander, but one officer in particular caught Utako's attention. Crown Prince Chichibu led a company of men, his sword drawn in salute to his older brother. An urge to open fire welled inside her, to rid Japan of these two Imperial parasites. But reason prevailed. The Emperor would be enough. Then Major Kuno and his comrades would take care of the rest.

Nearby activity demanded her immediate attention. Was it their turn? No, Colonel Hashizume and his horse remained motionless, but an Imperial Guard officer and civilian approached with rapid steps. The black fedora and overcoat were enough identification – Inspector Aizawa! How did he know?

It was all over now. But they'd never take her back to prison, she'd swallow the Nambu first. Utako drew the pistol, but a daringness overtook her. She hadn't come this far just to give up. It was a long shot, but so long as the horse dashed forward, the Emperor would be within her line of fire in seconds. Better still, Aizawa would be trampled underfoot. Pulling the reins, she moved the horse out of formation, trotting past Hashizume.

"Where are you going?" he demanded.

Utako ripped off her mask and growled back, "To start the Japanese Revolution."

A horrified realization warped the Colonel's iron features, finally understanding his role as a puppet. He'd served his purpose well, but now it was time to cut the strings. Utako spurred the horse's sides, and the beast broke into a fast-paced trot, straight toward Inspector Aizawa. She bit her lip and prayed for Ichiro Hayashi – wherever his spirit lay – to guide her bullet.

*****

Natsume's steed rushed forth, faster and faster. Aizawa needed to act fast, but what would stop a stampeding horse? On instinct, he reached for his shoulder holster, whipped out his Colt automatic, but a shooting pain exploded through his old shoulder wound. No, not now! His aim distorted, there was only one course of action. He might not be able to hit Natsume, but he could startle the horse, buying him some time. Arm throbbing, Aizawa jerked the pistol up and fired into the air. The terrified beast bucked and whinnied, drawing back and kicking its front legs up. Atop the saddle, Natsume tried to remain mounted, but one hand angled for a clear shot, sending her wobbling back and forth.

Aizawa lashed out and caught the horse's reins, pulling the startled animal back down hard. The jerking movement whipped Utako Natsume loose from her stirrups, sliding her backward. She sank a glare – full of hate, anger, and melancholy – deep into Aizawa, just as she toppled off the saddle, hitting the ground headfirst with a sickening snap.

Aizawa steadied the horse as it stirred back and forth, calming it with gentle pats. He glanced over to Natsume, a twisted heap crumpled beside the beast's hooves. No inspection was necessary. Her vacuous stare into nothingness, coupled with her contorted neck, was enough indication that Utako Natsume was dead. Whether it was from a shattered skull or a broken neck, the only thing that mattered was that the Emperor was safe.

Lieutenant Eisaku Miyake drew beside him, stooping over Natsume's corpse. A squad of soldiers surrounded them, rifles at the ready, alarmed by a gunshot in presence of His Majesty. But Eisaku shook his head, quickly placating them. These were enlisted men, after all, unwilling to act without strict orders. Two other Imperial Guards helped Eisaku drag Natsume's body off the Yoyogi Parade Ground, like litter fit for the dust bin. A few feet away, the 2nd Cavalry Regiment approached, confusion palpable in its ranks. Just in case the conspiracy was even wider than just Natsume, Aizawa handed the horse's reins to Eisaku and marched over to the officer at the head of the unit.

"Colonel Riku Hashizume?"

The stern officer nodded.

"You know why I'm here…"

Hashizume turned to a neighboring officer. "Lead the parade, Major. I have business to attend to."

The Major began to protest, but Hashizume trotted behind Aizawa. To spare a war hero such an indignity, he wouldn't be arrested, but rather "escorted" off the parade ground. A squad of Imperial Guardsmen approached, but beyond them, Aizawa could see His Majesty staring in his direction. His placid face was inscrutable, as if carved from bamboo, but there was something more to that look. Was it anger for having discharged a weapon in the Emperor's presence? Or just perhaps, was it gratitude? How much did the Emperor truly know about the insidious plot that had almost swallowed him and the nation?

Looking back, Aizawa felt his eyes strain. After all, no mortal could stare straight at the Emperor for too long, lest their unworthy eyes become blinded. Instead, he shifted his gaze over to the morning sun, rising over the Japanese Empire.

CHAPTER SIXTY-TWO

Major Kanemaru stared across the Yoyogi Parade Ground. Details were lacking, but he could see a figure clad in a black overcoat and fedora – Inspector Aizawa. Somehow, he had ruined everything yet again. Utako Natsume was probably captured or dead, as were those two fools, Genda and Izumi. But Colonel Hashizume was still alive, being escorted off the parade ground by Imperial Guards.

Junzo Kanemaru wouldn't share the same fate as the Red Terror Society. The Army – and Japan itself – still needed his services. He could still catch the ship out to Manchukuo this evening, escaping whatever trap Aizawa had for him.

Kanemaru made his way past formations of troops and toward the exit. The parade itself had never ceased, an unstoppable machine with endless fuel. Kanemaru glanced past the marching units, and saw the Emperor still atop *Shirayuki*, unconcerned with the miniature drama unfolding across the parade ground. But to his side, General Sadao Araki shot Kanemaru a stare so sharp, he felt impaled by it.

Would Araki sacrifice him just to avoid political scandal? The Army leadership had a way of covering up embarrassing incidents, from coup d'état attempts to battlefield defeats. But this was treason, after all. What better way for Araki to protect himself than by pinning everything on the so-called God of Intrigue?

But as long as he left Tokyo, he could escape this nightmare and start his new mission. Kanemaru pressed on toward the exit, Imperial Guards filtering in and out, rifles at the ready. The entry points were undermanned now, allowing him to sneak out and head eastward, toward Tokyo Station. He could take a train down to Yokohama and set sail for a bright new future.

However, Chizuru Okamura's disembodied scream rang out in his mind. No, he couldn't leave just yet. His little viper's soul would haunt him forever if he didn't settle things with Inspector Aizawa. And he knew just how to do it.

*****

The flashlight stung Reiko's eyes, but she followed the doctor's finger back and forth. Her exam was almost complete and thankfully, she'd passed without much trouble. Superintendent Miyake had brought her back to his office and sent for the Metropolitan Police doctor, rather than drop her off at a hospital. Perhaps he didn't want her blabbing any official secrets by accident.

"Very good," the doctor said. "No sign of a concussion. You're very lucky, young lady." He turned to Miyake, sitting behind his desk. "Apart from some dehydration, she's fine, Superintendent."

With a satisfied nod, Miyake dismissed the doctor, leaving them alone in his office. He grabbed a nearby kettle on his desk and poured her a cup of green tea. She took a sip, discovered it was lukewarm, then downed it in thirsty gulps. He refilled it again and she drained it just as fast.

"Drink up, Watanabe-san. We'll need you in good health for the future."

She set the cup down. "The future, sir?"

Miyake cracked a smile. "I couldn't understand at first, but now I see why Inspector Aizawa places such trust in you. A good spy makes police work more efficient."

"Thank you, sir."

"As I said, we'll have much use for you in the coming year." He leaned back, tenting his fingers. "The Atami Hot Springs Incident and this sordid affair with the Red Terror Society are just the beginning. By the end of the year, any remnant of the Communist Party will be mercilessly crushed into powder. From there, we can move on to all other dangerous thinkers, on the Left and the Right. You will be a lethal weapon in that coming war, Watanabe-san."

Reiko's stomach tightened with fear and disgust. She stood and said, "Will you excuse me, sir? I…I need some fresh air."

Miyake nodded again, and after a respectful bow, Reiko turned and left the office, like a damsel escaping the cave of some ferocious *oni* devil.

*****

Outside the Metropolitan Police Headquarters, Reiko lit up a Cherry cigarette and inhaled. Miyake's words played again in her ears. Spying on criminals was one thing, but thought criminals? She wasn't going to become some tool of Tokko, and if she knew Inspector Aizawa, he wouldn't either. Reiko Watanabe was nobody's weapon.

She eyed the *junsa* standing guard outside, *keijo* stick firmly in hand. A man untroubled by a conscience, comforted by obeying orders. Such was the Japanese way of life. Uniforms and weapons always had the same effect on men, transforming them into automatons, fit only for marching, shooting, and dying. Well, except for Inspector Aizawa. They were nails yet to be hammered down by the unceasing regimentation of Japanese society.

The doors parted and a man shambled out past the *junsa.* His suit was a mass of tattered rags and a smattering of bruises colored his skin a disgusting bluish tint. A bloodied thin nose hung above lips smashed into pulp, and a pair of cracked glasses shielded his eyes, ringed with fatigue and swelling. Although he resembled raw meat, Koichi Matsumoto was still recognizable.

"Matsumoto-san? What happened to you?"

Matsumoto jerked around, gaped through broken glasses, then grimaced. "You! You know damn well what happened to me, you bitch!"

The face was Matsumoto's – more or less – but the voice was bitter, angry, and full of such venom, it didn't even sound human. He began limping away from Police Headquarters, prompting Reiko to follow.

"What do you mean?"

"You set me up," he snarled without stopping. "That novel you loaned me, *The Crab Cannery Ship*? The Police found it when they arrested me. Now they think I'm a Red!"

"No, no, Matsumoto-san! I didn't set you up! I promise!"

"Liar! They knew all about my connection with Utako Natsume! That means you're working for them! And to think, I trusted you!"

The tirade stung Reiko like thousands of cuts, filling her eyes with tears. "No! It's not what you think! Who did this to you?"

"Who do you think? Inspector Aizawa and his partner from the *Kempeitai*! They worked me over, saying I would know where you are! And now, you turn up safe and sound!" A cynical laugh leaked between his swollen lips. "Some actress you turned out to be, Reiko Watanabe! You certainly fooled me! First Utako Natsume, and now Reiko Watanabe! The two women who killed my career!"

"Matsumoto-san…you can't mean that…they released you…"

"Bah! The executives at Shochiku Kinema will find out about this and won't give me another chance." Another sigh, loaded with bitterness. "I'll never direct another picture again."

Reiko squeezed the tears from her eyes and bowed. "Matsumoto-san…please forgive me. I had no idea this would happen to you."

She straightened up to see Matsumoto scanning her with utter disgust. Reiko felt less like a woman and more like bacteria being analyzed in a laboratory.

"You are a curse, Reiko Watanabe. Goodbye forever." Grimacing in pain and hate, Matsumoto turned and trudged out of her life.

Minutes went by as Reiko stood in silence until the smoldering cigarette burned her fingers. She dropped it to the ground and began walking, straining back another wave of tears. Not here. There would be time for crying later. For poor Matsumoto, for their relationship, for her pathetic little acting career, dead before it even started.

As she passed Police Headquarters, the *junsa* fixed her with a suspicious glower. No, she wouldn't become like him, a tool of brutality. But what about Inspector Aizawa? She couldn't shake Matsumoto's broken figure from her mind. Was her *senpai* really capable of such cruelty? She would find out for herself, no matter what the truth was.

CHAPTER SIXTY-THREE

A deep somberness carved itself into Colonel Riku Hashizume's face. The cellar of the Army Ministry wasn't a dignified location for *seppuku* – ritual suicide – and was unbefitting an esteemed samurai like the Colonel, not that he had any choice. After such a despicable crime, Hashizume was lucky to escape a public trial and hanging, obliterating what remained of his family's honor. But given his samurai lineage and the shame it would cause the Army, a coverup was necessary.

Kneeling at a low-lying *kotatsu* table, Hashizume scribbled out his death poem, part of the *seppuku* tradition. A fitting end for Colonel Haiku. After a weary sigh, Hashizume glanced at his captors – Lieutenant Eisaku Miyake, Lieutenant-Colonel Hatsu, and Inspector Aizawa. Holding the paper, he began reading.

"My great shame and crime,
Does not erase Pingdingshan,
I'll pay with my life."

The poem sent a flush through Hatsu's cheeks. "Those were Reds you aided, Colonel. Not some disgruntled liberals. You almost brought Bolshevism to our nation."

Shame lowered Hashizume's gaze and stooped his shoulders. "No words can express my disgust. I can only hope my *seppuku* will compensate for my foolishness." He glared up. "But that does not expunge the dishonor of the Manchurian Incident. There will be many more Pingdingshans to follow."

Anger seethed within Hatsu, but he contained it. Instead, Lieutenant Miyake stepped forward, his saber sliding from its sheath with a rasping hiss.

"You are lucky, Colonel," Aizawa said. "Your name will be kept out of this entire incident. For the good of the nation."

Hashizume's eyes slid to the floor. "It doesn't matter. Japan is doomed. We all are."

The cellar was cramped and stifling, but a chill prickled Aizawa's skin. That same evil omen had haunted his dreams and thoughts for years now, like some monstrous typhoon slowly approaching their shores. How strange to hear it echoed by someone like Colonel Hashizume, like a madman being told he was sane all along.

Hashizume slid off his tunic, and Lieutenant Miyake presented him with a *wakizashi* short sword, the perfect blade for disembowelment. The Colonel accepted and, after a series of deep breaths, plunged the *wakizashi* straight into his gut with a guttural cry. Blood sprayed out as the sword sawed through flesh and organs, twisting his face into an inhuman snarl. His head lolled back and forth, then wrenched forward, overcome by the overwhelming torture.

"Do…it…"Hashizume gurgled through a mouthful of blood.

Lieutenant Eisaku Miyake rose the saber above his head, high enough to gain suitable momentum. Tradition dictated a certain fluidity and grace to the executioner's strokes, but this had been an unconventional day. Instead, the sword swept down with a whistling whoosh of air, slicing through Hashizume's outstretched neck. Rather than popping clean off and rolling, the head plopped onto the *kotatsu*, nestling in a puddle of gore as Hashizume's torso pumped out waves of blood, painting his tortured face a deep shade of red.

Lieutenant Miyake wiped the saber clean, sheathed it, and offered a rigid salute – a loyal subordinate paying respect to his former commander. Despite his despicable crime, Colonel Hashizume had died like a true samurai, regaining some of his shattered honor. Most importantly, Tokyo was safe, for now at least.

Hatsu banged on the door and two *kempei* entered, armed with towels and mop buckets. As they began cleaning up the butchered flesh, Hatsu gestured for Aizawa to follow. They exited the room and made their way through the basement of the Army Ministry. The area was like the bowels of hell, full of secrets and forbidden knowledge. What strange clues lurked behind those closed cellar doors? Best not to ask, or else Aizawa might find himself locked down in there forever.

Only when Hatsu led him to the ground floor did Aizawa feel safe to speak.

"What comes next?"

"Next?" Hatsu looked like a contented cat. "Colonel Hashizume's death will be reported as a case of jaundice or some other ailment. Something to satiate the press and his wife."

"No, I mean with Major Kanemaru and," Aizawa paused to lower his voice, "General Araki."

Somehow, an even more pleased expression held Hatsu's face. "Oh, yes. Don't worry, Inspector. I've already ordered a dragnet out for our *Tokumu Kikan* friend. He won't escape Tokyo."

"So, all it took was high treason to motivate you?"

"Joke all you want, Inspector, but you don't understand the intricacies of Army politics. As for," Hatsu's eyes glanced upward, to the office of the Army Minister himself, "his time will come."

"I'd say his rap sheet is long enough already."

"Maybe, but long enough to arrest the Army Minister? Surely you can see the massive loss of face it will cause…not just for the Army but the entire nation! General Araki isn't some corrupt politician, Inspector…"

"Worse. He's a traitor."

Hatsu pursed his lips. "Perhaps, but we must proceed delicately. Today's incident was too consequential to ignore. Once we find Major Kanemaru, my men can pump every bit of information out of him. Then, we can use it to discredit the entire Imperial Way Faction and persuade Araki to resign."

"Resign? That's all?"

"Let's hope so. Or else things might get much bloodier, Inspector. The Imperial Way and the Control Faction are sharpening their swords, waiting for an opening to strike. Who knows how many more stomachs will be sliced open when it's all over?" Hatsu drew himself up, a man secure in his duty. "You'd better back the right horse when the race starts, Inspector."

An urge to escape coursed through Aizawa, as if the air, the walls, Hatsu himself, leaked poison. He bowed, turned, and marched straight out of the Army Ministry, hoping it was his last visit there.

"Goodbye for now, Inspector," Hatsu called after him. Somehow, Aizawa knew the *kempei* was smiling.

*****

It was well after sunset when Aizawa made his way back to Ueno. The working-class neighborhood always bathed him with a soothing familiarity, even if the sights weren't comforting. Yes, the economy was improving, but reminders of the Showa Depression were still raw. Children waddled around with swollen bellies and vagrants drifted in and out of alleyways. Up ahead, a miniature rally of gray-haired Russo-Japanese War veterans staged a protest, demanding assistance from the government in repayment for all their past service to the nation.

Drained and drooping with fatigue, Aizawa plodded onward until finally reaching his *nagaya* row house – small, cramped, but welcoming. He slid open the door and removed his shoes in the *genkan* vestibule, then entered the main room. The *daruma* doll greeted him, one eye still unpainted. Since the Red Terror Society had been brought to justice – more or less – it was time to fill in the other one. But as he stepped inside, an evil presence filled the *nagaya*. A book lay just outside the den, sprawled open. Aizawa snatched it up and scanned the title – *The Complete Works of Edogawa Ranpo.*

Last night's events flashed in his mind. Minori Miyake had asked him if she could drop by to loan him the book, and here it was – without her. Tension accelerated his heartbeat as he drew his Colt automatic. Creeping toward the den, he held his breath and yanked open the door.

Propped up on the floor, Minori Miyake stared back at him, brown eyes bulging in fear. Adhesive tape was plastered across her mouth, mumbling as she squirmed against the strips of tape that mummified her arms. Underneath her throat was a drawn sword, held by Major Junzo Kanemaru. His eyes shone with joy, like a starving man presented with a final feast.

"Welcome, Inspector Aizawa-han. We've been waiting for you."

CHAPTER SIXTY-FOUR

Aizawa aimed the pistol for a clean shot, but Minori's terrified face obscured every possibility. Even worse, Kanemaru's saber drew closer still to her throat until it nestled firmly under her chin. Minori kicked her feet back and forth, still secure in leather heels. Kanemaru must have been waiting for him inside the *nagaya*, then grabbed her when she came by to drop off the book, not even giving her time to remove her shoes. If only he had accepted that stupid thing back at Café Lion.

"Drop it, Inspector," Kanemaru commanded. "Either she dies by my hand or yours."

"Why should I believe you?"

"Because it's you I want, Inspector. And your little geisha."

The only hope now was that Kanemaru would glut himself on Aizawa's blood, sparing Minori Miyake any suffering. But this was Junzo Kanemaru after all, a man for whom double-dealing was as natural as breathing. Aizawa kept the pistol locked, but Kanemaru pressed the saber closer to Minori's pale skin, drawing a thin trickle of blood, a reminder of his ruthlessness. Minori let out a muffled scream into her gag, then went limp with dimming eyes.

"Bastard," Aizawa growled.

"She just fainted, I assure you," Kanemaru said, keeping Minori propped up against his sword. "But soon, I will lose my patience and mercy."

Moments ticked by as the gun wavered in Aizawa's hand, then dropped from his watery fingers.

"You win. Let her go."

Kanemaru hid any sense of victory, a cautious man. "Throw your handcuff key over, then cuff yourself."

Rummaging through his coat, Aizawa tossed the key over, pulled out the cuffs, then snapped his hands into place behind his back. He stood there, impotent, humiliated, and helpless, a condemned man awaiting execution. Shame competed with rage, but both were dwarfed by a towering fear for himself, Minori, and Reiko Watanabe, wherever she was.

"Good…now slide the gun over here," Kanemaru ordered, clicking on a nearby lamp, flooding the den with pallid electric light.

Aizawa kicked the Colt across the den where the Major scooped it up like treasure. Setting the saber aside, he let Minori plop to the floor, speckles of blood still dribbling from her throat.

"I should kill her just so you could watch your lover die," Kanemaru said, before emotion squeezed his voice, "like I watched my little viper bleed out in my arms."

"Chizuru Okamura died by her own hand. And her own stupidity."

No words from Kanemaru, but he spoke with the butt of the Colt, smacking Aizawa across the temple, sending him crumpling to the floor. Pain buzzed in his ears as he tried to calculate some plan of escape. But his brain was scrambled, and every thought led nowhere.

"My little viper died because of your constant meddling. You might fancy yourself as some righteous detective, but you're just a sniveling bootlicker, serving a government filled with weak-kneed, corrupt politicians." Kanemaru took a steadying breath, then continued, "But this isn't about politics. Tonight, we settle the score as men." He glanced back over at Minori, still passed out in blissful slumber. "Chizuru Okamura's soul won't be satiated with her. Where is that little geisha whore? Did those two idiots kill her off?"

Aizawa clenched his jaw and said nothing, trying to blot out the throbbing pain. The less he knew about Reiko the better.

Kanemaru bent down, then jammed the pistol deep into Aizawa's cheek. "What's that? Didn't hear you. If she's not already dead, why don't I invite her over?"

Aizawa tugged against the handcuffs and glared at the gun's metallic snout.

"Oh?" Kanemaru's thick eyebrows flared up. "Still pinning your hopes on this?" Chuckling, he tossed the gun out of the den and into the main room. "You're too tricky to take chances around, even handcuffed. Besides," he cracked his knuckles, "a bullet will be too merciful for you."

The Major slammed a rocklike fist across Aizawa's cheek, snapping his head back to the floor. A renewed wave of pain electrified his body like millions of little tortures. He should have guessed a brute like Junzo Kanemaru had one hell of a right cross.

"By the time I'm through with you, all that will be left is butchered meat. We have all night, Aizawa-han! Hell, I even skipped a boat to Manchuria, just to pay you a visit!"

Aizawa worked his jaw, and after realizing nothing was broken, gathered his thoughts into some paltry strategy. The only way to survive was to keep Kanemaru talking, which for an arrogant braggart, shouldn't be too hard.

"You signed your death warrant, Major…the *Kempeitai* are looking for you. They're going to bleed every secret out of you to use against General Araki and the Imperial Way Faction. Do you think he'll step in front of the firing squad for you?"

Kanemaru laughed, contemptuous and haunting. "I can outwit those fools in my sleep! Shadows are like a second skin for a *Tokumu Kikan* officer. I can slip in and out of Tokyo whenever I want, and nobody will stop me. Least of all you."

Kanemaru drew back his black jackboot and heaved it deep into Aizawa's stomach. Air blew out of his lungs, leaving him with a hollow, scooped out sensation, coupled by a throbbing agony that spread across his body, inflaming his old shoulder wound. Numbness crept along his spine, and he barely felt the second kick slam into his gut, then others into his back, legs, and chest. Rolling in agony, Aizawa searched the den for some hope, but his eyes settled on the unpruned bonsai tree, sitting atop his desk in mocking irony.

"Somebody! Help! He—"

The sole of Kanemaru's boot smashed against Aizawa cheek, stomping him like a bug. Blood poured from his lips, and the earlier numbness evaporated, replaced by bolts of searing pain that gripped every nerve ending.

"Too bad I used all that tape on her." Kanemaru nodded over to Minori, still unconscious. "But I have a much better way to shut you up." He marched over and retrieved the saber. He held it up, and in its metallic gleam, Aizawa caught his reflection – a bloody smear for a face, punctured by two wild eyes.

"I'll just hack a few inches off your tongue, then I can get to work," Kanemaru said, lapsing in and out of sadistic giggling. "Open wide, Inspector."

Straining against his manacled wrists was futile, so Aizawa firmed his body. The only thing he could do was fight to the bitter end. At least he wouldn't make it easy. Still cackling, Kanemaru splayed Aizawa out like a hog ready to be butchered and readied the saber for a quick slice. But an explosive crack smothered his hideous laughter, leaving him frozen in place.

Moments passed before the saber clattered to the floor. A spot grew across Kanemaru's abdomen, staining his brown uniform an even darker shade. Blood oozed over his lips before cascading into an endless stream. The Major collapsed to his knees, then sprawled across the floor next to Aizawa, twitching and jerking in agonized spasms.

Reiko Watanabe stood in the doorway with Aizawa's Colt automatic fastened in her hands. Her bobbed hair flanked a face devoid of expression, distant and cold. She gazed down at the two of them with equal aloofness.

A grotesque gurgling sputtered up from Kanemaru's throat as words fought to escape.

"K-kill…me…p-please…"

The Major was slowly choking, drowning in a vile concoction of his own blood and gore. Even Aizawa flinched at the realization. A hell of a way to go, even for a despicable creature like Junzo Kanemaru. Reiko craned her neck and examined the Major, now a tortured, choking heap of flesh. Moments elongated into minutes, with Reiko standing there silently, a beautiful Grim Reaper coming to collect. Kanemaru's breath wheezed out in shallow rasps, frothy blood bubbling out of his flaring nostrils and mouth. His body shook in violent jerks, but any sound was stifled by the gushing blood. His eyes flitted, then shrank into nothingness.

So, a brain full of schemes, double-dealings, and intrigue couldn't help Major Kanemaru in the end. Chizuru Okamura's soul would have some company now. Aizawa glanced over to Minori, still inert, then over at Reiko. He tried to smile, but a fuzziness glazed his sight before the bottomless blackness rushed forth to swallow him up.

CHAPTER SIXTY-FIVE

Standing underneath the statue of the headless Buddha, Reiko gazed upon Ueno Park with a mixture of melancholy and dread. Nearby, a food stall hawked roasted chestnuts and sweet potatoes, but her insides felt scooped out by bottomless anxiety. Inspector Aizawa would be here soon and she needed to steel herself for what was coming. She thought back to that incident, a mere two days earlier. Thankfully, Aizawa and Minori Miyake were revived from unconsciousness within minutes after she'd telephoned the Metropolitan Police. Major Kanemaru's corpse, however, had been hauled off, probably to a furnace or, more fittingly, a ditch.

A young couple – high school students, carefree and smart in their winter uniforms – passed the food cart, pausing to buy a sweet potato. Her eyes followed them with an envious glare as they disappeared deeper into the park. How she wished she could join them in their innocent little world. Thoughts pulled her deeper into a swamp of pensiveness, and she barely noticed the shadow that fell upon her.

"Reiko-san?"

She spun around and found Inspector Aizawa staring back. Bruises dotted his squared face, but he retained that usual stoic dignity.

"Good afternoon, Inspector. Thank you for coming here."

His face softened with a warm smile. "Yes, I was a little surprised you arranged this meeting. But it gives me a chance to personally thank you. For everything." Arms pressed against his sides, Aizawa lowered himself in a deep, respectful bow, the kind men rarely afforded women. It wasn't the first time she'd saved his life, nor was it the first time he'd saved hers. At this point, what was the use of counting anymore?

"Thank you too, Inspector…for rescuing me. But I asked you here today for two things. Firstly, what happened? I'm still trying to piece this whole incident together…"

Aizawa drew himself up with a breath. "Quite simply, it's this. Using Major Kanemaru as a go-between, General Araki took control of the Red Terror Society to assassinate the Emperor, putting his brother Prince Chichibu on the throne. This would also justify a war against Russia, which Araki has been itching for ever since becoming Army Minister. Through court whispers, Marquis Maeda became suspicious and asked Inspector Tezuka to investigate, but Kanemaru arranged his assassination on New Year's."

"I see…and let me guess, the entire backstory will be kept out of the newspapers?"

Aizawa gave a slow nod. "There's too much face to be lost if the whole truth ever came out. If Araki or the Crown Prince were ever implicated in such a treasonous plot, the entire Emperor System might collapse. We must maintain public order, no matter how distasteful the truth is."

"Just like all the other times," Reiko scoffed. "How are you feeling, Inspector?"

Rubbing his battered cheek, Aizawa said, "A little worse for wear, but I've been through worse."

"And that…woman?"

"Minori Miyake? She's recovering with her family. I'm ashamed that she had to suffer like that but what's important is that she's safe. Superintendent Miyake was torn between wanting to strangle me and offering me a kowtow for saving his daughter. However, I insisted that all the credit was yours. He extends his gratitude as well."

"I'll bet. But I'm happy Minori-san is safe."

"Yes, I am too. Not sure if she'll ever speak to me again, but that's not what matters."

"So, your face is better now?" she asked, drawing near him.

"It hurts a little, but nothing too—"

Without waiting, Reiko's gloved palm flew through the air, landing across Aizawa's face with a popping slap. Aizawa gaped back at her as a splotch of red spread across his blue-tinted cheek, bewilderment in his stare. An icy wind howled between them, a no-man's-land she could no longer cross.

"Reiko-san…"

The anger and bitterness rose like bile and spewed forth. "I had no idea you could be so cruel! What you did to poor Matsumoto-san was inhuman!"

The red sore continued to grow, but Inspector Aizawa focused only on her. He stepped forward and gripped her shoulders, a repeat of the gesture he'd performed outside the Denkikan Theater, back when things were much simpler.

"Reiko-san, I would have done anything to find you. I regret what happened to Matsumoto-san, but he was the only lead we had."

She squirmed out of his grasp. "But he didn't know anything, did he? You ruined his career and broke his body for nothing!"

"Damn it, Reiko! I did it because I…I…"

The words faded and Aizawa fell silent. Balling his fists, the red in his cheek spread across his face, a man boiling with rage. Was this the fury that he'd unleashed on Matsumoto?

"I went to your *nagaya* to confront you about this…but it seems more appropriate to tell you here," she glanced up at the headless Buddha, instilling her with the confidence to do what was necessary. "I don't like what's happening, Inspector. To Japan…to you…and to me."

"What do you mean?"

"I've killed three people!" Their faces paraded in her mind – the Chinese bandit who'd fallen into the Sumida River, Chizuru Okamura, and now Major Kanemaru.

"Those were all in self-defense," he snapped. "Believe me, I know what's justified and what isn't. But we are servants of the nation, Reiko-san. We must defend Tokyo, no matter what."

"Defend it from what? Today it's the Red Terror Society, but what about liberals like Matsumoto-san? Are they next? Would you arrest me for thinking 'dangerous thoughts?'"

A silence fell between them, interrupted only by the wail of a chilly breeze. She had her answer. Fighting back tears, she forced the words out.

"I don't think I can work for you any longer, Inspector."

More silence, then, at last, his voice. "Have you forgotten our promise, Reiko-san? To defend Tokyo?"

"No, I haven't forgotten." She took in slow breaths until the tears dissipated from her sight. "If I discover something…whatever it is, I will come to you. But until then, this is goodbye, Inspector."

The anger drained from Aizawa, leaving a saddened, hollow figure. "Reiko-san…I…I'm sorry…"

"I am too," was all she could say. Any more would reduce her to a whimpering child, and she couldn't lose any more dignity today. Instead, she turned and walked away, away from the headless Buddha, away from Inspector Kenji Aizawa, and away from whatever she was becoming. Tears filled her eyes again, but she cast a final glance back at her former *senpai*, standing alone and forlorn, deepening her sorrow.

Reiko ran past the food cart, billowing with savory smells, plunging deeper into Ueno Park. Tears obscured her sight as she ran but she soon found herself in a secluded, wooded area. Two blurry blobs lay up ahead, and as Reiko dried her eyes, their features took on a frightening shape. The schoolboy and his girlfriend lay sprawled out on the grass, holding hands in a grim embrace, staring up with unblinking gazes. A half-eaten sweet potato rested beside them, along with an empty bottle of poison. A young couple, out for a romantic stroll and lunch that ended in love suicide.

There was nothing she could do now. Somebody else would discover the bodies. All Reiko wanted to do was go home and cry. She turned around and started away. But an ominous thought chased her as she ran through Ueno Park – were they the lucky ones?

Afterword

Most characters in *Treason in Tokyo* are fictional, but a few like General Sadao Araki, Kinuyo Tanaka, Prince Chichibu, and, of course, the Showa Emperor, are historical figures.

The history of the Japanese Communist Party is usually glossed over in retellings of 1930s Japan. Always an underground movement, the Communist Party and other leftist groups attracted a relatively large number of followers in the 1920s and 1930s. Also attractive was the anarchist movement and the historical Guillotine Society, who, like the fictional Red Terror Society, plotted the murder of political and military leaders. The Omori Bank Incident – also called the Red Gang Incident – of October 1932 was a real event and the first modern bank robbery in Japan, leading to renewed crackdowns on Communists by the Tokko. While the 3-15 Incident of 1928 dealt a severe blow to Japanese Communism, the arrests of 1932-1933 killed it once and for all.

Jokichi Kazama and other major leaders were arrested at the Atami Hot Springs, followed by other Communists, like the prolific writer Takiji Kobayashi, who was tortured to death by the Tokko in February 1933. By 1935, the Japanese Communist Party had ceased to exist. But fears of Communism haunted the Japanese leaders long after. In 1945, while Japan burned from American air raids, Prince Fumimaro Konoe urged the Emperor to make peace, mostly because he feared a Communist revolution, despite there being no organized Communist movement in the country.

As mentioned, the Japanese film industry relocated to Osaka after the Great Kanto Earthquake, with Shochiku Kinema being the only major studio to remain in Tokyo. After the war, Kinuyo Tanaka would become the second female director in Japanese cinema.

In late 1932, the Imperial Japanese Army did split into two different groups – the Imperial Way and the Control Faction. The former being obsessed with revolution and restoring the Emperor to full power, whereas the latter was more concerned with working with the existing government and big business to create a national defense state for total war. This factionalism would almost tear the Army apart, until the 1936 coup.

A major plot point of *Treason in Tokyo* is the attempted assassination of the Showa Emperor. This is mostly fictional, but somewhat rooted in fact. There were attempts by the aforementioned Guillotine Society and a Communist to assassinate Crown Prince Hirohito in the 1920s, along with the Great Treason Incident of 1910 where anarchists plotted to murder the Meiji Emperor, leading to the creation of the Tokko.

There was also the Sakurada Gate Incident of 1932, where a Korean nationalist attempted to assassinate the Emperor, which inspired the plot of *Treason in Tokyo.* According to some sources, there were grumblings from radical officers like General Araki, who preferred the more dynamic Crown Prince Chichibu to become emperor. Chichibu was sympathetic to the Imperial Way Faction and fascism in general, but there is no evidence he conspired with radical officers to remove his brother from the throne. However, until the birth of Crown Prince Akihito in December 1933, Chichibu was the heir to the Japanese Empire.

Another point of interest is the infamous Shimpeitai Incident of 1933, which involved a right-wing terrorist group – the Shimpeitai or Divine Soldiers – who, according to some sources, plotted to murder the prime minister, his cabinet, and the Emperor himself, replacing him with Prince Chichibu. Historians still debate whether or not the Emperor was imperiled at the hands of these right-wing groups and Army officers. Regardless, it makes for compelling fiction.

Sadao Araki is largely forgotten now, but he played an important role in militarizing Japanese society. As de facto leader of the Imperial Way Faction, he was obsessed with attacking the Soviet Union and the "Crisis of 1936." This belief of an inevitable war saw him attempting to militarize the Japanese people, beginning air raid drills in the summer of 1933, and the very real film *Crisis-Time Japan*, which lambasted cosmopolitan liberalism. The film was even entered as evidence in the postwar Tokyo Trials. Araki's warlike tendency put him at odds with the Emperor and more moderate statesmen, who pressured his resignation as army minister in January 1934.

In September 1932, the Manchurian village of Pingdingshan was razed to the ground by the Japanese Kwantung Army pursuing Chinese guerillas. Over 800 people died but the massacre was covered up. Some sources say General Nobuyoshi Muto, the commander of the Kwantung Army, protested to the Emperor about this and other atrocities in Manchuria, but was ignored, and committed suicide. Others say he died of jaundice. Regardless, his actions show that not all Japanese Army officers approved of these crimes, which would be dwarfed tenfold at Nanking in December 1937.

The Battle of Shanhaikwan was a preamble to the larger invasion of Nekka (Jehol or Rehe) in February 1933. Claiming Nekka was part of Manchukuo, the Kwantung Army invaded and soon captured the entire province and pushed the Chinese defenders up to the Great Wall, where a stalemate ensued. At the same time, the League of Nations adopted the Lytton Report, whereupon the Japanese delegation walked out of the conference. Japan officially left the League in March 1933. The Tangku Truce of May 1933 established a demilitarized zone in North China and created a fragile peace between Japan and China, which would be broken in 1937 with the onset of full-scale war.

Several books I used for research include *The Double Patriots* by Richard Storry, *Revolt in Japan* by Ben-Ami Shillony, *The Japanese Communist Party 1922-1945* by Genji Okubo and George M. Beckmann, *Japan's Imperial Conspiracy* by David Bergamini, *Tokyo Rising* by Edward Seidensticker, *Japanese Police State* by Elise Tipton, *The Imperial Screen* by Peter B. High, and *Nippon Modern* by Mitsuyo Wada-Marciano.

Thank You

Thank you for reading *Treason in Tokyo*, the third book of the Reiko Watanabe/Inspector Aizawa series. If you enjoyed this novel, please leave a review on Amazon! Positive reviews from readers like you are absolutely essential for authors to survive in today's marketplace.

If you haven't already, check out the other books in the series, *Shadows of Tokyo* and *Smoke Over Tokyo*. Also, sign up to my mailing list and receive the free prequel, *Conspiracy in Tokyo*!

Thanks!

Reiko Watanabe and Inspector Aizawa will return in *Secrets Beneath Tokyo*!

About the Author

Matthew Legare has always loved reading, writing, and history. He's combined his passions to tell stories set during little-known, but fascinating, events of the past. His style is a smooth blend of old pulp magazines and contemporary thrillers, which makes for a pulsating read.

Matthew would love to hear from his readers! Please contact him at:

Website: www.matthewlegare.com

Twitter: @mlegareauthor

Printed in Great Britain
by Amazon

47774475R00182